3 8002 01302 692

D1139559

Samia Serageldin was born in Cairo, educated in Britain, and now lives in the USA. In addition to writing this novel, she is a columnist, a book editor and a lecturer.

For automatic updates on Samia Serageldin visit harperperennial.co.uk and register for AuthorTracker.

From the reviews of *The Cairo House*:

'An enchanting novel-as-memoir . . . what strengthens Ms Serageldin's book is Gigi's own personal story'
Economist

'This book has a lot to offer . . . Serageldin offers up an intriguing snapshot of contemporary Egypt'
Sunday Business Post

'An interesting prism through which to observe the shifting status of a complex nation'
Sunday Herald

'This novel is more about the personal changes – births, growing up, growing old, deaths – that make exiles of us all. Serageldin does a wonderful job of evoking Gigi's Cairo milieu'
Booklist

'A beautifully crafted novel . . . Flawlessly rendered prose'
Choice

'Serageldin's perceptive insights into the women who "have more than one skin" enrich this narrative of displaced and out-of-place women – expatriate intellectuals both spiritually and physically'
The Middle East Journal

SAMIA SERAGELDIN

The Cairo House

HARPER PERENNIAL
London, New York, Toronto and Sydney

Harper Perennial
An imprint of HarperCollins*Publishers*
77–85 Fulham Palace Road
Hammersmith
London W6 8JB

www.harperperennial.co.uk

This edition published by Harper Perennial 2005
1

First published in the USA in 2000
This revised edition first published in Great Britain by Fourth Estate 2004

A catalogue record for this book is available from the British Library

This novel is entirely a work of fiction. The names,
characters and incidents portrayed in it are the work of the
author's imagination. Any resemblance to actual persons,
living or dead, events or localities is entirely coincidental.

ISBN 0 00 718218 X

Set in Meridien by
Palimpsest Book Production Ltd, Polmont, Stirlingshire

Printed and bound in Great Britain by Clays Ltd, St Ives plc

For Kareem and Ramy

ACKNOWLEDGEMENTS

I would like to express my deep appreciation to Toby Eady for his patience, his whole-hearted support, and his thoughtfulness in ways great and small; to Laetitia Rutherford for her insight and unflagging responsiveness; to Susan Watt for her invaluable guidance and the benefit of her experience. Thanks to Ramy Serageldin for his unstinting help in matters digital and technical; to William Fisher, Jessica Woollard and Amelie Van Wedel. Finally, I am indebted to the friends, family and total strangers who have been so wonderfully supportive of this book and of my writing.

Contents

PART I

PHOTOGRAPHS

I

The Feast of the Sacrifice

For those who have more than one skin, there are places where the secret act of metamorphosis takes place, an imperceptible shading into a hint of a different gait, a softening or a crispening of an accent. For those whose past and present belong to different worlds, there are places and times that mark their passage from one to the other, a transitional limbo: like airports and airplanes.

Watch the travelers going through the arrival gates, being greeted by family and friends, or by strangers holding up a sign with their company name. Watch the subtle shift to accommodate a change in status or expectations, as we play our many roles in life: boss and child, parent and lover, hometown hot-shot and small fish in a big city pond. We emerge from the tunnel ramp and swing through the gates, a chrysalis bursting free of its cocoon, Superman erupting from the telephone booth; or we shuffle off to the luggage carousel, waiting to pick up the familiar battered luggage with which we left.

But the true chameleons are the ones who straddle

3

two worlds, segueing smoothly from one to the other, adjusting language and body language, calibrating the range of emotions displayed, treading the tightrope of mannerisms and mores. If it is done well, it can look deceptively effortless, but it is never without cost. There is no hypocrisy involved, only the universal imperative underlying good manners: to do the appropriate thing, to make those around you comfortable. For the chameleon, it is a matter of survival.

'Ladies and gentlemen, we will be landing at Cairo Airport in twenty minutes. Local time is 4 p.m., and the ground temperature is 22 degrees Celsius. Please fasten your seat belts and return seats and trays to their full upright position. We remind you to have your passports ready and your landing cards and customs declarations filled out.'

I stare at the landing card in front of me. 'Purpose of visit: Business or pleasure?' Simplistic questions in a complicated world. What is the purpose of my visit? How do you answer, I have come back to claim what's mine? To find out if it is still mine. To find two children I left behind when I ran away a decade ago: one child is my son and the other the girl I once was. The future and the past. Between them they hold the key to the question I have come to try to resolve: where do I belong? Where is this chameleon's natural habitat?

I fasten my seat belt and smile at the white-haired Minnesotan couple next to me as they grasp each other's knuckled hands. We have made small talk about cross-country skiing and hockey. At some point they asked me where I was from, and I answered, truthfully, that I live in New Hampshire. It is not evasiveness, nor even the instinct to resist being pigeon-holed. It is only that any

4

answer I give will be just as incomplete and misleading, so this is as good – or bad – as any other.

The wheels skim the ground and the engines are thrust into reverse with a violent roar as the plane hurtles down the runway, then skids to a stop. There is a round of clapping from the Egyptian passengers; it never fails, no matter how bumpy or smooth the landing. As much as a courtesy to the pilot, the applause is the self-congratulation of a fatalistic people on arriving safely. *Hamdillah `alsalama*. Home safely.

Cairo Airport, finally. I sling my shoulder bag and coat over my arm and head for the passport check booths. The Minnesotan couple follow me in line. I hand my blue American passport to the man at the first booth.

'Do you have a visa?' he asks in English.

'No, but I'm Egyptian-born.'

He looks mildly surprised; perhaps I do not look typically Egyptian. He flips through my passport.

'Seif-el-Islam?' He raises his eyebrows at my maiden name and asks in Arabic, 'Any relation to the Pasha?'

'I'm his niece.'

The man enters the data from my passport on a computer screen, then hands the document back to me with a smile. *'Hamdillah `alsalama*. Welcome home.'

As I pass through the gate I nod to the couple from Minneapolis, a little awkwardly, because I can see in their eyes that I no longer belong to their world. At customs I push my cart right through the Nothing To Declare aisle. I scan the mass of dark, eager faces beyond the barrier at the exit. One does not distinguish black or white, only infinite gradations of gray in this most ethnically-mixed and color-blind of peoples. Within a few hours I will no longer notice such things, just as I will no longer see the

5

inevitable film of desert dust in the stark sunshine, like a layer of ash over the gray buildings and the sooty cars, the leaves of the trees and the dark winter clothing of the people.

The muezzin's call from the minaret wakes me at dawn my first morning in Cairo. I listen to the drawn-out echoes rising and falling in the stillness. I try to go back to sleep but the layers of noise start to build up outside the wooden shutters: first the birds twittering, then dogs barking, voices raised in greeting; finally the first car will set off the incessant honking that punctuates every minute of the day on the streets of Cairo.

I can hear Ibrahim the doorkeeper carrying out his morning ablutions at the tap in the courtyard under my window. His wooden clogs clap on the cobblestones, then the creaky faucet is turned off. I can imagine him winding his turban around his shriveled old head. Someone passing by in the street calls out a greeting: 'Morning of jasmines!' Ibrahim responds: 'Morning of cream to you!' The flowery greetings make me smile. Such small automatic courtesies are some of the few luxuries which even the poorest of the poor can afford.

As a child I used to sleep right through all this. I even used to sleep through the Bayram Feast sacrifice. Except for that one year, that year that was to be the last of the 'good old days'.

There is a photo of me and my parents taken in the salon of the villa just before the Feast of the Sacrifice that year, 1961. Papa is holding a cigarette in one hand, his other hand on my shoulder. He chain-smoked Craven A's; I remember the red and white box with the black cat. In the photo he has the broad-shouldered, dark looks

6

of the Latin film stars of the fifties. His moustache is very neat, and his hair is slicked back. That style of suit, double-breasted, with boxy shoulders, was in style then, but I remember him wearing it a decade later and still looking impeccably tailored in it. He was that rare sort of man who carries himself well, without a hint of vanity.

Papa and I are standing behind Mama's Aubusson bergère. Papa never changed that much – because he died young, I suppose – but Mama is almost unrecognizable in the photo. Her black hair is short, she has the thick straight brows, the red lipstick and string of pearls that were the 'look' of the period. Her features are too irregular to be photogenic, but her smile is confident. She is wearing a salmon, lace-encrusted tulle dress she kept for years after she stopped wearing it. She is at her slimmest in that photo, and although her shoulders and arms look creamy and plump, the boned bustier of that dress is tiny. I know because I tried it on when I was eighteen. I could only hook up the waist if I sucked in my breath, while the fabric of the hips and the bust hung loose on me.

In the photo I am standing with an arm around the back of Mama's chair, head tilted to one side, one foot rubbing against the patent leather heel of the other foot. My shoulder-length hair is brushed back in a velvet Alice band. It was chestnut brown in those days and Mama rinsed it with camomile tea to bring out the highlights. I am wearing a sweater set over a short pleated skirt, and my legs are coltish and long. I am nine, on the verge of *l'âge ingrat*, as my governess called it, the awkward age.

Just before the photograph was taken, Mama had hurriedly tried to smooth my eyebrows.

'Stand still, Gigi!'

She had wet the tip of her finger with her tongue and

7

run her finger over my brows. I remember making a face. It's the same face my son makes today when I take a sip from his drink, or in some other way betray the fact that I still don't see him as his own person, physically separate from me.

Old photographs are like a deck of worn cards; you can try to read them like a fortune-teller at a fair, except in reverse: to read the past, rather than the future. With hindsight you recognize the people in them for what they were: the king, the joker, the knave, the hangman. The Pasha, of course, would be the King, the Sha`ib or Graybeard, as he is called in Arabic; Fangali the jester; Om Khalil's black figure the hangman, turning up like an ill omen at unexpected junctures. But only with hindsight. While the cards are face down, you cannot tell what hand you've been dealt.

That photo of me with my parents was taken just before the Feast of the Sacrifice the year I turned nine. It was the last time we ever posed together for a family portrait.

The Feast of the Sacrifice must have been in winter that year. The sheep had arrived two days before amid much commotion, an incongruous sight in a residential neighborhood in Cairo. Sheep or cattle were sacrificed on the family estate, but it was also customary to carry out the ritual in Cairo. This imperative was never questioned: it was one of the many instances in our hybrid culture when Western norms were unhesitatingly sacrificed on the altar of tradition.

The Bayram Feast was meant to ransom one's blessings, as Abraham did by his sacrifice. Health, wealth, and the greatest of blessings, children, could be withdrawn on a whim of the Giver. The Revolution of 1952 was

8

nearly a decade old, and the Land Reform Act had stripped the bulk of our landholdings, but the worst was still around the corner for families like ours, and as yet unimaginable.

The distribution of the meat from the sacrificial beast was a symbolically intimate form of charity, sharing with dependents and mendicants the meat from one's own table. For the sacrifice to be accepted, every detail of the ritual had to be carefully observed, such as the exact window of time during which it should be performed. That year that was to be the last of the good days, there was a hitch, the lapse of a fatal few minutes. In retrospect, it was an ill omen, and I was the one responsible for it.

I remember watching from the balcony when the van arrived with the two sheep in the back. The cook, his helper, the chauffeur and Ibrahim the Nubian doorkeeper then proceeded to drag the bleating, resisting beasts to the dog run where they would be penned until the morning of the feast.

There was a sudden commotion and panic; someone had forgotten to chain up the dog, who had come flying at the throat of the ram. The howling German shepherd was dragged away. Finally the sheep were safely enclosed. Two days later, before dawn on the day of the Feast, they would be taken to a shed in the backyard that was ordinarily used once a week by two washerwomen who came to do the laundry, then on the following day by a man who came to do the ironing. The dog was also bathed there. But on that one day of the year, between dawn and daybreak, as tradition required for the sacrifice to be valid, the sheep would be slaughtered and skinned in that room, and the stench

9

of blood would replace the scent of soap and starch. Then the walls and floor were hosed down and everything returned to normal for another year.

On the morning of the day before the Feast the bustle around the house had reached a pitch of controlled frenzy. In the salon, the Sudanese head-*suffragi* stood on top of a tall ladder, painstakingly unhooking the crystal drops from the chandelier, one by one, to be wiped with vinegar and water. Mama supervised, hair in curlers under a chiffon cap, wearing one of her favorite *déshabillés*: a faded, blue satin, shawl-collared affair with a sweeping skirt. Mama only dressed to go out, and then she spent at least an hour in front of her tulle-skirted vanity and her modern built-in closets.

The under-*suffragi* was pushing a heavy contraption across the parquet floor to polish it; twice a year the hardwood floors were hand-stripped with steel wool, cleaned, waxed, then polished with a chamois cloth weighed down by a massive brick of lead at the end of a stick. He pushed the unwieldy contraption forward and dragged it back with a clicking, sucking sound. One of the maids was using a bamboo duster to beat the back of a rug slung over the railing of the balcony.

I stood on the balcony at a safe distance from the dust raised by the maid, watching the arrival of the sheep. I remember the scent of jasmine from the bushes under the balcony – jasmine and dust. The cook came up to the balcony with some carrots to coax me to feed the lamb. A large, garrulous man with terrible burn scars on his chest, he was sweating from his recent efforts and the general excitement. All the household help seemed to go around with unusually dilated pupils in the days leading up to the Feast. 'Blood lust', my mother called it. The

10

cook proudly pointed out the two animals to me, a ram and a lamb.

'See the pretty little one, I chose him just for you.'

He went on to make a remark about the ram's horns and his virility. I had the uncomfortable feeling that the remark qualified as one of the 'indelicate expressions' to which the cook was unfortunately prone, and on account of which I was discouraged from engaging in conversation with him. The poor man was aware of this failing of his, without quite being able to determine how he offended. The comical result was that he prefaced his remarks with a precautionary 'excuse the expression,' as when he referred to a *breast* of chicken or a *leg* of lamb.

I went back inside, up to my room, and whiled away the afternoon styling my long-suffering governess' hair. Madame Hélène was over sixty, but she still had long, lush hair which she wore in a dowdy forties bun. I loved to pin her silvery hair up in complicated twists and braids. She always undid my fantastic creations before venturing out.

A persistent bleating from the backyard was followed by the dog barking. 'Oh, listen to that bleating,' Madame Hélène grumbled. 'At least tomorrow it will all be over and we'll have some peace and quiet.'

I took the bobby pins out of my mouth and slowly secured a twisted braid in place. 'I wonder what happens, when they sacrifice the sheep, I mean. It would be interesting to watch, just one time, what do you think?'

'*Quelle horreur*,' Madame Hélène shuddered. 'Don't even think about it. Your mother would never allow it.'

'Oh, it was just a thought.' I slipped one last pin in her hair. 'There, your *chignon* is done, you look like the *Belle Hélène* of the Greeks.'

11

That was not strictly true. Madame Hélène had big, bulging blue eyes, rather like boiled eggs, which I attributed to much weeping. She had told me all about her sad life. A Frenchwoman married to an expatriate Italian count with considerable property in Egypt, they had been dispossessed by the British during the Second World War. Her husband's death had left her penniless and childless. She had been reduced to working as a governess for a living, although among her coterie of expatriate widows she only admitted to giving private lessons. She kept a small apartment in downtown Cairo, where she spent her days off. She had no close relatives left in Europe, but was very attached to a godson who lived near Lyons. She often talked about '*le petit Luc*', and wrote him letters. She kept a photo of him on the table next to her armchair in my bedroom: a photo of a boy with a thick thatch of blonde-streaked hair over a square, smiling face.

'That photo is at least ten years old,' Madame Hélène would sigh as she looked at the photograph every day. 'He must be eight or nine years older than you, *ma petite*, I can't remember exactly.'

I sat down and flipped through a book, but I could not keep my mind on the pages. I had never been particularly curious about the ritual of the sacrifice. By the time I woke up on Feast Day mornings, it was all over. It was over by the time my father was roused, at about six o'clock, to attend the early prayers. Even Muslims who rarely set foot in a mosque during the year attend the feast prayers, and, on these occasions, the carpeting is extended out into the courtyard of the mosque in anticipation of the overflow. Papa tended to be late, so he usually ended up in the courtyard, along with the cook

12

and his helpers, who would also arrive late and exhausted, having just finished with the butchering.

Mama, who normally rose at about ten o'clock, would have been up at dawn, supervising the distribution of meat to the old retainers and the poor who regularly came to the house. A small crowd would have gathered by daybreak. The wetnurses were given the lion's share, followed by the household help. The sheepskins invariably fell to the lot of the Nubian doorkeeper, who took them back with him to his village in the Nubia on his biannual visits home.

I would stay up in my room until it was time for me to dress and go with Papa on another round of visits. By the time I came home, calm would have been restored, and the people who had come for charity would have dispersed. Dinner would be served, with several dishes of lamb as required by tradition. I never touched it; the odor of freshly-butchered meat still lingered about the kitchen, wafting into the dining-room every time the door to the butler's pantry swung open. The household staff would be in a hurry to clear the table and be gone for the holidays, except for the governess, who did not celebrate Muslim feasts, and for the doorkeeper, who had no family in Cairo.

It had never before occurred to me to be curious about what went on in that shed, between dawn and daybreak. But now I could not get the idea out of my head, not even when Papa took me with him on the first round of visits to relatives. The routine never varied; the aunts and uncles were visited in order of their seniority. Since Papa was the youngest of his eight brothers and sisters, his turn to receive visitors came on the last of the three days of the Feast. On the Eve of the Feast he took me to visit

13

the Pasha, Papa's oldest brother and the head of the clan. He lived in the family home in Garden City, which everyone called the Cairo House.

On the way we passed a truck full of smiling, excited people from the country. They were standing up in the back of the truck, swaying with its movement, singing and clapping. The girls wore neon pink, nylon gauze dresses, the boys new striped pajamas. We also passed pick-up trucks carrying bleating sheep marked for slaughter with a rose-red stain on their fat tails. By dawn the next day they would all be butchered. I stared at them with equal fascination and revulsion, trying to imagine the actual proceedings.

We drove down the Nile Corniche past the grand hotels and the long white wall of the British Embassy, then turned off into the narrow, villa-lined streets of Garden City. When we reached the family house Papa stopped the car and honked for the gatekeeper to open the gate. He parked in the back of the villa, alongside several other cars.

I followed him round to the front, past the fountain with its statue of a reclining Poseidon. One of the two heavy double doors was open; normally the front doors were only used on feast days, and at weddings and funerals. Inside the long hall the marble floor radiated cold. I looked up through the atrium at the blazing crystal chandelier suspended from the ceiling of the second floor, fifty feet above my head.

'Let's go upstairs to see your grandmother first.' Papa headed for the wide marble staircase with the two curved balustrades. I followed him up, then along the gallery.

At the top of the stairs we were met by Fangali, the majordomo of the house. He adjusted the out-moded fez

14

he wore on his head and tugged at his caftan as he came forward to greet us. There was something about him that eluded my understanding. The high-pitched voice, the ingratiating manner, contrasted with the thin moustache, the bold eyes. I wondered why he, of all the menservants, was the only one allowed to come and go freely upstairs, in the family quarters. I had vaguely overheard that, as a result of an accident at birth, he was not quite a man. I wondered if he was an *agha*. I had heard of the eunuches of my grandmother's day, without understanding what the word signified. I didn't dare ask. Years later I thought I understood, but later still, Fangali would spring a surprise on us all.

Fangali knocked perfunctorily on the door to Grandmother's room and opened it, announcing in his peculiar whine: 'Look who's here, Hanem. Shamel Bey and Sitt Gigi.'

Grandmother was sitting on a chaise longue, her legs covered with a knit shawl. Fangali tucked the shawl around the child-like feet in satin mules, and left the room. It never failed to amaze me that this tiny woman could have born my tall, strapping father and his eight brothers and sisters. But it seemed as though the effort had drained Grandmother completely; as far back as I could remember, she had always had that vague air of detachment about her.

Papa kissed his mother's hand and pulled up a chair beside her and I followed suit. She was saying to Papa, with an approving nod in my direction, 'That little one can name her own *mahr*.' I understood vaguely what the word meant: the dowry the bridegroom brings to the bride.

Papa laughed and rumpled my hair. 'I'm going down

15

to see your uncle in his study, Gigi. I'll send for you when I'm ready to go, and you can come to wish him a happy Feast before we leave.'

I nodded and sat down beside Grandmother. Fangali brought us glasses of *qammar-eddin*, apricot nectar, and a tray with sweets. I nibbled absently on a glacé chestnut, my mind on the act of the Sacrifice. Mama would never allow it if I asked to observe it, but she had never expressly forbade it, so technically I would not be disobeying. I knew Mama's rules well enough though: whatever was not explicitly allowed was forbidden. As for Madame Hélène, she slept in the room adjoining mine, with the door ajar, but she slept heavily, with a smoker's nasal snore. I made up my mind: I would do it.

At that moment Fangali ushered in a shriveled old woman wrapped in black from head to toe. The sooty black eyes, ringed with kohl, darted sharply around the room. No one seemed to know how old Om Khalil really was, but it was rumored that the secret of her spryness was drinking nothing but vinegar and water for one day a week. She went from house to house, making jam, pickles, rosewater, kohl from pounded roast almonds, or special concoctions for recovering new mothers. The servants in each household treated her with the awe commensurate with her reputation for an undeflectable evil eye.

I tried to resist an involuntary *frisson* when I set eyes on the black-shrouded figure. I knew this reaction to an old family retainer was highly reprehensible, but children, like animals, have not yet learned to override their instincts. Seeing Om Khalil at the moment I had made my decision was a bad omen, and I hesitated again.

'How are you, Om Khalil?' Grandmother reached for

16

some money from a tasseled purse she kept beside her for the steady stream of family domestics who came to visit on feast days. She had phobias about certain things; for instance, she insisted on having the maid wash any money that she handled, whether it was coins or bills. 'It's because she had such a bad experience during the cholera epidemic,' Mama had explained. 'She lost two children to cholera, they were just babies.'

Fangali came to fetch me. I kissed Grandmother and hurried downstairs. The door to my uncle's study was open, and there were a dozen men sitting around the room. My eldest uncle sat behind his desk at the far end. He seemed even larger than the last time I had seen him, on the Lesser Feast a few months before. A big man, his bulk suggested power rather than obesity. His gray double-breasted suit fitted him perfectly, and the silk square in the breast pocket matched his tie. I went up to kiss him; he smelled of Cuban cigars and Old Spice, just like I remembered.

'Happy Feast, little one, what a big girl you've become.' He patted my cheek and reached into his pocket for a handful of shiny coins. It was the custom to give children shiny new coins for luck on feast days, and my uncle always prepared great quantities of them for all the children of the clan, and the children of friends and retainers, who came to visit.

I had heard that in the old days, before the revolution, before I was born, when my uncle had been prime minister, he had once paid the Feast Day bonuses to some of the Cairo police force, out of his own pocket – out of the family's pocket, really, since it was all one and the same. During the revolutionary tribunals of 1952, this had been brought up as proof of undue influence. The

17

Pasha had countered that, there being a temporary short-fall in the budget, he had only advanced the money out of his own pocket, in order to make sure that the poor policemen and their families would have the wherewithal to celebrate the Feast. I did not understand what all the fuss had been about; I thought it was about the new coins that children were given.

That night it took me a long time to fall asleep. I couldn't make up my mind whether or not to risk trying to watch the sacrifice. Finally I dozed off. The call to dawn prayers from the minaret of the mosque nearby woke me. Every morning I slept right through the call to prayers, but that day it had woken me. It seemed like an omen. I sat up in bed in the dark, blinking at the dial of the alarm clock. Had the cook and his helpers started yet? The ram would be first. The larger, more dangerous animal is always killed first, before it has time to panic and resist. I strained my ears but I could hear nothing but Madame Hélène's regular snoring through the door to the adjoining room.

I slumped back against my pillow. I tried to go back to sleep, but my whole body was tense, straining for the slightest sound. I thought I heard a faint bleating, but I couldn't be sure. I sat up again, my heart pounding. It was now or never. I would just go down to the back garden, but I wouldn't actually look into the shed. I jumped out of bed, and pulled on my yellow wool dressing gown. I slipped on my ballet slippers and tiptoed out.

Within minutes I had slipped out of the kitchen door and headed for the lighted shed at the bottom of the garden. I could hear a sort of scuffling, then staccato bleating and the low, urgent voices of the men inside. I

18

recognized the voice of the cook, suddenly raised in warning:

'Watch out!'

Then the encouraging mutters of the doorkeeper and the other men.

'In the name of Allah!'

'Easy now!'

'I've got him.'

'Allah Akbar.'

I tiptoed to the door of the shed, my heartbeat throbbing so loudly in my ears I could hear nothing else. I clamped my hand over my nose and mouth against rising nausea, and peered in. To this day, I am unable to tell for sure what I actually saw from what my overheated imagination filled in: the harsh light of a naked light bulb on the straining backs of the men bent over in a circle; blood spattering the walls; bound hooves flailing. I screamed and turned to run, slipped in the pool of blood seeping under the door, and fell unconscious.

As Madame Hélène was to tell me later, she was roused from her sleep by the shouting of the cook under her window. She looked out and saw me, lifeless and blood-spattered in the arms of the bloody cook, and started screaming. The cook was apparently shouting for her to come down so he could unload me onto her and get back to his work, but she understood little Arabic at the best of times and at that moment was completely hysterical.

The combined screaming and shouting roused the household and the cook was able to leave me in Mama's care and get back to slaughtering his sheep. But by then the first light had broken, and the men shook their heads. It was a bad omen.

When I woke up, I found myself in my own clean

19

bed, in a fresh nightgown. Madame Hélène was embroidering in her armchair, looking as if she had been severely reprimanded by Mama, which boded ill for me. I buried my head in the pillow, ashamed and miserable, knowing I had taken the risk of breaking an absolute taboo, and yet was none the wiser for it.

Later that year, when the blow fell, when the storm-clouds broke, I could not help believing, in the unreasoning, solipsistic way of guilty children, that there had been a connection. That some sacred rituals – even *good* magic – should not be exposed to the eyes of the uninitiated, at the risk of incurring the wrath of the gods. Looking back, I realize that this experience left a deeper mark on me than anyone could have foreseen at the time: a fear of curiosity, a squeamishness, an avoidance of the messy, unsettling underside of life which left me singularly unprepared to deal with it as an adult.

2

Sequestration

Later that year, when the blow fell, when the storm-clouds broke, it started with a speech broadcast over the radio. That was the first time I became aware that my life was susceptible to being caught in the slipstream of history, that a speech broadcast over the radio could change my life forever. The year I first became aware of the burden of belonging: to a name, a past.

One day that summer I came home to find my parents sitting in front of the television set in the living room. President Nasser's oversized features dominated the screen, the intense eyes smoky under the thick eyebrows. I remembered that it was Revolution Day, July 23, 1961. Nasser was giving a speech, one of his three-hour harangues that were regularly broadcast on radio and television. The familiar hypnotic voice rose and fell, echoed through the open windows by the radios blaring from the street. Everyone seemed to have the radio on: the man in the cigarette and candy kiosk on the corner, the doorkeepers, the motorists in their cars.

21

I started to say something and Mama put her finger to her lips. It was then that I became aware of the tension in the air. I turned to the television set. I couldn't understand every word that was being said, but the virulence in the tone was unmistakable. There were repeated references to 'the enemies of the people.'

Over the next few days many inexplicable things happened. When I asked questions I was told not to worry and sent to Madame Hélène. I overheard snatches of anguished conversations, whispered phone calls. I gathered enough to understand that, the day after the speech, at dawn, all my uncles, including the Pasha, had been taken away to an internment camp. That night Papa brought out a little overnight case. He packed some underwear, toiletries and medicine, and put the case under the mahogany sleigh bed in his bedroom.

One morning all the servants were gone, except for the cook and Ibrahim the doorkeeper. I found Mama sitting on a stool in the butler's pantry, talking to the cook.

'I'm so sorry,' she was saying, 'but you know we can't afford you any longer. You won't have any trouble finding a job as a chef with one of the hotels. You're a first class cook and you'll have the best references.'

The cook stood in the doorway to the kitchen, dramatically baring his scarred chest and declaiming that he had been with my parents since they first set up house and that he owed them the flesh on his shoulders. I assumed he was referring to the terrible accident in which he had incurred the burn scars on his chest. He had been trying to light the gas stove before the Feast the year before when the stove caught fire and he was wrapped in flames. Papa had ventured into the blaze

22

to turn off the gas, taking the risk that the entire cylinder would blow up in his face. The cook was rushed to the hospital, where, despite the severity of his condition, his eventual recovery was assured. Mama had been very sorry for him at the time and only much later made the remark that the fire probably started because the cook was so lazy about keeping the stove clean from grease.

'What I need for you to do,' Mama was saying that morning as she sat on a stool in the pantry, 'is to find a *suffragi*-cook for me, someone who doesn't need a kitchen boy, a *marmiton*, to help him. Of course I don't expect him to cook very well. It doesn't matter as long as he will settle for the salary I mentioned and won't mind doing some housework on the side. Help with the heavy cleaning, that sort of thing.'

The next morning, when the cook arrived, Mama went into the kitchen.

'Did you find someone?' she asked.

'I found you a cook who will be happy with the salary, doesn't need a *marmiton*, will peel the vegetables himself and will even mop the kitchen floor!' the cook concluded triumphantly.

'Well, where is he?'

'You're looking at him!' The cook beamed, slapping his chest.

But Mama was just as stubborn as the cook, and adamantly refused the sacrifice. Eventually a '*passe-partout*' was found. Dinners were no longer served the usual way, with the head-*suffragi* bringing around each dish in turn to your left and serving you himself. Meals were served 'family style' instead: the dishes were all placed on the table at once, and we passed them around and helped ourselves. I, for one, was pleased: it always looked so

23

much cosier in American movies and on television when I watched families sit down to dinner.

Madame Hélène stayed. She would not consider looking for another position, at her age.

Later that week four men in dark suits came to the house, clutching pens and clipboards. They were solemn and almost apologetic as they dispersed through every room of the house, making careful notes on every piece of furniture, every object, every bibelot. They even went into my room and counted my dolls. At the end of their tour they handed Mama a copy of the inventory they had made. When they left, one of them drove off with one of the two family cars. They also took the revolver that Papa kept to take on his trips to the estate, in case of highwaymen on the road.

Mama looked at the list and then at Papa. She started to laugh. 'Just look what they've written down. They have no idea what anything is, or what value to put on anything. We could sell any of the carpets or any of the vases, and replace them with fakes, and they'd never know the difference.' Then she looked at me and changed the subject.

At the end of the month, when the servants had to be paid, Mama's younger brother Hani came to pick her up. She wore sunglasses and she was biting her lip as she slipped a bank passbook into her handbag.

'I wish you didn't have to go through this.' Papa put his hand on her shoulder as he saw them off at the door.

'It's all right, really. There's just a chance – it's such a small account, they might have overlooked it.'

I went up to my bedroom and cornered Madame Hélène, who was writing a letter to 'le petit Luc.'

'Why is Uncle Hani taking Mama to the bank? Why

24

not Papa?'

'Because he would be recognized. All the family's bank accounts are frozen, and your mother's as well, because she's married to your Papa. All the family keep their accounts at the Banque du Caire. But Maman has one small savings account that she's had since she was a minor, in a little bank, I don't know its name. And of course the account's in her maiden name. So perhaps the sequestration authorities don't know about it. Madame is going with your uncle to try to cash it. Let's hope the bank would not have instructions to freeze the account, and that they would not realize who she was married to.' Madame Hélène shook her head and sighed. 'Who would have believed all this? It's like what happened to us during the war, my husband and I. I never thought I would hear that word "sequestration" again.' She sighed. 'Now please don't tell Madame I told you all this, she said you were not to be allowed to worry about these things.'

Mama and her brother came back an hour later. She looked at Papa and shook her head. Before Uncle Hani left, Mama handed him a small, velvet jewelry box.

'It's platinum and pearl, I don't know what it's worth, but see what you can do. All my valuable things were in the bank vault. I had taken out all my best pieces for the Bindari's wedding last month, if only I hadn't been in such a hurry to put them back in the vault . . .'

'What's that you're giving Uncle Hani?' I asked.

'One of my bracelets, the clasp is broken, it needs to be taken to the jeweler's to be fixed. Kiss your uncle and run upstairs now, darling, I think Madame Hélène is calling you.'

Later that night I looked for my parents to kiss them

25

goodnight. Mama's bedroom was dark but the French doors were open and I heard their voices coming from the verandah. Before I reached them the word 'divorce' made me stop in my tracks and hold my breath.

'I mean it,' my father was saying. 'You heard Nasser's speech. If I were to divorce you right away you could keep your property. But if you stay married to me, you lose everything. It's not fair to you. Most of my brothers are married to their cousins, their wives would be subject to the sequestration decrees anyway in their own right. But you wouldn't be. Nabil and Zakariah's wives wouldn't either, but they have no money of their own. But you do. No one would blame you if you asked for a divorce, it would be understood that you were doing it for the child's sake. I would be the first to defend you if anyone said a word against you.'

'Don't let's discuss this. There's no point.'

'I want you to think seriously about this before it's too late. You didn't marry me for love. You married me because I was one of the most eligible bachelors in Egypt. Things have changed.'

'You know my answer, once and for all. Promise me you won't bring this up again?'

I crept back to my room.

When school started in the fall, there was a lot of whispering among the other girls, cut short when I approached. The nuns patted me on the head for no special reason and murmured '*la pauvre petite.*'

My birthday fell on a weekend early in December, and nothing seemed different about the preparations that year. It was only as an adult that I realized what a sacrifice this appearance of normality must have represented. As

26

usual I handed out an invitation to every one of the twenty-two girls in my class, no R.S.V.P. requested. Every girl in class had always come to my birthday teas. Mama and Madame Hélène put together twenty-two bags of party favors. After lunch I wasn't allowed into the dining-room while they festooned it with balloons and streamers and set the table with an organdy tablecloth. At three the deliveries arrived: Mama had ordered the decorated birthday cake, the *gâteaux* and the *petits fours* from Simmond's in Zamalek. At three-thirty I put on a velvet dress with a lace collar hand-made by Madame Hélène, and a little gold locket that was Mama's present. It was one of hers that I'd always liked.

At four o'clock I waited for the doorbell to start ringing. By four-thirty only one girl had arrived, Aleya Bindari, who was a distant cousin. At five o'clock, looking stricken, Mama suggested we go ahead with the birthday party. She said she had heard that there was a case of measles going around the school and the other girls must either have come down with it or have stayed away for fear of getting exposed to it. I pretended to believe her, then and forever.

At school the following week only one of my class-mates apologized. 'I wanted to come, but my parents said I couldn't, because it wasn't safe to associate – you know, because of the sequestration.' I nodded, although I didn't really know what sequestration meant, nor, I suspected, did she.

One day the Arabic teacher, the only male instructor, came into class and announced that a new subject had been added to the curriculum by the Ministry of Education. It was called Arab Socialism and was mandatory. It would be one of only three subjects taught in Arabic, the other

27

two being the language itself and Religion for the Muslim pupils.

The Arabic teacher taught all three. During the break between Arabic class and Religion class, while the half dozen Coptic girls filed out for Bible study with one of the nuns, he could be heard noisily performing his prayer ablutions in the washroom next door to my classroom. He gargled and spat, and cleared his nose and throat copiously. When he walked back into class, the girls would giggle and make faces.

The new course, Arab Socialism, seemed to focus on identifying 'the enemies of the people', and the Arabic teacher took evident satisfaction in teaching it. He drilled us in the triumvirate of evil: 'Imperialism, Feudalism and Capitalism.' Whenever he reiterated the words: 'landowners,' or 'capitalists', he looked at me and at Aleya Bindari, who sat one row behind me.

I showed the textbook to my parents, with its illustrations of peasants being whipped by cruel landowners. 'Now they're poisoning the minds of children!' Papa erupted.

Mama quickly put a warning hand on his arm.

'You'll only confuse Gigi that way. And if she starts to repeat things at school . . . She's too young to carry that kind of burden.' She put an arm around me. 'One day you'll understand all this. Things aren't going to stay like this forever. You'll see. Just don't worry about it now.'

One morning in November when I woke up, I looked at the alarm clock and realized that I had been allowed to oversleep, I was late for school. Madame Hélène was sighing in her armchair, her boiled-egg eyes reddened. I ran to find my mother. Mama was on the phone in her bedroom, whispering urgently, a hand over her eyes. I

28

opened the door that led, through my mother's boudoir, into Papa's bedroom. It was empty and the suitcase under the bed was gone.

In an otherwise forgettable essay on glamor, I read the phrase 'our parents are our earliest celebrities', and I suppose that's true. In my own case, the recollection of my early years is colored by more than the rose-tinted glasses of childhood. I realize now that it is the easy life, the freedom from petty problems and concerns, that imparts the glamor of optimism and generosity.

I think what I regret most from 'the good old days' is the loss of lifestyle of the open house, of the easy welcome to guests at any time of day, on any day of the week. Merely to ask a drop-in guest if he would be staying for dinner rather than to assume, indeed to importune, him to do so, would have been considered irredeemably tactless. The cuisine and the etiquette may have been more or less cosmopolitan, but the spirit of hospitality was as uncompromisingly Egyptian as that of the country people with whom we shared our roots.

It's true that the easy welcome of the open house was made casual and effortless by the swarm of domestics hovering in the background. But it's just as true that the back door was always as wide open as the front. No beggar off the streets was turned away without a meal or a handout. Anyone with the most tenuous claim, whether of kinship or former service, could be sure of a regular stipend or a place to spend the night.

The nether regions of the house: the kitchen, the butler's pantry, the kitchen balcony, the maid's room and the all-purpose 'holding-room', were a domain into which I trespassed cautiously. At any time of day, but especially

29

at mealtimes, I never knew whom I might stumble upon: the doorkeeper's third cousin come up from the country, my aunt's wet nurse, the seamstress who did alterations and ran up the servants' clothes, the laundryman who did the ironing, the shoeshine man.

It's also true that, long after the front door was closed, the back door stayed open. And that the last luxuries we clung to were pride, and the good name of the family.

3

Past As Prologue

The good name of the family. Growing up, I was constantly aware of bearing the burden of belonging. You couldn't help it, when the mention of your last name invariably provoked a reaction not always easy for a child to read: dread or pity, envy or commiseration. You grow up unable to reconcile family loyalty with the virulent rhetoric from public podiums. You grow up with the myth of the 'good old days', before the revolution, antebellum, before you were born. All you have are photographs, but they cannot tell the whole story, because even the most candid snapshot always presupposes angles and editing.

You can pick one faded black and white photograph after another, and look at the people in it, so young, so carefree, and wonder how they never saw the storm clouds gathering. There is one particular snapshot I find in a worn leather album of my parents' wedding pictures, an incongruous photo tucked in the flap. This photograph, in black and white, was taken a couple of years before the Revolution, around 1950. A woman sits

31

between two men at a table in a restaurant, the men in light summer sharkskin suits, holding cigarettes, the woman in a scoop-necked cocktail gown. All three are smiling at the camera.

The broad-shouldered young man with the neat black moustache is my father, Shamel. The slender girl with the dark hair in a French twist is his niece. Her name was Gihan but he always called her Gina. The only time I ever heard him call her by her real name, she ran out of the room and he never saw her again. But this photo was taken before I was born, before my father was married.

The other man in the photo is shorter than my father, wiry, radiating energy. His lanky black hair falls over his forehead and his teeth flash in a smile that etches deep creases in his face. His name was Ali, and he was my father's best friend, but they had been estranged for years before his death.

Shamel splashed some water over his face and neck and came out of the bathroom. The room was quiet except for the sound of the fan, whirring clockwise in one direction, then counterclockwise back again. Ali Tobia was sprawled in an armchair, propping an open book on his bare, smooth chest. Maurice Baruch was slumped in front of the chess board, his head down on his arm, apparently snoozing. Shamel sat back down opposite him and moved a rook to the right. 'Your move,' he touched Maurice's arm. The other ignored him. He turned to Ali.

'Want to take over from Maurice? He seems to have fallen asleep.'

'Leave me alone, will you, I have to study. Some of us need to earn a living, you know.' Ali was an intern at the Kasr-El-Eini Hospital, not far from Garden City.

32

Shamel lit another cigarette. May was hotter than usual in Cairo that year. The three young men in the room had taken their shirts off. In the salamlek or 'bachelors annex' of the Cairo House, Shamel was free to entertain his friends as he pleased. The older, married brothers of the Seif-el-Islam family lived in the main house, while the unmarried, younger brothers slept in the salamlek, a separate small building a few feet away on the grounds.

Shamel poked Maurice again. 'Are you going to finish this game or not?'

There was no response. Shamel reached over and shook his friend's shoulder. Maurice rolled over onto the floor, the chair crashing down with him. Shamel dropped to his knees beside him and Ali leaped out of his armchair.

A few minutes later, Ali sat back on his heels and shook his head. The two men were pouring sweat from their efforts to resuscitate their friend. 'It's no use. We've tried everything. He must have been already dead when he fell.'

It was about a month later that Shamel stood, hesitating, one foot on the bottom step of the wide, curving marble staircase flanked by a pair of stone griffons. His grandfather had brought the griffons back from Italy, along with the Italian architect he commissioned to build the house. Seif-el-Islam Pasha's portrait hung in the hall, with his formidable handlebar moustaches, his tarbouche, and the sash and sword of a pasha of the Ottoman Empire.

The grandfather had been the one to make the momentous decision to uproot the clan from their family home on the cotton estates in the Delta and establish them in Cairo. The Egyptian Cotton Exchange in Alexandria was booming. Seif-el-Islam Pasha and his brother-in-law left for Europe with a suitcase full of Egyptian pounds, to which they each had a key; they helped themselves at will as they toured the continent. It was in Italy that the Pasha finally saw the palazzo he would set his heart on. Within three years the family moved into the brand-new mansion in Garden City that came to be known as the Cairo House.

Twenty years later, he sent for his Jesuit-educated son from Paris, married him to an heiress and found him a seat in Parliament. It was time for men like him to lead the nationalist movement against the British and against the Albanian dynasty that ruled Egypt. His son died at fifty, but the old Pasha had the satisfaction of seeing his grandson chairman of the most powerful party in the country.

The wealthy heiress that Seif-el-Islam Pasha had chosen for his son's bride was an only child; this unusual circumstance was a result of her mother's gullibility. Her mother had been a beautiful redhead Circassian from one of the Muslim regions of the Russian steppes. The women in her Egyptian husband's household could barely contain their spite against this lovely and somewhat dim-witted foreigner. When her first child, a girl, was born, they convinced her that, according to local superstition, her daughter would die if the mother subsequently had a male child. The poor woman believed them, and resorted to midwives' tricks to prevent another pregnancy. Her husband, however, did not immediately take another wife, as the spiteful women had hoped. When he died unexpectedly, his daughter was the only heir to his considerable fortune.

At fifteen she was married off to Seif-el-Islam Pasha's handsome son, and bore him thirteen children, of whom nine survived. Two babies had died in succession before

34

the youngest, Shamel, was born. She insisted on having him sleep in a small bed in her boudoir until he was eight. That was the year his father died of a heart attack, and his older brothers decided that it was time for him to move into the bachelors annex with them.

Shamel strode up the stairs and stopped briefly in his mother's bedroom to kiss her hand, as he did every morning. Then he crossed the gallery to his oldest brother's suite. He knocked, just in case his sister-in-law was still in bed, and went in. There was no one in the bedroom. His sister-in-law must be up already, seeing to the needs of the household, and he could hear the Pasha washing in the bathroom. Shamel referred to his oldest brother, who was eighteen years his senior, by his title, as did most of the family.

The Pasha came out of the bathroom in his satin dressing gown. 'Good morning,' he smiled. 'Well, well, it's been a while since you joined us for breakfast. Shall I ring for some more tea?'

Shamel glanced at the breakfast tray with the flat, buttery pastry, the white slab of thick clotted cream and the clover-scented honey. It was his favorite breakfast, but he could not muster an appetite. He had lost considerable weight lately. He shook his head.

The Pasha reached for the first cigar of the day and sank into a comfortable club chair. 'Your sister Zohra was complaining just last night that you haven't been to visit her in a fortnight. What have you been doing with yourself?'

Shamel suspected that his brother already had a fairly good idea of the answer to that question. Not that the Pasha was in the habit of keeping tabs on his family. But

35

the chief of the Cairo police reported directly to him; as a courtesy he routinely included briefings on the movements of any and all of the cars belonging to the Pasha's address. Their special single-digit Garden City license plates identified them immediately to the police all over Cairo. Shamel had found this to be a mixed blessing. If he was in a hurry he could park his car almost anywhere without getting a ticket. On the other hand, the police report was not for the Pasha's eyes only; it was turned over to the `Abeddin Palace.

Shamel supposed that the Pasha was aware that, of late, his youngest brother had neglected his familiar haunts and regular nightclub companions; had taken solitary trips to the country; and had spent several hours with an illustrious doctor of theology at the Azhar University.

'There's something on your mind.' The Pasha puffed on his cigar. 'I'm listening. You've not been yourself lately. I know it must have been a shock for you, your friend Maurice dropping dead like that. And so young too, in his twenties.'

'That's just it. You never think it could happen to someone your own age. I mean, you live your life, you sow your wild oats, you think you have all the time in the world, to settle down later, to make everything right with Allah and your fellow-man. And then, just like that . . . You realize that you can run out of time at any moment.' He shook his head. He was quiet for a minute, then he turned to face his brother. 'I've come to ask for your permission. To get married.'

The Pasha listened, nodding from time to time. If he had an inkling of the nature of Shamel's revelation, he did not show it. Shamel had learned very early on that

36

his oldest brother could listen to the same piece of information five times from five different people and leave each one of his interlocutors with the impression that he was imparting news.

'Well, well, so you've decided it's time to settle down. Of course, what a shock, that poor Baruch boy – You know, someone else would have dealt with that very differently. But you were always mature for your age. I think you're making the right decision. Congratulations.' The Pasha puffed on his cigar, deep in thought. 'When I get back from the ministry this evening we must get together with all your brothers and decide about dividing up the inheritance. We always said we'd do it when you came of age. We should have done it five years ago, but there never seemed to be a good time. Now that you're thinking of getting married, it's high time.'

The Pasha got up and started to put on the suit that was set out for him on the clotheshorse. He picked out a bow tie and matching silk pocket square. 'What do you think of the land around the Kafr-el-Kom villages? It's good cotton land, and there are mango orchards. It's right next to the land your brother Zakariah has his eye on; the two of you can take turns running both estates.'

He picked up two soft, silver-backed brushes, one in each hand, and brushed his thinning dark hair with both brushes at once. 'Do you have a particular bride in mind? No? Then I assume you're leaving that to the women?'

'As soon as I had settled it with you, I was going to speak to Zohra – and to Dorria too, of course,' Shamel added, remembering his sister-in-law.

'Good, good. You couldn't make them happier if you offered them Solomon's treasures. It will keep them occupied for months.' The Pasha clearly relished the thought.

37

'I swear there is nothing women enjoy as much as match-making.' He buttoned up his waistcoat and pressed his tarbouche down on his head. 'There, I'm ready. Let's go.'

As the Pasha and Shamel opened the door, Om Khalil straightened up from her position at the keyhole. The Cairo House teemed with intrigues, what with its three sets of married brothers, the bachelor brothers, distant relatives and assorted hangers-on. The Pasha sometimes found it more of a challenge to manage the politics of his household than those of his cabinet. The thirty-odd domestics played an indispensable role in the scheme as spies and couriers. So Om Khalil did not bother to disguise or excuse her eavesdropping behind the door. She threw her head back, put her hand to her mouth and released the blood-curdling whoop of rejoicing called a *zaghruta*. The men groaned. They knew that in a few hours every household of their acquaintance would have been informed that the youngest of the Seif-el-Islam brothers had thrown his hat in the ring.

Shamel drove across the Kasr-el-Aini Bridge, flanked by its British stone lions, and down the Nile Corniche to his older sister Zohra's villa on the island of Zamalek in the middle of the river at its widest point in Cairo.

'Is Zohra Hanem home?' Shamel asked the maid who opened the door. 'Good, I'll go up then. And go tell Sitt Gina that if she's ready in twenty minutes I'll take her out to dinner.'

There were twenty years between Shamel and his oldest sister Zohra, so that his nieces were only a few years younger than he was. Zohra had four daughters, and each of her three youngest brothers had a favorite niece whom he chaperoned and squired around to restaurants and shows. Shamel's favorite was the oldest, Gina, not because she was the prettiest – the youngest was considered the beauty – but because she was the most intelligent and spirited.

Shamel found his sister sitting in front of her secretary desk, tallying up the household accounts. When Shamel told her the news she jumped up and hugged him. 'Have you told anyone yet but the Pasha? Do you have anyone in mind? No? Will you leave it to me and Dorria then, to find you a bride?'

'All right. But no cousins. There's too much inter-marriage in our family already. You know how I feel about that.' Zohra herself was married to a cousin on her mother's side; it had been a difficult marriage. 'And none of these "modern" girls,' he added. 'I've known too many of them.'

'Of course, of course. Leave it to me. These things take time, they have to be handled very delicately.' Zohra's eyes gleamed at the prospect. She was already weighing and dismissing various possibilities. 'Why don't you go see the girls? You've been such a stranger lately, they've missed their favorite uncle.' It was obvious that Zohra could barely contain her impatience to get on the phone.

Shamel headed down the corridor towards his nieces' rooms. It occurred to him as he caught whiffs of lemon juice and talcum powder, nail polish and hot curling irons, that four daughters in the house was something like a cottage industry. His arrival was greeted with squeals of alarm, cries of welcome and doors being pulled hastily shut. His youngest niece, Mimi, skipped down the corridor towards him. She tossed her chestnut brown plait over her shoulder and offered a plump cheek for a kiss.

'The bath woman is here today,' she confided. 'They're

39

all getting their legs waxed with sugar wax, then smoothed with pumice stone. I'm glad I don't have to do that yet. It hurts! Come in here.' She pulled him by the hand into a small sitting room where a dressmaker was running up a nightgown. 'Gina's almost ready.' She sat him down and perched on the arm of the chair. 'Why is it always Gina? When are you going to take me out?' She pouted.

'When you're older. And when you stop eating so much Turkish Delight. You're turning into a piece of Turkish Delight yourself.' He pinched her chubby pale arm.

'Gina's taking so long because her hair takes forever to hold a set,' Mimi announced spitefully. 'It's so floppy she has to set it with beer. But Nazli's hair is so coarse and curly, she has to straighten it with the curling tongs. She even waxes her forearms. Why –'

'Mimi! Wait till Mama hears how you've been talking!' Gina came in, smoothing the puffed skirt of her flow-ered-print silk dress. 'Sorry to keep you waiting, Uncle Shamel,' she gave him a peck on the cheek. 'Where are we going?'

'The Romance. I haven't taken you there yet. They have a new band, all the latest sambas and rhumbas. And Samya Gammal is the featured belly dancer for tonight. She's back from Europe, she just finished filming a movie with Fernandel.'

Gina looked around the dance floor. The band was playing an animated 'Mambo Americano, Hey Mambo'. She sighed. One thing her favorite uncle could not do was dance, and of course it was out of the question for her to dance with anyone else. She put down her fork. Her portion of the Chateaubriand steak for two they had

40

ordered was daunting. She put her hand on Shamel's arm and motioned with her head. 'That man that just came in – I think he's trying to catch your eye.'

Shamel looked over across the dance floor.

'Oh, that's Ali Tobia. He's a good friend of mine.' He waved to Ali, who crossed over to their table. Shamel offered him a seat and introduced him to Gina. They shook hands. It seemed to Shamel that it took Ali a heartbeat too long to muster his easy smile and that Gina turned her attention back to the dance floor a little too self-consciously. It was hard to read young girls, Shamel thought, but his friend was a different story; he knew Ali well enough to sense his momentary loss of composure. At the first opportunity he would mention that Gina was spoken for. It would avoid complications, and in any case it was true enough.

A sudden scurrying and whispering on the part of the staff was followed by an expectant hush. All eyes turned to the door as King Faruk and his retinue made their way to a table by the dance floor. The diners at the other tables stood up and applauded. The three at Shamel's table clapped perfunctorily. The king lowered his great bulk into his chair, people took their seats and the band resumed playing. Faruk's head turned slowly toward Shamel's table; he stared in their direction for a moment, then turned away. Pouli, his Italian valet, whispered something to the maître d'hotel. Faruk would be informed in a minute who was responsible for this public display of disrespect.

'I think we might as well go somewhere else,' Shamel suggested, motioning to the waiter for the bill. He handed Ali his car keys. 'Why don't you go ahead and take Gina to the car? I'll follow as soon as I've settled the bill.'

41

Several other tables with young women in their party were following suit. The king had a reputation for forcing unwelcome attentions on any woman who happened to catch his eye. As a preliminary, he would send a bottle of champagne, with his compliments, to the woman's table. If his overtures were repulsed, disagreeable incidents ensued. Faruk could be dangerous; it was widely believed that he had arranged for the 'accidental' death of a young officer, the fiancé of a woman Faruk was currently besotted with.

By the time Shamel joined Gina and Ali in the car, the incident with the king had had the effect of completely dismissing from his mind his earlier misgivings about having introduced them.

That summer, as every summer, there was a mass migration of households to escape the heat of Cairo during the mosquito-infested months of the Nile flood. Those families that were not vacationing in Europe sent the staff ahead to air and clean their summer homes in Alexandria. A few days later the entire household would follow. Shamel shuttled between the seaside and his new duties on the estate in the Delta. Ali Tobia came up from Cairo every weekend that he could get away from hospital assignments.

The days were spent at cabanas on the private beaches. At around ten in the morning the beach boys unlocked the cabanas and set up the parasols and chairs on the sand. By noon the beach would be busy.

'*Fresca! Ritza! Granita*! "Life"!'

All day long the vendors walked up and down, hawking tiny honey and nut pastries, raw sea urchins, water ices and magazines in four languages. The waiters from the

42

cafeteria on the pier hurried back and forth in their embroidered caftans, carrying pitchers of frothy yellow-green lemonade the color of the foamy waves that lapped at their feet.

At two o'clock in the afternoon the Corniche was clogged with chauffeur-driven cars bearing full-course hot lunches which would be served on folding tables in the cabanas. Reluctant, brown children were called out of the water by nurses with large towels at the ready. In swimsuits and burnouses, families sat down to lemon sole and sweet sticky mangoes. Lunch invitations were passed along from cabana to cabana.

By sundown the beach boys folded the parasols and pulled the light wooden paddle boards up the sand and stacked them. The beaches were deserted for the night spots.

All through that long, lazy summer the photographers trudged up and down the shore with their pant legs rolled up, their equipment slung over their shoulders, looking for likely prospects. They snapped the photos and came back with a print the next day. Shamel had a photograph with Gina and Ali sitting on either side of him, at a table in the garden of the Beau Rivage hotel at night; wrapped around Gina's wrist was a string of jasmine blossoms that Ali had bought from a street vendor. Looking at the photograph, later, Shamel wondered how he could have been so blind.

It was late August when the three of them were having dinner on the terrace of the Beau Rivage. There was an end-of-summer air about the folded parasols and the black flags fluttering on the beaches. The strings of lights suspended from the trees swayed in the breeze and Gina drew her wrap around her bare shoulders. Shamel got up to use the washroom.

When he came back to the nearly deserted restaurant, Gina and Ali had their heads together, whispering urgently. She shook her head and turned away. He reached for her hand. She laid her forearm flat on the table between them and turned her palm up. He covered her hand with his and pressed her fingers apart. She closed her eyes.

When they heard Shamel coming they jumped apart. He sat down between them.

'How long has this been going on?' He put up a hand. 'Never mind. I tell you one thing. It stops right here, or else you speak to Gina's father tonight.'

'Do you think I haven't tried?' Ali burst out. 'I've wanted to tell you. I've wanted to ask for her hand from her father, for weeks now. But Gina won't let me. We were arguing about that again just now.'

'He doesn't know Papa,' she pleaded. 'You know what he's like, Uncle Shamel. We don't stand a chance. Give us some time. Maybe if I can talk Mama around to our side first –'

'No.' Shamel had seen enough. He was not going to be responsible for what might happen between them. 'You talk to your father tonight, Gina. I'll come with you, I'll do my best to convince him. But if the answer is no, then that's that. Ali?'

'Of course,' Ali nodded miserably. 'You have my word. You should know me better than to ask.'

Gina's father, Makhlouf Pasha, never felt as out of place as he did in his wife Zohra's boudoir. He was not sure what grated most on his sensibilities: the uncomfortable

44

preciousness of her Louis XVI-style bergères or the feminine froufrou of the chiffon skirt of her dressing table. It reminded him that he lived in a household of women.

A few minutes in his wife's boudoir were enough to make Makhlouf Pasha long to be on horseback in the country, touring some corner of his land. In the freshness of the dawn he would ride out to the white pigeon towers of the Bani Khidr village, wheel his mare around and whip her into a flat gallop all the way home. They said of Makhlouf Pasha that he rode his peasants as hard as he rode his horses, but he only really felt at home among them. He was proud of not being an absentee landlord, like most of his wife's citified, Europeanized brothers.

His cousin Zohra had been barely sixteen when he married her, but even then Makhlouf realized that he could never completely cow her. Had she born him a son, she would have been intolerable. But every time she had been pregnant with a boy, she had miscarried in her last term. Allah knew Makhlouf had indulged her every whim during her pregnancies. She could not suffer his presence in the first months: she claimed the sight of his thick, red lips made her ill, it reminded her of raw meat. Baffled and humiliated, he would take off for the country and return after the months of morning sickness were over. But his sons had been still-born. Only the four girls survived.

Allah had not seen fit to give Makhlouf the sons who should bear his name and inherit his land. But his brothers had sons, many of them, and his daughters would marry their cousins. His grandchildren would bear his name, and the land of their great-grandfathers would not be parceled out to the sons of strangers.

45

Makhlouf Pasha had always made clear his expectations in that respect. So he was astonished and annoyed as he sat in his wife's boudoir and listened to his young kinsman and brother-in-law, Shamel, intercede on behalf of some fortune-hunting suitor for Gihan.

'Ali is no fortune-hunter,' Shamel objected, 'and you know as well as I do that the Tobia family goes back a long way.'

'Much good that does them!' Makhlouf was stung by the hint at his own *parvenu* status. 'All I know is that they've run through their fortune. Oh, they live well, vacations in Europe every summer and all that. But there won't be one fedan left for that boy to inherit by the time his father is done selling off their property. And even if he owned half the Sharkia province, I wouldn't marry a daughter of mine into a family with such "modern" notions. It's a scandal how his sisters drive their own cars and smoke in public. I ask you!' He threw his hands up in exasperation. 'No, Gihan will marry one of her cousins, that was decided a long time ago. Now I'm not an unreasonable man. I'm not imposing my choice on her. My brother Hussein has three boys and Zulfikar has four. She can pick and choose.'

Makhlouf Pasha leaned back and closed his eyes. He stopped listening to Shamel's arguments and Gihan's pleading, he ignored Zohra's interjections. He took a deep breath and tried to control his rising temper. His blood pressure was dangerously high, the doctor had warned him repeatedly not to get worked up. He opened his eyes.

'Listen. I've been very patient, but enough is enough.' For once even Zohra was silenced. She knew him well enough to know when he could not be budged.

'Gihan will get engaged to one of her cousins within

46

the month. I don't want to hear any more about Ali Tobia. If you ever see him again, Gihan, I will disown you.'

A week later Gina was engaged to her uncle Zulfikar's second eldest son. She did not see Ali Tobia again till Shamel's wedding.

By the end of summer Shamel had settled on his choice for a bride. The fact that the new fiancée was no kin helped to minimize the inevitable slight to the matchmakers whose candidates were passed over. It was grudgingly admitted that Shamel's choice was perfectly appropriate in every way, and that she had the best kind of reputation, in other words, none. After lengthy, delicate negotiations and a short engagement period, the wedding was set for an evening in late October.

The double front doors of the Cairo house were flung open, as they had been so many times before, for weddings and funerals. The chandeliers in the hall blazed down on the scores of huge, free-standing flower arrangements sent from all over Cairo and the provinces. At the far corner of the salon, a *kosha* had been set up, a bower of white flowers where the bride and groom would be enthroned in state for the first part of the evening. The bride had arrived an hour earlier in a limousine followed by a procession of cars, and had emerged, in a pale pink chiffon gown, on her uncle's arm, to a volley of *zaghrutas* and clapping. She had been hurried up the stairs to change into her Paris wedding gown with the help of hairdressers and maids of honor. Armand, Cairo's premier photographer, followed in due course with his assistants, and the bride was photographed standing alone against a sweeping drapery of red satin and ten-foot-tall, bird-of-paradise arrangements in baskets.

47

Meanwhile downstairs, suffragis in brilliant caftans circulated with trays of jewel-toned nectars and mounds of almond dragées. The guests who had been milling around the two salons now crowded the bottom of the staircase in the hall; the rumor had spread that the bride and groom were about to make an appearance. Everyone prepared for the *zaffa*, the slow procession down the staircase that was the highlight of an Egyptian wedding. The belly dancers adjusted their sequined sashes, the torch-bearers lit their torches, the flower girls picked up their baskets. Under Zohra's direction, the unmarried girls and boys of the clan lined the steps of the staircase on both sides, holding tall, flickering tapers. Gina took her place with her sisters and cousins at the top of the stairs, one hand shielding the flame of her candle from a sudden breeze.

There was a burst of ear-splitting *zaghrutas* from the maids at the back of the second floor gallery, drawing everyone's attention to the top of the stairs. Belly dancers clicking castanets and musicians clashing cymbals and banging drums wound their way slowly down the steps. Then came the flower girls, tossing wafer-thin, gilded coins. The bride and groom finally made their appearance at the top of the landing, the bride in a bare-shouldered gown of creamy satin entirely embroidered with tiny seed pearls, long satin gloves and a diamond pendant at her throat; the tall, beaming groom in a black frock coat. They stood there for a few moments while the guests broke out in applause and the photographers popped their flashbulbs. Then the groom gave the bride his arm and they started slowly down the stairs, one step at a time, stopping every so often to let the maids of honor adjust the long, heavy satin train and the frothy

48

tulle of the veil sweeping behind them. As Gina followed the procession around the curve of the landing, she saw Ali Tobia at the far end of the hall, in a group of young men. She looked away almost as soon as their eyes met.

The zaffa procession made its leisurely way down the stairs and through the hall to the kosha set up at the far corner of the inner salon, and there was a pause while the bridesmaids negotiated the task of drawing the train out of the bride's way and arranging it in a pool of shimmering satin at her feet. The bridesmaids took turns sitting on little stools at the feet of the bride and groom. Gina discreetly slipped away when it was Ali's turn to approach the kosha dais and greet the wedding couple. The photographers snapped endless photos and the belly dancers entertained the crowd, as the Pasha beamed and greeted, and Zohra supervised and ordered the wait staff and the photographers about.

Eventually the bride and groom got up from their gilded chairs in the bower of flowers to go upstairs and change for the second part of the evening. Gina followed the bride to one of the suites while the groom's attendants followed him to another. Half an hour later, the bride made her reappearance in a pale lemon, sleeveless satin gown trimmed with wide black bands of pearl and jet embroidery; she wore long black satin gloves to match and her diamond pendant mounted on a black velvet ribbon around her neck. The groom had changed into a white smoking jacket and black tie. They made their way down the stairs again and headed to the dining room where they cut a ceremonial ribbon to open the grand buffet, and the guests took their places at the tables set out around the dining room and the hall.

The long evening stretched into the early hours of the

49

morning, and the bride and groom got up again to cut the wedding cake. Finally the center of the hall was cleared and a full orchestra of traditional musicians set up their chairs and stands as the guests gathered around. The legendary singer Om Kalthoum, clutching her trademark chiffon handkerchief, belted out song after song in her deep, powerful voice, urged on by cries of 'Allah' and 'Encore.'

When the first light of day broke, the bride and groom went upstairs for the last time, to one last tribute of *zaghrutas* and applause. The first guest got up to leave, picking up the wedding favor at his place at table, a silver ashtray embossed with the couple's intertwined initials and filled with pink and white dragées. As the long hours of the wedding wore to a close, as the drawn-out litany of leave-taking took place, the 'mabruk' and 'may your turn be next' echoing over and over, Gina and Ali breathed a sigh of relief; throughout it all, they had somehow avoided coming face to face.

Two months later Makhlouf Pasha sank into an armchair in his salon, his thick fingers splayed on his beefy thighs, his muddy shoes planted squarely on the rose border of the Aubusson carpet. He had just arrived in Cairo an hour ago, and the servants had scurried because they had not expected the Pasha to be back from the country till evening. Zohra Hanem was out shopping with the three youngest ladies, and Sitt Gihan had gone out on her own a while ago.

The doorbell rang and he heard the voice of his oldest daughter as she greeted the maid. Then she walked through the French doors of the salon, dropping her handbag on the console on the way.

50

'Hello, Papa.'

'Where were you?' he barked.

She stopped in the middle of the salon. One look at her face brought the blood rushing to Makhlouf's head. Gihan could never hide anything.

'Answer me. Where were you? Did you see that Ali Tobia?'

She stood there, not saying a word, head up, eyes down, twisting her gloves. Even as a child, Makhlouf thought, she did not lie or whine when she was accused; she should have been a boy. He felt the blood surge behind his eyes so he could hardly see. How dare she stand there, facing him down! He grasped the arms of his chair and tried to heave his bulk out of it.

'Papa, be careful!' Gina instinctively took a step forward, to help him up.

He swung his arm back and lunged at her, swiping blindly at her face as he lost his balance. She screamed and turned, running for the door.

'Get out!' He was frothing at the mouth. 'Don't ever come back! You're no longer my daughter!'

She ran out, not stopping to pick up her handbag.

A few hours later, Zohra let Shamel into her husband's bedroom. 'No one has been able to go near him,' she whispered, her eyes red. Shamel patted her hand and closed the door behind him. In the semi-darkness of the room he made out the figure of his brother-in-law lying on the bed, still wearing his muddy shoes.

'Who is it?' Makhlouf Pasha growled, lifting the ice pack off his forehead. 'Oh, it's you! I should throw you out of my house! It's all your fault. I trust you with my daughter and you play the Pander between her and that—'

51

'I wanted to tell you that Gina –'

'Don't ever pronounce that name in my house! I have no daughter by that name.'

'She only disobeyed you that one time, I swear. And nothing happened. Even after you threw her out and she ran to Ali, he brought her straight to me, he didn't even let her through his door. The last thing he wants to do is compromise her. Don't you see that you're wrong about him? He would marry her this minute, in the dress she's wearing, but he must have your blessing. He won't make her choose between him and her family. And he has too much pride to marry her without her father's permission. The Tobias have their pride too.'

'By Allah she'll have nothing from me! Not one feddan after I die and not one piastre while I'm living. She'll be sorry. No wedding trousseau, no shopping trip to Europe, no furniture, no decorator, no antiques, nothing. Let's see how long this true love will last.'

'It won't make a difference to Gina. If it were any of her sisters, I'd agree with you. But she's different, things like that don't matter to her. And I can speak for Ali. All he wants is Gina – but not without your blessing.'

'Then let him have her! In nothing but the dress she is wearing!'

'And your blessing –'

'My blessing, my curses! Now get out before you kill me!'

It was a happy ending, for a while. Gina and Ali set up house in an apartment with simple modern furniture. My parents were newlyweds themselves, and the two couples were inseparable. When I was born, my father named me Gihan.

52

That year the coup d'état of 1952 changed everything, although no one at the time realized the magnitude of what was happening.

The day came when the bulk of the large estates was confiscated from the landowning families. Mostly the *fellahin* accepted this momentous change with their usual mixture of resignation and indifference, but there were isolated incidents of violence. When the rumor spread that government agents were on the way to confiscate Makhlouf Pasha's country house, a mob of peasants besieged the place. Their intention seemed to have been to loot the house before the agents arrived. Makhlouf came out on the terrace and roared at them, and they took a few steps back. But he was suddenly struck by a massive stroke and collapsed, speechless. The *fellahin* surged forward; some of them were carrying torches and they set fire to the house. Makhlouf and his family were smuggled out in a car, the two youngest girls lying on the floor. Makhlouf never recovered from the effects of the stroke; he remained a paralyzed husk of a man.

Ten years later the selective sequestration decrees targeted certain families, notably the Seif-el-Islams and the Makhloufs. Gina's sisters, married to their cousins, sold off their jewelry and their furniture, piece by piece, to live from day to day.

Meanwhile Ali's reputation as a brilliant cardiologist had risen steadily. The waiting rooms at his clinic overflowed and he was increasingly called in for consultations by the most prominent members of the new regime. His success cost him long hours away from home, but he encouraged Gina to go out without him. She was often seen at parties and restaurants, always with a group of close friends from the new elite of doctors and their wives.

One day the rumors started about Gina and the scion of a Lebanese banking family. She did not lie to Ali.

'You're my only friend,' she pleaded, 'help me.'

He acted like a perfect gentleman: he divorced her on the spot, pronouncing the ritual words 'I release you,' three times in quick succession. He told her she could take anything she wanted, as long as she left quickly. She took nothing but photographs of the two children she was leaving behind, Leila and Tamer. There was no question of taking the children with her; they were both of an age when custody would have gone automatically to the father, even if the mother were not the one to ask for divorce, even if she were not leaving the country, even if she were not remarrying.

I remember the day Gina left for Lebanon; she came to our house to say goodbye. I was fourteen at the time. I watched from the balcony as she arrived in the Lebanese playboy's sports car. He stayed in the car, but I got a glimpse of dark sunglasses and a gold bracelet on his wrist glinting as he tapped his fingers on the side-view mirror.

Gina ran up the stairs and into the living-room where my father was waiting. She came towards him, arms outstretched. 'You're the one person I couldn't leave without saying goodbye!'

'Goodbye, Gihan,' he said very quietly.

She stopped dead in her tracks. Then she turned on her heel and ran out of the room and down to her lover waiting in the car.

At the time I misjudged my father's harshness. I even attributed it to the fact that the man was a Maronite, and that Gina would marry out of her religion. But I realize now that it had nothing to do with it. My father was a romantic. He had believed in their love, his Gina and his

54

best friend. He could not forgive her for disillusioning him.

Many years later, Tante Zohra was to tell me that for Gina it always had to be the grand passion. She was one of those women who need to feel in love, the way an addict craves an elusive state of euphoria. She could not bear to see her romance with Ali succumb to routine and neglect; she could not bear to be taken for granted. She looked for the immediacy, the missing thrill, the passion, in the eyes and the arms of another.

Today I can try to understand the fugue for which Gina was condemned without appeal by everyone she knew. But what I remember thinking at the time was that I could never bear to disillusion my father that way. Did Gina give a thought that day to the adolescent girl watching from the corner? Do we ever realize, when we take a plunge, that the ripples we create can spread as far as the distant shore? But there was no way anyone could have imagined then that Gina's story would lie like a palimpsest under mine, long after it had faded from memory.

As for Gina, Papa never saw her again. A few years later the civil war broke out in Lebanon; it must have been particularly hard for her, a Muslim married to a Maronite.

But he did see Ali again. A year after Gina left him Ali remarried, a younger woman with ties to the new regime. He became President Nasser's personal physician. So it was hard to believe when Dr Ali Tobia came to visit my father one night. It had been years, even before his divorce from Gina, that he had not come to our house. Few people who had anything to lose risked association with the families that Nasser had designated as 'enemies

55

of the people'. It was no secret that the intelligence agent at the door took note of every visitor, that the telephone was tapped and the servants were spies. Even in the privacy of our own bedrooms, between parent and child, we still whispered. That Nasser's personal physician would risk calling on my father was unthinkable.

Yet one summer night, there was Ali Tobia. He looked tired, the creases in the craggy face were deeper, but his smile was unchanged. He chucked me under the chin as if I were still seven rather than seventeen. Then he and my father went out to the verandah to talk in private. I remember seeing the tips of their cigarettes glowing in the dark for over an hour.

Only after Ali's death did I learn from my father why he had come that night. He needed to confide in someone he could trust. He was convinced that Nasser was paranoid, clinically paranoid, and increasingly irrational and dangerous. A few months later Ali Tobia died overnight of an unexplained illness. It was generally believed that Nasser had his physician poisoned for spreading rumors about him.

4

The Proposal

The girl watching from the corner, the girl I once was. Where do I start looking for her? In retrospect, she seems to have drifted along like a leaf borne downstream. When could she have changed course?

I flip through an album of my own wedding pictures. These photographs are in color, and that difference in itself seems to mark a distinct shift in time and mood, the inherent glamor and nostalgia of the black and white images replaced by the stark, bright immediacy of the color prints. I am looking at a photo of a young bride with a round, sweet face and long, dark brown hair. She is looking straight at the camera, unsmiling, and the only expression behind the blankness of her wide eyes is a flicker of apprehension. But I am only guessing. I can close my eyes and get under the skin of the child of nine, but when I look at the photo of the bride of nineteen it is like looking at a stranger. Somewhere in the intervening years I have lost the key to her thoughts and emotions.

Perhaps it is the evolution girls go through in the process of molding themselves in the image of a feminine 'other'. The wild, willful 'I' is mercilessly renounced like the outgrown, embarrassing, favorite things of childhood. They become strangers to themselves. Years later, a change in their lives can trigger a return full circle, and they rediscover their lost voice.

The Gigi I remember at eighteen was a little set apart by her circumstances and consequently unusually sheltered and naive. She lived largely in her books and her imagination; the outside world filtered through as feebly as light through the thick wooden shutters of Mediterranean windows.

In the way that the particular, rather than the general, colors our fundamental experience of growing up, hers was a cherished, normal girlhood. All children have nightmares about a bogeyman. For Gigi the bogeyman was real, he had a name and a face. The black-browed face was inescapable on a million posters throughout the country: the intense, sooty eyes, the prominent nose, the moustache, the lantern jaw. The name was whispered: Nasser, El-Raiis; his thousand eyes and ears lurked behind every corner. She did not have nightmares, only she was a very light sleeper, and she always woke at dawn, straining her ears; when they came for her father, it was at dawn.

She never heard her father talk about his experiences in the internment camps. At home he spent hours smoking in an armchair, lost in his thoughts. He had no land or business left to run. According to the sequestration decrees that applied to most of the men in the families affected, he was barred from practicing law or belonging to a professional syndicate or even a social club. Like a prisoner on

58

parole, he could not leave the city without clearance from the authorities, nor leave the country under any circumstances. His revolver and passport were confiscated. Nasser's sequestration decree went far beyond the confiscation of wealth or the stripping of civil liberties. It was the sharply-honed instrument of his malice: it emasculated, it isolated, it muzzled, it humiliated, it stigmatized; it forced retirement on men in their prime; it immured them in their own homes.

If the diffuse gloom that hung in the air at home had an effect on Gigi, it was to teach her a sort of precocious tact. She learned to be unquestioning and accepting, in order to spare the adults who imagined they were shielding her. She cultivated a bubbly surface. Mama in particular regarded any sign of moodiness as alarming.

She waited patiently for life to begin, without giving a single conscious thought to what she was supposed to be waiting for, until her aunt Zohra's visit set the wheels of this unspoken destiny in motion.

'Gigi! There you are.' Madame Hélène stood at the door, a little out of breath. 'Reading again? You'll ruin your eyes, *ma petite! Monsieur* is looking for you. He's in the study.'

Gigi put down *Le Rouge et le Noir* with a sigh. She went downstairs to the study. Papa was sitting at his desk. The window behind him let in the afternoon sunshine and a whiff of jasmine from the bushes outside. Gigi perched on the arm of his chair, watching him fill his pipe, his movements careful and precise, the back of his hands shadowed with dark hair. He had given up cigarettes years ago, since his first heart attack. Gigi loved the smell of the aromatic pipe tobacco.

'Well, Gigi, your Arabic tutor tells me you need to do some reading if you're going to pass your Arabic exam for the baccalaureate this year.'

Gigi made a face.

Her father laughed. 'Considering that Madame Hélène was just complaining you stayed up all night reading a novel by Zola—'

'Not Zola. Stendhal.'

'Stendhal, then. Surely you can make yourself read a dozen pages a day of Naguib Mahfouz.'

'His books are so – depressing.' She flipped through a book titled *Midaq Alley*.

On her way elsewhere Gigi had been driven through some of these back alleys, her nose firmly buried in a French novel, avoiding the sight of the beggars; of the carcasses of meat hanging on hooks in front of the butcher shops; of the flies on children's faces; of the peasant woman sitting cross-legged on the railroad station platform, suckling a baby on one swollen, bare breast. The woman had been totally unselfconscious, and no one had stared at her. Whether it was motherhood or misery that removed the provocation from her nudity, Gigi had not been able to tell.

Papa took the book from her and put it back on the shelf. 'One day you'll appreciate Mahfouz's writing. But never mind for now.' He pointed to the bookcase behind him. 'Pick a book by Yussef El-Siba`yi. They're harmless romantic novels about cavalry officers and pretty young girls.'

'They sound like books by Delly. I don't like the *roman à l'eau de rose* type either! But all right, if you insist.'

Gigi leaned against his shoulder.

'Papa, were you ever sorry that I wasn't a boy?'

60

'Every day.'

'Please be serious!'

'Then why do you ask?'

'It's that I just found out that the sacrifice of the Feast is to ransom the *male* members in a family. Only the sons.'

'Strictly speaking, that's correct.'

'But we always sacrificed a sheep and a lamb, and you always said the lamb was for me.'

'As far as I'm concerned we ransom our blessings. And you were a blessing – most of the time!'

Domino suddenly started barking and the doorbell rang. In a minute the maid announced that Tante Zohra was at the door. Gigi ran upstairs to tidy up.

She looked out of her bedroom window. Tante Zohra's ancient black Mercedes was parked in front of the house, and the driver was helping her out. Her tall, lean figure unfolded slowly out of the car. Gigi recognized the driver, Omar, although he was not her aunt's regular chauffeur. He was an agent of the government intelligence service, the dread *Mukhabarat*, who had been assigned to follow Tante Zohra around several years ago. Like the rest of the family, she was the object of constant surveillance since the sequestration decrees.

Gigi had heard the curious story of how it came about that the government informant ended up driving her aunt around. One evening during the month of Ramadan Tante Zohra had been looking out of the window and had seen the man standing alone in the deserted street. It was sunset, and the calls from the minarets echoed all over the still city. The birds were twittering in the Indian jasmine trees and an eerie moratorium had fallen over the normally bustling traffic. Everyone was indoors waiting for the cannon to go off, announcing the breaking

61

of the fast. Apparently no one had thought to relieve the poor *Mukhabarat* agent. Zohra felt sorry for him and sent someone to call him around to the back door for the Ramadan meal.

From that day on, the man bowed politely whenever he saw her waiting outside the door to her villa, while the doorkeeper tried to hail a taxi. Her husband, Makhlouf Pasha, was wheelchair-bound since his massive stroke. She herself had never learned to drive and now could no longer afford a chauffeur.

One day when she was late and having trouble stopping a taxi, she had a brainstorm. She beckoned the man over and suggested that he could drive her where she was going in her own car, which was sitting idle in the garage; that way he would know her exact whereabouts at all times without having to chase after her. The man fell in with her plan immediately and that was the beginning of a long, mutually profitable association. It was one more instance in which the Kafkaesque shadow of the police state was undermined by the irrepressible common sense of the people.

Gigi dragged her hairbrush through her hair hard enough to make Madame Hélène wince, then slipped on a headband. She washed her face but decided against changing out of the dreary uniform of the Sacré Coeur school.

She skipped down the stairs and stopped short just behind the Aubusson screen that separated the two salons. She had remembered to unroll the waistband of her skirt, which she had rolled over twice while dressing in the morning in an attempt to shorten it. Papa was very old-fashioned about things like that and called any hemline above the knee a 'miniskirt'.

62

'Gigi's too young,' she heard her father say.

'She's eighteen.' Her aunt's voice. 'Her cousins were engaged or spoken for at her age.'

'Fine. I have only one daughter. I'm in no hurry.'

'That's evident. Look, I'm not talking about marriage yet. I'm just asking you to consider an engagement. At least you would have some peace of mind – you know what I mean.'

'I'm not worried about anything like that with Gigi.'

'I know she's very sheltered, but if you think just because of that –'

'Not at all. Girls who get into that kind of trouble lack attention and affection at home, they look for them in the arms of the first boy who turns their head. I know Gigi; underneath her bubbly ways she's a cool, self-sufficient girl.' Gigi could hear Papa puffing on his pipe, the way he did when he was thinking. 'Besides, she really is too young. She should wait until she finishes college. She's a bright girl and should do very well in her studies.'

'All the more reason why she won't have any trouble studying for her college degree while married. The boy is suitable from every point of view, and these days, what with the situation in the country what it is –' She sighed. 'You should be glad to see her get away, to have her study in Europe. You should think of her future, of her own good. Things are going from bad to worse over here. If things were different, if we weren't under sequestration, a girl like Gigi would have her choice of suitors, but these days . . . ' She sighed. 'Really, Shamel, we're only talking about an engagement. But it's not as if we could take our time about this. Yussef is only here for a couple of weeks, then he'll be going back to England. His father

63

is putting a lot of pressure on us to arrange a meeting right away.'

Yussef? Gigi tried to guess whom they were discussing.

'His father is a hard man,' Papa was saying. 'A hard man in business, a hard man with women. Twice divorced, and his wives complained bitterly during their marriages. No, Kamal Zeitouni is a hard man. I don't know if I want to hand over my only child to a son of his.'

Yussef Zeitouni. Gigi remembered being introduced to him at a wedding, and running into him again on feast days at her aunt's. His mother Zeina, Kamal Zeitouni's first wife, was a friend of Tante Zohra's.

'It's not always like father, like son,' Tante Zohra was remonstrating. 'Besides, do you want her to marry one of those pious young men who've never been with a woman before?'

'And have him experiment on my daughter? Allah forbid!'

'At least let me arrange a meeting between Gigi and Yussef –'

Gigi had been standing awkwardly behind the screen, too embarrassed to interrupt once she realized she was the subject of the discussion. But now she heard her mother coming down the stairs and decided it was time she made an appearance in the salon.

Yussef, Kamal Zeitouni's son by his first marriage, was now in his late twenties and lived in London, where he was studying for a doctoral degree. Since Tante Zohra's visit, Gigi had met him again several times at formal teas and dinners that common acquaintances had arranged. She found him as she remembered: good-looking, tall, with his mother's sweep of raven hair. He had come to

64

the house for lunch, twice. After lunch they had made strained conversation in the salon while Madame Hélène sat discreetly in a corner, ostensibly engrossed in her embroidery.

Normally the next step would have been a formal engagement, followed by a few months of courtship during which the engaged couple, still more or less chaperoned, came to know each other better. Either one could break it off at some point before the wedding, and some of Gigi's friends were already on their second engagement. But the circumstances were different in this case. Gigi knew that she had run out of time to make up her mind: she needed to give an answer before Yussef left for England. If it was favorable, he would be back in a few months for the wedding, after which they would leave immediately for Europe.

Papa assured her repeatedly that the decision was entirely hers; it was his prerogative to veto any of her suitors, but he would never influence her in anyone's favor. Mama seemed to be favorable. Gigi's girlfriends thought Yussef was handsome and that she was lucky to be going abroad not just for a honeymoon, but to live and study.

Gigi kept stalling; she felt she didn't know Yussef at all, a reasoning which made Mama impatient. What she could not tell her mother was that she had only the vaguest notion of what marriage was about and did not feel ready for it, regardless of the suitor. Indeed the idea that her parents actually expected her to marry so soon came as a surprise, tinged with a slight sense of betrayal.

Tante Zohra took the matter in hand with her usual decisiveness. 'Gigi dear, I have an idea. I know it's hard for you to exchange more than a few words with Yussef

65

with people around all the time. Why don't you go spend a couple of days at my beach house in Agami? Yussef could come to visit, without all the pressure, in peace and quiet. With your governess, of course, to chaperone; and take Tamer along too, so it won't seem too obvious. Leila has to study for an exam, but Tamer can go, he never studies anyway.'

Ever since their father's sudden death nearly a year ago, Tante Zohra had raised Gina's children, Leila and Tamer. Gigi got along very well with Leila, a level-headed girl only a year younger. Tamer, on the other hand, alternated between uncommunicative sulks and obnoxious high spirits. Gigi was a little disappointed that it was Tamer and not Leila who would go along on this trip.

'See Alexandria and die,' the ancient Greeks used to say. Gigi tried to remember the book in which she had read that. She loved Alexandria in the off-season, before the summer crowds arrived. She sat in the back of the car between Madame Hélène and her fifteen-year-old cousin Tamer as they drove up the desert road from Cairo. Omar, Tante Zohra's occasional driver, was at the wheel, with Om Khalil, all in black, in the passenger seat next to him. Tamer gripped the dog between his knees, his long, lanky legs bent nearly in half.

Tante Zohra's chalet, as small beach houses were called, was in Agami, on the far side of Alexandria, but they detoured through the city. Once past the salt marshes and long before they could see the Mediterranean, they caught whiffs of the sea breeze. Then they were driving along the Corniche, relatively quiet because it was only April. They stopped at Glimonopoli to buy *granita*: lemon and mango ices.

66

They parked on the Corniche. Gigi and Tamer leaned against the railing at the top of the sea wall and let the breeze blow in their faces as they licked their ices. The sun glinted on the crests of the steel blue waves that broke briskly against the sea wall. Gigi closed her eyes and inhaled deeply, her senses overwhelmed by the light and the warmth, the smell of salt and seaweed, the tang of lemon on her tongue.

At the chalet they were greeted by the familiar musty smell, soon dissipated when the creaky wooden shutters were flung open. Gigi found a battered straw hat in the hallway closet overflowing with sand-encrusted sandals, fins, goggles and inflatable rafts. She rolled up her pant legs and ran down the beach across the fine, sifting white powder. At the water's edge she dug her toes into the cool, wet sand and the gritty, crushed cockleshells. She ran in and out of the surf, keeping a lookout for the loathsome jellyfish washed up by the tide.

'Gigi! Will you come back in now? It's getting dark.' Madame Hélène's plaintive voice called from the top of the path down to the beach. 'Gigi! Come in now, you'll be bitten by crabs.'

After dinner Tamer found the dog-eared deck of cards and the Scrabble game with the three missing letters; they played for hours in the dim light. The electrical voltage in Alexandria was 110 rather than the 220 prevalent in the rest of Egypt and the light always seemed weak there.

Gigi tried on the new dress she was planning to wear when Yussef came tomorrow. Mama's 'little dressmaker' had just finished running it up for her. It was an apricot sundress with crisscrossing shoulder straps and a short, swinging skirt. Gigi twirled round and round in front of the mirror, making the dress flare up and out, and her

67

long hair fly about her face. A Beatles record played on the small portable record-player. Tamer sipped a coke through a straw; it was flat and syrupy, the only kind available in Egypt for years now. When Gigi stopped twirling, she saw him gazing at her, and she pinched his cheek.

That night she dreamed that Yussef was coming down the beach towards her, but all she could see of him were his bare feet. He had black hairs on the toes. She turned and started running away. But suddenly something surfaced in front of her, terrifying eyes in pools of black ink.

Gigi fought off the clutches of the nightmare to find herself staring into the fierce, kohl-ringed eyes of Om Khalil. Om Khalil applied a lot of kohl before going to bed and washed it off in the morning. This morning she had apparently not yet done so, and the kohl was smeared all around her eyes.

'Sitt Gigi, are you going to sleep all day? What time do you want lunch? What time is your company coming?'

Gigi looked at her watch on the bedside table. 'Nine o'clock! I'd better hurry. Yussef said he'd come early. We'll have lunch at two, Om Khalil, does that give you enough time? Just a simple lunch. I'll come down and see about the menu. Where's Tamer?'

'Sleeping on the slope of the roof; if he slips down and breaks his neck it'll teach him a lesson.'

Gigi yanked on her dressing gown and went out on the roof terrace. Her cousin was still half-asleep in the morning sun, his curly dark hair rumpled, a blanket over his shoulders. He didn't turn in her direction. Gigi leaned against the sun-warmed wall. She wanted to ask him if

68

he missed his father, if he wished his mother would come back from Lebanon. But the eyebrows drawn down like shades over the eyes warned her off. She touched his shoulder.

'Come on, Tamer, we'd better get dressed. Yussef will be here any minute. Will you find Domino and chain him up?'

'Whatever for?'

'Yussef doesn't like dogs.' She sighed.

Tamer looked at her as if he were about to say something, then changed his mind. He went off to find the dog.

Gigi went downstairs to check on the preparations for lunch. She stopped short in her tracks when she saw Yussef standing in the middle of the foyer. 'Oh! When did you get here?'

He smiled. 'Just now. Your governess went to look for you.'

Involuntarily, Gigi's eyes dropped to his feet. He was wearing canvas espadrilles. She couldn't tell if his feet looked anything like those in her dream.

'Excuse me a minute, I just have to dress.'

She ran back upstairs. Before the mirror she surveyed her messy hair and childish dressing gown in despair. This day was not getting off to a good start.

A few minutes later she came down, wearing the new apricot dress. They went for a walk on the beach. She carried her thin-strapped sandals and waded ankle deep in the water. He kept his espadrilles on and walked on the sand, a foot or two up from the water's edge.

'Father says I'd better be flying back to London as soon as I get back to Cairo.'

'Oh, so soon?'

69

'My thesis supervisor threw out all the data I'd collected over the past two months, he insists that I redo the experiments. Just because I took a shortcut! He just likes to give me a hard time, the old stick-in-the-mud.'

They walked along, Gigi swinging her sandals by the straps. She tried to imagine what life would be like for her in London. 'Do you have to study all the time?'

'Oh, no, London's lots of fun! Parties, discos on the King's Road.'

'You have a lot of friends?'

'Quite a few. Many of them are foreign graduate students like me. The one thing we all miss is home cooking. My mother is having a dozen stuffed pigeons, a leg of lamb and I don't know what else prepared for me to take back to London. Then as soon as I get there I'll call everybody to come over and we'll have a big dinner.'

He sounded eager to go back, Gigi thought. She couldn't see herself in the picture he was painting. Maybe she could put off making the decision till later, maybe they would have another chance to get to know each other better. 'When do you think you might be coming back to Egypt?'

'I don't know, it depends on what my father decides. I doubt I can come back before summer next year. But I think he said a day or two before the wedding would be plenty of time. That is, of course, assuming . . . ' He trailed off a little awkwardly. Gigi too was embarrassed. It seemed bizarre to be discussing wedding plans with a man with whom she had not exchanged an intimate word. It occurred to her that he had not asked her a single personal question, about her likes or dislikes, her hopes or her dreams. Disappointment formed a lump in her chest. She knew she was hopelessly romantic, waiting for

70

some intrepid explorer to discover her like some uncharted island; like the woman languishing dreamily on a deserted tropical isle in the advertisement for Fidgi perfume: '*Toute femme est une île*' – every woman is an island.

Just then Domino appeared at the top of the dune, barking frantically as he ran towards them. Yussef stiffened and Gigi rushed to head off the dog.

'I'm sorry, I can't imagine how he got loose.' It could only be Tamer, she thought grimly, as she caught Domino's collar and dragged him back towards the chalet.

Om Khalil cleared the lunch table and set down a tray of baklava and a basket of the earliest mangoes of the summer: green, comma-shaped Hindi; sweet, round, orange Alphonse; huge 'calf's egg'. Gigi regretfully decided to skip the mangoes – no matter how careful she was, there was no way to eat a whole mango without risking a stain on her new dress or at least getting her fingers all sticky. At home Mama would have made sure the mango was served peeled and diced in a bowl. Gigi started to serve the baklava to Yussef and Madame Hélène.

Tamer chose a round, fleshy Alphonse. He held it upright in his fist, stuck a knife into the middle and cut about an inch deep all the way round. 'Aren't you going to have a mango, Gigi? You like them so.' He twisted the top half off, ending up with one half like a cup and the other with the large pit still attached, protruding. The sticky, indelible, bright-orange juice ran down his hands. Gigi watched with horror out of the corner of her eye while trying to make conversation with Yussef.

'So what was the weather like in London when you left?'

'Wet and cold, as usual. But you get used to it. There

71

aren't many days in the year you'd get a chance to wear a dress like the one you have on.' He glanced at her bare shoulders, lightly tinged with pink from the sun.

Gigi blushed, she wasn't sure why. She tried to think of something to say but every topic seemed fraught with implications of one sort or another. She was a little resentful that Yussef seemed to be making no effort, while she felt it was incumbent upon her, as hostess, to keep up the conversation. For his part, he seemed perfectly at ease answering questions but devoid of curiosity himself. She wondered if it simply meant that he had already made up his mind. But based on what? Her looks and her pedigree? She was disappointed rather than flattered. But she tried to put herself in his shoes: it must be awkward to be the suitor, waiting to be accepted or rejected; perhaps that explained why he didn't want to appear to be trying too hard.

'Did you find it hard to learn to drive on the wrong side of the road in England?' she hazarded.

'A little at first. Not that I drive much there, I don't have a car. But one time, I borrowed a friend's car and found myself going the wrong way down a one-way street.'

Gigi's attention was distracted. Tamer had acquitted himself of the first half of the mango easily enough, scooping out the flesh with his spoon, but when he came to the half with the pit he abandoned all decorum and simply sucked on the pit like a dog worrying a bone, juice coating the incipient down on his upper lip and dribbling down his chin. He picked at a mango fibre stuck between his teeth.

When they left the dining room Gigi pointed Yussef to the washroom and, as soon as his back was turned,

72

lobbed a small, hard mango at Tamer's ribs. He gave an exaggerated yelp.

'Now, now, children,' Madame Hélène remonstrated automatically, *'jeux de mains, jeux de vilains.'*

Gigi flushed, mortified. But Yussef only looked amused. At least that was one point in his favor, she thought; Tamer's antics didn't seem to disconcert him.

'Well?' Mama asked impatiently on the phone late that afternoon, after Yussef had left. 'What did you talk about?'

'Oh, nothing special. We went for a walk on the beach. You know, he was wearing espadrilles all the time.'

'Espadrilles?' Mama sounded puzzled. 'Darling, have you made up your mind yet?'

'Not yet, Mama. But I will by the time I come home tomorrow, I promise.'

Gigi decided to take Domino for a walk on the beach; he had been cooped up a good part of the day to keep him out of Yussef's way. She changed out of her dress and put on a pair of comfortable Bermudas.

The sun was setting and the beach was deserted. In the distance she saw a windsurfer skimming the water, headed for shore. A lonely swimmer bobbed in the foreground.

Gigi turned and headed away from the chalets, splashing calf-deep in the surf, looking away from the blood-orange horizon periodically to check the sand under her feet for the dread jellyfish. She knew she had been gone long enough for Madame Hélène to fret, but she was reluctant to head back.

Mama would expect an answer about the marriage proposal when she arrived in Cairo. Gigi tried to concentrate. She realized it was the first time she had had to

73

make a real decision in her life, and it would be the most important decision she would ever make. It frightened her to feel as detached from the outcome as if it concerned someone else.

The idea of marriage seemed unreal, somehow. Whether she said yes or no, Yussef would go back to England and life would go on as usual for her. Even if she said yes, she would have a year to change her mind.

Years later, many years later, Tamer was to ask her: 'Why did you marry Yussef? I always wondered about that.' It would be years later, on a balcony overlooking the Nile, overlooking a by-pass bridge like a gigantic Ferris wheel spanning the city; a bridge that would not be built for another decade, and would be named after a war that was yet to take place: the Sixth of October Bridge. Years later Tamer would ask her that question, long after they had both crossed over to adulthood; when they had changed as unrecognizably as the transformed vista over the familiar old river; when they were trying to reach across the distance the years had stretched between them. He would ask her that question then, and for the first time, even to herself, she would have an answer.

But the girl walking her dog on the beach that day had no answer. Except perhaps that she was tired of waiting for life to begin.

5

The Wedding

The month before the wedding went by in a whirl. Gigi tried to concentrate on her final exams, but she was distracted by the sessions at the dressmaker's and other preparations. She left the details to Mama, even the styles and colors of the embroidered satin negligées for her trousseau. But the choice of a stone for the solitaire engagement ring was to be entrusted to the Pasha, by family tradition. He was considered as much a connoisseur of jewelry as he was of period furniture.

Rather than pick a ring, Yussef's parents had presented Gigi with an equivalent sum of money, discreetly concealed in a navy Sèvres *bonbonnière*. She called her uncle.

'Of course, dear, I'll call my jeweler right away. Do you have any preference as to cut? No? All right then, I'll tell him what your budget is and he'll pick a few stones for us to choose from. You can pick them up from the shop in town tomorrow morning and bring them right over. It's the Sirgani jeweler downtown, but make

75

sure you ask to speak to Sirgani Senior himself. Just tell him you're my niece, he'll be waiting for you.'

Gigi had driven downtown to the busy square and circled a couple of times, not looking so much for a parking space, which was near impossible at this time of day, but for a *minadi*, one of the self-appointed parking attendants who offered to watch your car when you triple-parked. In exchange for a small tip, they staved off the roving policemen so you did not get a ticket or your car towed. She finally caught the eye of a *minadi* and parked. She hopped out, telling him she would be in the jewelry shop and he was to fetch her if one of the cars she was blocking needed to pull out or if the tow truck showed up.

The man shook his head and explained that there was a particularly active police patrol that day; she needed to leave the key with him so he could move the car if they showed up. Gigi hesitated, but she recognized his face; he had taken care of her car before. She left the keys with him and went into Sirgani, *Père et Fils, Bijoutiers*.

The owner, Sirgani *Père*, was expecting her and handed her a small blue velvet pouch. 'There are four stones in there, all about two carats. I think the Pasha will find something to suit. Please give him my regards.'

Gigi took the light pouch with what felt like tiny pebbles inside. She hesitated, but the man did not seem to expect her to sign a receipt of any sort, he merely ushered her to the door. Outside she looked around for her car but it was nowhere in sight, nor was the *minadi*. She looked up and down the street, in case he had moved it, but there was no sign of it. Gigi waited, with increasing misgivings, as the minutes ticked by. Five minutes. Ten.

A noisy parade of cars passed by, horns tooting and flags waving out of windows. Red flags identified the riders as supporters of one of the two national football teams, the Ahli; red and white were the colors of the rival team, the Zamalek. There was a football match scheduled that afternoon. Owners of white cars might find that vandals had painted a red stripe on their parked vehicles, or vice versa. Party politics were banned in Egypt; there was only one party, the regime's National Socialist Party. Football mania was a substitute for party politics. Gigi was somewhat concerned: her little Simca was red.

She looked at her watch. Fifteen minutes. Could the *minadi* have made off with the car? She shouldn't have given him the keys. Should she try to hail a taxi and go home, then call the police? But she didn't even know the man's name.

Just as she was about to hail a taxi, the *minadi* pulled up in her car and jumped out. 'I'm sorry, but the police came through with the tow truck and I had to take your car and circle around with it until they were gone. You were done quicker than I thought.'

Gigi tipped him and drove off. She was a little late but she knew her uncle would be home. He was under house arrest, had been so for the past three years. Someone had falsely reported to President Nasser that the Pasha had been seen laughing with some cronies at the Gezira Club on the night of Nasser's speech acknowledging Egypt's terrible defeat after the Six Day War. An infuriated Nasser had ordered the Pasha thrown into an internment camp. When brave souls interceded to point out that the Pasha had been nowhere near the Gezira Club in ten years, Nasser commuted the sentence to house arrest. That had been over three years ago.

Vast as the Cairo House was, there must have been times when the Pasha would have settled for a short stay

77

in an internment camp rather than this indefinite house arrest. But he was never heard to complain. The Pasha lived alone. He had been a widower for many years now, and he had no children. His mother had died a long time ago, and his married brothers had moved into their own homes. But he was never alone for long during those years of enforced seclusion. The clan and the closest cronies rallied around, coming over every night for long soirées of chess and monopoly, while the *Mukhabarat* agents posted outside the gate took conspicuous note of everyone who went in or out.

Gigi negotiated the narrow streets of Garden City and parked in the yard of the Cairo house, ignoring the man at the gate who copied down her license plate. She took the little pouch and went up the long marble staircase. Fangali met her at the top of the stairs and ushered her into the Pasha's bedroom suite. She found her uncle in his club chair, dressed but for his shoes. Gigi leaned down to kiss him.

'Hello Gigi dear, did you pass by Sirgani? Good, I'll have a look right away. Just ring the bell, will you, I'll ask the maid for my magnifying glass.'

Gigi pulled the long tasseled silk bell cord and a wiry girl of about fourteen hurried in.

The Pasha did not look up; he was intent on opening the pouch. 'Get me my special magnifying glass and tweezer kit for jewelry.'

'What?' the girl bleated in a nasal country voice.

He looked up in alarm and stared at her. 'Who are you? Where's Fatma?'

'Fatma went back to the village yesterday to be married. I'm Khadra. I've been in this house for two weeks now.'

Gigi smiled because Khadra meant green. Her thick,

78

glossy black hair was cut very short, and gave off a faint whiff of benzine. Gigi guessed that when the girl had arrived from the country her head had been shorn and deloused with benzine.

'Why doesn't anyone ever tell me these things,' the Pasha grumbled. 'Call Fangali – No, just bring me my slippers, I'll get up and find the kit myself.'

'Let me look, Uncle,' Gigi offered.

'I don't think you'll find them, only Fatma knew where she placed things.'

The girl brought the slippers.

'Which village do you come from, child?' he asked.

'Mit-Gibala. We live by the second irrigation ditch from the road. I'm Fangali's niece.'

'I see,' he sighed with resignation, 'help me up.'

The Pasha found the kit and settled himself in front of the high window, spreading the four small diamonds on a blotting pad on the desk before him. Gigi sat down beside him, watching silently as he picked up each stone with the tweezers and held it up to the light. After what seemed like a long time he put two back in the pouch and placed the other two in the palm of Gigi's hand.

'One of these two will do.'

'Then the bigger one, of course!'

He hesitated then shook his head. 'The bigger one isn't as well cut, and it has a yellowish tinge; the smaller one is much finer.'

'But I don't notice any yellowish tinge! Besides, Tante Zohra always said her ring was as yellow as a topaz!' She had never seen her aunt's ring, only heard about it; it had been sold, of course, after the sequestration decrees that had cut off all the family's sources of income.

The Pasha laughed. 'Imperfect color may be overlooked

79

in a ring of close to twenty-two carats! Anyway I never liked Zohra's ring. But with a stone of the size we're looking at, quality is essential. Are you disappointed because it's the smaller of the two? I'll have Sirgani set it for you in a special platinum raised setting, it'll look bigger than the yellowish one, I promise. And he won't charge you anything extra, the setting will be my wedding present. All right?'

Gigi smiled and kissed him.

He handed the pouch back to her, along with one of his calling cards, the top right hand corner carefully folded down. Gigi knew he always did this to make it clear there was no message written on the back; that way if the card fell into the wrong hands it could not be misused.

'Just take all the stones back to Sirgani, and he'll take your ring size. I'll give him a call to tell him which one we picked and give him instructions about the setting. *Mabrouk*, dear, congratulations.'

Her ring had been ready two weeks later, and the Pasha was right, the setting made all the difference.

The Pasha was also to officiate at the signing of the marriage contract, as Gigi's proxy.

'But Papa, why do I have to have a proxy at all?'

'The legal aspect of the marriage is a matter of signing a civil contract. It's men's business. There's no need for you to be there. It might even be awkward for you, surrounded by all these men, not just your uncles but male relatives you've never seen and friends of the family, important people. You'll be so busy, anyway, the day before the wedding. Just leave the contract to us, and concentrate on getting ready for the wedding.'

Papa had explained that in her case the contract would

80

be a very standard, simple affair. It comprised the mandatory stipulations, like the *mahr* the bridegroom offered the bride, for instance: since it was not an issue, 'as agreed between us' would cover it. The same with the divorce settlement, which by law had to be specified: it would be put down that the bridegroom was to pay the bride five piasters in case he divorced her.

'Five piasters!' Gigi was indignant. 'You can't buy a stick of gum for five piasters! Is that all I'm worth?'

Papa smiled. 'It's precisely because we value you so highly that we specify a purely nominal sum. Substantial divorce settlements are typical of matches where the bride marries for money.'

'What if I'm the one who wants to get divorced?' Gigi knew the husband could divorce the wife any time, but that the opposite was much more complicated.

'The marriage contract can stipulate that the wife has the same right to divorce unilaterally as the husband. It's legal under the Islamic Shari`a. But you won't find a man willing to agree to that, unless he is of a much lower status than the woman he's marrying.'

Gigi knew that Papa had a law degree, although he had not practiced much.

'But I still don't see why I have to have a proxy,' Gigi was unconvinced.

'Listen, darling. When Yussef takes your uncle's hand – as your proxy – and their hands are covered with the white handkerchief, in front of all these witnesses, it stands for something. That in this marriage he is not dealing with a friendless girl, he is dealing with the men in her family, and is accountable to them.'

'All right,' Gigi conceded, 'but if I must have a proxy, why can't it be my own father?'

81

'But your uncle is the head of the family. It's both an honor and an obligation for him. That's just the way it's always done in our family. So when the two witnesses – two of your uncles – come to ask you whom you choose as your proxy, you must designate the Pasha.'

'Can I at least look down from the upstairs gallery to watch them do the handshake and the white handkerchief? I'll hide behind one of the columns, no one will see me.'

'No, Gigi,' Papa laughed. 'There's no point.'

So it was that Gigi did not see Yussef again until he was her husband. He arrived the day before the wedding. His plane was delayed and rather than having time to see her before the signing of the marital contract, he had to go straight from the airport to the Cairo House, where twenty men were assembled and waiting. Gigi held them up a little longer by teasing the two witnesses who had come to ask her to name her proxy. 'Papa,' she insisted.

'Oh, we don't have time for these childish games,' Uncle Hani exclaimed impatiently. 'Come on, Zakariah, we'll just say she named the Pasha.'

'No, we won't,' Uncle Zakariah, Papa's third eldest brother, shook his head. 'These things are dead serious. I'm not leaving till she names her proxy properly.'

Gigi, shamed into seriousness, meekly named her uncle.

An hour and a half later Yussef was at the door, smiling. She put out her hand and he leaned forward to kiss her. Gigi drew back, shocked. Only then did the realization sink in that they were actually married. 'I'll feel married tomorrow,' she told herself. 'After all, that's the real marriage, the wedding.'

*　　*　　*

82

'Gigi, will you please try to smile? You look as if you're at a funeral, not at your own wedding. People will start to wonder.' Yussef took her hand in his.

The bride and groom were enthroned on matching gilded armchairs set on a raised dais in a bower of white flowers: chrysanthemums, calla lilies, gladioli. A pair of turtle doves, a symbol of marital harmony, cooed in a silver-gilt cage above their heads. It was about two o'clock in the morning, but none of the guests sitting at the round tables in the garden of the Cairo House seemed ready to leave. The night was balmy and the colored light bulbs strung between the trees swayed gently. The last of the three belly dancers had performed her number and left; the waiters were clearing away the buffet, carrying off the carved carcasses of the spit-roast lambs. Gigi and Yussef had sliced into the three-tier cake, and portions were distributed to each table. The guests lingered over ice cream and coffee while the band played a slow number to which a few couples were dancing on a carpeted platform.

The wedding was given by the groom, as Egyptian custom dictated, but it was held at the Cairo House rather than at a hotel, partly because the Pasha was still under house arrest and it was the only way he could attend. Gigi looked at her watch. It was so late, and she was tired. The heavy headdress and the veil were giving her a headache.

'Yussef, don't you think we should start taking our leave now? Because people must be tired and most of them won't leave before we do.'

'I suppose so,' Yussef agreed.

Gigi got up carefully, adjusting the pearl-encrusted flowers in her headdress and sweeping the train of her

83

skirt around so she would not step on it as she came off the dais. They stepped down and started to wind their way between the tables, stopping at each to take their leave. First the head table at which the Pasha presided, dapper in his bow tie and boutonnière, holding one of his trademark cigars. Tante Zohra, tall and resplendent beside him, had the satisfied smile of the successful matchmaker. The Pasha introduced Gigi to Prince Bandar, a brother of King Feisal of Saudi Arabia and a friend of her new father-in-law.

Kamal Zeitouni sat beside his ex-wife Zeina, Yussef's mother. At nearly sixty he was still a large, vigorous man, his black hair and moustache only beginning to gray. Zeina was impeccable with her sleek, black, upswept hair and her diamond-drop earrings. She straightened Yussef's tie as he bent over to kiss her.

'You look so handsome! But I've just had an argument with the photographer; I don't think he did his job well at all, he didn't light you properly. You don't leave for England till the day after tomorrow. If the proofs he shows me tomorrow aren't good enough, you won't mind dressing up again and having the photos redone at the studio of another photographer in town?'

Yussef shrugged. 'If you like.'

Gigi groaned inwardly. It might not be much trouble for Yussef to put on his tuxedo again, but for her it would be a time-consuming ordeal to get ready to be rephotographed: having her complicated hairdo styled all over again, the makeup, the heavy headdress, the layers of satin and tulle in this hot weather. Besides, she was planning on going home tomorrow to finish packing.

She turned to Yussef. 'Do you think it's really necessary?'

'I'll have a look at the proofs and let you know,' Kamal Zeitouni intervened in a decisive tone.

'What time would they be ready tomorrow?' Gigi persisted. 'Could Yussef or I have a look?'

'That won't be necessary,' her father-in-law answered pleasantly enough, 'I said I'd let you know.' He had a look in his eye as if it had just occurred to him that he might have taken on more than he bargained for in a daughter-in-law.

They moved on to the next table, where Uncle Hani sat with two of Papa's brothers and their wives. Zakariah was the only one of Papa's brothers to have inherited the flaming red hair of their Russian grandmother; in his youth he used to try to extinguish his glaring head with gobs of brilliantine. Nabil, next to him, looked like a black and white copy of Zakariah's color print. His expression was as dour as Zakariah's was good-natured.

Near the dance-floor Mama and Papa sat at their table. Mama looked exhausted, relieved and anxious, all at the same time. She had been so engrossed in the preparations for Gigi that she had almost forgotten to pick up her own dress for the wedding from the dressmaker. Gigi had never seen her in quite such a frantic state. Happy as her mother was for her, she couldn't hide her anxiety. Partly, Gigi realized, because she had suddenly admitted to herself that Gigi was desperately unprepared.

'I don't know how you'll manage in England,' Mama had fretted earlier that evening as she helped Gigi to dress. 'You don't know how to do housework or laundry, you've never been in the kitchen – the very sight of raw meat makes you sick, ever since that feast day when you were nine!' She hesitated. Clearly there was something even more worrisome on her mind. 'Gigi, did you understand

85

that booklet I gave you about birth control? I mean, you have some idea?'

Gigi's *éducation sentimentale*, as it was referred to in French novels, was limited to precisely that, novels. She knew that most of her girlfriends had more specific information – though not necessarily any more practical experience – than she had. But Gigi had always been a little apart, less curious and more sheltered. The other girls called her a *Sainte Nitouche* and stopped whispering and giggling when she came into the room.

The booklet on birth control and Gaylord Hauser's 1940's primer on conjugal relations were Mama's total contribution to Gigi's education in intimacy. Neither had been of much help. But when Mama had posed the question, Gigi had nodded quickly to spare them both further embarrassment: she had intuitively understood, even as a child, that Mama had certain limitations and tabu that even a sense of motherly duty could not prevail upon her to overcome. For her mother, the world in general, but in particular the world of the senses, was a place fraught with unspoken dangers which could only be traversed safely under the protective bubble of blind innocence. Thus she would justify thrusting her daughter into marriage in complete ignorance like a lamb led to the slaughter. But now Gigi could see an eleventh-hour doubt in her mother's eyes as she kissed her goodnight.

Papa was looking immensely proud of her, and had the air of a man who felt he had done his duty. Gigi gave him a big hug.

'Will you miss me?'

'Not in the least.' Then he added: 'Don't ask silly questions.'

86

The newlywed pair wove their way through the tables, Gigi's short train sweeping the grass behind her.

'*Jolie comme un coeur, bellissima,*' Madame Hélène rearranged Gigi's veil. The governess was wearing a dramatic gown with rhinestone shoulder straps, clearly exhumed from her pre-war wardrobe. She sat at a table with Gigi's maids of honor: her cousins and schoolmates. The long white tapers they had carried in the bridal procession lay, extinguished, on the table.

'Ooh, you're so lucky,' Leila Tobia whispered in Gigi's ear. Dina, whose blonde hair and 'liberal' upbringing were both attributed to her English mother, drew Gigi aside.

'Who's that tall boy over by the dance floor?'

Gigi followed her gaze to where Tamer was standing with his hands in the pockets of his suit.

'That's a cousin of mine, Leila's brother. He's only sixteen.'

'He can't be just sixteen! I don't care, ask him to ask me to dance anyway, will you?'

Gigi beckoned Tamer over and transmitted the message. 'I'm going now. Wish me luck? Goodbye, Tamer.' She stood on tiptoe and gave him a peck on each cheek.

Yussef took her elbow and pointed her towards another table where some of his relatives were seated. It took over an hour to say goodbye to each of the two hundred guests. Finally they were in the limousine heading for the hotel. Gigi leaned back against the seat of the car. Yussef bent over to kiss her, and she moved her head away awkwardly, pretending that her veil had got in the way. 'I still don't feel married,' she thought, a little panicky.

87

6

London

Toute femme est une île . . . at least every romantic young girl is an island; she dreams away the hours, scanning the horizon for a sail, waiting to be discovered, waiting for life to begin. When the beachhead is breached abruptly, when the flag is planted by a careless or a callous hand, she turns inward, away from the horizon, her hopes crushed.

From their wedding night on, Yussef did not seek to win her or woo her; because he was content to take from her only what he could, it was all he would get from her. All that had been soft and impressionable in her closed and hardened against him like a scar over a wound. In turn he retaliated for her indifference with deliberate neglect and occasional meanness. The dynamics between them quickly locked them into a vicious cycle which neither of them was willing to be the first to break. Gigi was too inexperienced with men to resort to feminine wiles to get the upper hand in their relationship. She crawled into her shell, too confused and too proud to

88

confide in anyone. She was very lonely, for the first time in her life.

Gigi switched on all the lights in the little ground floor flat in a quiet street off the King's Road, although it was early afternoon. She could not get used to needing electric light during the day. Outside it drizzled steadily, as it seemed to have done every day since she had arrived in London. She turned her attention back to Machiavelli's *The Prince*. The paper was due in two days but she should have no trouble finishing it on time; unless, as she had a tendency to do, she got carried away with the reading, not leaving herself enough time for writing up.

Machiavelli was wrong about one thing, she thought: when he claimed that a man will more easily forgive a ruler the killing of his father than the stripping of his possessions. Machiavelli argued that the death of the father is soon forgotten, whereas the loss of fortune rankles every day. Gigi's experience did not bear this out. Nasser had done everything to her family, and others like them: confiscation of property; stripping of political and civil rights; house arrest; internment. The Pasha had even been condemned to death by a revolutionary tribunal, but the sentence had been commuted.

Men like her father had remained patriots. Gigi remembered the night they had watched Nasser admit, in a televised speech, crushing defeat in the Six Day War. The unthinkable had happened: enemy troops had occupied Egypt. Her father had been devastated.

'You should be thanking Allah instead,' Mama had blurted out. 'If he had won the war, Nasser would have thrown you and your brothers in an internment camp and tossed away the key. In defeat, he doesn't dare to.'

'Don't speak that way in front of the child!'

89

'I'm sorry, but it's the truth. You're too idealistic.'

Nasser had died three months after Gigi had left for London. He was gone, that omnipresent bogeyman of Gigi's childhood. As far back as she could remember, his over-sized features had loomed in the background of her waking hours and her nightmares. His name was whispered: Nasser, El-Raiis; his thousand eyes and ears were everywhere. Every time he gave one of his three-hour harangues, she had strained to pick up the buzzwords that would tip them off that her father should pack the overnight case he kept under his bed, or that yet another sequestration decree would be imposed on their lives. Now he was gone. Egypt was waking as from a long spell.

Yet to the man on the street Nasser had remained the charismatic demagogue. In Nasser the masses had seen their champion, their vindicator, their father. His genius had lain in finding successive scapegoats on whom to blame the eternal misery of his people.

This bitter reality had come home to Gigi in the days after Nasser's death. Apparently Om Khalil had come by to visit Papa; she made the rounds of the family's houses to collect a regular stipend now that she was too old to work. When the subject of Nasser's death came up she had sighed loudly and declared that 'our father is gone'.

When Gigi heard of this she had been dumbfounded. It had never occurred to her that Om Khalil, who made her livelihood from the family, could have been harboring such sympathy for their avowed enemy. It made Gigi think of Julien, in *Le Rouge et le Noir*, hiding his picture of Napoleon under his mattress in the house of his employer the duke. Om Khalil, however, knew she could express her feelings with impunity before Papa. Gigi put down *The Prince* and picked up Hobbes' *Leviathan*.

90

Suddenly the lights went out and the clunky radiator shut down.

Gigi tried to make out the hands on her watch. Was it five o'clock already? This morning the notice posted on her door announced the power outage schedule for the day: three hours on, three hours off, starting at 8 a.m. The power workers union had been on strike for weeks, and before that it had been the rail workers union, the nurses union . . . Gigi closed her book, it was too dark to read. She pulled the comforter off the bed and drew it around her. She debated going to sit out the three hours with friends in Kensington, where the power outage schedule was reversed. She decided against it, it was too much trouble to walk down the King's Road in the cold to catch the tube from Sloane Square.

She reached under the bed and felt around for the extra blanket in its case. Her hand came into contact with a small metallic object and she drew it out. It was a heavy silver earring. Not hers; she didn't have pierced ears and in any case she never wore that kind of jewelry. It must belong to one of Yussef's former girlfriends. He had not hidden from her that he had made the most of his months in London before their marriage to 'live it up'. What better place to do it than in swinging London?

'But he's clean,' his friend Bassil Sirdana, a resident at St Mary's Hospital, had assured her. 'I made him promise to live like a monk for at least a month before the wedding, then I ran all the tests on him. After all, I told him, it would be criminal to risk passing on something nasty to a girl like you. I mean –' He trailed off as Gigi flushed in embarrassment. But she liked Bassil, with his stocky build and his blunt manner.

It seemed to Gigi that, far from making a secret of his

91

English girlfriends, Yussef was deliberately careless about leaving telltale items lying around: notes, hair combs, a lipstick. She guessed it was a misguided strategy to make her jealous. It had the effect of chilling her to the core. He did not seem to understand that she did not have enough feeling for him to experience jealousy; it was her pride that he hurt. He did not understand her at all, or try to.

She heard a door slam in the basement flat, which looked out onto the small garden in the back. One of the two tenants, Jonathan or Jeffrey, must be home. Jeffrey had brought her a pie yesterday, made with sour goose-berries picked from the bushes in the garden. Jeffrey, the thin one with the nasal East End accent, was in charge of cooking. Jonathan, whose auburn shag had been trans-formed to a platinum frizz this week, was the handyman.

Gigi reached for a date-filled biscuit from the box Mama had sent with a friend; they were the traditional buttery *kahk* prepared in great quantity for the Lesser Feast. These were probably made by Om Khalil, Gigi decided, the criss-cross pattern on top of each little cake was her signature. She bit into the biscuit then put it down quickly, a wave of nausea washing over her. She didn't know what was wrong with her, it had been happening all the time lately.

She got up and threw off the comforter. She went into the kitchen, where there was a little more light, emptied the rest of the gooseberry pie into the garbage, rinsed and dried the plate, then filled it with some of the butter biscuits. She would return the dish to Jeffrey. At home one never returned a dish empty.

Gigi took the dish and an umbrella and made her way down the stairs to the door of the basement flat. It was neither Jonathan nor Jeffrey who opened the door, but

92

a burly man with a reddish beard and a reddish nose.

'Excuse me, I'm looking for Jeffrey? Or Jonathan?'

'Here's a word to the wise, love,' the man leaned forward with a grin. The smell of his breath made Gigi recoil. 'You're wasting your time on Jonathan and Jeffrey. Know what I mean?' He winked.

'Oh! You don't understand, I'm their neighbor upstairs. Would you just give Jeffrey this dish?'

'Come on in then and be neighborly,' the man took Gigi by the elbows as she clutched the dish and started to lift her over the doorstep and through the doorway.

Jeffrey appeared behind him. 'Put her down, you awful man! Can't you see you're scaring her to death? Put her down, I said! Her husband's an Arab, and you know what they're like about their women.'

The red-headed man released Gigi with a belly laugh. She shoved the dish into Jeffrey's hands and fled up the stairs.

In a few minutes Jeffrey rang her doorbell and stood at the door, apologizing. 'That was me brother-in-law. He's harmless, really, only he was a little the worse for drink, as you may have noticed. My sister threw him out last night and he came over here. He says to tell you he's very sorry indeed, he was only fooling, he meant no harm. Oh, and thanks for the biscuits, such a treat! We'll save some for Jonathan.'

As he turned to leave, he added: 'Oh, my brother-in-law thinks you're ever so pretty. What a smashing neighbor you have, he says. I says: "You should see her husband!"'

Gigi closed the door behind him and sat back down on the bed, pulling the comforter around her again. The nausea came back. She closed her eyes and lay back.

93

When she opened her eyes again all the lights had come back on in the flat, and it was pitch dark outside. She looked at her watch. It was past eight o'clock. She got up. She should fix something for dinner. Then she sat down again. If Yussef did show up for dinner, she would just reheat yesterday's uneaten fish fingers and peas in white sauce. He had come home at eleven last night, saying he had already had a bite. Why didn't he ever call her so she wouldn't wait? But it was no good her asking him. He seemed to feel that it was important to assert his independence.

Suddenly Gigi got up and picked up the phone. It was rather late to call Egypt but she dialed the number anyway.

'Gigi?' Mama's voice sounded wide awake. 'Hello, darling! Is everything all right?'

'Oh, yes, everything's fine, only I really wanted to talk to you and Papa.'

'Is something wrong, dear?'

'Can I come home for a while? I'm just very homesick, and miserable. I just need to come home for a while.'

A pause.

'Does Yussef know about this?'

'I haven't talked to him about that yet. Things aren't working out very well between us just now, I just need to leave for a while.'

There was a short silence at the other end. She could hear Mama whispering with her hand over the receiver. Then she was back. 'Papa says he'll send you a ticket tomorrow, darling. How soon can you come?'

'As soon as I hand in my last term paper, the day after tomorrow.'

'All right, dear. We'll be waiting. But don't get too upset. All newlyweds go through these misunderstandings.

94

Coming home for a while will do you a world of good.'

'Mama? There's something else. I've been feeling so sick lately. I want to throw up and I sleep all the time.'

'Oh, Gigi. You're pregnant.'

Gigi could read the reproach, then the resignation, in her mother's voice as clearly as if she could see her expression.

'Come home till you feel better, dear. But whatever's wrong between you and Yussef, you'll have to work it out. If you're pregnant, you're in no position to do anything else. You'll have to go back to him.'

Then it was Papa's voice at the other end of the receiver. 'Gigi? It will be so good to have you back home for a while, darling. And what's this I hear about a baby? Take good care of yourself, and of my grandchild, until you get here!'

Gigi put down the receiver and started to cry.

7

Cairo

If you examined the turning points in a life, could you pin-point the exact twists of the kaleidoscope that set the pattern? If you could go back in time and change course, would you? Or would there be some part of the past that you would be unwilling to give up for a second chance? A child, it has been said, is your hostage to fortune: henceforth your choices are never free.

Gigi felt Tarek slip into bed beside her and cuddled him against her sleepily. She nuzzled his soft brown curls and pudgy cheeks. His cheeks were red and chapped today and Gigi promised herself not to kiss him all day till they were healed. She sighed. It would be a hard resolution to keep.

She stretched in bed, her own familiar girlhood bed. She had been back in Cairo only a few weeks, but she already felt as if she had never left. Perhaps it was because she knew she was home for good this time. Over the past five years of living in England, she had come home for visits every year or so, first alone, then after Tarek was born, with the baby. But now that both she and Yussef had earned their degrees, they were home for good. The political climate had changed for the better since Nasser's demise.

Gigi was glad to be home. In her five years with Yussef, she had sometimes been very lonely. But Tarek had filled the emotional void in her life; between them the active child and her studies had kept her busy. She had confided in no one about her problems: living in England as they had, distance had facilitated discretion in a way that would have been impossible had their marital relationship developed in the goldfish bowl of societal scrutiny and in-law interference that were the norm for a newlywed couple in Egypt. Part of the reason for her reserve was that she understood the mind set of Mama and Tante Zohra well enough to know what they would be likely to think: any reasonably attractive and intelligent woman had only herself to blame if she could not deploy her feminine wiles effectively enough to manipulate her husband into dutiful devotion. She would be even more to blame if it turned out that, with a husband entirely susceptible to her charms as a woman, she refused to resort to these same feminine wiles out of sheer, wrongheaded, hurt pride and dashed romantic expectations.

At any rate, confiding in Mama, Gigi had learnt, was a risky proposition. She always seemed to have her mind made up before she had even listened to you, and then she was apt to go off half-cocked, either quick to blame or, sometimes to worse effect, quick to defend with immoderate, mother-tigerish loyalty. In any case she could never be counted on to keep anything to herself; she would immediately try to enlist public opinion, in the form of Tante Zohra et al, in whatever issue happened to be at stake.

97

Papa was a different story. Gigi had always found it easy to talk to him; he listened attentively and could be counted on to be absolutely discreet. But her marital problems were one subject Gigi was reluctant to broach. She could guess at the turmoil it would stir up in her father: outrage that his little princess had been treated so cavalierly, remorse that he had not seen it coming, a conflict between powerlessness and interference. Papa was not one to blow off steam; he would keep his own counsel and let his frustration eat away inside him. Much as she was tempted to confide in him, Gigi was reluctant to shift her burden onto his shoulders now that his health was a cause for concern.

When she had come back to Egypt, she had decided to make a fresh start in her marriage, for Tarek's sake. Gigi had never had a nesting instinct, she had never seen herself reflected in material things. But now she clutched at the idea of a structure, of roots. She had resigned herself to putting away her dreams of emotional fulfillment and intellectual companionship, as one puts away the outgrown, embarrassing things of childhood. If she and Yussef were to have a life together, she would have to fill the empty husk so it would not collapse over the void inside, fill it with furniture and family and friends. Together with Leila Tobia, who had recently become engaged, she poured over French decorator magazines; they chose nearly identical built-in bookcases to be ordered at the cabinet-maker's. They looked around their parents' homes and other familiar interiors as if they were seeing them for the first time. They attended auctions and estate sales, sharing the excitement of bidding and acquisition, and combed the souk for antique silver and intricate passementerie.

Tarek wiggled restlessly. She sat up.

'Let's go see if Grandpapa Shamel is awake.'

Tarek was already pattering in front of her toward Papa's room. She followed him.

Papa was sitting up in bed. Gigi still registered the change in him every time she saw him. He had lost weight, although, big-boned as he was, he would always look solid. His coloring had turned sallow, his hair was gray and thin. He looked a decade older than his fifty-odd years. As she leaned over to kiss him she caught a whiff of staleness, of age, so different from the combined scent of aromatic pipe tobacco and fresh cologne that she associated with him. A tray full of prescription bottles of all sorts and a thermos carafe sat on his bedside table.

Far more than the sporadic spells of internment, it was the years of enforced inactivity and stress that had turned him into an old man while still in his prime. When he had his first heart attack, when the severity of his condition was confirmed, he secretly welcomed the diagnosis: he finally had an occupation, a justification, a job description: invalid.

'Did you sleep any better, Papa?'

Papa stroked Tarek's head. 'Couldn't get much rest tonight. I've been up since five.'

'Did you come in and close the windows in my room?' She knew Papa roamed the house, when he couldn't sleep.

'Yes, I did, and in Tarek's too. It gets chilly at dawn. Well, ready for breakfast, Tarek?'

Tarek nodded eagerly. Even at four he realized that it was a special treat to have breakfast with Grandpapa on the weekends, just the two of them. They were the only ones in the house to get up so early. He would watch his grandfather dress; his clothes were always laid out on the clotheshorse for him the night before. Then they would drive downtown, to Groppi, *pâtisserie-confiserie*, and order breakfast. Before they went home, they would choose a selection of small cakes to take home for lunch.

'Tarek, run to Khadra and ask her to dress you. Hurry up, Grandpapa's almost ready.' Khadra had come to work for Mama the year after Gigi's marriage, and was now a sturdy young woman who had lost her country ways.

Gigi handed her father his trousers. 'Papa, there's no need to get any *gâteaux* today, Tarek and I are having lunch at Zeina's, remember?'

Since they had come back from England she had hardly seen Yussef. At first, they had stayed at his mother's, but Yussef spent most of the day with his father. Kamal Zeitouni, along with a great many other entrepreneurs, new or established, was making the most of Sadat's new *'Infitah'* or 'Open Door' economic policy to launch import-export ventures. The Egyptian consumer was avid for imported goods after two decades of Nasserite 'socialism' during which nothing had been available but generally shoddy, domestic substitutes produced by a public sector as inefficient as total protectionism could make it.

One of Kamal's ventures involved importing medical equipment from Europe and hiring Egyptian technicians to install and run it in Saudi clinics. His old friend, Prince Bandar, had paved the way with the necessary contacts. Two weeks ago Kamal had sent Yussef to Jedda in connection with the deal. He was staying in one of Prince Bandar's guest-houses.

Since Yussef had been gone Gigi had used the excuse to move back home. But every Friday she took Tarek to have lunch at her mother-in-law's. Today, after lunch,

100

they would visit her father-in-law as well. Gigi and Tarek were to spend a week with Yussef in Jedda. She could not take Tarek out of the country without his father's signature on the passport; failing that, the paternal grandfather's signature was required.

'Looking forward to seeing Yussef again?' Papa asked as he buttoned his shirt.

'Oh, I don't know, Papa.' She hesitated. At that moment she wished she could confide in her father. But she thought better of it and just shrugged when Papa looked at her questioningly. 'It's just that I don't see that much of Yussef anyway when he's here. And since we've been back, we've had no privacy.' That was true enough. At Zeina's Gigi couldn't make a phone call without her mother-in-law listening, couldn't tell Tarek what to do without her interfering. Kamal called Yussef at all hours of the day and night with errands to run. Sometimes they were things the driver could have done just as well, like picking up a prescription or dropping off a letter, but his father seemed to need to have Yussef at his beck and call all the time. Once he had called at one o'clock in the morning, for something unimportant, she couldn't even remember what it was. Zeina had come into the bedroom to wake Yussef, she had hardly even knocked. When Yussef had free time, he went out with his friends, without her, just as he had in London. She was used to that, but not to the absence of privacy and lack of independence.

'But Yussef seems quite happy living at his mother's and having her fuss over him, and he never seems to stand up to his father, no matter how unreasonable he's being.' Gigi handed Papa his keys, his wallet and a handkerchief. Papa sat down on the chaise longue to tie his shoelaces.

101

'Don't you see, Gigi, Yussef can't stand up to his parents till he can be truly independent, earn his own living. That's not possible if he stays here in Egypt; he works for his father. He couldn't even afford a decent apartment without his father's financial support.' He pulled on his cold pipe, preoccupied.

'I know. It's all right, Papa, don't worry about it.'

Tarek burst into the room, his navy and white outfit crisp, his curls damped down and brushed, his little face one big grin of anticipation.

Gigi leaned back in the stiff petit-point armchair. It was covered in the same pale lemon slipcovers as the rest of the suite in her mother-in-law's salon. The last time she had seen the furniture without slipcovers had been at a party before her engagement. She vaguely remembered that the petit-point design represented a hunting scene. She wondered if the elaborate velvet draperies on the wide windows could be drawn. It was the middle of the afternoon but the electric lights were on. The windows were kept permanently closed against the pervasive dust and the harsh light. Zeina's home had the airless, hushed atmosphere of a museum, Gigi thought. She wondered if it had been like that when Yussef was growing up.

In the foyer Tarek was pretending to play football, sliding on the hardwood floor and throwing himself in front of an imaginary goal. Gigi called to him. 'Tarek, don't slide on the parquet, you almost knocked over that little table.'

He stopped and plunked himself down beside Gigi.

'Mummy, I'm hungry.'

'Go get a banana from the sideboard in the dining-room, but don't let Zeina see you, she'll be very disap-

102

pointed after all the special dishes she's having prepared for you.'

Gigi heard her mother-in-law's footsteps in her satin mules, less nimble than she remembered them. Zeina came in, smoothing her neat black hair and adjusting the sleeves of her cardigan.

'We're almost ready to sit down to dinner.' She straightened the delicate table Tarek had displaced. 'I have to supervise everything myself, even with Om Khalil. Thirty years she's been coming to this house to make pickles, she should know my ways by now. How many times have I told her, first you scrub the cucumbers under hot running water, then you peel them, then you rinse them, then you seed them and slice them. What do you think she was doing? She was peeling them without scrubbing them first. Where's Tarek? Oh, there he is. Gigi, how could you let him snack before dinner? I never let his father snack, he had such a small appetite in the first place. Well, dinner's served. Om Khalil is going to have to wait on us, I lost my *suffragi* last week, it's getting harder to keep help these days.'

Gigi followed Zeina into the dining room, wondering if her mother-in-law's fussiness had anything to do with her difficulty in keeping her staff. They sat down and Om Khalil started to serve them.

Gigi unfolded her napkin. 'Everything looks delicious, Tante Zeina, you shouldn't have gone to so much trouble. Tell me, is there anything you want me to tell Yussef when I see him? Or anything you want me to bring back for you?'

'I'm worried about Yussef, Gigi, his voice sounded scratchy the last time he called. I think he has a bad cold, but he's not taking antibiotics. You really should be with

103

your husband, taking care of him, that's a woman's place. A wife should make herself indispensable to her husband.'

Gigi ignored the undercurrent in her mother-in-law's pleasant voice. She wondered what Yussef had been telling her.

'Tarek, did you try the *kibbeh*?' Zeina had turned her attention to the boy. 'Your father used to love *kibbeh*. But that banana must have spoiled your appetite.'

'Don't worry, Tante Zeina, Tarek eats like a wolf, one banana won't spoil his appetite.'

'Takes after his grandfather Shamel,' Om Khalil chimed in as she removed a platter from the sideboard. 'I remember him well as a youngster. Had the best appetite of all his brothers, and they were big eaters, mind you, the Seif el-Islam men.'

Zeina looked at Om Khalil in alarm, clearly reminded of her reputation for the evil eye. It wasn't only the domestics who believed that it was enough for Om Khalil to remark on a child's rosy cheeks for him to wither and sicken, or for her to blink her sharp eyes at the brilliance of a chandelier for it to fall and smash to pieces. Zeina changed the subject in a hurry. 'These stuffed vine leaves are too salty. They must have been preserved in brine. I had specified fresh vine leaves, I must speak to the cook. What is it, Om Khalil? I wish you wouldn't hover when we have company.'

Om Khalil twisted the ends of her kerchief in her big-knuckled fingers. 'Well, Sitt Gigi, when I heard you were going to Jedda to see Yussef Bey, it was like a sign, I told myself Allah wants me to go visit the Holy City . . . if you'll take me with you.'

'I suppose it's no problem to arrange a day trip for her to Mecca, it's not the pilgrimage season,' Zeina added,

104

'but I don't know, she doesn't have a passport, and you'll be leaving in a week.'

'Of course, Om Khalil, I'd be glad to take you. The passport might be a problem though.' Gigi did not especially look forward to Om Khalil's company but it would have been ungracious to refuse such a pious request.

'Why don't you ask Kamal when you see him this afternoon?' Zeina suggested. 'He has ways of arranging these things.'

Gigi had arranged to meet her father-in-law in his office in town. Two male clerks were working at the fax machines. The female receptionist made a lot of Tarek while Gigi went into Kamal's office. He put down the papers he was studying and greeted her with a peck on the cheek.

'Well, Gigi, how have you been? How are your parents?' He took off his glasses and rubbed his eyelids. 'When are you going to join Yussef?'

'Next week. Uncle Kamal, before I forget, I want to ask a favor of you, for Om Khalil actually. She wants to come with me for the week I'm spending in Jedda, but she needs a passport.'

'I suppose it can be arranged, if you're willing to take that old witch with you. Where's Tarek?'

'He's with the receptionist outside.' They could hear Tarek giggling as he tried to photocopy his hand on the photocopying machine.

'Hm. Well, are you all set for your trip?'

'I think so, except that I need your signature on Tarek's passport to take him out of the country.'

'I've been thinking about that, Gigi. It's not a good idea to take the child. You'll be staying in Emir Bandar's

105

guesthouse. I know what the lifestyle there is like. There's nothing for Tarek to do over there, and he's an active little boy. He'll just distract Yussef. I want him to have his wits about him, this deal's important.'

'Uncle Kamal, I'm really counting on taking Tarek. I'm sure Yussef wants to see him.'

'He'll see him soon enough. Leave Yussef to me, I'll call him tonight.' He put his glasses back on. 'Let Tarek stay here with your parents. Do him good to get away from your apron-strings for a while. You're too attached to that child, Gigi, you'll turn him into a mama's boy.'

'Not *Tarek*.'

Kamal did not miss the inflection in her words. His eyes narrowed, the same way he had looked at her at her wedding. Then he turned his attention back to the papers he was holding. 'Well, it's high time you spent some time with Yussef. All I can say is, in his place I wouldn't have been so accommodating about having my wife stay behind like that. No, he doesn't take after me.' He looked at Gigi, who was trying to suppress a smile. 'Don't imagine I don't know what you're thinking, Missy. You're telling yourself: "And a good thing too!"'

Gigi burst out laughing.

Kamal pulled her ear lobe in mock reproach. 'Well, well, Gigi, sometimes I wish you were my daughter, not my daughter-in-law. Where's Tarek? Call him in here.'

106

8

Jedda

At Jedda Airport the young man behind the passport inspection counter was firm but polite. 'You can't come into the country without a male relative to act as your guarantor, your *mihrem*.'

'I know that,' Gigi answered, 'my husband is in Jedda, he will be my *mihrem*. He's supposed to meet me here.'

'And I've been with the family forever,' Om Khalil proclaimed. Instead of her usual black, she was dressed all in white in anticipation of her pilgrimage to Mecca.

'That's all right,' the dark young man with the thin moustache smiled. 'With a lady your age, we don't worry too much about whether or not you have a *mihrem* to guarantee your moral behavior.' He turned to Gigi. 'Please sit down and wait for your husband.'

Gigi sat down on one of the lounge chairs and Om Khalil sat down beside her, a little piqued by the man's tactless reply. Gigi was getting worried. What if Yussef had forgotten, or mixed up the flight numbers? There would be nothing to do but to get on the next flight back.

107

But he was probably just late, he was often late.

The call for afternoon prayers sounded over the loud-speaker. The passport control officer came out from behind the counter, slipped off his shoes and stood up to pray, head bowed, hands folded. Several people followed suit.

'Look,' Om Khalil whispered to Gigi, 'at the currency exchange counter over there. The man who was behind it just left and walked out through the gate to go pray. And he left all that money lying there on the counter, just stacks and stacks of bills in rows!'

'Don't even *look* too hard at the money, Om Khalil,' Gigi teased her, 'you know what they do to thieves here.'

'Allah preserve us,' Om Khalil shuddered.

Gigi looked at her watch. It was half past three. Then Yussef came striding through the gate, smiling and waving. Gigi tried to erase the tension from her expression. They avoided touching in greeting. Public displays of affection were frowned upon here, even if the offending couple were legitimately married.

The passport control officer carefully examined their passports, then let them through.

'You were so late, we were getting worried,' Gigi tried not to sound as if she were complaining.

'Sorry about that. Guess who I met in the lounge on my way over here? Bassil Sirdana! I hadn't seen him since he left London. He's married now. Anyway we made plans for tomorrow night, I'll tell you about it later. So, how are you, Om Khalil?'

As they headed out of the airport the sliding doors opened, letting in a warm, humid breeze. A white Mercedes was waiting for them.

'Gigi, did you bring a veil?' Yussef asked.

'Yes. But do you think I need it just to ride in the car?'

108

'This is one of Emir Bandar's cars, and they're recognizable by their special plates. Anybody riding in them is assumed to be a member of his household. So out of courtesy for our host we have to be careful. Jedda is a lot more relaxed than Riad, though.'

Yussef helped her in, and Om Khalil got in beside the driver. Gigi covered her head with the veil although the windows of the car were tinted and she was sure nobody could see into them.

Within a few minutes they drove into the palace complex. The guest house, or salamlek, was only a few meters from the palace but completely private. Yussef had explained that there was no one else staying there at the moment.

'Come on, Gigi. We'll let Om Khalil unpack and we can have a nap.'

'This late?' Gigi stood in the gilt and mirror bathroom, surveying the array of French perfumes, bath oils and lotions set out on the counter.

'We'd better. We're invited to dinner with Bandar and his family tonight and nothing starts happening here till very late. There's nothing much to do in the afternoons.'

She slipped on a salmon-pink silk nightgown and sprayed a mist of Chanel No.5 on the inside of her wrist.

'Gigi, what's taking you so long? Come to bed.'

At around ten o'clock in the evening Gigi followed the maid towards the Emira's quarters. Yussef had gone to join the Emir in the men's quarters. The understanding was that they would get together later for dinner, in honor of her first night there. As a rule the women in the Emir's household did not socialize with men who were strangers to the family, but Bandar was an open-minded man who

109

had spent many years in Cairo, in virtual exile as a result of falling out of favor with his brother the king. During that time he had become fast friends with Kamal Zeitouni. Gigi had met him once before, at her wedding with Yussef. Since then the old king had been assassinated and Emir Bandar had returned to Saudi Arabia.

Gigi followed the maid across the marble floor of a vaulted atrium in the center of the house. Jets of water from a fountain sprang up to spray the tops of the surrounding trees, fell back in defeat, sprang up again. Gigi looked up through the glass dome at the night sky, the brilliant stars.

At the end of a long gallery she was ushered into a large room dominated by a projection screen on one wall. In the center of the room a depressed seating area formed a semicircle of cushions facing the screen. Two women and three young girls were watching an Egyptian film, apparently a noisy musical romance.

The woman who turned to greet Gigi was in her forties. Her black hair was arranged in an elaborate hairdo and she was wearing a complete matched set of emerald and diamond jewelry. Gigi wondered if Yussef was right about it being an informal evening.

'*Ahlan*, welcome,' Emira Khadija smiled at Gigi and offered her a seat on the circular sofa. Gigi sat down and nodded politely to the elderly lady in an embroidered black caftan sitting at the far end. The Egyptian film was coming to a clamorous conclusion. The youngest of the three girls jumped up.

'May I choose the next film, please, Mama, may I?'

Khadija nodded. 'That's my youngest, and Riha here is my eldest of the girls, she's our little bride, her wedding is planned for next month. We were just looking through

110

some catalogues to order sets of jewelry for her.' The low table in front of her was piled with catalogues from Asprey's, Garrard's, and Cartier's. She flicked through one of them, then tossed it back. 'Tell me, did you find everything you need in the guesthouse? Did the housekeeper restock the toiletries and snacks?'

The selection of perfume and toiletries in the bathroom had been very thoughtful; Om Khalil had also reported that the pantry and refrigerator were packed.

'Absolutely everything, really, thank you, you've been very kind.'

'It's been two years since it was built, and I was thinking it needed to be redecorated. What do you think? Do you have any ideas?'

Gigi thought for a moment about the proportions of the rooms, the way the light threatened behind the tinted glass, and visualized men in flowing `abbayas` sailing through them. 'Well, I don't know too much about these things, but I would think a few Directoire or Empire pieces would look good, wouldn't you? I mean, because it's a massive, masculine style, but there's that element of fantasy and oriental splendor: you know, the winged Sphinxes and the whole theme from Napoleon's Egyptian campaign.'

Khadija looked blank. Gigi trailed off lamely.

'Everything has to be new,' the Emira pointed out, 'and made to order. All the seating in the formal rooms has to face in one direction, so no one has their back to the Emir when he is seated. And no statues, of course.'

Gigi was embarrassed. She should have remembered the Wahabi Muslim injunction against the portrayal of animate beings.

The maid came in with guava juice and dishes of nuts and dried fruit. Khadija took a handful of pistachios.

111

'Have you seen this film? No? Good. In any case you can choose the next one we get to see. I don't think the Emir will be done with his visitors and ready to sit down to dinner before one o'clock tonight.'

Gigi stifled a yawn. She wished she had been able to fall asleep when she had tried to nap in the afternoon.

Gigi stepped out of her dress and dropped it on the chaise longue. In the bathroom she leaned over the sink, wiping the make-up off her bleary face. Yussef was throwing off his clothes, tight-lipped.

'Look, Yussef, I'm sorry I giggled. I couldn't help it! I mean, I didn't expect it, he just suddenly picked up that chunk of lamb and tossed it on my plate!'

'Bandar was just trying to be hospitable, to serve you with his own hands.'

'I know, I know, and I'm sorry. But I was so startled, that giggle just popped out, I couldn't help it. But I really don't think he was offended at all, because he was very pleasant afterwards.'

Gigi took a couple of aspirin for a headache that had been building for hours. She collapsed on the bed. 'I'm so tired.'

He tossed the extra pillows on to the floor. 'How did you get along with Khadija?'

'All right, I suppose.'

'Good. Because I think things might work out here. In that case we'd be staying for a while.'

'Really? For how long?'

'I don't know – this project is just starting to take shape.'

Gigi digested this in silence for a minute. 'I see. Don't you think we ought to discuss this?'

112

'Papa thinks it would be a good move.'

'But Yussef, there's nothing to do here. And it's so hot nearly year-round. I know everything's air-conditioned, but that means Tarek would have to be shut up indoors all day.'

'If you want him to stay in Egypt, he can stay with my mother. Or yours, if you insist. You can go back and forth and visit him.'

'But there's nothing for me to do here. I'd go crazy!'

'Gigi, can we just drop this and go to sleep now? I've got things to do tomorrow.'

'And what am I supposed to do all day tomorrow?'

'What?' He yawned into his pillow.

'Never mind. Good night. Or good morning, rather.'

She heard the call to dawn prayers, amplified by loud-speaker, start up and echo from minaret to minaret.

'So does Bassil live here in Jedda now?' Gigi asked as they drove to the hotel.

'Well, he's based here, but he travels around a lot. I gather he's doing very well, he's managing one of the major hospitals in the entire region.'

In the hotel lobby Bassil was waiting for them, looking sleek and impeccably tailored.

'So nice to see you again,' he smiled at Gigi, 'it was such a pleasant surprise to see Yussef in the lounge at the airport. Come and meet my wife.' Bassil led them to a seating area in the back of the lobby. A full-figured woman with long chestnut hair and a pleasant smile rose to greet them.

'This is Mona,' Bassil introduced them.

The elevator took them up to the Swissair Restaurant on the tenth floor. They sat down and ordered. When

113

the waiter had taken away their menus, Gigi turned to Mona.

'How do you like it here in Jedda?'

'Oh, well, there's the weather, of course, for so much of the year. And I can't drive a car here, but we have a driver. Our building complex has all sorts of boutiques, a beauty salon, even a spa, which I should use more often, I've put on a few kilos since I've had the babies. It's just that I'm home with the children all the time, I snack too much. We have two little boys; of course the Filipina nanny is very reliable, but I'm home a lot anyway, there isn't much to do here . . . ' She patted her hips in the tight foam-green lace dress she was wearing. 'Now Bassil plays tennis at six o'clock in the morning to beat the heat in summer, but I can go for weeks without sticking my head out of the air-conditioning. I don't mind, really. We take vacations in Europe twice a year, and we go home to Cairo for short visits all the time.'

Gigi listened with half an ear to Yussef and Bassil, who were reminiscing about their school days at the Jesuits. Yussef seemed to be doing most of the talking.

'Do you remember Father Anselme? He used to make us write one hundred lines for dropping a pencil. He made us run up and down the stairs for ten minutes just for talking in class.'

'You used to get out of it, though, Yussef, I always wondered how.'

'My mother sent a note saying that I might have had rheumatic fever as a child.'

They laughed. The waiter brought the first course. 'After dinner let's all go back to our apartment and have some liqueur. We keep a half-way decent bar at home,' Bassil offered. Gigi raised her eyebrows.

114

'Oh yes, even here, as long as you're careful,' Mona nodded.

At the airport Gigi claimed her baggage and pushed the cart through the 'Nothing to Declare' line at customs. Om Khalil followed, pushing an overloaded cart. Gigi glanced at it. She could have sworn Om Khalil had not had that big red suitcase with her when they set out for Jedda. The customs inspector motioned Om Khalil over to the side and Gigi, sighing, followed suit. If Om Khalil had customs duty to pay she probably would not have enough money on her.

'Why really, young man, you don't have eyes in your head! Can't you see I'm a pilgrim in white, just back from the Holy City? What do you expect to find in my suit-case?' Om Khalil grumbled as she fumbled with the lock of the red suitcase and reluctantly flung it open. On top lay a prayer rug encrusted with a compass and a clock displaying international time zones. The two combined would allow a Muslim to orient himself towards Mecca wherever he might be and to calculate the exact time for the five daily prayers anywhere in the world.

The customs inspector lifted the rug and Gigi's eyes widened at the sight of the array underneath: bolts of cloth, watches, small radios – Om Khalil had obviously done her shopping in Jedda. Then Gigi saw the liter bottles of Chanel No.5, fragrant boxes of Fragonard soap, gold-wrapped assortments of Godiva chocolates, bags of pistachios. Om Khalil had helped herself to the contents of the bathroom and pantry cabinets at the Emir's guesthouse.

'Oh, Om Khalil, how could you!' Gigi whispered.

'Well, they were there for guests anyway, and it was such a waste,' Om Khalil shrugged.

* * *

115

In the car on the way back from the airport Om Khalil sat in the front, entertaining the driver with stories of her trip. Gigi sat beside her mother in the back, cuddling Tarek on her knees. She sniffed his tousled hair, his warm little neck, his chewing-gum minty breath, all the re-assuringly familiar smells. Then she turned to Mama.

'How's Papa?'

'The same, darling. He didn't quite feel up to coming to the airport.'

'Has Tarek been a lot of trouble?'

'Not at all. We had a lot of fun together, didn't we, Tarek? Oh, by the way, Zohra called, she's inviting us to a party for Leila's engagement. She asked to borrow my silver punch bowl, so it must be a big party, she has two of her own. So, how did it go in Jedda?'

116

9

Papa

Gigi found Papa sitting on the terrace in the dark. Lately he spent hours every evening sitting on one of the lounge chairs on the terrace, nursing his cold pipe. He didn't read, or watch television, or check with his lawyer over the phone on the status of the ongoing appeals for partial restitution from the Sequestration Authority. He hardly ate any more, leaving the table abruptly halfway through the meal. Madame Hélène, shocked, tried to keep up appearances by repeating: '*Faîtes, faîtes, Monsieur,*' as if he had asked to be excused.

He had given up the weekend breakfasts at Groppi's with Tarek. 'I felt an attack coming on as I was driving home the last time,' he confided to Gigi. 'I put a pill under my tongue and it passed. But all I could think of was what would happen to the boy if I keeled over at the wheel while he was with me in the car. I can't take that risk again.'

Every evening he sat on the terrace in the dark, lost in his thoughts. Of the past or of the future, Gigi couldn't

117

tell. For the first time in decades, there was hope of change. The pall of the police state had lifted. Sadat had kicked out the Soviets and welcomed in the Americans. He had promised free parties, free elections, free press. The buzz-words were 'democracy' and *'Infitah'*, economic open-door policy.

Sadat also hoped to encourage local entrepreneurs and foreign investors. To restore confidence, he announced that he would gradually lift the sequestration decrees, and look into making some measure of reparation to the individuals and families whose property had been arbitrarily confiscated.

To Gigi, having grown up under the Nasser regime, all this seemed miraculous. But the older generation, roused to action, reacted as if to an expected, if long-delayed, return to normality.

The Pasha had been the first to take up the challenge by establishing an opposition party to contest the upcoming elections after a quarter of a century of single-party rule. The Cairo House, so long dormant, shook off its cobwebs and sprang back to life: the great doors were flung open, the ponderous wooden window shades were drawn up on their creaky chains; the chandeliers blazed; the halls and salons teemed with people; the phones rang off the hooks; the new party newspaper was snatched off the stands. Sadat, surprised and derisive, referred to the Pasha in a speech as 'a phoenix rising from the ashes'. Yet the Pasha had bided his time; sheer will and incurable optimism had carried him through the past two decades.

Only Papa seemed detached, as if he had given up, just when things were taking a turn for the better. Gigi sensed that he was drifting away. It frightened her. He

118

seemed to have lost the spirit to cope with the occasional, inevitable slights and annoyances.

Gigi had needed her passport renewed before her trip to Jedda. Yussef was already out of the country, and she could not, as a young woman, go to government offices on her own; Papa had to accompany her. They were ignored and kept waiting by a minor functionary. The system was well established. On the one hand, the bureaucratic underclass was not paid enough to subsist, and supplemented its income with under-the-table kickbacks extorted by surliness. On the other hand, an entire profession of 'facilitators' existed for the express purpose of dealing with this petty bureaucracy: running errands, greasing palms, and smoothing the way for those who kept them in their entourage. Between the two, government offices were a no man's land for the uninitiated or unprepared.

Gigi could see that Papa was not up to handling the paper pusher's calculated insolence that day. He was trying to control his temper and fumbling around in his pocket for an Angicid pill to stick under his tongue. She drew him away.

'Come on, Papa, it's not worth upsetting yourself. Let's go home now, we'll take care of it later some other way.'

She promised herself not to expose her father to that kind of situation again. The next day she went to lunch at the Pasha's and mentioned the difficulties she'd had at the passport office. He made a phone call and sent her over with his driver half an hour later. It was taken care of immediately.

Gigi pulled up a lounge chair beside Papa on the terrace. 'Hello, Papa.'

'Hello, darling. Come tell me about your trip. Where's Tarek? Have you put him to bed?'

119

'Mama is doing that tonight.'

'Tell me all about Jedda.'

'Yussef seems to think we should live there for a while, I don't know how long. I don't think I could take it, especially if he expects us to stay as Bandar's guests. The Emir and his wife are very kind, that's not the problem, but you wouldn't believe how monotonous the life the women lead there is.' Khadija and her friends woke very late, about two o'clock, and spent the rest of the afternoon getting massages and manicures. Their one passion seemed to be shopping, and occasionally they covered themselves from head to foot and got driven to a mall, but mostly they waited to go on shopping sprees to Europe. In the evening they watched endless videos while waiting for the men to be free. Every so often they dressed elaborately for a party; lavish affairs, with hired entertainment, belly-dancers and singers, but all women, from the guests to the musicians. Then sooner or later some of the guests themselves got up and belly-danced to entertain each other. She sighed. 'Papa, I couldn't breathe while I was over there. And it would be no life at all for Tarek, I'd have to leave him behind.'

There was a long pause. 'Gigi, if Yussef stays here, his father will keep him under his thumb forever. I know Kamal Zeitouni.' He sighed. 'The only alternative is for Yussef to try to make a career for himself abroad. You could go back to London. A lot of young couples are trying to establish themselves abroad, but they generally don't have as much going for them at home as you and Yussef do. But if you want to be independent of his father, that's the price you'll have to pay. It will be hard, the first few years especially will be very hard, you won't have the lifestyle you could have had here.'

'So you think we should go back to London?' Gigi was glad of the dark, so he couldn't see that she was close to tears.

'Don't ask silly questions. Do you really think for a minute that I want you to go away? My only daughter? Just when you come back after being gone to England for years and years? Do you really believe I want you to go away again, and take the child with you, this child that is such a joy to us, your mother and me?'

Gigi rubbed her head against his shoulder in the dark.

'If Yussef were mean to you, if he had vices, I wouldn't encourage you to put up with him for a minute, you know that –'

Gigi hesitated. But certain things, once said, could not be retracted. She shook her head.

'Then you have to do what's right, Gigi, for Tarek's sake. You're my daughter, and your mother's daughter.'

She remembered the conversation overheard, so many years ago now, through the French windows of Mama's bedroom. She wondered if Papa were thinking that Mama had stood by him through thick and thin. For the first time she wondered, too, if her father's disillusionment over Gina's story had colored his perception when it came to her own engagement to Yussef and now her marriage. Perhaps it was the disappointed romantic in him that had settled for a loveless marriage for his own daughter. She remembered the look on his face when Gina had come to say goodbye, the day she left for Lebanon, abandoning her children and her country; Gigi couldn't bear to disappoint him that way.

In the dark she could sense, more than hear, Papa draw furiously on his unlit pipe. She knew how frustrating it was for him to see her unhappy. It frightened

121

her to think that she might be responsible for bringing on one of his attacks.

'It's all right, Papa, really. It'll all work out, don't worry. Oh, did I tell you about Om Khalil and what she did in Jedda?'

'Papa, do you need anything before I go to bed?'

'Rub my leg for me for a minute. It aches tonight.'

Gigi sat down at the foot of the bed and rubbed his calf muscle as he lay with his knee bent. She knew Papa's circulation was very poor, his hands and feet were always cold.

'Do you know,' he murmured, 'I used to be something of a chess player, when I was young.'

Gigi was surprised. She had never known her father to play chess. Perhaps he was half-dreaming; she heard his breathing change and realized the strong sedative he took had taken effect. But he would sleep only fitfully, and long before dawn be unable to rest.

Gigi tiptoed to the door then turned around for a last look. Her father's breathing was loud and laborious, every breath seemed to take so much effort, she wondered how he could keep it up.

He couldn't. During the night the blood clot that had caused the pain in his leg had migrated in his blood. By morning it had reached his heart and the death watch had begun. The two doctors came and went, setting up an oxygen tent and hooking up intravenous lines. Shamel had refused to go to the hospital; he wanted to die at home.

The salons filled with the nearest relatives: the Pasha, Nabil and Zakariah, Tante Zohra, Uncle Hani. Mama did not leave Papa's side and left it up to Gigi to make sure

122

the *suffragi* served tea or coffee to each new arrival, that the maid, Khadra, brought guest towels and a prayer rug to Tante Zohra, that an ashtray was found for the Pasha. Leila came to take Tarek out of the way.

Gigi had just finished answering the telephone – another concerned relative – and hurried back to her father's room with the bottle of rubbing alcohol the doctor had asked for. At the door what she saw made her cry out and drop the bottle. The two doctors were pounding on her father's chest and his legs were bouncing on the bed, the intravenous drip tube flying out of his arm.

'Stop! You're hurting him! Stop!' she screamed.

The younger of the two doctors pushed her out of the room and closed the door, calling tersely to Uncle Hani, who was just outside: 'Keep her out till it's over.'

The next few hours blurred into a haze as the sedative she was given took over. She vaguely remembered throwing up while Madame Hélène held her head, as she had done when Gigi was a child. She was barely aware of Leila bringing Tarek back, and tucking him into bed beside her. She half-woke in the middle of the night and stumbled over to her mother's room at the other end of the house. Mama was asleep, heavily sedated. Khadra lay on a mattress on the floor at the foot of the bed. She raised her head when she saw Gigi and put a finger to her lips. Gigi crept back to bed.

Then it was sunrise. Tarek stirred beside her. Gigi drew him closer but he wiggled away and slipped out of bed. It was only when she heard the patter of his little bare feet on the hardwood floor of the corridor that she realized he would head straight for his grandfather's room, as he did every morning when he woke early. Gigi flung herself out of bed.

'Tarek, no!'

But it was too late, he was speeding through the corridor and had reached the sitting room that led to Papa's bedroom. Madame Hélène, slumped mournfully in an armchair by the door, heard the little feet. How, despite her creaky old knees, she was able to shove herself out of the armchair; how she managed to catch the little blue-pajama'd figure in full flight; this Gigi would never know. She only knew that an angel was standing guard that morning.

'*Viens, mon petit, Monsieur* is sleeping late today, we must be very quiet.' Madame Hélène led Tarek away.

The doorbell rang, making Gigi jump. She hurried downstairs. She was surprised to see Tamer's tall, lean figure at the door.

'Tamer! What are you doing here?' She pulled him in by the hand and closed the door.

'I hope I didn't wake you. Only when I heard, I wanted to be the first one here in the morning to see you. And to make sure that I could be one of the pallbearers.'

'You're a sweetheart.' Gigi gave him a hug. 'Did you tell anyone you were coming?'

'No, it was my idea.'

Gigi had guessed as much because no one had told him that pallbearers needed to wear a black tie.

'Wait here for a minute, I'll get you a tie.'

She went upstairs to her father's room. Papa had any number of black ties that he kept for funerals and visits of condolences. She would lend one to Tamer.

She entered Papa's room without hesitation. He looked as he would if he were asleep, except for a bandage around his head holding his jaw closed. The other discordant note was an electric fan whirring on the bedside table. Gigi leaned over the bed. 'Hello, Papa.' She brushed his hand.

124

'Touching the dead causes them pain!' A strange voice boomed behind her.

Gigi spun around. A *fikki* sat cross-legged on the chaise longue, partially screened by the clotheshorse. He adjusted the white turban on his head, balancing an open Koran on his knees. His shoes were on the floor.

'Who let you in here?' Gigi asked.

'I was called to pray for the soul of the dead through the night.'

'Oh, I see.' Gigi turned back to Papa, trying to ignore the presence of this stranger in her father's bedroom. But as soon as she leaned over the bed again the man began remonstrating.

'Touching the dead causes them pain!'

'It's all right, I'm his daughter. I wouldn't hurt him.'

'The soul of the dead feels the slightest touch!'

Gigi lost patience. 'Look, why don't you go downstairs now and have a cup of tea. You must be tired. Tell Khadra – that's the maid – tell her I said to make you breakfast. Go on, please. The mourners will be here in a minute and you won't have another chance.'

She ushered the *fikki* out. She looked around Papa's room. It was so tidy, the dressers clear of clutter: no books, papers, letters or trinkets; only his keys, a pen and the cold pipe in a silver ashtray. She stared at the bedside table with its neat array of prescription bottles, the clotheshorse with his pants crisply folded at the crease. She opened his closet. Everything was impeccable. The suits and ties were not new and yet looked hardly used. The tie rack was arranged according to colors, and there were a dozen black ties hanging side by side. She chose a relatively recent style for Tamer.

She had never noticed before that her father was a

125

tidy man, or that he used his possessions lightly, as if they were borrowed. Some people took up so much space in this world, surrounded themselves with clutter and bustle, staking a claim on life. But with her father, when his body was borne away and the tray of medicine was removed, the room in which he had lived for nearly thirty years would look as if it had never been occupied.

It was as if he had packed his bags and been ready to go, a long time ago. Gigi reproached herself for having been too engrossed in her problems with Yussef to notice the luggage standing ready in the corner.

At nine the men came. The last Gigi saw of Papa was his body being carried out of the house, wrapped in white sheeting, on a pall borne by six men, including Tamer. The men left the house for the cemetery. Mama stood by the door, as speechless and dry-eyed as Gigi. The lack of a display of emotion apparently offended Khadra's sense of what was fitting and due to her kind employer. She took it upon herself to remedy the situation. She started to wail at the top of her voice as the silent procession went down the stairs to the waiting cars.

The two salons of the Cairo House overflowed with women in black. In a powerful baritone, a *fikki* seated behind a screen chanted verses from the Koran.

> 'Those who believe, and the Jews,
> And the Christians and the Sabians
> Those who believe in Allah and the Last Day
> And are righteous in their deeds
> Shall have their reward with their Lord
> They need neither fear nor grieve.'

126

For the first time Gigi concentrated on the chanted verses. She tried not to fear or grieve for her father. Papa had been righteous. She had never known anyone with a more absolute sense of right and wrong. But she knew that it was a morality undictated by fear of divine retribution. Had he believed?

In the intervals the *suffragis* circled with trays of Turkish coffee and ice water. Gigi sat at one end, surrounded by her cousins and school friends. Mama and Tante Zohra each held court at opposite ends of the salons.

The men held their reception for condolences under a huge awning of carpeting set up in a square in front of one of the major mosques in Cairo. Hundreds of chairs were packed under the awning to accommodate the crowds that came to pay their condolences to the Pasha; now that he was back in the political limelight his brother's memorial service was no longer a family affair.

The Pasha had organized everything for the three days of official mourning. All Mama and Gigi had to do was to dress in black and drive over to the Cairo House to receive visitors. This arrangement contributed to the unreality of the situation for Gigi.

The *fikki*'s disembodied voice rose again from behind the screen.

> 'Seek refuge with the Lord of the dawn
> From the evil among his creations
> From the darkness as it spreads
> From witches breathing spells
> From the evil eye of the envious.'

Tante Zohra let out a long, loud sigh. Gigi crossed the salon and sat down beside her. Her aunt dabbed at her

127

eyes with a handkerchief. 'Ah, my poor Gigi, what a loss! I never thought I would outlive Shamel, he was the youngest of us all. But he was always too sensitive, he took everything to heart. It wore him down. People like that aren't tough enough to deal with this cruel world.' She patted Gigi's hand. 'He worried about you so, you know.'

On the last day, a slim woman with dark brown, upswept hair arrived late in the afternoon. She went straight to Tante Zohra and hugged her, and they both started weeping. It was only when she turned to Gigi and Mama that Gigi recognized her. It was Gina. Gigi had been fourteen the last time she had seen her.

She hugged Gigi. 'How you've grown! It must be ten years since I last saw you. The last time I saw Uncle Shamel, Allah rest his soul. You can't know how much he meant to me. But it's so good to see you, darling Gigi!'

Driving home, Gigi couldn't wait to tell Papa that she had seen Gina again after all these years. That she looked older, but that you could still see traces of the charm that Papa, and other men, had found so irresistible. Then it hit Gigi that Papa would not be home to hear about Gina. He would never be home again. She would never be able to talk to him again, about anything. That night, for the first time, she cried.

In her sleep she thought she saw Papa come in and close the windows. When she woke in the morning she realized it must have been a dream, evoked by the sound of the wind rattling the shutters.

Mama could not sleep alone, since Papa's death. Khadra slept on a mattress at the foot of her bed.

That day was the first day they had lunch together at

128

home, rather than at the Cairo House. Mama, Gigi and Madame Hélène tried to make conversation, for Tarek's sake. Suddenly Tarek piped up:

'Grandpa came and closed the windows in my room last night.'

Gigi dropped her fork and stared at him.

Mama understood. 'You too?' she asked Gigi. 'He closed the windows in your room too?' The tears came to her eyes. 'He never came to my room. Why didn't he come to me? Is it because Khadra sleeps in the room?'

'Oh, Mama, what an idea.' Gigi jumped up and hugged her. But it shocked her that her mother, usually so rational, had accepted without question that it was Papa's spirit, rather than a dream, that had visited both Gigi and Tarek that night.

Yussef came back from Jedda a week after Papa passed away. He had only learned of his father-in-law's death upon his return. The day of the burial Kamal Zeitouni had taken Gigi aside.

'It's best not to tell Yussef about this just yet. He'll be back in a week anyway. Telling him will only take his mind off his work, and there's nothing he can do.'

Nothing, Gigi thought, except to console his wife, if only by a phone call. But it was typical of her father-in-law. She wished Yussef had been there, she needed to cling to him for perhaps the first time in their marriage. With Papa gone, she felt exposed and vulnerable.

When Yussef arrived a week later, late in the evening, Tarek was already in bed. Gigi took Yussef into the salon. She switched on a lamp and they sat on the sofa in the half-dark.

'I'm so glad you're here. I wish Uncle Kamal had called

129

you. I would have called you myself, but you never gave me the number at the Emir's guesthouse.'

'Father had it.'

'I know. But he didn't think you should be told till you came back.'

'Yes, he was afraid it would be a shock. He likes to spare me as much as possible, that's the kind of father he is.'

Gigi bit her lip. She changed the subject.

'So, did the deal go through all right?'

'It worked out, which means I'll have to go back again in a week. When can you join me?'

'Not right now, I can't leave Mama so soon.' She sighed. 'It's so confusing, all the estate duties, the legal documents. I have to go to the notary public tomorrow, there are all kinds of paperwork to sign. Will you come with me?'

'No, I don't think I can, Father wants me to drive him to the oculist tomorrow.'

'But I can't go alone. I suppose I'll ask Uncle Hani if he can come with me, or perhaps the Pasha will send someone.' She worried about it for a minute. 'Well at least you'll be here all week, you'll be here when Tarek has his tonsils removed. It was all set for last week but of course we put it off because of Papa . . . We can reschedule the operation for Tuesday, at the Dokki Clinic. We have to be there early, at seven. Can you pick us up at six-thirty?'

'It would take too long for me to drive over to Zamalek from Garden City to fetch you. What time is the operation scheduled for? Nine? Why don't I meet you there just before nine?'

The telephone rang and Khadra called Yussef to the

phone. He got up to take the call in the study. He came back in a few moments.

'That was Mother. She was reminding me not to be late, some people are coming over for dinner tonight.'

'Oh. I was hoping you'd stay. There's so much we need to talk about. Can't you stay with me for a little while?'

She went to him and put her arms around his neck, rubbing the top of her head against his chin. She felt him stiffen and looked up. She could see that he distrusted her gesture; she was rarely spontaneously affectionate with him. Then she caught the glimmer of triumph in his eyes. He was thinking that she needed him, now that she was feeling alone and helpless. He drew her closer. But she had read his hesitation too clearly. She dropped her arms and pulled away. She would take no comfort in his staying now, and she lacked the will to play games just to win a point.

'You'd better go, Tante Zeina's expecting you.'

'All right.' He hesitated, as if he realized that there was more at stake in his leaving than he thought. It was not like Yussef to be perceptive, Gigi knew. He shrugged it off. 'Look, I stopped by Tarek's room to give him a kiss. He was sleeping, he didn't even wake up. Tell him I'll see you both when you come for lunch on Friday, okay?'

Gigi sat back down on the sofa in the near dark. Sometimes it takes an almost imperceptible shift in the kaleidoscope for the pattern to come into focus. Sometimes all it takes is the removal of one sliver of colored shapes for the entire image to change. It seemed that in her life, endings and beginnings were marked not with a bang, but with a whimper. But this time, at least, she had not merely floated along like a leaf downstream. This time she had taken a decision.

* * *

131

'I swear someone must have switched the doves in the cage at your wedding and replaced them with hawks.' Tante Zohra shook her head. It was the fortieth day of Papa's passing away. The fortieth day marked a milestone and the visits to the bereaved were renewed. Tante Zohra had been to visit Mama and had asked Gigi to drive her home. Her purpose, it soon became clear, was to sound out Gigi on her estrangement from Yussef.

'Listen, child, no man is perfect. His parents are not easy to get along with, I grant you that, but a little patience, a little diplomacy . . . Yussef still cares for you. I don't understand why you can't get your way with him. Pretty as you are, clever as you are, you should have him eating out of your hand. Why, Makhlouf, Allah rest his soul, was the biggest bully imaginable when I married him. But I learned how to handle him. A woman should be supple!'

Gigi pulled up in front of her aunt's building. 'Here we are, Tante Zohra.'

'Come up with me and have a cup of tea. No, Gigi, I insist.'

Tante Zohra held off the subject until they were comfortably installed in her salon and she had ordered tea.

'Now, Gigi, what's this all about? I feel responsible, in a way, since I was the one who brought the two of you together.'

'Well then, Tante Zohra, perhaps you could answer a question for me.' Gigi wrapped and unwrapped her key chain around her finger. 'Why did Yussef marry me? Was it his father's idea?'

'What a question! Of course his father thought it would be a good idea for him to get engaged before he went

132

back to England. To forestall the possibility that he might make an unsuitable match out there, as so many young men do. And of course you were at the top of the list of girls his parents suggested to him. But after that first meeting we arranged between you, he wasn't interested in seeing anyone else, that's how keen on you he was. And I'm sure that after you were married –'

'No. He didn't love me.'

'I can't believe that, Gigi. Why, you were adorable! I remember you at your wedding as if it were yesterday. Everyone thought you looked so right together. If I believed in the evil eye!' She sighed. 'And afterwards, everything seemed normal. I mean, you had Tarek so quickly –'

'Oh, Tante Zohra, everything was normal that way, Yussef made sure of that right away. That was part of the problem, he never gave me a chance to get used to him first – he never cared how I felt, he just –'

'He just what, child?'

'He never – he never courted me.'

Tante Zohra threw her hands up in exasperation. 'That's the problem with your generation! You grow up filling your heads with romantic nonsense!' She took a long sip of her tea. 'Your father – Allah rest his soul – he spoiled you, you know. Sheltered you too much and let you have unreasonable expectations.'

'I know.'

Tante Zohra hesitated. 'Gigi, did you ever think that Yussef might only have been reacting to your – coldness? I hear his side of the story, too, you know, through Zeina. I'm not the only one.'

Gigi looked down at her lap. Tante Zohra patted her knee. 'All I'm saying is, there's usually some blame on

133

both sides. But never mind that.' She took another sip of her tea. 'Gigi, trust me, there's no perfect marriage. Most young brides get caught up in their new homes, then their babies; and the routine takes over and the obligations pile up. That's what life is all about. That's all there is.'

'I know. It's not enough. I thought I could make a fresh start with Yussef, by playing house, doing all those things. But it wouldn't work. It's not enough.'

Tante Zohra leaned back on the sofa and sighed. A long sigh. 'No, I can see that. It wasn't enough for my Gina, either. It always had to be the grand passion. But that doesn't last. Gina found that out.' She shook her head. 'But you won't see that now. I know when it's no use arguing. What are you going to do?'

'I'm going to go to the Pasha and ask him to speak to Yussef about a divorce.'

'Well, a separation is a first step. But I warn you, Gigi, Yussef won't divorce you.'

'Why not? It's not as if he really cares for me.'

'He does, in his own way. And in any case, child, that has nothing to do with it.'

Gigi got up. 'I have to go now, Tante Zohra.'

'All right, dear. But wait a minute, I need to give you a check to drop off at Nellie Sirry's, it's a donation for an orphanage, she's on the board. She lives one street down from you. You don't mind, do you?'

'I'd be glad to, Tante Zohra, it's right on my way.'

'Do you remember her oldest son? Sharif? He had an eye on you for years, but Kamal Zeitouni had more or less put the word about that you were spoken for. Just like him to be so manipulative: to drive away the other suitors who were interested in you while not committing Yussef.

134

Why, if the Sirry boy knew you were free, even now – but listen to me, matchmaking already, and you're not even separated, let alone divorced! You'd think I would have learned my lesson and minded my own business!'

Driving back from Tante Zohra's, Gigi felt a new understanding and an odd sort of sympathy for Yussef. In this arranged marriage he had been following his parents' wishes, just as he always did – in a way, just as she had, herself. If he had been callous and egotistic towards her, it was the way he had been raised. If she had not succeeded in changing him, in 'getting him to eat out of her hand', as Tante Zohra would have expected, it was because she had not tried. She hoped the divorce would be an amicable one, for Tarek's sake; she had no intention of piling the blame on Yussef in order to paint herself in the colors of the victim.

This sort of reasoning, Gigi knew, baffled Mama: she found it wrong-headed and naive. She disapproved of the idea of divorce, but she realized that Gigi, normally pliable and vacillating, was for once utterly and implacably determined. If it must come to a divorce, then, Mama felt, it should be '*À la guerre comme à la guerre*', and the public opinion campaign should be launched with no holds barred. Gigi dreaded her mother's interference; having a loaded gun on your side was a liability when it could so easily be turned and used against you by your adversary. She tried her best to keep Mama from ratcheting up the rhetoric. Somewhat to her surprise she realized that, with Papa gone, her mother was less formidable.

'Come on in, Gigi.' The Pasha led the way into his bedroom and sank into a comfortable club chair, as was his custom at this time in the afternoon. Gigi had dropped by for

135

lunch, as she often did lately. In the evenings now the Cairo House teemed with people from the party. The only time to catch a few moments in private with her uncle was to come by at lunch-time. He was always glad to see her.

'A face as pretty as yours across the table always gives me an appetite,' he would say. Gigi smiled at her uncle's old-fashioned gallantry; a *bon mot* was as natural to him as breathing.

'Are you going back to work this afternoon?' the Pasha asked as he lit a cigar. Gigi had recently started working in the international department of the El-Ahram newspaper, as a news analyst and translator. It helped to occupy her time, what with Tarek in kindergarten all morning and Mama and his nanny all too ready to take care of him in the afternoons. The El-Ahram building was not far from her uncle's house in Garden City, and it always pleased him when she dropped in for lunch.

'No, I'm all done for today.' She plunged ahead. 'There's something I've been wanting to tell you. Things aren't going well between me and Yussef. I mean we've actually been separated for the past few months. When he's not on business trips for his father he lives with his mother, and Tarek and I are at home at Mama's.'

Gigi hesitated to continue. Since the Pasha's reentry into the political arena, Kamal Zeitouni had become one of his most important allies. He was running for a seat in the National Assembly under the new party banner, and was managing editor of the party newspaper. His contacts in Saudi Arabia were also valuable.

'Listen, Gigi,' the Pasha spoke deliberately, as if he read her mind, 'I have some idea about the problems you've been having with Yussef lately. In fact Kamal Zeitouni

136

complained to me the other day about the situation. I told him I needed to hear your side of the story. I told him that, your father being dead, you're in the position of my daughter. I want you to tell me the whole story.'

'It's not just these past few months. From the beginning it was a mistake, we never had a real marriage. But I kept trying, because of Tarek. And because of Papa. Now that he's gone, there's no point in going on any longer. Uncle, I want a divorce.'

'I need you to level with me, Gigi. Is there someone else?'

'No!'

'Good.' He nodded. 'Then we can take our time, negotiate. You understand that I can get Yussef to divorce you tomorrow, if he thought you were involved with someone else. But you would pay a very high price. You would lose everything, including your reputation.'

'All I want is Tarek.'

'That's just the point. If we keep this amicable, you get custody of Tarek; Yussef could visit him whenever he wanted. Once he turns ten, custody reverts to his father, but long before then, you'd have remarried. Trust me on this – young as you are, pretty as you are – you'll remarry in no time.' He smiled as Gigi tried to protest. She realized he had a point. Her chances of making a good match now, even as a divorcee, were much better in the new political climate of the country than they had been in the days when she was a young girl under sequestration. These days everyone seemed to want to be associated with the Pasha and the family again.

'When you remarry,' the Pasha continued, 'you would automatically lose custody. Yussef wouldn't let you take his son to live in a stranger's house. But he might agree

137

to let your mother keep him; you could work out some kind of arrangement where you could see Tarek every day but still keep up appearances. Take your cousin Nevine, for instance; when she remarried she took an apartment in her father's building in Zamalek, and her son lives with his maternal grandfather, officially, but Nevine can see him all day if she wants to, and her ex-husband has no problem with that. But it was an amicable divorce, and they're cousins, of course.' He puffed on his cigar. 'The main thing is to be patient. We can't afford to put too much pressure on Yussef to divorce you right away because if he gets his back up – or his father does – it can get ugly. You have no grounds for a divorce that will stand up in court. This has to be done by persuasion. I'll speak to Kamal Zeitouni. You and Yussef are already separated, for all intents and purposes. Now it can be official. But Gigi – be careful. You're still a married woman. You can't afford even a breath of scandal.'

10

Madame Hélène

'Gigi, I'm worried about Madame Hélène. It's been months since we've heard from her. Not since Papa's fortieth.'

Ever since Gigi had left for England, Madame Hélène often went to stay in her apartment downtown, for weeks, even months, at a time. She didn't have a telephone in the apartment, so she couldn't be reached, but she would call from time to time. It was unusual for her not to get in touch for so long. Gigi realized that she had been so unsettled by turmoil in her own life that she had not kept track of the time that had elapsed since Madame Hélène last called.

'I sent Ibrahim the doorkeeper over this morning with a message,' Mama continued. 'Just to make sure that she wasn't ill or in need of something. He came back a while ago. He said he tried ringing the doorbell for a long time, but no one answered. What's really worrying me is that he said the apartment door was sealed with wax. He tried to get some information from the doorkeeper but it was a new man who didn't seem to know who she was. All

139

he knew was that when he was hired the apartment was empty and had been sealed by the superintendent of the building.'

'I don't understand it,' Gigi shook her head. 'She would never leave just like that without letting us know. And where would she go? She always used to say that if she were seriously ill or dying, she would go to the Italian Hospital in Abassia.' Madame Hélène had often mentioned that they would take care of her there because her husband's family had been major benefactors of the hospital for generations. She had said to ask under her married name, Fernandini. 'I'll go over there right now.' Gigi picked up her car keys.

Guilt is a strange thing. All the while she was driving to the hospital Gigi kept remembering the exquisite lace collar Madame Hélène had made by hand for her thirteenth birthday, a lace collar the governess must have pored over for hours with her weak, boiled-egg eyes. It had been all she had to offer, a labor of love. She expected Gigi to wear the lace collar over a velvet dress, the way she had in years past. But Gigi was thirteen, and in the past year the last vestige of the little girl had given way to the self-conscious teenager. For her birthday she wanted to dress like other girls her age, in a bright sweater and matching, short skirt that had been Gina's present from a trip to Europe. Guilt is a subjective thing. For some of us it is not breaking great commandments but small acts of thoughtlessness that continue to haunt us.

For some reason an image came to her mind, an image of Madame Hélène watching a soccer match on television with Papa. Madame Hélène was short-sighted to the point of near-blindness and had not the first idea of how

140

the game was played, but she had heard that the goal-keeper for the red-shirted Ahli team, Aldo, was Italian, like her dear departed husband. From that day forward she sat through every match in which Aldo played. Papa would be hunched forward in concentration, clutching his pipe till his knuckles turned white, and every time there was a burst of excitement from the commentator Madame Hélène would pester him with: 'C'est Aldo, Monsieur Shamel?' He would answer patiently that it wasn't Aldo, Aldo was the goalie.

Gigi had only a vague idea where the Italian Hospital was, and got quite lost trying to find it. By the time she managed to get there it was past nine o'clock at night. The hospital was a large, turn-of-the-century building surrounded by a pleasant garden of overgrown magnolias. It took Gigi a while to rouse the night guardian, then to be taken to the head nurse.

'Was she a relative of yours?' the Italian nurse in her crisp white cap asked as she ran her finger down the list of names.

'No, my governess. But she raised me, she was family.'

'Fernandini, Fernandini. No, there's no one here by that name.'

'Please check under her maiden name then. Dumellier. Hélène Dumellier. Although I'm sure she would have used her married name.'

'No Dumellier either.'

'She has to be here. I mean, she has nowhere else to go.'

'Wouldn't she have called you?'

'Of course. Unless she were too sick, or confused.'

'We certainly have plenty of senile old women here. Some of them may not know their own names, but

141

there's no one here who's not accounted for in the records.'

'Are any of them French? I don't know how old she is exactly but she must be over eighty. She has bulging blue eyes and long silver hair that she wears in a bun rolled in the back. She has a bit of a humped back and she smoked quite a lot, so her teeth are very stained, but she still has most of them.'

The nurse shrugged. 'Old ladies all look alike.'

'Can I look in the ward?'

'Our patients have gone to bed for the night.'

'Please. We're very worried about her.'

'Go ahead and look around then,' the nurse conceded grudgingly. 'The women's geriatric wing is through that archway to the left. There's a night light in every room, and most of the bedside lamps stay on all night, so you'll be able to see. Not that you'll find her.'

Gigi walked along the corridors, peering into room after room. The smell of disinfectant and old age was inescapable. The two or three occupants in each room all looked alike, especially those who were asleep. At the door of each room Gigi called softly: 'Madame Hélène? Madame Hélène? *C'est moi.*' One or two answered in French, but that meant nothing, the Italian community in Egypt spoke French routinely.

In one of the last rooms on the corridor a sleeping woman in a pink, knitted bed jacket bore a resemblance to Madame Hélène. Gigi's heart skipped a beat. 'Madame Hélène?' she called quite loudly, to wake her. '*C'est moi.*'

The woman snorted in her sleep and raised her head. '*Viens, ma petite,*' she beckoned.

Gigi hurried to the side of the bed and leaned over her.

142

'*Viens, ma petite, que bellina,*' the woman mumbled, reaching out to pat Gigi's cheek. But even as she sat on the edge of the bed to let her face be stroked, Gigi knew it was not Madame Hélène. This woman had sweet brown eyes and no teeth. In a minute her hand dropped to her side and her head fell back on her pillow and she started snoring peacefully again. Gigi wondered who she had been dreaming of, a child or grandchild.

Gigi went back to the head nurse's office so drained that the woman took pity on her. 'Look, you said she was very old. Have you considered that in all probability she's resting in peace?'

Gigi slumped down in the chair. 'Yes. But she always said that if anything happened to her she would be brought here for the final rites, then taken to the Italian Cemetery to be buried.'

'She was Catholic?'

'Of course.'

'It would have been recently?'

'A month – two months at the most.'

'I can check the records at the Italian Cemetery in the morning. Leave me a telephone number and I'll let you know if I find out anything.'

'Would you? At least if I knew that she's buried properly – it sounds awful, but it's better than not knowing what happened to her, wondering if she's alone and suffering somewhere.'

'Of course, I understand. I promise I'll let you know if I find any trace of her. Now you'd better go home, it's very late.'

Over the next few months Gigi called the Italian Hospital several times. It was always very difficult to get through to the head nurse, and when she did she was

143

always told that there was no news. When she did hear of Madame Hélène again it was in the last place, and from the last person, she would have expected.

II

The Day of Remembrance

'Have some more of this *Om Ali*, it's my cook's specialty. No?' The Pasha waved away the *suffragi* who was offering the dessert to Gigi. One of his aides brought him the telephone to the table. He listened, his expression turning grim. 'Send Mr Ebeid over right away.'

By the time lunch was cleared away one of the party parliamentarians had joined them. 'Well?' the Pasha asked.

The man looked at Gigi, hesitating.

'That's all right,' the Pasha said impatiently, 'this is our daughter.' The Pasha was not using the royal plural, only an idiom which his circle would understand. 'My daughter' would have meant just that, but the Pasha was childless; 'our daughter' meant a close relative like a niece.

The man was clearly excited. 'They'll give us everything we asked for. Ten more seats in Parliament. Three Cabinet positions.'

'At what price?'

The man hesitated. 'That the party purge itself of its present leadership.'

Even Gigi understood right away. Sadat had resorted to bribing the opposition party to rid itself of its leader. The so-called democratic experiment was largely for the purpose of foreign media consumption. In effect Sadat could only tolerate what he expressed by the oxymoron 'loyal opposition'. She looked at her uncle, who sat silently digesting the news. She wondered what he would do. The Pasha could truly say of his party as Louis XIV said of the state: *'L'état, c'est moi.'*

Gigi had intended to take the opportunity after lunch to ask her uncle if there was any progress in her divorce proceedings. But this was clearly not a good time. She got up.

'Uncle, I'll leave now, if you'll excuse me.'

'Of course, dear, it was good to see you,' he answered absently. She had reached the staircase when he called her back. 'Gigi! Can you come Sunday afternoon? I've decided to hold a press conference, and I expect there will be foreign press too. I'd like to have you here to translate for me.'

The Pasha made it his policy never to make public announcements in a foreign language, however fluent he might be. He could not understand how Sadat could be oblivious to the criticism he invited by his practice of giving press conferences in English. Sadat sometimes did this even when he was on Egyptian soil, which sent the message to the man of the street that the President considered his constituency to be the foreign press, not his own people.

'Of course.' Gigi nodded. 'What time would you like me to come over?'

'About five o'clock, but I'll call and let you know exactly. Goodbye, dear.'

That Sunday the local and foreign press corps was there in force in the vast hall of the Cairo House. Gigi peered down from the gallery at the cameras and lights set up below, the cables winding around the bases of the thick, rose marble columns.

Having decided against the sweeping staircase at his age, her uncle took the rickety little elevator down to the ground floor, catching the assembled journalists by surprise. He took his seat on a gilded bergère that had been set for him in the middle of the hall. Gigi sat on a small chair to his left. When questions were posed in English or French, the Pasha answered in Arabic, and Gigi translated his answers back to the foreign journalists.

'Why are you taking a stand against the Japanese project for the development of the Pyramid plateau, in spite of the fact that President Sadat himself is promoting it?'

Gigi translated. 'The Pyramids are not Disneyland. The idea of a tourist theme park built at the very foot of the Pyramids, complete with a Disney-style monorail, is quite simply a sacrilege and a scandal. The Pyramids are not Sadat's to exploit by selling the concession to the Japanese; they are the heritage of all Egyptians, indeed of the whole world.'

Gigi made a slip of the tongue, translating 'the whole party' for 'the whole world'. Her uncle reached out and rumpled her hair to bring the slip to her attention. She flushed because the familiarity of the gesture had obviously piqued the curiosity of the journalists who did not realize she was his niece.

147

The next question was asked by a French journalist.

'How do you respond to the rumors that you have secretly been negotiating a "marriage of convenience" with the Muslim Brethren, the *Ikhwan*, for the upcoming elections?'

'No basis whatsoever. Our party has traditionally been the most secular of parties, the one to which minorities gravitate, the only one in which top positions were held by Copts, both in the party and in the government, whenever the party was in power before 1952.'

'But there is justifiable concern that opening up the electoral process in Egypt for the first time in decades will allow the Muslim Brethren to infiltrate legitimate parties. Will you comment?'

The Pasha answered and Gigi tried to translate, but she was still flustered and had trouble keeping up. The journalist started to press the question, then shook his head, smiled at her, and let it go. It was then that she noticed him, and the way he looked at her.

There was a hush as the Pasha announced that he had a statement to make, after which he would take more questions. He made his short announcement and Gigi translated it into English, then French. There was a moment of silence as the words sunk in. He had announced the dissolution of the party, in effect calling Sadat's bluff. Rather than relinquish control over his party and allow it, under more malleable leadership, to join the ranks of Sadat's rubber-stamping 'loyal opposition', he had dissolved it. Somehow he had mustered the votes to do so within forty-eight hours. There was a pandemonium of questions.

An hour later, as the crowd was dispersing and Gigi started up the staircase, she heard someone behind her.

148

'Mademoiselle!'

She turned around to see the French journalist.

'Yes?'

'Excuse me, but I feel I know you. You must be Gigi. Aren't you? I've heard so much about you over the years. From Tante Hélène's letters. My godmother, Hélène Dumellier?'

'Madame Hélène? Oh! *Le petit Luc*!'

He laughed. 'Luc Joussellin, in effect, at your service.'

Gigi stared at him, trying to reconcile the man before her with the photo of '*le petit Luc*' that had sat on a dresser in her bedroom by her governess' armchair all her life. He looked disconcertingly familiar: the same thatch of blonde-streaked hair sweeping down to thick eyebrows, the same square, smiling face, except for the short moustache, darker than the hair on his head. He was not very tall, but sturdily built.

'I'm sorry,' Gigi was a little embarrassed. 'But she always called you that. She was so proud of you. You look like your photo.'

'I have one of you, too, that she sent me, somewhere with her letters.'

'Oh no, which one?'

'With your parents, standing behind your mother's chair. You must have been nine or so. She considered you her family.'

'We loved her like family. Do you know what happened to her?'

'No. I only knew she must have passed away when her letters stopped coming. Then when I was given this assignment to Cairo, one of the first things I did after I arrived was to make inquiries at her old address, but no one knew anything.'

149

'I know. I looked everywhere. At the Italian Hospital, everywhere. Here, let's go into the study. I'll tell you all about it.'

It would be an unseasonably hot day. It was only six o'clock in the morning and already the haze in the sky bore the threat of heat. As Gigi started up the car Ibrahim the doorkeeper hurried up and saluted, surprised to see her up so early. She wore a black shirt because she was still in strict mourning for her father until the first anniversary of his death. Her riding breeches were khaki, but that couldn't be helped and in any case she was unlikely to meet anyone to whom it would matter.

As she pulled out of the garage she thought, for some reason, of the chaotic days following Nasser's death six years ago. She had heard of incidents of thugs harassing cars with passengers that were not in mourning. Tante Zohra went about, wearing a black shirt with a white skirt, reasoning that they could only see you from the waist up as you sit in the car.

The political climate of the country had changed dramatically in the intervening years. The very idea that Sadat had flown to Israel to make peace had been unthinkable. But the about-face seemed to have been too radical and too abrupt for many. The man in the street watched Sadat grinning his unnervingly face-splitting grin on television, hand in hand with 'my friend Kissinger' and 'my friend Begin'; he looked at the shop windows suddenly full of imported goods he could not afford; he watched the overnight millionaires of the *Infitah* glide by in their shiny new Mercedes; he waited for the promised trickle-down prosperity to reach him. There was a general malaise in the country, the tension before an impending storm.

The morning's unseasonable heat reminded Gigi that the season of the *Khamaseen*, the fifty-day winds, had started: the dreaded sandstorms could sweep out of the desert any day, blinding, stifling, filling every orifice, every pore. Each year the desert launched its storm troops to reclaim the city for the sand dunes, and the dust-whirl winds laid siege to the city, seeping under the most tightly sealed doors and windows, invading every nook and cranny. There was no predicting when they would start or stop, or start again, till the fifty days were over. Then they retreated back to the desert for another year, leaving the inhabitants to scoop up the red dust by the shovelfuls.

Gigi hummed John Denver's 'You fill up my senses, like a storm in the desert,' as she drove to the Tobias' apartment in Dokki. The drive took ten minutes instead of the thirty it would take in normal traffic. Tamer was not waiting for her in front of the garage as they had agreed. It was not like him to be late.

In the past few months they had gone riding together often. Her status was precarious until her divorce became final; she dared not allow the slightest pretext for tongues to wag. Her younger cousin was the perfect escort: whenever she did not want to be seen alone somewhere, she would ask him to come along. Other times he was the one who would call to ask her if she wanted to go riding or to the Gezira Club.

Gigi looked at her watch. It was six-thirty. She would have to go up and fetch Tamer. It was Om Khalil, with her kohl-smeared eyes, who opened the door. Gigi was taken aback, with the familiar childish sense of foreboding.

'Sitt Gigi, what are you doing here at this hour?'

'I'm going riding with Tamer. Is he up yet?'

151

'Tamer Bey? He must be asleep, I heard him come home at dawn. He keeps impossible hours. Eh, well, young bones never ache, as they say!'

'Let me see if he's awake.'

Under the disapproving gaze of the old woman Gigi made her way to his room and knocked quietly. Nothing. Not daring to knock any louder she opened the door and went in. Tamer's long frame was sprawled over his bed; he wore only swimming trunks. She shook him by the shoulder; feeling something grainy on the smooth skin, she licked her finger and tasted sea salt. There was sand in his dark curly hair and his tanned back was pink and raw in patches where the skin had flaked off. She guessed that he must have taken advantage of the unseasonably warm weather to go to a beach party in Alexandria or Agami, three hours away by car.

She shook him again. He opened his eyes, looked at her blankly, then, remembering, he groaned. 'I'm dead. I just got to bed. Can't you go on your own?'

'You know I can't.'

'Are we supposed to meet that French guy?'

'Luc. Yes. We're late already. Please?'

'All right. Get out and I'll dress. I'll meet you downstairs.'

Gigi drove while he slumped in the seat beside her. Already traffic had picked up on the road to the Pyramids in Giza, the road that Khedive Ismail had built in honor of the Empress Eugénie's visit, along with the Opera House where Verdi's Aida was first performed. The road to the Pyramids was now punctuated by trees pruned into a pyramid shape, no doubt the inspiration of some tasteless tourism official.

At the stables, Haj Hassan came to greet them, his

152

sharp gray eyes under his turban unchanged over the years she had known him since she was a child. Only the crew of grooms he ruled changed from year to year, the little boys who could ride bareback almost before they could walk growing into youths who could speak passable English and a smattering of other languages, since their business was mostly with tourists.

At the moment two boys were saddling up the horses for a heavy-set, middle-aged Austrian couple. The woman asked if she could ride bareback, it would be so romantic. Haj Hassan's stern look quelled the lewd remarks in Arabic with which the grooms greeted this request; he declared that it was not advisable. The couple were led away by one of the grooms.

Haj Hassan had known Gigi and her cousin since they were children; he would allow them to ride on their own without a guide. He knew Tamer to be a good rider, but he had misgivings about the mare he had requested: she was very high-strung and completely unused to traffic. He finally let Tamer have her with the warning that he must stick to the desert and avoid the road completely. Gigi he knew to be timid and a poor rider; he chose a gelding.

'He'll follow your cousin's mare; you'll be all right,' he reassured her. 'The *frenji* was here only a while ago,' he added, his eyes shrewd, and she flushed. The *frenji* – the Frenchman – did Haj Hassan know she was meeting him?

She had gone riding with Luc once before, with Tamer. She had seen Luc many times over the past months, but never alone. He had dropped by her desk in the international department at the El-Ahram newspaper. They had met at a series of open-air concerts on balmy spring nights: it seemed to be the year for entertainers past their heyday to give concerts in Egypt. Under the banyan trees at the Gezira Club, Dalida vamped her way through old favorites like 'Ti Amo', and 'Que sera, sera' before bringing down the house with 'Salma ya Salama' – a Nubian-inspired refrain for a French song sung by a Cairo-born-and-bred Italian. Aznavour growled and purred to enthusiastic applause – even when he sang of Armenians massacred by Turks. The Egyptian public was starved for Western culture after the long years of deprivation behind the Iron Curtain. The only cultural dividend of Egypt's status as a Soviet satellite under Nasser had been the annual performances by the Bolshoi at the Cairo Opera House. But Egypt's reward for Sadat's abrupt about-face to the West had come in the form of massive economic aid, a flood of imported goods and Frank Sinatra lip-synching 'My Way' at the foot of the Great Pyramid of Giza.

Now Tamer took off at a canter and Gigi followed, for once not complaining about the pace he set, till they reached the meeting place. They were late. But Luc was there, smiling, smoking a cigarette. His horse tossed its mane to shake off the flies.

Before they set off again he adjusted her stirrup straps, which were too long, and his fingers inadvertently brushed the inside of her thigh; they were both awkward for a moment. He mounted his horse and they took off at a trot. Out in the open desert, the sun was already fierce, but the wind in their faces kept them from feeling the heat. Tamer galloped off on his own.

The horses labored up the dunes, knee deep in the liquid sand, then slithered down the other side, breaking into a canter as they reached a flat stretch. After a while

Luc signaled to her and they reined in their horses side by side. Immediately they were enveloped by the oppressive, dead silence of the desert. Their knees were jostled together as one or the other of the horses moved to stamp a hoof or swish a tail. Finally he asked:

'So, you'll be coming to Cyprus then?'

Senior members of Gigi's department at work were planning to attend an international conference in Cyprus the following week, and a few days earlier the editor-in-chief and famous novelist, Yussef El-Siba`yi, had personally asked her to go along as an interpreter. Siba`yi, a courtly man with snowy hair, had known Papa, and it was his novels that Gigi had read, albeit reluctantly, as a teenager. Gigi was looking forward to the trip, in spite of the tensions surrounding the conference. There had been death threats against Siba`yi and other prominent figures who had participated in the delegation that had accompanied Sadat to Israel. But Gigi had her personal misgivings about this trip.

'There's a problem. My husband –'

'You mean your ex-husband?' Luc frowned.

'I suppose so. But the divorce isn't final yet. I think it's called a *decree nisi*. It won't be final for another three months, and only if he doesn't contest it in the meantime. I don't know how he'd feel about my going on this trip. When I started working earlier this year he was unhappy about it, he made a point of warning me not to accept any assignments that involved travel –'

'That was then. Surely that doesn't matter now?'

'No, you're right, I suppose.'

Luc's assignment in Cairo had ended. He would be leaving for France in two days. He had mentioned, however, that he would have a couple of days off when

155

he arrived in Europe and could make *'un petit saut'* to Cyprus, if she were going. 'It's a beautiful island. I've vacationed there before. I could show you around.'

They had been standing still for too long in the sun. She felt dizzy. She told Luc she wanted to go back. They looked for Tamer in the distance. They could see him wheeling his horse in figure eights, taking wider and wider circles. Gigi suddenly felt a pang, remembering how tired he must be. They waved to him and he galloped over. Luc suggested they take the short way back to the main road and go down the hill; they could have breakfast at the old Mena House Hotel.

By the time they reached the steep road down from the Pyramids, it was crowded with cars inching along at about the same pace as the horses and camels the tourists were riding. The clatter of horses' hooves and the blaring of car horns were unnerving after the dead silence of the sand dunes. Tamer was having trouble controlling his mare; she was shying away and kicking out in panic. Haj Hassan had not exaggerated her fear of noise and traffic. Tamer finally shook his head.

'You two go ahead. I'll take her back to the stables by the desert route and wait for you there.'

Gigi felt uneasy about going to the hotel for breakfast without her cousin and in any case it was getting late. They slowly made their way back along the crowded road. Before they reached Haj Hassan's stables Luc stopped so she could go on alone.

'I'll be staying at the Nicosia Palace. Give me a call when you get there.'

Gigi hesitated. It disconcerted her that from the day she first met Luc he had seemed as familiar as an old photograph you glance at every day of your life; that

156

from the start their exchange had been as easy and comfortable as if they had grown up together – which, in a way, they had, through Madame Hélène's stories and letters and photographs. With Luc she felt free, she could breathe. She had been holding her breath, concentrating on getting through the divorce. Now she had begun to glimpse what lay beyond, and something within her rebelled against the prospect of falling back into a future of Tante Zohra's match-making.

But meeting Luc in Nicosia seemed to be taking a step, taking their relationship a step further than she was comfortable with. 'I don't know. It depends,' she murmured. '*Peut-être* . . . '

He laughed. '*C'est pas la mer à boire, tu sais.*'

She smiled at him. He was right, it was no big deal. Except that he didn't understand that everything in her world was complicated. She cantered off, waving goodbye.

It was immediately apparent that something was wrong when she turned into the stables. Haj Hassan asked her grimly where her cousin was. She looked at him blankly until she saw the unruly mare, lathered up in sweat, saddle askew, legs quivering. Riderless. A sick feeling of apprehension gripped her stomach. If the mare had managed to throw Tamer and run off, he must be badly hurt. Haj Hassan and two of the grooms galloped off to look for him. She got into her car and drove to the nearest police station to telephone for an ambulance.

When she got back they had found him and laid him on some dirty blankets. He was half conscious, one eye covered in blood, his right leg at an odd angle which could only mean that it was broken. She made her way through the small crowd which had gathered, and knelt beside him, praying for the ambulance to hurry. A man

157

in a tattered *gelabeh* murmured that the boy's leg was obviously swelling by the minute and that they should get the boots off. She nodded gratefully and the man pulled off one of the boots. It struck Gigi as vaguely odd that he was pulling the boot off the good leg. Then he began pulling the boot off the hurt leg. Tamer cried out in pain and fainted. Haj Hassan rebuked the man sharply and, bringing out a knife, began ripping through the boot.

The man in the *gelabeh* muttered regretfully: 'What a waste!'

Only then did Gigi realize that he had intended to steal the boots and that in order to do so he had knowingly hurt her cousin. Haj Hassan carefully ripped through the leg of the jeans up to the waist, revealing the horribly mangled leg and the incongruous swimming trunks. There was nothing Gigi could do but wave away the flies that would have settled on the bloody eye. The heat was oppressive. Finally the ambulance arrived.

Two days later she was visiting Tamer in the hospital. She opened the door tentatively, in case he was asleep. But he was awake, and alone. He turned his head and motioned for her to come over to the other side of the bed because he could not see out of his bandaged eye. His leg, in a cast, was suspended in a sort of pulley. He had stitches on a long gash running from the tip of his thumb to his wrist.

She gave him a careful peck on the cheek and sat down gingerly on the edge of the bed. He winced.

'Sorry!' She grimaced in sympathy. She touched his cast. 'Does it hurt a lot?'

'Nah. They keep me pretty much doped up.'

'Look, I brought you some *marrons glacés.*' She put the

158

box of candied chestnuts in silver foil next to the flowers on the dresser.

'Thanks. You look nice.'

It disconcerted her a little, the unexpectedly adult way in which he paid her the compliment.

'I had my hair cut. I'm glad you like it.'

The eye would be all right and the broken leg was set. When Tamer had turned back to the desert he had given the mare her head, figuring that he would let her race off her panic, confident that she would not be able to unseat him. But she had headed for a single low, scrubby tree in the open desert, and had tried to scrape him off on it. He had not ducked low enough and a branch had caught him just over his eye, knocking him unconscious. He had broken his femur bone as he fell, and gashed his hand.

Chattering voices in the corridor were followed by a loud knock on the door. Half a dozen young people, including Leila and Gigi's schoolmate Dina, burst into the room at once, carrying an assortment of flowers, chocolates and music tapes. Dina brandished a box of crayons. 'I'm going to be the first to autograph your cast!' she announced to Tamer. She leaned over the bed, sweeping her long, blonde-frosted hair to the side, and began to draw a heart in fuchsia.

Gigi blew Tamer a kiss from the door. 'I'll come to see you as soon as I get back from Cyprus.'

He winked at her, or maybe he was wincing because a stocky young man had just tried to sit at the foot of the bed.

When Gigi arrived at home her mother was on the phone, placing an order with the baker for a kind of brioche

159

which is distributed to the poor at the cemeteries. Gigi suddenly remembered that Wednesday of the next week was the anniversary of her father's death. As tradition required, in the afternoon there would be the visit to the cemetery and the distribution of the brioche and money. Earlier, at home, there would be a reception for female relatives and friends. The first anniversary marked the end of the official period of mourning; the women in the family need no longer wear black.

How could she have forgotten? There could be no excuse for not attending the first anniversary of her father's death. She would have to explain to the editor of the Ahram that she could not go to Cyprus. She picked up the phone and asked to speak to Dr Siba`yi. He sounded annoyed.

'Gihan, perhaps you should reconsider. It's not that we can't find someone else to go in your place, but we'd have to do the visa and security clearance all over. For your own sake – well, it doesn't look good. I asked for you personally.'

'I understand. And I'm sorry. But I just can't be away on Wednesday.' She knew she would not be given another opportunity. After she hung up, for the first time she thought of Luc, who would be waiting for her to call.

On the day of remembrance the two salons were full of elegantly dressed women in black carrying on animated conversations in hushed undertones while a *suffragi* circled with trays of black Turkish coffee. From behind the Gobelin screen came a loud clearing of the throat. The turbaned *fikki* seated behind it, hired for the occasion, was indicating that he was ready to begin chanting verses from the Koran. The ladies reluctantly hushed till the next interval in the recital when they could resume their conversations.

An hour later, the visit of condolences over, the women began dispersing; the immediate relatives would go to the cemetery. Tante Zohra rose slowly from her seat, unfolding her long, lean, black-clothed figure to its full, imposing height. She moved with the deliberation of a woman who had to live up to a reputation for being formidable.

Tante Zohra asked Gigi to ride with her to the cemetery. Gigi understood from the tone of voice that it was a summons rather than an invitation. She ran upstairs to her bedroom to fetch the sheer scarf she would need to cover her hair out of respect for the dead, and some change for the caretaker's children. She asked Khadra to give her a basket of the brioches and she was ready.

Gigi got into the car with her aunt, and they drove off. She recognized Omar, the *Mukhabarat* agent, behind the wheel. Although surveillance had been lifted from Tante Zohra years ago, and she could now afford to hire a regular driver again, Omar still drove her around from time to time, on his days off.

Eventually they drove through unfamiliar parts of the city, past the ruined arches of the ancient city wall of Cairo, turning into narrow alleys barely wide enough to accommodate a car. There were no street signs. Her aunt was talking to her but Gigi was barely paying attention: this part of 'old Cairo', as it was called, fascinated her. The car was crawling along because it was stuck behind a slow-moving donkey cart. A woman called out from the second floor of a rickety, centuries old house to a street vendor below. The car was further delayed while the woman lowered a basket on a rope; the vendor deposited his wares in it and she hauled it back up. The driver rolled up the windows against the rank smells and the dust.

The car turned into the maze of dusty alleys of the

161

necropolis, row upon row of high walls shielding tree-shaded courtyards. Each family had its mausoleum which housed the separate monuments of its dead under one roof. A hut on the grounds was occupied by the caretaker and his family. The walls turned a blind face to the street and Gigi was never prepared for the moment when the car would suddenly stop before the unmarked gate that led to the courtyard of her own family's mausoleum, where her father was buried. The City of the Dead, it was called; of the dead, and increasingly of the homeless living.

'Gigi, you weren't planning on taking a trip out of the country any time soon, were you? Because Omar has something to tell you.'

Her aunt's question startled Gigi. So that was the reason Tante Zohra had insisted Gigi ride with her.

The week before, in the course of a routine check, Omar had stumbled across a piece of information which he immediately brought to Zohra's attention. Her niece Gihan's name was on the list of women who were to be stopped at the airport if they attempted to leave the country. By law, a married woman needed her husband's signature on her passport to go abroad without him; in practice, airport authorities did not check for the husband's authorization unless they had been notified by him to be on the lookout for a specific name and passport number. In that case, if the woman in question attempted to leave, she was detained, her passport confiscated and her husband notified.

Gigi stared at the back of the driver's head as he delivered his warning. She couldn't believe Yussef would subject her to such humiliation. She imagined with horror the scene at the airport, in front of Dr Siba`yi and her colleagues.

162

'I can't believe he'd do such a thing!'

'You don't have much experience of men.'

'But why, Tante Zohra? We're as good as divorced –'

'My child, I'm afraid he never intended to go through with it. He was only playing for time, hoping you'd change your mind. But before the decree becomes final he'll insist you go back to him.'

'I won't do that.'

'But he can still refuse to divorce you. You could try through the courts, but you have no valid grounds. He can drag it out for years, free to lead his own life while you twist in the wind. Meanwhile, if you make one false move – ' Zohra shook her head.

The car stopped abruptly before a narrow wrought iron gate in the wall. They had arrived. Tante Zohra stepped out stiffly, helped by Omar. Gigi slipped the veil over her head and followed. The caretaker had heard them arrive and swung the gate open. Two small children hid behind him. Gigi held out the basket of brioches and they each grabbed a handful and ran off, giggling, to hide under the dusty olive trees.

Tante Zohra took Gigi's arm to walk the few yards to the small house where the dead of the family lay buried in an underground vault. They entered the single, large room with its marble edifices in the form of a tomb and headstone. Even in death men and women were separated. The men's headstones were on one side of the chamber, the women's on the other.

A *fikki* sat cross-legged on a bench in one corner, murmuring over his rosary. Gigi stood by her father's tomb and traced her fingers over the inscription on the marble headstone. She knew her father was not buried there. He lay in the crypt several meters under her feet,

163

in a simple shroud. She felt as if Papa's spirit had somehow intervened to save her from making a fatal mistake. She wished she could speak to him more urgently than at any time since his death. Now that she realized Yussef would not divorce her, she did not know what to do.

She closed her eyes and tried to pray, but she was breathing heavily, like someone who realized that she had just escaped an unseen danger. But it was only when she went back to the car that she understood that she had been doubly reprieved.

Gigi and Tante Zohra found Omar standing grimly by the open door of the car, his ear cocked to the news blaring from the radio. Gigi listened to the somber voice of the announcer. 'At five p.m. today, in Cyprus, an undetermined number of gunmen opened fire on the Egyptian delegation headed by Dr Yussef Siba`yi. Dr Siba`yi was killed and several of his entourage were wounded. No one has yet claimed responsibility for the attack but it is well known that Dr Siba`yi had been under a death threat since his visit to Tel Aviv. Details to follow . . . '

PART II

EXILE

12

Paris

Some people's lives are inexorably caught in the slip-stream of the headlines. For Gigi, even though she did not go to Cyprus, the course of her life was changed nevertheless the day Siba`yi was assassinated and Sadat saw the writing on the wall.

In his last year of life Sadat was a man in fear of his own shadow. The experiment in democracy was aborted. Towards the end Sadat's prisons made for strange bedfellows: the right and the left, Nasserites and Communists, Islamists and Coptic bishops, journalists and students.

Even the Pasha, at his age, was not spared. A search of the offices of Heikal, the notorious Nasserite former editor-in-chief of El-Ahram, happened to turn up a calling card of the Pasha's, attached to a copy of an article. Sadat claimed that the card was proof of a conspiracy against him and that there was a compromising message written on it. Heikal himself was the first to point out that the corner of the card had been turned down, as was the Pasha's custom, to indicate that it had been left blank.

167

But no one seriously doubted that the flimsiest pretext would have been good for Sadat's purpose. The Pasha found himself sharing – with mutual cordiality – a cell with the Nasserite Heikal who had so often attacked him in the press.

When the end came for Sadat, it still blindsided him. The genie of Islamic fundamentalism was finally out of the bottle. Faruk had flirted with the Muslim Brethren; Nasser's henchmen had patented new methods of torture for the *Ikhwan* in the prisons in which he had thrown them; Sadat had encouraged the Islamists in order to counterbalance the diehard Nasserites. He had forgotten that the antidote could be worse than the disease. Like the annual *Khamaseen* sandstorms sweeping out of the desert to reclaim the city for the sand dunes, religious fanaticism periodically launched an onslaught to reclaim the country for an atavistic Islam.

The smallest fish can be caught in the slipstream of a whale. Although Gigi did not go to Cyprus, the bloody events there nevertheless had a domino effect on her life. She would not go back to Yussef, and she now knew he had no intention of going through with the divorce. Now that the Pasha was incarcerated along with hundreds of others in Sadat's blind panic following Siba`yi's assassination, her last hope of putting pressure on Yussef was gone. The only way out seemed to be for her to leave the country before the deadline for revoking the divorce ruling. It was a calculated risk: that once Yussef realized there was no hope of getting her back, he would let the ruling stand. She fled to France.

She had miscalculated. He had the ruling revoked. She was still his wife in the eyes of the law. Now there was no going back before she was divorced and free. To go back, a runaway wife returned, would be to put herself at Yussef's mercy. The scandal she had caused by leaving as she did put her beyond the pale. Even her nearest and dearest found it hard to defend her conduct.

Her mother had disapproved but finally had not tried to stop her. For Mama, there was no salvation outside the court of social judgment: to flaunt convention, no matter what the provocation, was to run an unacceptable risk. She faulted Gigi for her reluctance to enlist general sympathy in her dispute with Yussef, for acting on her own counsel, for her stubbornness in pursuing this drastic course of action. She refrained from blaming Gigi for the failure of the marriage itself, but the unspoken reproach strained the cord of civility between them nearly to the breaking point.

Gigi saw no choice now but to stay abroad. She enrolled at the University of Paris to study. Yussef could take his time about divorcing her, but she would not languish forever at home in Egypt. She would come back when she was divorced and no longer at his mercy.

The price she had to pay was to leave Tarek behind. It had been difficult enough, even with the connivance of Tante Zohra's *Mukhabarat* man, for her to leave the country without her husband's signature on the passport. Taking Tarek without his father's authorization on the passport would have been unthinkable.

But she had not realized how hard it would be, nor that it would take so long. She had believed that Yussef would make up his mind to divorce her when he realized there was no point in going on with the cat and mouse game. But Kamal Zeitouni had been wrong when he had deplored the fact that his son did not take after him: Yussef had his father's vindictiveness. With Papa

169

gone, and the Pasha incarcerated, there was no one who could shame him into doing the right thing by her.

When she had left, she had fled as if she were escaping a trap about to close on her. Now she felt as if she were in exile, waiting for her sentence to be commuted in order to return.

Gigi watched Sadat's funeral on television in Paris. She saw Carter and other heads of state pay their respects. The camera panned over the largely indifferent crowd of Egyptians following the procession. The commentator pointed out that it was a very different scene from the mass hysteria of Nasser's funeral ten years earlier. He found that inexplicable.

Gigi switched off the television set and looked out of the window. It was a sunny October late afternoon and she needed to get out of the cramped apartment. She locked the door and made her way carefully down the worn stairs of the old apartment building. She pushed open the tall, heavy door to the street and blinked in the afternoon sunshine. She walked past the tables set outside the café, where the first regulars were drifting in after work.

It was a five-minute walk to the Parc Monceau. Gigi strolled past the ice-cream stand and the carousel with its old-fashioned horses. She found a bench in the shade and settled down to watch the parade of people walking dogs and babies up and down the promenade. Some babies slumped in strollers but most infants surveyed the world around them in solemn splendor from the height of their stately carriages. Little girls in jumpers played hopscotch and skipped rope while boys in buckled shoes kicked balls around and rode bicycles.

One boy on a bike rode back and forth in front of Gigi.

170

He had rumpled dark brown curls and flushed cheeks. She took a deep breath, trying to fight down the surge of hot tears, the wave of emptiness that washed over her every time she saw a child that reminded her of Tarek. It still blind-sided her every time, the sudden unbearable longing to hold him in her arms, to nuzzle his warm little neck and sniff his chewing-gum minty breath. When it hit her sometimes it propelled her to the nearest telephone just to hear his voice. But in her last letter Mama had written: 'Gigi, it's best if you only call on Fridays, as we agreed. When you call at odd times it disrupts him, he cries because he misses you. He jumps whenever the phone rings, and sometimes he won't go out or go to bed because he thinks you might call. It's best if he knows you'll only call at pre-arranged times.'

Gigi lived by the postman's schedule. Sometimes in the middle of the day she rushed back to the apartment to check if there was any mail from Egypt. Mama wrote painstaking, detailed letters about Tarek, but however long they were, they always left Gigi hungry. Tarek's scribbles, with his shaky block printing, made her cry. The letters that contained photos of him were a feast, and she pored over them for hours. The last photo had been a heartache: his bouncy curls were gone and his round cheeks looked slimmer; he had changed so much in only a few months.

The little boy on the bike rode past Gigi again. One of his shoelaces was untied and dragging. She wiped her blotchy face with a tissue and got up. As he rode back in her direction she signaled to him. He came to a skidding stop.

'Let me tie your shoelaces for you before you get them caught in the spokes.' She tied the laces and straightened up, brushing her hand over his curls.

171

'Emmanuel! Viens ici!' A voice called sharply. *'Laisse la dame tranquille.'*

She looked over to the woman who had called, the boy's mother, presumably. Gigi tried to smile at her reassuringly as the child rode off. She couldn't blame her for being suspicious of a tearful woman gazing hungrily at her child.

Gigi turned around and started to walk home. She tried to focus on tomorrow: tomorrow there might be a letter in the mail. The last one had been a week ago. Tomorrow, after class, she would go to the bank and see if there was another transfer for her from Mama.

When Gigi had heard the newsflash about Sadat's assassination, she had tried to call home right away, but could not get through. She felt very isolated. Suddenly she thought of Luc. She had seen his name as a contributor to a report in the *Evènement du jeudi* magazine a month ago. He had told her – it seemed so long ago now – that he shared an apartment in Paris with a friend, but he was on the road a lot. The day she had seen his name in the magazine she had looked up his number in the phone book. But she had not called. She felt a strange reluctance to contact anyone connected to the world of her past. It was too painful.

But the day she heard the news of Sadat's assassination she needed to talk to someone. She called Luc's number. The man who answered the phone told her that Luc was out of town. She left her name, number and address. That was two days ago.

She picked up a newspaper at the *tabac*, and a baguette at the bakery. The café by her apartment building was full now, the tables busy with people smoking, chatting, sipping drinks. The street door to her building was locked

172

after five o'clock and could only be opened by entering a code on the metal plaque on the wall. As she punched in the code and heard the buzz and click of the door being released, a man who had been sitting at a table in front of the café got up and came towards her. She was taken aback for a minute. Then she recognized the smiling face under the thatch of hair. It was Luc.

'It's high time you met Maman, really.' Luc shifted into fifth gear and the little Renault responded noisily, speeding along the highway south from Paris. 'I've talked so much about you over the past – what has it been? Five months now. And of course she knew all about "*la petite Gigi*" from Hélène's letters, all those years ago.'

They drove through the early summer countryside with its rose bushes and cherry trees in bloom; the uncertain sunshine looked likely to yield to the first threat of showers. They made good time and reached Lyons early for their lunchtime rendezvous with Luc's mother. Luc parked across from the café where they were to meet, a quiet little place on a pedestrian side street off a square in the old quarter.

'Luc, I'd like to have something to offer your mother; can we go around the shops? We have time, don't we?'

They strolled through the streets, gazing at window displays and stepping in and out of shops. At a *confiserie* Gigi was struck by the display of green velvet, pillow-shaped boxes of marzipan-covered chocolates.

'They're called *coussins de Lyon*, cushions of Lyons, in commemoration of the offerings made to the Notre Dame of Fourvières for saving the city from the something or other, I forget just what.'

Gigi bought the chocolates and white tulips for Luc's

173

mother. Their last stop was a bookstore, where Luc chose two of the latest novels.

'Maman's a great reader. All right, I think that's everything. Ready, Gigi?'

'Ready. Where's the car? We must be miles away from the café.'

The bookseller overheard them. 'Where is it that you parked? Rue du Boeuf? You can take a shortcut. Go through the door at the back of my store, it leads to a *traboule*. Just keep going till you exit on the street at the other end. It tunnels right under two blocks of houses to rue du Boeuf.'

Gigi followed Luc through the back of the store and into a dim, covered passageway.

'What were these used for? To hide from enemies? Or from religious persecution?'

'Not at all. There's a warren of passages like this running under the buildings in this old part of the city where the textile factories used to be. When it rained the silk workers used them to carry the bolts of cloth from one square to another without getting the silk wet.'

Filtered sunlight dappled the mauve-washed walls in the quiet corridor. Luc turned towards her and she felt his moustache brush her cheek and the corner of her mouth. It was the first time he had kissed her, apart from the customary peck on the cheek that they exchanged on greeting. He drew back and paused a minute, gauging her ambivalent response, then he shifted the packages in his arms and winked at her.

'Lucky for you I have both arms full, isn't it?'

She laughed; it was easy to be comfortable with Luc, he was so non-threatening. She followed him down the passageway to a door that opened to the sunshine outside.

174

They hurried back to the café but when they turned the corner Luc's mother was still not in sight and they slowed down to a more leisurely pace.

'Inside or outside?' the waiter asked as he led them to a table.

'Gigi?'

'Whatever you like. Outside if it's the same to you.'

'I knew you'd say that. You're like a Mediterranean sunflower.'

From their seats at a small table on the narrow cobblestone sidewalk of the shady alley they were all but jostled by the passers-by. Gigi leaned back in her chair to catch the sun on her face. Luc turned his attention to the wine list with an utter absorption that, she suspected, she would never truly understand. In a few minutes they were joined by a small, sturdily built woman with short, fair hair.

'Maman!' Luc got up and kissed her. 'This is Gihan. Gigi, my mother, Mathilde.'

Mathilde's blue eyes in a tan face appraised Gigi for a moment, then she smiled, a reserved smile. 'It's nice to meet you. Oh, how thoughtful, thank you.' She admired the bouquet and the box of marzipan chocolates for a moment. 'Couldn't you find a table inside? Oh, I see, no, no, this is perfectly fine.'

They studied the menu posted on a chalkboard.

'Ah, *tête de veau*! Maman, shall we order that for you? Gigi, will you try some?'

'No thank you!'

'You don't know what you're missing. You're very squeamish about some things, you know,' Luc teased.

'Perhaps we should have gone somewhere else?' Mathilde looked concerned. 'The menu here tends to typical traditional dishes, quite heavy, a lot of charcuterie. You

175

might be homesick for a good couscous, Gigi?'

'*Maman*, couscous is a Moroccan dish, they don't eat it in Egypt.'

'I'll have the salad with the baked brie, that sounds perfect,' Gigi interposed quickly.

Luc ordered and the waiter took away their menus.

'Well, you can't imagine some of the things I had to eat when I was in Niger during my *coopération*, my national service.' Luc crossed his arms and leaned across the table. 'I was posted in a dirt hut village, supposedly to teach the children to read. I ended up teaching the adults about hygiene and birth control. But it wasn't all bad. Sometimes another *coopérant* friend drove over from another village and we toured the countryside together. We'd get lost and spend the night in hammocks. You couldn't sleep on the ground in a sleeping bag because of the giant insects. Ah, here come the aperitifs! I have quite an appetite, don't you?'

Luc seemed even more talkative than usual, as if he were trying to fill any awkward pauses. But mother and son soon fell into their familiar rhythm of conversation and Gigi felt free to follow or join in, without pressure. After lunch they ordered coffee and Luc excused himself to go to the post office before it closed.

Mathilde lit a cigarette. 'Do you smoke, Gigi? No?' She took a long drag. 'Well, I'm sorry neither of Luc's sisters could join us, I know they wanted to meet you. Lucienne lives too far away, of course, but Catherine would have driven down from St Etienne if the baby hadn't been colicky today. You're an only child, aren't you, Gigi? I remember that from Hélène's letters. She was my mother's generation, really, her best friend from school. She left for Egypt when I was very young. But all those years,

176

she always wrote regularly, long letters, and sent pictures. When Luc was born, she insisted on being his *marraine*, even though she'd never seen him.' Mathilde took a sip of her espresso and another drag on her cigarette. 'You have a son in Egypt, Gigi, don't you?'

'Yes. Tarek. He's with my mother back home.' To her mortification, Gigi felt the tears come to her eyes.

'Forgive me for asking this, ma petite, but how could you leave him? Why didn't you try to bring him with you?'

The question startled Gigi. 'But it was out of the question. There was no way I could have taken him out of the country without his father's permission on the passport; if I had tried I could have been arrested for kidnapping.'

'Couldn't your family have helped you?'

'They wouldn't help me kidnap my child out of the country even if they could. No one would have condoned that. I know it's hard for you to understand, but these things are seen differently over there. Most people see a child as belonging with his father. The mother gets custody of a young child up to a certain age, but not if she remarries, and certainly not if she leaves the country.'

'But if you knew that, how could you leave him? Didn't you know how much you would miss him?'

'I thought it would only be for a short time, a month or two, I had no idea things would turn out like this. I didn't think it through, it was a mistake.' Gigi felt her face flush and her chest constrict.

'And now you're too stubborn to go back? Or too afraid? And Luc. How does he fit into all this? I'm sorry, ma petite, but you must understand I have to think of my son first. Does he know what your feelings for him are?'

177

'I like him so much, I don't know what I would have done without him over the past few months . . . '

'But you don't love him?'

'Well, what have I missed?' Luc came around the corner and pulled up his chair. 'Anyone for a second coffee?'

'I'm glad you had a *tête à tête* with Maman. I think she likes you.'

They were driving back to Paris; it had started to rain, a hard, steady rain that showed no signs of abating for the rest of the trip.

'I don't know about that.'

'She'd let herself like you even more if she didn't suspect that – well, that I intend to marry you some day.'

'Luc! You know that's not serious.'

'Why not?'

Because, she thought, it's not the grand passion. Yet in the past few months her world had shrunk; she could not imagine her life here without Luc.

'I'm not even divorced yet.'

'You'll be getting your divorce soon. Didn't you tell me Yussef has been seeing someone else?'

'That's what Mama writes. A woman who works for his father. Apparently she's from a decent enough background that she would insist on his divorcing me before he marries her.'

'Well, there you are. Once you're free, we can get married.'

She shook her head.

'Why? You mean the problem of religion? I'll become a Muslim on paper, if that's what it takes.'

'I couldn't ask you to do that!'

'It's not as if I were a practicing Catholic. And I believe

178

there's good in all religions; there are many teachings in Islam I can subscribe to. Besides, it's only *pour la forme*.'

Gigi shook her head and looked out of the window.

Three months to the day after Yussef had the divorce papers served to Gigi's home in Zamalek, she sat with Luc in a waiting room in the Paris mosque, around the corner from the Jardin des Plantes.

Gigi's first impulse when she knew the divorce had gone through was to go home. But Mama had written: 'Be patient. Yussef is content to let me keep Tarek, he knows it's best for him. But if you come back now to claim him, Yussef will exercise his right to sole custody. He insists he won't let you raise the boy. He's been saying that you're an unfit mother, that you abandoned your child. His parents have even been spreading rumors about your reasons for leaving, hinting that there was someone else. It's sheer vindictiveness on their part. But time will heal Yussef's sores, he'll get remarried eventually, and have other children. Then you can expect him to be much more mellow and reasonable, you'll see. Only you have to be patient. It was a mistake to leave as you did, Gigi, but it's no use going over that now. It's Allah's will. Now you need to do what's right for Tarek. If you come back now Yussef will take him, and it would be traumatic for this poor child to go through another separation. Be patient.'

Gigi had been unbearably disappointed. The recurrent hollow feeling overcame her. Without Tarek she felt empty, incomplete, like an amputee. But she knew that Mama was right. She was glad, for his sake, that he was adjusting to her absence. He no longer cried when she called him on the phone, he chatted about school friends

179

and about the latest toy Grandma had bought him. As for Mama, Gigi knew that Tarek now filled the vacuum in her life, with Papa and Gigi both gone.

Gigi would have waited indefinitely. But she had run out of time. Luc had applied, a few months before, for the post of correspondent in the United States. A month ago he had learned that he had been given the assignment. 'We have to get married, now, Gigi, so you can come with me. Just as soon as your divorce is final.'

The brief civil ceremony in the town hall was set for tomorrow. Today they were to have a marriage contract performed according to Islamic law, as soon as Luc's conversion was accepted.

'I'm surprised at how simple it is, really, compared to conversions to other religions,' Luc was speaking in an undertone although it was unlikely they would be overheard in the empty waiting room. 'I study the basic tenets, I get interviewed by the priest –'

'Not a priest!'

'No, that's right, there are no ordained priests in Islam, only lay ministers. Then I pass the test, I bear witness to the faith, and that's it!'

'Oh, absolutely! Islam is anything but exclusive. There's a catch though; it may be an open door, but it's a one-way turnstile. Going back isn't an option.'

'That's fine.'

'Yes, but what about your mother?'

'She might not like it at first, perhaps. But she'll come around – *elle se fera une raison*.'

'Oh, Luc, I don't know. What are we doing? How will I ever tell Mama about this? She'll never understand, she'll never accept it.'

'Give her time. She'll come around eventually.'

180

'No, you don't know her.'

'At any rate it's better to present everybody with the *fait accompli.*'

'I'm not sure. Perhaps we should have waited –'

She was terrified at the thought of burning her bridges. How would she ever be able to go home again? Luc took her hand; it was cold.

'Gigi, we discussed this. I leave in a few days. You can't go home. Do you want to stay here in Paris alone?'

A door opened at the far end of the waiting room and a man came in wearing a caftan and a flat turban. The sheikh was middle-aged, swarthy, with a slight paunch. He smiled as he greeted them in a Moroccan dialect that was nearly as incomprehensible to Gigi as it was to Luc.

'Now then. Are you ready?'

181

13

New Hampshire

If you examined the turning points in a life, could you pinpoint the precise twists of the kaleidoscope that set the pattern? What if she had not run away to France? What if she had never met Luc again? What if she had not followed him across the ocean to the northern town of snow-capped steeples and ice hockey that she has called home for the past ten years? Sometimes the sea changes in a life can be sudden, and at the time, can seem temporary. Ten years can go by like an interlude, a sharp zigzag in the flat line of experience, a detour around an insurmountable bump in the road.

Gigi went downstairs and turned the thermostat up to seventy-five degrees. In the mud room she put on snow pants, pulling the suspenders over her shoulders, and zipped up her ski jacket. She slipped on wool socks and moon boots. She tucked her hair under a knitted cap and slipped on thick mittens. Then she picked up the shovel propped against the back door and trudged in the calf-deep snow

182

around the house to the front door. She started to shovel the snow off the steps. The front door was rarely used; even the mailbox was at the end of the driveway. Usually Gigi did not bother to clear the path or the steps; it was enough work shoveling out the driveway every day and keeping the path to the mud room door clear. But this evening they were giving a party for faculty colleagues, and the front door needed to be accessible.

As she worked some part of her mind momentarily stood apart, observing, and had difficulty recognizing the Gigi of old in this woman in moon boots. Even to herself she had become something of a stranger; her native language no longer came naturally to her tongue; the memories of her old life seemed to have taken place in another dimension.

When Gigi had moved with Luc to the States ten years before it had been on the understanding that it would be a temporary assignment. Eventually they found it easier to make a life together on territory that was neutral for both of them. As Gigi's hopes that she would soon be reunited with Tarek faded, it no longer mattered to her how far she lived from Egypt.

As the years slipped by and they metamorphosed to adapt to their new life in an alien world, they gradually became strangers to each other. Luc could no longer recognize in her the princess in the oriental palace; nor she, in him, the globe-trotting reporter who had fascinated her with stories of elephants in Africa. What remained was the habit of affection, the familiarity and irritation of routine, the sterility of a childless marriage.

They had realized, almost from the beginning, that they would never have a child together. It was an admission that, in the final analysis, they stood apart, each in

183

his own nature, like species that can mate but not reproduce.

What bound them together, even more binding than a child, was the burden of the knowledge that they had burnt their bridges for each other. Reading an article about Wallis Simpson, Gigi had thought what a strain it must have been for the Windsors after his abdication: constantly to have to present a common front to the world; never to be able to admit they had made a mistake.

Even to each other. There was a careful silence, now, between Gigi and Luc, when they were alone. Outwardly they exchanged the minutia of daily existence, the automatic gestures, the peck on the cheek, the wifely adjusting of the tie. Inwardly there was silence. Silence disguised, over long winter evenings, by the white noise of the stereo, the flickering screens of the computer and the television, the drink in his hand and the book in hers.

Silence, and 'space'; figuratively, but also literally. Gigi slept in the spare bedroom now, an arrangement that had never been explicitly discussed between them. She was a light sleeper and Luc's snoring kept her awake. At first she would start off each night in the master bedroom, then, unable to sleep because of his snoring, she would creep away. But as soon as she had slipped out of bed he would fill the space she had vacated, stretch out his legs and arms, appropriate her pillow, spread himself across the queen-size bed so that there was no place left. Once when he had complained of her slipping away every night she had teased him about this. He had protested. 'But I only do it to find the scent and the warmth you leave behind!' He still had that kind of gallantry toward her, but it was a reflex, like good manners.

Gigi straightened up and leaned on her shovel, catching

184

her breath. She watched her neighbor's car heading down the street, the chains on the snow tires crunching on the salted and sanded road. The woman waved and Gigi waved back with a mittened hand. She remembered the time she had first met this neighbor, the day after they moved in, when she had come knocking at the door with a cake and a basket of Welcome Wagon coupons. 'I don't know if you'll have any use for this Honey Baked Ham coupon?' she had asked, pointedly. It was only later that Gigi understood that the woman had wanted to know if she were Jewish. Here in the snowy New England backwoods, the hint of the exotic about her eluded placing.

It was that same neighbor and her husband who came out in a blizzard a week later, boots and parkas over their pajamas, to help Gigi push her car out of the snow bank by their house when the car had slid on the icy road. Local townspeople, their code of neighborliness was reinforced by the remote location and the harsh winters. But once they established that you were not a candidate to join their church, they lost interest.

Which is why the people at the party tonight were all university people. There was a clear distinction in this place between town and gown. Over the ten years they had lived in this town where the accumulation of snow on the medians made it impossible to make a left turn between November and May, Gigi had made friends, even made a place of sorts for herself in the community. But she felt like one of those 'sleeper' agents that were popular in Cold War fiction. Even with friends like Janet Glasser she only showed one facet of herself. There was no place in this world of snow-capped steeples and ice hockey for her memories of dust and jasmine.

Half an hour after she started clearing the path, she

185

stopped to survey her handiwork, perspiring under her layers of clothing. The path was reasonably clear; just before the guests came Luc could take a broom to the steps to sweep off the fluff of snow that would have accumulated in the interim.

By eight o'clock the hallway closet, the screened front porch and the mud room were full of steaming coats, scarves and boots. Most of the guests had brought their dress shoes in a bag and changed into them before going into the living room. Luc was struggling with the fire, which kept threatening to sputter out. Gigi circulated with platters of stuffed mushrooms and miniature quiches.

'These are wonderful, Gigi,' Janet Glasser called over her shoulder as she bit into a quiche. She turned back to Toussaint Hopkins, the chair of the Romance Languages Department. 'So, tell me, what do you intend to do with your review of John Newley's monograph on Garcia Marquez?'

'Oh, damn with faint praise, that sort of thing . . . I mean, quite apart from anything else, he doesn't reference me.'

Gigi circulated with the tray.

'Sixteen inches – at least sixteen inches accumulation by morning, that's what I heard. The state police has already closed the roads.'

'No, he didn't get tenure. Uncollegial, you know, the usual stuff; fact is no one can stand his wife –'

'The Faculty Wives Club needs help on the refreshments committee, Gigi, are you interested?'

'Gigi, is there any more hot cider?' Toussaint Hopkins held up his cup.

'I'll get some.' Gigi took the empty punch bowl and

186

looked around for Luc. He was by the fireplace, holding a drink in one hand and poking and worrying the fire with the other. Smoke was backing down the flue into the room. Gigi sighed.

'Luc, why don't you just let it die out? It's warm enough without it, and the smoke is starting to annoy people.'

'I almost had it going. Get me a broomstick or something, Gigi, I think there's a bird nest blocking the flue. Remember when we had that bird caught up there in Spring?'

Gigi carried the empty punch bowl to the kitchen. She added another jug to the cider simmering in a stockpot with cinnamon sticks and cloves.

Toussaint came in, empty cup in hand. 'Ah, there's the cider.'

He ladled some into his cup and leaned on the counter, running his fingers through his thick gray hair. 'Would you like to attend the symposium on Montaigne on Friday? I know you're no *seizièmiste*, but you might enjoy it.'

'Of course, I'd love to.'

'How's your dissertation getting along, by the way?'

'Fine. I'm almost done writing up.' She tipped the stockpot and started pouring the steaming cider into the punch bowl.

'Good. Do you need some help with that bowl?'

Toussaint carried the bowl out to the dining room. Gigi was wiping the counter when Janet Glasser walked in.

'Where's Toussaint? I thought I saw him go in here. Never mind, it doesn't matter, I just wanted to ask him something. Let me get some water.'

Janet filled a glass at the sink, holding back the long brown hair, gray at the temples, that hung halfway down

187

her back. It occurred to Gigi that Janet's perennially long hair was one of the badges of her generation and education; shorthand for an entire Seventies sensibility: beige, pewter, oatbran, liberal, erudite and environmental.

'Gigi?' Janet took a last sip of water. 'Is everything all right?'

Gigi shrugged. She was arranging cheese puffs and salmon rolls on a platter. 'Oh, I guess I miss Tarek, that's all.' Janet was one of the few friends who knew that Gigi had a child.

'When was the last time you saw him?'

'A year ago, when he was in Italy with his father; I flew over to Rome to meet him, but it was only for a week. I haven't been to Egypt for over three years now. Not since I went back for Mama's funeral.'

Her mother's death had been a shock, coming as it did after a violent but mercifully brief bout with illness. The first two years after Gigi had married Luc, Mama had not wanted to have anything to do with either of them. Gigi had understood the rigidity of her mother's principles but also her sense of grievance: not only had she lost the daughter she should have been able to count on for support in her widowhood, she was left to face the whispered censure of the social circle in which her standing had always been unassailable. But with time Mama grew less bitter. Gigi realized that Tarek had supplanted her completely in her mother's affections; in fact she was content to have Gigi stay away, so she could keep the child to herself.

The reconciliation, when it came, was tepid and gradual: it had been years before Mama agreed to meet Luc; and then only in Europe, she refused to have him to come to Egypt. But at the end she was resigned to the

188

situation. It made Gigi sad, in a way, because it was part of a general sort of resignation, the way people get towards the end, when nothing matters as much – a kind of detachment sets in.

'I remember.' Janet put down her glass. 'That must have been a difficult time for you. You weren't yourself for a long time. I'm just glad that you'd more or less made up with your mother before you lost her.'

'Yes. I'm so grateful for that.' Gigi finished arranging the platter and wiped her hands on a dish towel. 'You know, I'm thinking of going home during the holidays.'

'Really? To see Tarek?'

'To see him, plus there's some business involving the inheritance from my father that I need to attend to. But I've been thinking. Tarek's so grown up now, you wouldn't believe it! He's sixteen, he'll be going to college next year. Wouldn't it be wonderful if he could go to college here in the States? That way I'd finally have him with me, or at least I could see him whenever I want to!'

'Oh Gigi!' Janet gave her a quick squeeze around the shoulders. 'You've been dreaming of this for a long time, haven't you?'

Gigi nodded. Ten years of waiting and hoping. Putting each day to bed with a sense of dissatisfaction, of unfinished business. The unbearable ache of the first months of separation dulled to a sense of something missing, of never having permission to be happy. Ten years of putting her life on hold, of arranging her existence, year in year out, around the rare occasions when she saw Tarek. Living for those times. Never a day going by when she did not think of him, wonder where he was, what he was doing, if he thought of her. Dreaming of a future for them together. The photos, every few months; always a

189

pang mixed with the joy, because they reminded her that time galloped on, that the child grew day by day, a gangling teenager already when the photo she had been kissing goodnight was of a gap-toothed little boy.

She had never given up hope, and she felt that now was the time. 'I'm not even sure Tarek will want to come here for college. But if I can talk him into it, and if I can convince his father to give his permission, wouldn't it be wonderful?'

'It certainly would! How long will you be staying in Egypt this time?'

'Oh, a few weeks; it depends. It will give me a chance to get reacquainted with the country, in a way. On my last trip, what with the shock and the funeral arrangements and everything, I didn't have time to turn around.'

'That's interesting. Because you know there's going to be a symposium in Cairo right around then, on francophone writers, in fact I was looking for Toussaint right now to talk to him about that. Gigi, can you keep this to yourself? Toussaint and I —'

Luc came in. 'Gigi, do we have any more red wine? In the cellar? But Gigi, it will be much too cool. People always underestimate the importance of bringing wine to the right temperature,' he grumbled as he headed down the cellar steps.

Janet smiled at her. 'Talk to you later.'

190

PART III

THE RETURN

14

Cairo Revisited

I close the album of photographs. Business or pleasure?'
the landing card inquired. How do you answer: I have
come back to claim what's mine. To find out if it is still
mine to claim. To find two children I left behind: one is
the girl I once was. The other is the little boy I left ten
years ago, Tarek. The future and the past. Between them
they hold the key to the question I have to try to resolve:
where do I belong? Where is this chameleon's natural
habitat?

I look around the small two-bedroom apartment built
on top of the villa in Zamalek where I grew up. Since
Mama's death the villa has been rented to an American
company which has transformed it into offices. The
company had asked for permission to build a small *pied-à-
terre* on top of the villa for visiting executives. I had asked
if I could use it for my stay in Cairo this time; it was
currently unoccupied and they had had no objection.

It feels strange to be home and yet not home, to be
the guest and the landlord at the same time; to look out

of the window at a familiar view and then turn back to an unfamiliar room. The few pieces of Mama's furniture which I kept to furnish the small apartment look out of scale and out of place. The large, velvet-upholstered sofa and armchairs crowd the room like overdressed house-guests living in reduced circumstances.

Most of Mama's furniture has been sold at auction; what I have chosen to keep is stored at the Cairo House along with my own furniture. There is a kidney-shaped vanity with a rose tulle skirt which I have kept, although it is of no intrinsic value, because some of my most vivid memories are of Mama sitting at that *coiffeuse* before the mirror. I used to know by heart the contents of the drawers: which drawer was dusty with Coty's loose powder and puffs, which had a permanent pink nailpolish stain, which held a tangle of hair brushes, pins and curlers. But after Mama's death, when I opened the drawers of the *coiffeuse*, the familiar paraphernalia was gone: the drawers were neat and bare but for a brush and a pot of Pond's cold cream. I realized that it had been years since Mama had worn makeup and perfume. If she'd had a daughter's support and encouragement, she might not have given up on personal vanity so prematurely.

This morning it has been disorienting to visit the company offices in the old villa. The salons have been partitioned into clapboard cubicles; telephones ring and typewriters clatter, fax machines buzz and employees shuffle paper. I went upstairs to see what had become of my bedroom. It is unrecognizable, an office with three desks. The walk-in closet is now a filing cabinet. The young woman at one of the desks looked up and smiled when Ibrahim the doorkeeper explained who I was. 'I've

194

always been curious, what was this room used for?' she asked.

'It was my bedroom. That was my governess's room through there.'

'How lucky you were to grow up here. But how you must hate what we've done to the house!'

I looked out of what used to be my bedroom window. I used to be able to see the Nile through that window but now my view was obscured by tall buildings that had sprouted up around the older villas.

On the ground floor I found a small office at the end of a long corridor. There was a plaque on the door: 'Susan Baygley, Director'. The door was partially ajar and I tentatively stuck my head in. A blonde woman with glasses looked up from her desk, annoyed.

'Sorry to disturb you,' I apologized, 'but I used to live here and I asked Ibrahim to show me around.'

'That's all right,' the woman said stiffly.

Ibrahim reminded me, in Arabic, that this used to be Khadra's room. I laughed. The woman raised her eyebrows.

'Ibrahim was just reminding me that this used to be the maid's room,' I explained sweetly as I turned away.

I paced around the little apartment. I had called Tarek as soon as I arrived last night, but the maid who answered said he was away on a trip to the Red Sea with some friends and wouldn't be back for four days. I left a message and a number, but I didn't ask to speak to Yussef or his wife.

I should call the Pasha, and Tante Zohra, who had had a stroke. For the first few years after my remarriage, I hadn't come to Egypt, because of the estrangement with

195

Mama. Later, when I did come, I always came alone, and the subject of my marriage to Luc was tacitly ignored. The Pasha, I had come to realize, was really a very worldly man. Tante Zohra had had her own scandal in the family, with Gina. In general too, I realized, in this matter as in others, the Draconian standards I remembered were no longer upheld. Perhaps they had never been.

My relationship with Leila was as warm as ever, but we kept in touch only sporadically. I called her occasionally, or sent letters, but she was too busy to write back: Leila was a pediatrician, married to an internist, and mother of twin daughters. As for Tamer, he had not turned out to be the ally I automatically assumed he would be when I decided to marry Luc. He became somewhat distant. Over the years we ran into each other a few times, in Europe or in Egypt. I knew he had married, divorced, remarried.

I decided to call Leila. She would bring me up to speed on everybody's news. I picked up the phone.

'Leila? It's Gigi. How are you?'

'Gigi! How are you, dear? Are you in Cairo? How marvelous! Listen, I'm expecting some friends over for *sohour* this evening. Mostly doctors and their wives. Why don't you come right over? We'd love to see you!'

'Tonight?' I looked at my watch: eight o'clock in the evening. We were in the middle of Ramadan, the month of fasting from sunup to sundown. The fast is broken at sunset, so the *iftar* meal is served around five thirty in winter; the night-time meal, *sohour*, would be served any time between midnight and two a.m. I had plenty of time.

'All right, Leila, I'll do my best.'

The problem was how to get to her apartment across town. I would be coming home at two or three in the

196

morning, and taking a taxi alone at that time of night was not advisable. I could use Mama's old car, it was kept in running condition, but I hadn't driven in Cairo for years, I wasn't sure I could still do it. No one but a native Cairene would even attempt it. Even Luc, who ten years ago would have tried anything, had lost his nerve at the idea of driving through Cairo traffic.

I jumped up. It was now or never. If I were going to be mobile and independent while I was here, I would have to drive. I should do it right away, before I had time to think about it.

I called to Ibrahim through the window. 'Ibrahim, would you get the car ready for me, please? I'll be going out in an hour or so.'

I decided on a black sheath dress and picked out some jewelry: a pearl necklace, earrings, my solitaire ring; more than I would have worn in New Hampshire, but in Cairo women dress up. The neckline was somewhat low-cut, so I took along a fine white mohair shawl to wrap around my shoulders in case I had to stop somewhere along the way.

When I came down Ibrahim had drawn back the gate to the villa and was wiping the windshield of the car. I got in and switched on the ignition, fumbling with the unfamiliar, stiff gear shift. Then I backed out into the street and plunged into the terrifying cacophonous chaos of Cairo traffic.

I drove up onto the overpass and was immediately engulfed in traffic swirling in all directions, the cars dispersing arbitrarily across the lanes like billiard balls scattering across a pool table. The Cairene is the worst of motorists, in that he observes no law but that of the jungle, and at the same time the most talented, in that

197

he for the most part miraculously manages to avoid collisions. This requires hairline judgment, peripheral vision, nerves of steel, and a strategy of yielding with good grace when unavoidable and forging ahead with blind faith when an opening presents itself. He who hesitates is lost.

Cairo traffic is a microcosm of Egyptian society. Rules are only observed when they are enforced with the active presence of the authorities. Stop lights are ignored; a policeman directs traffic with a whistle and a wave of the hand. There are no fast lanes, slow lanes or passing lanes; cars swarm across lanes, jockeying for position. No one observes speed limits; one travels as fast as one's vehicle and the surrounding traffic allow.

No one uses turning signals. Everyone honks continuously and arbitrarily, out of impatience, frustration or boredom. As a means of attracting attention, the horn is as devalued as the currency.

This is a society without safety nets; the most expensive cars are prohibitive to insure and the run-of-the-mill, past-its-prime compact not worth insuring. It follows that the millionaire in his Mercedes is far more vulnerable than the poor drudge in his beat-up Fiat.

Oddly enough, however, it is the pedestrian who is the least vulnerable. Watch the jaywalker, solitary or in a horde, who thrusts himself fearlessly into rumbling traffic, pitting his bones and flesh against steel and rubber, nonchalantly slapping the hood of a car as it screeches to a halt at his feet. He knows what the horrified tourist witnessing this scene does not: that in Cairo your car can collide with another vehicle with relatively minor consequences, but if you run down a human being, your worst nightmare has come true. Say that woman rushing into your path carrying a baby on one arm and dragging a

198

toddler with the other happens to lose her grip on the child and it falls under your wheels. The mild-mannered crowd around you will instantly turn into a mob, the mindless rage of the have-nots welling up from unsuspected depths of frustration and despair.

By the time I made it to Leila's I was flushed with nervous tension and triumph. I had managed to avoid getting lost or having an accident.

As the *suffragi* opened the door a wave of light and laughter washed over me. He ushered me in. The two salons were full. The men had spontaneously gravitated to one salon and the women to another, a sure sign that the soiree had been in full swing for a while. Leila came towards me, arms outstretched. She looked a little fuller than I remembered, but very elegant in a white silk pantsuit accentuated with heavy gold jewelry. Her unmistakably professional French twist made me aware that I was probably the only woman in the room this evening who had not had her hair styled by a hairdresser.

'Gigi! I'm so glad you came! You look lovely. It's so good to see you!'

'And you! I've missed you all so much. How's Tante Zohra?'

'Still bed-ridden since her stroke. It's such a shock, she's always been so active.' She shook her head. 'Of course she's well into her eighties. It's just that she's been more of a mother than a grandmother to us, Tamer and me.'

'How is he?'

'Fine, very busy. I only seem to see him when he drops in for lunch. You know he divorced again recently?'

'No, I didn't. So soon? Didn't he remarry only a year

199

ago?' I'd never met Tamer's new wife. I'd known Dina, his first wife, but they had divorced years ago.

'Yes, it was very sudden. None of us knew her very well, you know. She was Italian, and she only came to Egypt for a month or so, then she went back to Milan. I think it was that more than anything that finally led to the divorce. They still seem to be on friendly terms though.' She called to her husband. 'Amin, look who's here!'

Leila's husband detached himself from the cluster of men in the far salon and came to greet me with a smile. 'Gihan, *Ahlan*, what a nice surprise! When did you get here?' He drew me into the salon to introduce me around while Leila ducked into the dining room to check on the preparations.

Around midnight Leila called out: '*Sohour* is served!' The *suffragi* drew aside the sliding doors separating the salon from the dining room. The women led the way, filing towards the buffet table and exclaiming over the flower arrangements and the more exotic dishes. Leila took me by the waist and led me in. I glanced at the sideboard, with its array of typical Ramadan desserts, the honey and nut pastries called Syrian desserts in Egypt: baklava, *konafa*, 'Palace Bread'.

'If only I'd known you were coming, I would have ordered your favorite *Om Ali*,' Leila lamented. 'Well, come for *iftar* on Sunday, it's my day for having my mother-in-law over, and often Tamer comes too. Nana Zohra can't come anymore, of course, since her stroke. There'll be a place set for you every Sunday while you're in town.'

I was unable to fall asleep, too wound up after the *sohour* on top of the jet-lag. For some reason I thought of calling

200

Tamer. It was past two o'clock, but then this was Ramadan and a Thursday night, the beginning of the weekend; he might not be asleep yet. I looked up his number in my phone book and dialed it.

'Hello?' He picked up after the first ring, sounding wide awake.

'Hi, Tamer!'

'Who is this is?'

'Guess.'

'Gigi? But – where are you calling from? When did you get back?'

On an impulse I answered, 'I'm still in the States.'

'But the phone didn't ring the way it does for a long-distance call. That's odd. Anyway, how are you? Will you be coming back anytime soon?'

'Well, I was thinking of coming for a visit this month.'

'Good! It would be great to see you. It must be – what – three years since I saw you? At least. How long will you be staying this time?'

'Just a few weeks.'

'To see Tarek?'

'Yes. And there are some things to do with Papa's estate that I need to look into. Tell me, how have you been?'

'All right. Busy.'

'Leila tells me you're on your own again. I'm sorry your marriage didn't work out.'

'Yes, well, it turned out we got along better as friends and business partners than we did married. So we've gone back to just being friends and partners. Hey, wait a minute – when did you speak to Leila?'

'Oh – she wrote to me.'

'Leila never writes!'

201

'Okay, I give up. Guess where I'm calling from? I'm here in Zamalek!'

'I knew there was something funny about the way the phone rang! That's great. When can I see you?'

We agreed that he would pick me up the next evening.

I went to visit Tante Zohra this afternoon. She now lives in a large, high-ceilinged apartment in a building she owns in Zamalek; she rents her villa on the same street to a foreign company. I circled the block three times, unable to find a parking space. Then I caught the eye of the *minadi* who works this particular territory. Even after years of living abroad, you still recognize a member of this *confrèrie* instantly. He helped me double-park and I left the parking brake off and the clutch in first gear so he could push the car out of the way if one of the cars I was blocking needed to pull out. I took the elevator up to Tante Zohra's apartment.

The door was opened by a plump, poised young woman.

'*Ahlan*, Sitt Gigi, welcome.'

It was Khadra. After Mama had passed away she had gone to work for Tante Zohra. It was hard to believe that this was once the little girl fresh from the country who used to chew on the leftover watermelon rind as she cleared the table.

'How are you, Khadra? And how's Tante Zohra?'

'As well as can be expected, Allah be thanked. But since her stroke, you know, she's never been the same.' She shook her head. 'She'll be so pleased to see you. She's by herself right now, but they try not to leave her alone for a minute, bless their hearts. Her daughters and grandchildren take turns, there's always someone coming

202

and going. Except Sitt Gina, she's in Lebanon, of course.'

She ushered me to Tante Zohra's bedroom. 'Here's Sitt Gigi to see you.'

Tante Zohra was sitting up in bed, propped up with pillows. I was shocked to see her so much changed, so old. She held out her arms. 'You're just as pretty as ever, Gigi! Take after your aunt, your father always said so.'

'Hello, Tante Zohra.' I pulled up a chair and sat by her bed.

The phone rang. Khadra hurried out to answer it. She came back in a minute. 'That was Sitt Nazli.' She raised her voice for Tante Zohra's benefit. 'She says she's running a few minutes late, but she's on her way. She's bringing the hairdresser with her to do your hair and manicure. I just heard the call to afternoon prayers. Would you like to get ready now?'

Tante Zohra nodded and Khadra left the room. She came back with a pan of clean, dry sand. Because of her condition, instead of washing, Tante Zohra patted the sand and went through the motions of the ablutions required before prayer. I had never seen anyone do this before but I remembered that this dispensation from using water was accorded to invalids, and in cases of shortage of water. Tante Zohra then started praying, still sitting in bed, instead of standing on a prayer mat.

I looked at the large portrait photo of Tante Zohra hanging in an elaborate frame over her bed. It must have been taken when she was in her thirties, and was signed by Armand, a popular Armenian society photographer in Egypt at the time. The pose and lighting emulated the glamorous studio portraits of Hollywood movie stars. The young Zohra threw a sultry look over a bare shoulder emerging from a cloud of tulle; her dark hair was elaborately styled; diamond earrings dangled to her bare collar bone; she had the arched, pencil-thin brows and cupid-bow lips of the period. Only the indomitable eyes belied the deliberately vapid pose.

As I waited for Tante Zohra to finish her prayers I wondered what led a woman like her back to the veil, when it had been her generation that had been the first never to have to wear it. She had told me proudly how, as a schoolgirl, she had been one of the youngest to take part in a public demonstration against the veil. She had stood on a train platform in the midst of a group of women wearing the filmy white veils of Ottoman court custom. Most of these wives and daughters of pashas were there with the grudging permission of male relatives. They waited for the Egyptian women's delegation to arrive, back from attending a suffragette conference in Europe. Hoda Sha`rawi and the other delegates got off the train, throwing back their veils. The women waiting on the platform imitated the gesture. The street crowd would have jeered at them, but it was clear the women had the tacit approval of the King and of their husbands. The triumphant women rode home in their chauffeur-driven sedans, never to cover their faces again.

Tante Zohra had told me that story many times. Yet here she was, if not veiled, at least with her head covered: she wore a white turban all the time now. If it were only women of her age, with eternity looming close at hand, it would be understandable. But I had seen women of all ages and backgrounds in Islamic dress all over Cairo.

The doorbell rang, and I heard a voice in the hall, questioning Khadra, then brisk footsteps coming down the hallway. But it was not Nazli. It was Leila, but barely recognizable, wearing no makeup or jewelry, dressed in

204

a plain tailored suit, hair covered with a silk scarf knotted at the nape of her neck. She was carrying a medical bag.

'Hello, Nana. Hi, Gigi! What luck to run into you here.' She seemed tired as she sat down on the edge of the bed. She opened her bag and drew out a stethoscope, taking Tante Zohra's wrist between her finger and thumb. 'How are you feeling today, Nana?'

'The same, dear, the same.'

I had never seen Leila wear a scarf over her hair before. She must have noticed that I was taken aback.

'It's just that I've come straight from the university hospital. You come into contact with all kinds of people doing the rounds, and they tend to take you more seriously if you're dressed like this.' Leila smiled at me absentmindedly, her eye on the blood pressure meter as she pumped up the gauge attached to her grandmother's arm. 'Nana, did you take your pills this morning? No nausea? Good. What did you have for lunch today?'

'Oh, I don't know. It's all such boring food.'

'Let me check with Khadra.' Leila left the room.

'She's such a good girl, Allah knows,' Tante Zohra confided. 'Always checks on me on her way home from the hospital, although she must be so tired, poor thing. And of course her husband and children are waiting for her.' Tante Zohra looked at me with the shrewd eyes I remembered. 'She's very unlike Gina, isn't she? But you know the life she leads is so different. They turned out well, you know, Gina's children. Tamer too. It's Allah's grace, when you think of what they went through. After Gina left – and their father was always so busy – they were at my house more often than in their own. But I'll say this much for Ali – busy as he was, he always let them know he loved them. Wherever he was, whatever

205

he was doing, he called them every night before they went to bed, at the same time. After he died so suddenly – Oh, that was awful, Allah rest his soul – well, I raised them. I never needed to worry as much about Leila. She's like her father, you know. Focused, pragmatic. Nothing derails her.'

That was true. I remembered Leila studying for her exams, the year her father died in such suspicious circumstances. I had admired her for that. She just forged ahead with life, instead of vacillating and soul-searching like I did.

'Tamer I worried about. Leila was a little older but Tamer was just a boy,' Tante Zohra continued. 'He kept things inside, you couldn't reach him. People say I spoiled him, but that's not true. They say he crashed the car I gave him for his graduation from college, but there's more to that story than he'll admit. I have my suspicions. Oh, nobody tells me anything, they think I don't know, but I know more than they think.'

Tante Zohra seemed lost in her thoughts for a minute, absent-mindedly tucking loose strands of hair under her turban. Her black hair needed to be re-coloured, it showed white at the roots.

I wondered how Tante Zohra felt about the proposed sale of the Cairo House. Apparently a very good offer had been made, through Kamal Zeitouni. This had caused a considerable rift in the family. According to Egyptian inheritance laws, every one of the Seif-el-Islam brothers and sisters, or their heirs, had a share. But in practice it was the Pasha, as oldest brother, who had lived in the house all his life; for the past forty years, he had been the only occupant. Offers to buy the house had trickled in over the years, but had not been seriously entertained.

206

The unspoken consensus was that it would not be sold till the Pasha died. But the years passed and he outlived several of his younger siblings. Their children and grand-children were growing impatient. Now Kamal Zeitouni's proposition had brought matters to a head. The Pasha himself had called for a family meeting in two weeks to consider the offer, and to take votes. As Papa's heir, I was one of those with the most at stake.

'Tante Zohra? I'm going to have *iftar* at the Pasha's tomorrow.'

She looked at me with alert eyes. 'You know about this business of the sale?'

'That's what I was wondering – I mean, how do you feel about it?'

'Well, I have to think of my grandchildren. Nazli's chil-dren and the others. Decent apartments in Cairo are so expensive nowadays. And some of them need start-up capital for a variety of projects. But on the other hand to see the house go to strangers, or be demolished to build a hotel in its place – I don't know. As long as the Pasha is alive . . . I would be for waiting. But after his death, there's no telling – that woman he lives with could claim to be his common-law wife.' I was intrigued by her reference to a woman, but Tante Zohra had closed her eyes and her speech came slower, slurred. 'I don't know. I'm too old to care. I'll sign any way the Pasha wants me to.'

'Tante Zohra, are you getting tired? Can I get you anything?'

'No, dear, I'll be fine. Since you'll be having *iftar* with the Pasha tomorrow, would you mind taking him the envelope on the *secrétaire* over there, it's money for the Ramadan soup kitchen that the party sponsors.' She

207

sighed. 'Ah me, only last year I sponsored a Ramadan soup kitchen myself one night at the mosque nearby, we had two hundred people come to eat. This is the first year I haven't done it since the sequestration decrees were lifted. But it's Allah's will, my health isn't what it used to be.'

I took the envelope, rang for Khadra and bent over to kiss Tante Zohra good-bye. On the way out I met Leila in the corridor. She walked me to the door.

'How's Gina?' I asked. 'Does she call often?'

Leila hesitated, then seemed to make up her mind. Her words came in a rush. 'Mother is dying of cancer. She's in a hospital in Lebanon. She can't even call anymore, she's under morphine all the time. Nana doesn't know, we don't want her to know. We pretend that Mother has called when Nana was asleep or praying or in the bathroom.'

'Oh God, I'm so sorry!'

'Well, we pray it won't be long now, because Mother's suffering so much, even with the morphine.' Leila rubbed her red eyes with a tissue. 'I'd better get back to Nana. Don't forget to come on Sunday if you're free.'

15

The Dervish

Around eight o'clock this evening I heard the dog barking. Domino II looked like his namesake and already treated me as if I belonged. Perhaps I reminded the poor brute of Mama. Since her death Ibrahim took care of him. The barking was followed by Ibrahim's heavy, slow tread on the stairs. He was wheezing by the time he rang the doorbell. He announced that a *bey* was there to see me.

'I know, I'm expecting him. It's my cousin Tamer. Will you ask him to come up?'

Tamer's quick steps followed and he was at the door. His face was more angular, his hair darker, less curly, receding slightly at the temples. He looked older; it suited him. He was wearing a soft sports coat over a crisp shirt and jeans.

'Hey!' He bent down to give me a peck on the cheek. 'How are you?'

He had a new car, a sporty Japanese model. He went around to the driver's side and started to unlock the door.

'I'm sorry I can't unlock the door on the passenger side,' he started to say, 'but –'

'That's all right, I'll get in on your side!' I assumed his car had been in an accident and that the passenger side door was stuck. I remembered that Tamer's cars always seemed to have idiosyncrasies related to the traumas they had suffered. I slipped in ahead of him on the driver's side and wiggled across the seat under the steering wheel and then settled into the passenger seat, yanking down my skirt, which had ridden up my legs.

Tamer got into the car and turned on the ignition. He looked amused. 'As I was saying, I'm sorry I couldn't unlock the door on your side first to let you in, but this car has a security system so that the driver's door has to be unlocked before any of the others.'

'Oh! Then why did you let me make a fool of myself, not to mention getting a run in my pantyhose?'

'Well, you didn't give me a chance to explain, and – I must admit I was enjoying the view.'

I made a fist at him. It was funny how the dynamics between us tended to fall into the old pattern.

'Where would you like to go?' he asked.

'Anywhere we can sit and talk. You know where I haven't been in years and years? Khan-Khalili. The souk. Could we go there?'

'Sure.'

Tamer parked in a narrow alley not far from the souk near the El-Hussein Mosque. The streets all around the mosque were bright with strings of Ramadan lanterns swaying in the evening breeze. At one end, a banner proclaimed a 'Table of the Compassionate' over a huge awning, one of the thousands of privately-sponsored soup

210

kitchens that spring up all around the city for the duration of the month of Ramadan; no one need go hungry, at least during the holy month.

As I followed Tamer down the street leading to the great mosque, we stepped around country people encamped on the ground. It was the Night of Power, towards the end of Ramadan, the sacred night when prayers are answered and worship is rewarded a thousand times over; these *fellahin* had made the traditional pilgrimage from their villages to the city to spend this holiest of nights on this hallowed ground. To them it was no desecration to set up their cooking pans and bundles of blankets on the threshold of the Great Mosque, nor did anyone try to prevent them.

Skirting the mosque, we plunged into the maze of narrow alleys of the Khan-Khalili, past the glittering shop windows with their dazzling array of silver and gold, glass and ivory, wood and leather. We ran the gauntlet of good-natured solicitations with a smile and a shake of the head. It was axiomatic that prices went down as you penetrated deeper into the darker, danker alleys of the souk where the tourists rarely ventured.

In a dusty boutique I stopped to examine a turquoise hand-blown glass jar with a *cloisonné* medallion portrait of the Ottoman Sultan Abdelhamid. It was gorgeous and rare, but I decided not to try to bargain for it. I had no idea what a fair price would be if it were genuine, and if it were an imitation it would be worthless.

'Looking for anything in particular?' Tamer asked.

'One of those old Turkish military medals. I thought it would look beautiful, framed.'

A little boy asked what we were looking for. Tamer told him and he immediately directed us to: 'Haj Zein's – second

211

alley down on the right.' The boy ran ahead, presumably to inform the shopkeeper that he was sending business his way.

In the tiny shop Haj Zein pointed to worn stone steps leading to a second floor room. 'The medals are in the drawers of the cabinet upstairs. Take them out and look around. If you find something you fancy, just bring it down, we'll have a look at it.'

I started up the steep steps, ahead of Tamer, and bumped my head against a step that was hidden by the cloth curtain hanging from the top of the stairs. I slipped back against him. He steadied me and touched my forehead. 'Ouch! That must hurt.'

In the tiny, deserted room we found the dusty trays of jumbled medals in a glass-topped display cabinet and pored over them together. There were Turkish, Persian and British medals among the plethora of Egyptian ones of all periods.

'Look at this.' Tamer picked up a heavy, silver Yemeni dagger from one of the display cases. He grasped the intricately carved handle and drew the long blade out of the sheath. I reached for it.

'Careful.' As he released it into my hands his fingers touched my palm. The sudden tingling caught me unprepared; his hands were so familiar, after all, the long fingers, the scar running from his left thumb to his wrist, a legacy from the riding accident in the desert. I weighed the dagger in my hand and passed it back to him.

I sifted through the medals in the drawer. 'What do you think of this one?' It was a crimson enamel medal set in a frame of gold leaf and semi-precious stones. We took it and made our way gingerly down the steps.

'Turkish?' I asked Haj Zein.

212

'Farsi,' the Haj answered.

'No, it's Turkish!' I had no idea what difference it made, if any. This slightly silly tourist banter was meant to cover up the unexpected awkwardness a few minutes earlier.

After considerable repartee Haj Zein declared, with a great show of exasperation, that he would be willing to accept anything over a hundred pounds. I had insisted that I wouldn't pay a piaster over a hundred. Tamer allowed us both to save face by plunking down a pound of his own over the hundred. Haj Zein gave the medal to a boy to polish and wrap. While I was settling the bill he offered Tamer a cigarette, then lit up himself. He shook his head soberly.

'Did you hear what just happened? There was another incident. A bomb blew up a tourist bus in front of the church in Abassia.'

'When? Just now? Was it on the radio?' Tamer asked.

'Not yet, but it will be soon. I heard it from the street. They must be crazy, those *Gamaat islamiyya* people.'

'They want to ruin the country, so they can take over.'

'Allah preserve us! Well, I'll tell you one thing. They're going about it the right way, if they're trying to ruin the country. Have you looked around the souk? Where are the tourists?'

We filed out of the narrow doorway of the boutique and headed towards the Mahfouz Café, so-called in honor of the novelist and first Egyptian Nobel laureate. He had been a regular, decades before, when he used to sit at one of these small tables to pen the novels that were redolent of the smells and the sounds of these alleys: the scent of mint leaves in small glasses of strong tea, the tinkling teaspoons, the jingling anklets of the women

213

swaying their hips under their black shawls. Mahfouz, now aged and blind, had been attacked by a knife-wielding assailant only a few days earlier; on account of his allegorical novels that had been interpreted as subversive of Islam, or because of his support for the peace with Israel, or both.

There had been a brief, rare shower while we were in Zein's shop and the cobblestones looked washed, the rain collecting sluggishly in the gutters. The complex, smoky odors of the street were suddenly cut by the full, sharp aroma of Turkish coffee. I had an inexplicable impulse to breathe it all in, to explore an entire world I had found impenetrable in the days when Papa had tried to get me to read Mahfouz's novels.

'Can we order a water-pipe?'

'Sure.' Tamer didn't react as if I were playing the tourist.

'What flavor?' the waiter asked. 'Honey, apple?'

I hadn't realized that water-pipes now came in flavors. Since my arrival in Cairo I had been struck by the variety in the supermarkets, on the newspaper stands. Variety had been in such short supply in the days of state-controlled production under Nasser's 'socialism': one kind of car, one kind of sofa-bed, one government-controlled newspaper, El-Ahram. A monopoly on everything, even the name: every other product seemed to bear a variation of the name Nasser: Nasr cars, Nasr sofa-beds, Nasr City, Nasr sesame halva.

The water-pipe proved an unsatisfactory experience; I wasn't able to actually smoke it, but the glowing coals and pleasant aroma were companionable. I didn't feel self-conscious, although ordinarily only a tourist or an Egyptian of the 'common' type would smoke a water-pipe. Here in the souk, they were used to both.

214

A syrup peddler circulated among the customers of the café, splendid in his gold-embroidered caftan, a long-necked brass jug balanced in each hand. I snatched up my camera. He saw me and stopped, posing with courteous but unsmiling dignity. When I had taken the photo he nodded and moved on, not expecting a tip or a Polaroid.

As the shops closed the café filled with people smoking, drinking tea or coffee, playing checkers, talking. They were relaxed as people can be in cafés outdoors, in ancient cities of the south, where time is a friend to rendez-vous with eagerly at the end of the day. I felt my pulse slow down.

The call of the muezzin rang out slow and sweet, a long-drawn out echo that seemed to suck the breath out of me and suspend it somewhere in the air with the last, endlessly vibrating note. *Laylat-al-Qadr*, the Night of Power; here in the café, it seemed as if it were indeed a miraculous night of forgiveness and compassion, as if the whole world shared the simple mysticism of the peasants camped on the steps of the mosque and the easy-going tolerance of the merchants of the souk. It was easy to forget that only hours before and minutes away, the faith of the fanatics, of the sword and the law, of the house of peace and the house of war, had struck again.

A drumbeat started up and a small procession wound its way to the courtyard. First a couple of musicians with tambourines and drums, then a man wearing a pleated white skirt, a red embroidered vest, a sash and a high fez. The musicians set up a plaintive, hypnotic chant and the dervish began to whirl, slowly, dreamily, his dark eyes fixed on a point in the air, the white skirt billowing around his waist. 'Allah, the merciful!' The drums beat faster, the chant became more urgent. 'The Compassionate!' The

215

dervish whirled faster. From the voluminous sleeves of his white shirt he drew out two long, gleaming knives and held them pointed straight up, one in each hand, as he whirled faster and faster. The small crowd that had gathered around him drew back to a safe distance, like leaves blown back by a whirling fan. The drums were frantic now, and the dervish a blur of white and glints of silver.

'He can't keep it up,' I murmured. 'He's going to fall on those knives and hurt himself.'

Some people moved away, sat back down at their tables and picked up their drinks or their pawns. But I couldn't take my eyes off the dervish.

'Let's go,' Tamer said finally. 'He can keep it up all night. At least he can try. What a form of worship! Well, why not? Perhaps his prayers will be heard, tonight of all nights, the Night of Power.'

We made our way back along the narrow alleys. We no sooner reached the car than, as if by telepathy, a *minadi* materialized and hurried up, tipping his cap and making a show of wiping the windscreen.

Tamer started the car and headed slowly down the narrow, one-way alley, parallel-parked on both sides. Just then another car headed towards us from the opposite direction. Both cars stopped; neither backed out. Tamer reached out and folded down his side-view mirror and the other driver did the same. The two cars began to inch past each other, the drivers signaling each other on, while bystanders offered tactical advice. I held my breath. Our car barely scraped past the other, then with a sudden gunning of the accelerator we broke out of the bottle-neck. I heaved a sigh of relief; driving in Cairo, even as a passenger, unnerved me.

216

On the overpass of the Sixth of October Bridge a police checkpoint was set up, stopping cars with suspicious license plates or passengers with the trademark beards and skull-caps of the Islamists. The policeman looked into our car briefly, then waved us past the checkpoint. A few minutes later we had arrived at the villa and Tamer dropped me off and drove away. Ibrahim came up to the gate.

'I don't want you to stay up for me next time, Ibrahim. Will you make me a copy of the key to the padlock of the gate? That way I can let myself in if I'm late. Oh, Ibrahim, would you please put the garbage in plastic bags instead of just wrapping it in newspaper and tossing it in the trash cans? This morning there was melon rind and bits of paper strewn around the cans.'

He nodded. 'Will there be anything else tonight?'

I rummaged around in my head for the correct reply rather than a curt dismissal. Like someone remembering a forgotten language I found the formula from my childhood: the gracious and untranslatable, 'Not that we can do without you, but not right now.'

These formulaic greetings, requests and responses were second nature. Each formula required its conventional response, each action an equal and opposite reaction, like a law of physics. To fail to provide the proper response was an awkward lapse of social skills. That sort of automatic courtesy would be easy enough to relearn; far harder to master, for me, would be the intricate minefield of arcane social dictates governing everything from hospitality to visits of condolences.

I tried to fall asleep but it was no use. It would soon be daybreak. I listened for the clip-clop of the donkey carts. The garbage collectors come at dawn, but so early I never see them.

217

16

The Pasha

That evening I was invited for Ramadan *iftar* at the Pasha's. I left twenty minutes before sunset. I calculated that there would be lighter traffic on the road just before the breaking of the fast, whereas if I left earlier I would get caught in the frenzied rush of irritable motorists hurrying to get home in time. At any rate Ramadan etiquette requires the guest to arrive just as the call to sunset prayers is sounded, or a few minutes before, no earlier.

I drove along the Nile Corniche as the sinking sun splashed ochre on the broad expanse of water. I turned the corner of the long wall of the British Embassy, once white and now a dingy gray. The call to sunset prayers rang out against a chorus of twittering birds flocking home to the thick foliage of the old banyan trees. I pulled up at the gate to the Cairo House. The doorkeeper asked me who I was before letting me park inside the grounds; ten years ago he would have recognized me. I went in by the side door and hurried up the marble staircase.

Fangali met me at the top of the stairs and knew me

218

immediately. '*Ahlan*, Sitt Gigi, what a long time it's been.'

His high-pitched whine had not changed. Yet I knew that, shortly after I had left for Europe, there had been a great transformation in Fangali's life. He had apparently visited a medical specialist who had recommended an operation. Subsequently, much to everyone's consternation, Fangali, at the age of forty, had married and in short order fathered two children. There were mixed feelings about Fangali's good fortune. It was felt that he had somehow pulled the wool over everyone's eyes. 'Will Allah's miracles never cease! And all these years when we all thought he wasn't a man! Why, he was even allowed to massage the Grandmother's legs!'

Fangali headed down the upstairs gallery. 'This way, Sitt Gigi. Let me just tell the Pasha you're here.'

The vast downstairs dining room, with its twenty-four chairs, was hardly ever used any more. A smaller dining room set, seating twelve, was set up at the far end of the upstairs gallery, in front of the tall French windows leading out to the terrace. Today it was set for only three people.

I saw my uncle shuffling slowly from his bedroom, supported by Fangali on one side and an elegant woman in black on the other. I recognized Lamia El-Salem, the widow of a Lebanese prime minister, and for some years now the Pasha's companion.

'Gigi!' The Pasha stopped and freed his arm to greet me and kissed me on both cheeks. He waved away Fangali and made it to the head of the table on his own. I sat down on one side of him and Lamia El-Salem on the other.

'Don't forget your pills,' she fussed in her lilting Lebanese accent. She had changed nothing about her style since I saw her last. She was still in elegant mourning

219

for her husband, assassinated over twenty years ago. The same black lace scarf was draped dramatically over her jet black, meticulously styled hair. She had to be at least seventy years old.

When she had first come to Egypt she had kept a suite at the Nile Hotel across from the British Embassy, a three-minute walk from the Pasha's house. As the years passed she spent more and more time at the house until one day her presence there became a fait accompli. For appearance's sake she and the Pasha maintained the fiction that she was only occasionally a houseguest, but everyone knew better.

Two waiters filled the glasses with *qammar-eddin*, apricot nectar, the traditional Ramadan beverage for breaking the fast. I was somewhat taken aback that the two *suffragis* were wearing pants and shirts, rather than the caftan and turban of traditional Egyptian butlers. The table was set correctly but the china and flatware were of a cheap, everyday kind I did not expect. Apparently the good china and silver were locked away. But the *suffragis*, in spite of their unconventional attire, seemed to be well trained. One of them brought the soup tureen around to my left, and when he had ladled the lentil cream into my plate, the other followed with the croutons. The next dish was one of my favorites, *imam bayaldi:* tiny, elongated aubergine stuffed with meat, raisins and pine nuts. By the time the lamb cutlets came around I shook my head.

'You should eat, you've lost weight,' the Pasha remonstrated. 'I know you'll like dessert. Nobody makes *Om Ali* like my cook. I remember you always liked that.'

I was touched that my uncle had remembered my favorite Ramadan dessert. He served me himself, a large helping of flaky pastry baked with cream, nuts and raisins,

220

still warm from the oven. I finished more of it than I really wanted.

The thoughtfulness was so like him. Yet he was otherwise very much changed. Before he roused himself for this gesture he had been absorbed in his own thoughts, chewing silently and without relish. I tried to make conversation but it was heavy going. I could no longer draw him into a discussion of politics. He had been so different in the hey-day of the new party, those short-lived days of heady optimism. I avoided mentioning the sale of the house, racking my brains for a neutral topic. Then I remembered the old gentleman I had met at a conference in Montreal last Fall.

'Uncle, do you remember a man named Paulus Hanna?'

'It's a fairly common name, dear. Give me the particulars.'

'He's the dean of the Egyptian Coptic community in Montreal. When he heard my surname he asked me if I were related to you. Then he told me how, in the years before the Revolution, when the Coptic community in Egypt was trying to build a church in a particular spot in downtown Cairo, they couldn't get anyone to sell them the land. So he – this Paulus Hanna – was delegated to speak to you about the problem. He says you were very sympathetic, and that you helped them out. I understood that you bought the land in your own name and then turned it over to them for the church, is that what happened?'

'I don't remember the details, but I remember helping them to get their church. Even in those days, there was some intolerance. But nothing like the religious polarization which exists today.'

Imposing new churches figured prominently now in

221

the cityscape of downtown Cairo, a legacy of Sadat's years of *rapprochement* with the West. But a rift had grown between the majority and minority religious communities in Egypt during those years. The backlash from the Islamic fundamentalists had been fierce.

More than a decade after Sadat's assassination, the fundamentalist menace loomed over the horizon like sandstorms in a perpetual *Khamaseen* season. The parties of the opposition, both to the right and to the left, were effectively paralyzed by the threat of an Islamist takeover. No one dared rock the ship of state. The Pasha had the defeated shoulders of a man who was no longer so much concerned that his movement might not outlive him, as that he would outlive his movement.

Lamia, one hand on his arm, was telling him something in an urgent, insistent undertone. She seemed to be asking for a pension for some retired retainer. He nodded, but she persisted, trying to get him to commit to a specific sum. 'All right,' he muttered impatiently, 'I said I'd take care of it.'

Yet I could understand why he needed a woman around. The three place settings at table told it all. In the old days there would have been relatives, people from the party, journalists dropping in. Now there must have been days when he dined alone. How lonely this vast house must seem, echoing now with the footfalls of the brothers outlived, the ghosts of faithful companions mourned and fair weather friends flown away.

I was relieved when dinner was over. It had been a strain to try to keep up the semblance of a conversation. I wondered if it had been simply distraction on his part, or deliberate reserve because he thought my visit was connected to the sale of the house. He had not taken an

222

explicit position on this particular offer, but it was hard to see how it could be in his interest to support it.

I followed my uncle back to his bedroom. It was the same: piles of documents, newspapers and books neatly stacked on chairs, tables and dressers all around the huge high-ceilinged room with its panels of faded blue brocade on the walls.

'You know, it may look disorganized, but I can lay my finger on a letter or a clipping in a minute.' He settled in his club chair.

'Of course, I know.' It surprised me that he felt the need to justify anything to me; it occurred to me for the first time that he saw me differently now, a grown woman with the acquired glamor of a life abroad.

Fangali set the demitasse cups of Turkish coffee on the table in front of us. He brought the telephone round to the end table within reach of the Pasha and left, closing the door behind him. Lamia had retired to the adjoining room.

I showed my uncle a clipping of an article in a French newspaper mentioning the party, and a letter from the Moroccan ambassador, whom I had met in Washington the summer before, asking me to send his best regards to the Pasha. He was visibly pleased.

He lit a cigar carefully. 'So tell me, Gigi, how are you finding things here in Egypt?'

I talked about this and that, about Tante Zohra's failing health, about the police sweeps on the bridges at night. He probed gently and I realized that he was trying to find out if there was something I needed from him, some special favor, some intercession. It saddened me.

'Uncle, I know you must be tired. I have to be going. Can I take a photo of you before I go?'

223

'Well, I'm hardly dressed for the occasion,' he protested.

'That's all right, it's just a souvenir for me.'

He straightened up and turned down his collar and allowed himself to be photographed, unsmiling. The first time Luc had seen photos of my family at engagements and weddings he had commented on how glum everyone looked. 'Only in photos,' I had explained.

I made my way down the sweeping staircase, sliding my hand along the cold marble banister till it rested on the head of the griffon at the bottom. I sneaked a quick photo of the shadowy hall, knowing the flash would be completely inadequate to light its expanse. I would have liked to turn on the lights in the monstrous crystal chandeliers, to photograph the marble staircase, to unlock the double doors to the salon on one end of the hall and the dining room on the other.

I thought of all the weddings and the laughter, the funerals and the tears, the politics and the intrigue, the passion and promise this house had known. The murmurs and the shouts, the song and the prayer, now all silenced.

I heard the trilling zaghrutas and the drumbeats of the scores of zaffas that had made their way down this same double staircase over the years. I thought of the generations of flower girls tossing thin gilded coins, growing into maids of honor carrying long white tapers, and finally, in their turn, bashful brides carrying bouquets. I had been one of these ghosts in white.

In my mind I conjured photos of my parents' wedding and those of other relatives. Against that very marble pillar the legendary singer Om Kalthoum had stood, belting out song after song in her powerful voice as the nights of celebration wore on.

I thought of all the feast days, year after year, when

224

the double doors were left open from morning to night to welcome guests, and of the shiny new coins children were given for good luck.

I thought of these same doors left open from morning to night to receive mourners when there had been a death in the family. I heard once more the blind fikki's resounding voice reciting the familiar, haunting verses from the Koran, the day my father was buried.

I heard the footfalls, heavy or furtive, triumphant or urgent, of the men who had once hurried to gather behind the closed doors of the study to discuss matters of state with my uncle. I thought of the Pasha holding court in this house, in power or out of it, in the limelight or as an eminence grise in the shadows; of the princes in their sweeping abayas who paid informal visits after dark and the opposition leaders who came secretly through the back door.

I remembered the day my uncle announced the formation of his new party, and the optimism and the trepidation with which we greeted a new dawn that was to prove so short-lived. I remembered, only two years later, standing on this very spot in the hall, leaning against my uncle's bergère as he made the announcement that he was dissolving the party. I remembered the assembled press, the power cables winding around the bases of the thick rose marble columns, the cameras and the lights in my eyes. I remembered making a slip of the tongue, and my uncle's affectionate gesture to cover up for it. Odd to think that Luc had been standing there at that moment, somewhere behind the lights. Could the Gigi leaning against her uncle's chair that day ever have imagined that her life would one day be intertwined with that of this stranger?

225

I wished that my inadequate camera could capture these halls, these walls that had seen so much history. I wanted to commit to memory this house that I might never see again. It was the last private home in this row of houses that had once belonged to friends and relatives and had now been turned into embassies, one after the other. One day soon I would only be able to drive past the Cairo house, and it would be flying a foreign flag.

17

Tamer

'So, what did you do today?' Tamer leaned back in his chair and pushed away his bowl of creamy yoghurt. We were having *sohour* at the Gezira Club in the glass-enclosed restaurant. The restaurant served a traditional, home-style *sohour*, rounding it off with thick, fresh yoghurt and the ubiquitous *Om Ali* served in individual earthenware ramekins.

'I went to see the Pasha in Garden City.'

'How is he?'

'Older. Detached. It was depressing. How's Tante Zohra?'

'Dear old Nana. Her body may be failing but her spirit is holding up, thank God. Whenever I go see her the first thing she asks me is if I've heard any new jokes. She likes the political jokes best but I throw in some off-color ones because it makes her sit up and pretend to be angry with me.' He lit a cigarette. 'Have you seen Tarek yet?'

'No, he's still in Hurghada. He'll be back tomorrow. I can't wait to sound him out about going to college in the States next fall. I just hope he'll want to go.'

227

'How does Luc feel about that?'

The mention of Luc took me aback. No one else had asked me about him since my arrival; it was as if I weren't married. I was used to that while I was in Cairo. The fact that I was always introduced and referred to by my maiden name was perfectly natural, since in Egypt even married women go by their maiden name.

I debated my answer. I had mentioned my plan to Luc, just before I left, but more in passing, to make sure he would have no objections. It had been a long time since I had felt the need to discuss anything with him in order to make up my mind. 'Well, I'm sure he doesn't have any objections. I mean, of course I told him about it, but we haven't actually discussed the details. It's not as if Tarek's agreed yet, or Yussef.'

'Uh-huh.'

'Wouldn't it be wonderful, though? Especially if Tarek went to college at the university in town, so he can live at home – or if he insists on living on campus, at least he could be home every weekend. I've missed him so much.'

'You never thought of having another child? With Luc?'

'No.' I avoided his eyes.

'What do you do with yourself all day? I mean, it sounds like you live in a pretty remote place.'

'It is. I'm working on a dissertation, I volunteer a fair amount, I do some cross-country skiing in the woods nearby . . . ' I shrugged. 'Look, I think the waiter is trying to hint that they're closing.'

The restaurant was nearly deserted. The waiter was pulling down the shades and turning the chairs upended on the tables.

'Yeah, let's go.'

228

The night air was chilly outside. The trees were rustling in the breeze. We got into the car.

'What would you like to do?' he asked.

'I don't know – park somewhere and talk?'

'Not in this country, Gigi, you've forgotten. The vice squad would be on top of us in a minute. But I know lots of places we can go that are open till dawn.'

'No, I'd rather not be seen out in public so late.'

'I can drive around. I can drive around for hours, you know. Or we could go to my place.'

'All right.'

Tamer had an apartment in a newish building with a florist and newspaper stand in the lobby, both closed at that hour. As we passed the doorkeeper on our way to the elevator the man looked up and saluted. The elevator stopped with a hiccup at the sixth floor. The apartment wasn't big but it had a rare view of the Nile. I headed straight to the balcony and leaned out, looking down at the broad expanse of black water, the boats bobbing in the marina of the Yacht Club, and further down the house-boats and showboats anchored at their docks. The brightly lit hotels and high-rises with neon advertisements winking on the roof lined the far shore. The headlights of cars glimmered as the traffic looped up and around the bridges and overpasses of the Sixth of October Bridge like a gigantic Ferris wheel. Cairo at night acquired a glamor it lacked in the dusty, clamorous, congested hours of daylight.

Tamer came and stood beside me. I shivered and rubbed my arms. He took off his coat and put it around my shoulders. I leaned forward on the balcony railing, taking in the lights on the river, the smell of the night air. There is a distinctive quality of light specific to certain places,

229

as artists and photographers have always known. But for me there was a quality to the air, too, especially at night; I thought I would recognize the night air in Cairo always.

I realized what I missed most in the small town in New Hampshire I have called home for ten years now. I could never feel at home in a landlocked place without a great river or a sea, a waterfront. There was no hub, there was no point of orientation; there was no 'there' there.

'It's strange, it feels as if I'd never gone away.' I drew the coat closer around me. 'You know, when I left New Hampshire, it was under two feet of snow. I can't believe I have to go back in a couple of weeks.'

'Then don't.'

I looked up at him quickly. He knew I had not been thinking of the weather.

'I have to.'

'Why? It doesn't sound like you have much to go back to.'

'But don't you see? I have to.'

'You've made your bed, you have to lie in it? Is it because of what people might say?'

I shook my head and turned back to the apartment. It was furnished in an eclectic style with Bedouin rugs on the floors and exotic woven fabrics draped across the windows, long plush sofas against the walls and Moorish, tooled-leather camp chairs. The total effect, with the brick red and warm brown tones, the moody lighting, suggested the inside of a Bedouin tent. It couldn't have been more deliberately different from the Louis-Seize-style, Aubusson, gilt salons with which we had both grown up.

I fingered the heavy, supple fabric of the draperies. The design was striking, vaguely suggestive of palm trees swaying in a sandstorm, but too stylized to pin down.

230

'I like this, it's very original; it feels hand-woven.'

'It is. It was made at my factory in the village.'

'Really? Is that one of the things you export?'

He explained that it was a sort of side-business: he had built a small factory on a plot of his father's land near Lake Fayyoum. The local villagers – women, mostly – did the weaving on hand-looms according to his designs and the specifications of the importer. He had a partner in Milan – who I guessed must be his ex-wife – who distributed the fabrics to select interior designers in Europe, to be used for draperies, decorator cushions, rugs, shawls, bed linen.

'Sounds like a great idea.'

'Well, I don't know if it's going to be a success, but at least it provides work for the villagers. And I'm glad I was able to start a project that involves exporting from Egypt, rather than importing. Everybody is importing like crazy, no one's exporting.' Tamer closed the French doors to the balcony. 'Shall I put on some music? What are you in the mood for?'

'Anything.'

Eric Clapton moaned about 'Layla, you've got me on my knees, Layla'.

'What would you like to drink?'

'A liqueur if you have it.'

'Sure.'

He moved to the bar at the other end of the room and I followed. It was well stocked. I wondered if he had a lot of flight attendant friends to keep him supplied.

Drink in hand, I crossed the room and sat down on an overstuffed leather cushion. He came over and crouched beside me. Just then the phone rang.

Tamer jumped up and answered, pacing behind me,

231

speaking in upbeat but impatient monosyllables. I shifted on the pouf, and was suddenly aware of his eyes on my back.

He put the phone down and came back.

'Got to go to the office early tomorrow to send a fax to the company in Milan.'

'You sound pretty busy.'

'On top of my own import-export business, and this sideline, there's my dad's land to run, and I take care of some business for Nana Zohra too.'

'Have you heard about the offer for the house?'

'Yes, I have. What do you –' A beeper went off on his watch and he pushed a button to silence it. 'I didn't realize it was this late. I call Mother in Lebanon every night before I go to bed. You know about Mother?'

'Yes. I'm so sorry.'

'Lately she's not been conscious most of the time, but I call anyway to ask the staff how she's doing. I try to call every night before I turn in, since she took sick, a year ago. But I'm so busy sometimes, I might forget. So I set the beeper on my watch.'

I wondered if his father had had a similar system to remind himself to call his children when they were little.

'Excuse me a minute.' Tamer got up and put through a brief phone call to Lebanon. I gathered he spoke to the hospital staff, not to Gina.

'How is she?' I asked.

He shook his head. 'Under morphine. She's suffering so much, you know.'

'Poor Gina. The last time I saw her was at Papa's funeral. But I remember her the way she used to be when I was a child.' She had always seemed so gay and lively then, with that quick, bird-like way about her. 'And your father

232

– he had the most charming smile of any man I ever met. I remember thinking that, and feeling disloyal to my own Papa!'

'You know, I think my dad never stopped loving her. He wouldn't speak of her, but he wouldn't let anyone say a bad word about her in his presence.'

I remembered the day Gina left for Lebanon, the day she came to our house to say goodbye. I had been fourteen at the time. I had watched from the balcony as she arrived in the Lebanese playboy's sports car. He had stayed in the car; a gold bracelet on his wrist glinted as he tapped his fingers on the side-view mirror. I remembered the look on Papa's face as Gina came towards him, arms outstretched. I remembered thinking at the time that I could never bear to disillusion my father that way. Did Gina give a thought that day to the adolescent girl watching from the corner? Do we ever realize what a far-flung web we weave by our actions? But there was no way anyone could have imagined then that Gina's story would lie like a palimpsest under the dynamics between a man and a woman twenty years later.

I turned to Tamer.

'Tamer – can I ask you a question? I've never been able to ask you this; you were such a porcupine when you were a boy. Did you ever forgive your mother for leaving like that?'

He grimaced. 'It's not a question of forgiveness. Who is it who said, to understand everything is to forgive everything? When I was eleven, I admit I didn't understand. But when you get older, you accept your parents for what they are. They're human, they have their own lives to lead, their own happiness to try to seize. You just learn

233

not to count on anyone being around forever, that's all.'

'Is that why –' I wondered if that was the reason he had found it so hard to make commitments in his own relationships with women, his short-lived marriages.

'Why what?'

'Never mind.'

'Why what?'

'Why you never had any children, in either of your two marriages?'

'Maybe. Maybe I couldn't guarantee that *I* would be around forever.'

I bit my lip. I hadn't been around forever for Tarek either.

Tamer put down his glass. 'Now it's my turn. I've wanted to ask you something for a long time too. Your marriage to Yussef. There was no connection between you at all; I remember that day in Alexandria.' He looked at me. 'Why did you agree to marry him, Gigi? I've always wondered that.'

No one had asked me that question before. Over the years, I had asked it of myself. But I had no real answer. I had lost the key to the thoughts and emotions of the girl of eighteen walking her dog on the beach at Agami. Except perhaps that she was tired of waiting for life to begin. I thought of that day, so long ago now, of the two adolescents licking their *granita* ices by the sea wall in Alexandria: a girl who had learned to be unquestioning and accepting in order to spare the adults who thought they were shielding her, and a boy who had learned not to count on anyone being around forever. They were long gone. But now, for the first time, when Tamer asked me that question, I had an answer.

'I married Yussef because I was expected to,' I finally admitted.

234

'I guessed that. You always did what you were expected to do.'

'That's true. Not that anyone put any pressure on me. Papa would never do that. I still miss him, you know. Do you remember the day of Papa's funeral, you were the first one to come in the morning, and you didn't even have a black tie to wear?'

'I loved Uncle Shamel. I don't think I cried over anyone's death, before or since, except for my own dad.'

'Papa loved you too. He told me once he saw Gina in you – more than in Leila. Leila is more like your father.' I looked at the vista from the window. 'You know, Tamer, it was my fault, in a way.'

'What was?'

'I know he had a bad heart, but it wasn't just that. He seemed to have given up, at the end, to have lost his will to live. I was so wrapped up in my problems with Yussef, I didn't see it. It was making him sick, the whole ugly situation. He felt so helpless. It killed him.' I had never admitted that to anyone before. I turned away so he would not see my face twist and the tears running down.

'No, Gigi, it wasn't anyone's fault. Hey, come here.'

He took me by the elbows and drew me down off the leather cushion and onto his lap. I shook my head but he held me tight and I relaxed against him. It felt like coming home. He kissed me on the temple, the cheek, the corner of the mouth, the neck. His hands pressed up and down my back.

'No, Tamer.'

'Okay. Okay. Only listen for a minute, will you? I have something to tell you, only I have to hold your hand while I say it.'

235

I drew away and sat back on the cushion, leaving my hand in his.

'Gigi, listen. I think I've always been in love with you. When I was twenty I had a crush on you I didn't know what to do with. When you left for France like that, all of a sudden – I thought my heart was broken. But it started before that. Long before. You were the first girl I ever noticed. Do you remember that dress you had, it was orange, with crisscross straps, and you were twirling round and round in it, and it made the skirt flare up and out?'

'You remember that dress? My apricot sun dress I first wore that day in Agami? I'd forgotten all about it. How can you remember that dress? You were so young!'

'I remember a lot of things.'

He did. And there, before the window, he made me a gift of his memories, a gift I trusted.

When he drove me home an hour later, the streets were deserted. The city's frantic pace seemed to be muted to a hum. It was nearly four o'clock in the morning, the rare dead hour during the month of Ramadan: *sohour* revelers had gone to bed and the call for dawn prayers would not wake the devout for another hour.

'I'm so late!' I fretted.

'Don't worry, I'll get you home in no time.'

He drove easily, with one hand on the wheel, his other hand holding mine. I felt my palm tingle. I looked around at the loops of the fantastic Ferris wheel over the black water. He ran the red lights, there was very little traffic and no traffic police. In a few minutes we had crossed this city of twelve million souls.

Tamer parked in front of the gate to the villa. The dog came padding swiftly to the gate. Recognizing me, he didn't bark.

'Don't get out,' I warned Tamer. I drew my hand out of his. I felt cold, suddenly.

I managed to unlock the gate without too much trouble but once I slipped inside the dog was all over me, silently jumping onto my shoulders and licking my face. I tried to put the padlock back on the gate but he reared up and planted both paws on my chest, making me drop my handbag and the padlock.

Tamer stepped out of the car. The dog went ballistic, barking and snarling. Ibrahim came hurrying, winding his turban around his head. I waved Tamer on and he drove away.

'Why didn't you ring the bell or call me?' Ibrahim grumbled.

'I told you I'd get in on my own. It's just this silly dog who had to bark.'

'Was that Tamer Bey's car?'

I ignored his curiosity. It was not impertinence on his part; it was his job to keep abreast of goings and comings. He was accountable to the other doorkeepers in the neighborhood for the good name of the household.

'Oh, Ibrahim, there were bits of rubbish around the garbage cans again. Some kind of animal must be getting in there and prying off the lids. Maybe you should put some rat poison in there.'

He shook his head in his most obtuse Nubian way, and I wasn't sure whether he had not understood me or whether he disagreed with me. I sighed and went upstairs. I lay down on my bed, too tired and too wound up to sleep.

18

Tarek

I still couldn't sleep through the night. If it were just jet lag, it would have worn off by now. Sometimes I fell asleep for an hour or two, then I found myself stark awake. I lay there in bed for hours, trying to fall asleep again, or I gave up and turned on the light to read. By dawn, when the city came alive, I finally dropped off to sleep.

The new moon was officially sighted last night. This morning was the first day of the Feast. I settled down by the phone to call the Pasha and Tante Zohra, promising to come by later and wish them a happy feast in person. Then I got up to dress. The phone rang.

'Mummy?'

'Tarek! Sweetheart, where are you?'

'Just got back from the Red Sea today.'

'Can you come right over? I miss you like crazy!'

It seemed like hours before Tarek arrived. Finally he was at the door, and I pulled him into the apartment.

'Let me look at you!'

In the year and a half since I had last seen Tarek he had grown tremendously, and there were no traces now of the little boy in this six-foot, lanky sixteen-year-old. His dark hair was cropped short, and he was very tan from the beach. There was a fine shadow on his upper lip. I felt my heart turn over.

I sat him down on the sofa beside me, resisting the impulse to try to pull him onto my knees. His breath smelled of chewing gum, as it always had since he was a little boy.

'So, tell me what you've been doing!'

'Well, it was great to have a break at the beach, because I have to work really hard this year; I sit for my baccalaureate exams in June.'

'I know. Have you thought about college yet? You could go to college in the States!'

'In America? I hadn't thought about that! Anyway let's see how I do on my exams first.'

'Of course. We'll talk about it later. Everything all right at home?' Even before Mama had died, Tarek had divided his time between his father's home and his grandmother's. But I knew how much he must miss Mama.

'It's all right. Papa nags me a bit about studying, but he's okay. I get along all right with Tante Mervat, she leaves me alone. Would you believe she's started wearing a scarf over her head, off and on, since she went to Mecca for the pilgrimage last year? She wears it during Ramadan, anyway.'

'Really?' I had never met Mervat, Yussef's second wife. They had been married for eight years now, and had a little girl. 'How old is your little sister now?'

'Zeina's six. She's a pest, Zin-Zin, she clings to me like molasses. But she's cute.'

239

I looked at my watch. It was almost two o'clock.

'Listen, sweetheart, let's call your father, I need to wish him a happy feast, and I also need to talk to him about other things. Isn't it great that we have the whole day together to do whatever we want? But lunch first. You must be hungry. Where would you like to eat? We could go to the club? I need to renew my membership dues anyway. Or to a proper restaurant? Anywhere at all, you choose.'

'McDonald's.'

'McDonald's?'

'Yeah, a new McDonald's concession just opened in Mohandesseen last week. All my friends went to the opening; they say there was an unbelievable crowd, you couldn't park for blocks and blocks around. But I was away at the Red Sea, so I haven't been yet.'

'McDonald's it is then! Let's go.'

The phone rang and I jumped up to grab it; Tarek was asleep in the next room and I didn't want it to wake him. The ring had warned me that it was a long distance call. It was Luc.

'*Âllo*? Gigi? Did I wake you?'

'No, no, it's only eleven o'clock. But Tarek's asleep in the next room.'

'So he's staying with you in the apartment?'

'Well, only tonight, tomorrow he has to go back to his father's because school starts after tomorrow. But I'll see him some evenings and next weekend he'll spend with me.'

'Did you discuss college in the States with him?'

'I brought it up and he seemed open to the idea, but I didn't want to get into it till I speak to Yussef.'

240

'When do you see him?'

'Tomorrow evening. I spoke to him on the phone and explained that I needed to talk to him about Tarek. Yussef suggested I join him and his wife and some friends at a restaurant for dinner. We'll see. So, how are you?'

'Fine. We've had some very heavy snowfall so I called the guy with the end loader to come clear it off the driveway and the paths. Janet Glasser called. You'll never guess what she wanted! Your number in Cairo! She said she'd nominated you to head the refreshments committee for the Faculty Women's Club, and thought she should check with you so you wouldn't be mad at her.'

'Oh! Well, then I guess I'm stuck with it. I'm surprised she'd want to call just about that, though. Anyway, did you remember to pay the credit card bills?'

'No, I'm glad you reminded me, I'll do that tonight. Where are the statements, on your desk?'

'In the red folder in the second drawer on the right.'

'Okay. Well, everything else all right? I'll call you next week around the same time.'

I hung up. It had been an effort to concentrate on these details. It all seemed so far away, another world. Here and now felt like reality. I checked in on Tarek. He was sleeping, his back to me. I gave him a light kiss on the nape. I felt like a child with a longed-for new toy who has to take it out of the wrapping every few minutes to look at it, not quite believing it's finally really hers.

I went to the phone and called Tamer. His home number didn't answer. I tried the office number. He picked up right away.

'Hey!'

'Working late?'

'No later than usual. So, what have you been up to?'

241

'Actually I'm supposed to meet Yussef, his wife, and some friends of his for dinner tomorrow night at Le Pasha. I feel awkward going on my own. Can you come with me?'

He hesitated a minute. 'Sure. No problem. What time shall I pick you up?'

'Yussef said to meet at nine.'

'Then I'll pick you up just before nine.'

'Good! Thanks, Tamer.'

That night I fell asleep around midnight but woke up again at dawn. I heard the faint rumbling of the donkey carts growing fainter. The garbage collectors had come and gone again. I wondered if Ibrahim had put the poison in the cans. I lay there, trying to go back to sleep.

19

The Restaurant

Tamer arrived at fifteen past nine. 'Sorry, I got caught up at the office. Relax, no one arrives on time in Egypt anyway. You've forgotten.'

I glanced at his profile as I sat next to him in the car. He looked different, somehow, and I realized it was the gold frame glasses he was wearing.

'Since when do you wear glasses? Let me see.' I reached for them and he let me have them with a smile. I tried them on. As I suspected, the prescription was so weak I could hardly notice a difference.

'These are just for show, aren't they? To impress clients?' He didn't answer but I guessed that he'd worn them tonight to look older, for me.

'So, you've been working hard?'

'Yeah. Well, except last night, of course, being the feast. Some friends dragged me off to a party. It was a disaster. I got hit on by two women who were belly dancing – not my type! And two guys – definitely not my type!'

243

We drove along the Nile and parked by the embankment across the street from the Gezira Sporting Club, where a houseboat which had been converted into a restaurant was anchored. The strings of lights swayed slightly as the boat bobbed on the water. We walked up the gangplank and a smiling security officer perfunctorily patted down Tamer. He did the same with the other male customers as they came on board, but let me and the other women pass unchecked. Since the restaurant was frequented by tourists, which could make it a target for terrorists, the management was taking precautions, although apparently inadequate ones. The maitre d'hôtel led us downstairs. The large dining room was reasonably busy; there was an even mix of tourists and Cairenes.

At a table by the window we saw Yussef, Mervat and the Sirdanas. As Yussef stood up to greet us I noticed his hair was even greyer at the temples than the last time I had seen him, but he was still as slim. His smile was reserved. 'Hello, Gigi. Hi, Tamer. Haven't seen you in a while.'

I shook hands and turned to his wife. Tarek had warned me she might be wearing a head scarf; she was actually wearing a sort of loose, crocheted snood which left most of her smooth black hair exposed; it seemed to serve the purpose of a token more than anything else. Apart from that she was wearing a stylish turquoise ensemble and somewhat too much jewelry. She stared at me with large, carefully made-up eyes, a flicker of hostility behind the curiosity. It surprised me.

Bassil Sirdana was standing up, smiling. 'Hello, Gigi! It's been a long time.'

Since I had last seen him in Jedda his smile had gained the expansiveness of success. I had heard that he had

244

made a fortune in the Gulf States and in *Infitah* Egypt; he now spent the Fall shooting and hunting at a manor in the Cotswolds, the summers at Marbella and the winters in a villa in Garden City.

'It's so good to see you again.' Mona gave me a peck on the cheek. She still wore her auburn hair in a sweep down to her shoulders, but she had put on quite a bit of weight.

We sat down and the waiter brought the menus. While we debated what to order he set down the *mezze*, a dozen small dishes of appetizers. I could never resist them, even at the cost of being too full to enjoy the grilled lamb kebab I ordered as a main course.

Bassil and Mona showed me photos of their two sons, who were a little younger than Tarek. Mervat showed pictures of their little girl; she was cute but already ominously plump around the jowls.

The conversation turned to politics, as it inevitably does in Egypt, perhaps because the weather is too invariable to offer an alternative. Bassil was optimistic.

'I don't foresee any major upheavals in the next four years. I don't think investors have anything to worry about in the immediate future, and in the meantime, with the privatizations, there are some real killings to be made on the stock exchange.'

'Four years!' Yussef scoffed. 'Anything can happen in four years.' He didn't need to elaborate; since the Revolution, succession of the heads of State had followed one path: death by natural causes or assassination. It was generally suspected that there were more foiled attempts on Mubarak's life than the press reported.

'Yussef, you never change your tune. Remember how you kept insisting the Egyptian pound would drop in a

245

free fall against the dollar? It's held its own for years.'

'You know how I've heard the Egyptian economy described?' I piped in. 'This was by an economist at Dartmouth University who is an expert. He said it was like watching a man walk on water. You wonder how it's done and how long he can keep it up.'

'Well, it's not going to keep up much longer,' Yussef insisted. 'What with the tourists scared away.'

Conversation was interrupted while we were served.

'Cheers!' Bassil raised his glass. He had ordered wine for himself and Mona, and Tamer had ordered a beer. I had mineral water in order not to give Yussef and his wife, neither of whom drank, ammunition against me.

'Well, here's to time. How it flies!' Bassil took a sip. 'It seems like only yesterday we had dinner together in Jedda!'

'When did you leave Saudi?' I asked.

'Mona and the boys moved back to Egypt eight years ago, when the boys started school. We also bought a home in England. But I shuttled back and forth till the Gulf War started. We got out just in time!'

Mona spread her napkin on her lap. 'Can you imagine what the sight of American women G.I.s in shorts and T-shirts must have looked like to the Saudis? I mean, in a society as puritanical as that? I remember the imported magazines at the newsstands with half the pages ripped out by the censors. And the difficulties smuggling in liquor! Some of our expat friends even resorted to making their own – with Welch's grape juice and tea for tannin – horrible stuff!'

The waiter brought the main course, and for a few minutes conversation was interrupted.

'Bon appétit!' Bassil turned to me. 'How long will you be staying in Cairo, Gigi?'

246

'Not very long, just a couple of weeks.'

'That's a pity. The country house we're building in Mansouriya will be ready in a month or so, and we were planning our first party there. We would have loved to have you come.'

'So would I, it must be lovely.' I had heard that they were building a splendid mansion on a large estate an hour away from Cairo, complete with Moorish courtyard, swimming pool, tennis courts, Japanese gardens and English rolling lawns. Full-grown trees had been imported from Japan and from England.

'The biggest challenge has been draining the marshes to get rid of the mosquitoes. That's one problem our landscape engineer hadn't had to deal with before! He's English.'

'He's expensive,' Mona complained. 'You can imagine what it's costing us to put him up in a first class hotel for the past two years. But he's worth it. You should see the Japanese bridges over the lily-ponds. And I have my own secret garden just outside the bay window of the Jacuzzi.'

'A window around the hot tub? Aren't you concerned someone might look in?' I asked. 'What about the *fellahin*?'

'We don't have any *fellahin* on the complex. They aren't allowed inside the walls. The staff and the gardeners are all Filipino. Besides, we're planting tall bamboo all around the little garden, so it forms a natural screen.'

'I see.' This was a different world from that I remembered as a child, when visits to the country estate were circumscribed by the precautions taken to accommodate the sensibilities of the *fellahin*.

Mona started to discuss the children's schools with

247

Mervat. 'Bassil is thinking of sending our boys to boarding school in England, he's not happy with the schools here. Of course it's different from the old days when he attended the Jesuit School. What do you think, Gigi?'

'I really don't know.' I was trying to listen to the conversation between the men.

'Well, I think it's a scandal,' Tamer was saying.

'What is?' I asked.

'There's this professor at Cairo University, a professor of law, I think, who wrote a critical book on Islam. I don't know exactly what he says because I haven't been able to get hold of a copy. A pirated copy, I mean, because the book is banned, as you can imagine. Anyway some theologians at the Azhar read it and decided it was heresy and pronounced him an apostate. He's Muslim, of course. Then they took him to court and – get this – they tried to get the courts to rule his marriage to his wife invalid, on the basis that he is an apostate and a Muslim woman can't stay married to a heretic!'

'I don't understand. It's his wife that wants a divorce?'

'Not at all. She's adamant that she wants to stay married to him. They've been married twenty years and have children. But these clerics insist on a divorce against the wishes of both the husband and the wife.'

'Can they do that?'

'Apparently they're trying!'

'But they've no right to do that. That's awful.'

'You don't know what he wrote,' Yussef objected.

'That's right,' Mervat agreed. 'There are limits. You don't know what he wrote.'

'It shouldn't matter, should it?' I was aghast at their reaction. 'It's the principle of the thing.'

'You've been away too long, Gigi,' Bassil smiled.

248

'There's no such thing as freedom of opinion here.'

'The only way to fight that is to keep testing the limits over and over,' Tamer countered.

'You can't have freedom of opinion here. Free speech is a luxury in a country like Egypt. Who do you think would take advantage of it? The extremists. The fundamentalists.'

'Let them, as long as the moderates get into the arena as well and fight it out. The problem is that too many people have a vested interest in the status quo, they don't want to rock the boat.'

The band struck up on the dais at the front of the restaurant, announcing the first of the nightclub acts for the evening. For the occasion of the Feast the restaurant was putting on special entertainment. A male singer in a tuxedo stepped up to the mike and started belting out Arabic pop songs. The volume effectively put an end to all conversation across the table.

The singer wrapped up his number with a grand flourish. There were a few minutes of merciful quiet while the next act, a belly dancer, was getting ready. The conversation between Mona and Mervat had moved from children's schools to the relative merits of Filipina maids as opposed to Egyptians. Tamer was lighting a cigarette; Bassil had gotten up to make a phone call. I took the opportunity to broach the subject of Tarek's schooling with Yussef.

'Tarek looks great! He's grown so much. He seems happy.' I wanted to preempt putting Yussef on the defensive by letting him see that my plan to take Tarek to the States was in no way prompted by feeling that he was unhappy with his father and stepmother.

'There's no reason why he shouldn't be.'

249

'No, of course.' I tried a different tack. 'He adores his little sister. She's called Zeina after your mother, isn't she? How are your parents?'

'Mother is well. Papa had a stroke a few years ago but is still going strong. He's amazing for his age.' There was the familiar note of admiration in his voice when he mentioned his father.

'Well, give both of your parents my best.'

'I will. Have you been to see your uncle yet?'

'Yes, I had *iftar* with him.'

'Was that woman there?'

'You mean Lamia El-Salem? Yes.'

'Did he mention the sale of the house to you?'

'No, the subject didn't come up.' I realized the connection. 'It's your father who's involved in the sale, isn't it?'

'That's right. He's representing a buyer with a very good offer. It's not likely to be repeated. I hope your family sees the advantage in selling now. But with that woman influencing your uncle, there's no telling what he'll do. Any time a man his age allows a woman to influence him like that, it can affect his judgement.'

Yussef always tended to blame the woman in any situation – *cherchez la femme*. It occurred to me that he really didn't like women. In the early days of our marriage the naive child I had been had not understood about men like that, physically passionate but with a deep-seated distrust of women. It had confused and chilled me.

I wondered who the prospective buyer might be. An embassy? A private party? Bassil Sirdana, even? That would be ironic. I looked across the table at Bassil and Mona. How time had passed since I had last seen them. How my situation had changed. I was the outsider now.

Memories of my stay in Jedda passed through my mind.

250

Prince Bandar serving me a chunk of lamb with his hands. Emira Khadija and her jewelry catalogues. Om Khalil and her red suitcase at Jedda airport.

'Yussef, do you remember Om Khalil and her red suit-case in Jedda?'

Yussef laughed. I caught Mervat giving me a look. I wanted to reassure her that there was nothing between Yussef and me to cause her concern. That the memories of Jedda, all the memories, were as impersonal as if they had happened to someone else. That the man sitting across the table from me was as much a stranger as if we had never been intimate, never had a child together. That I was sure it was the same for him. I had learned that after a relationship was over, after the passion or the acrimony have burned off, only the essential residue remains. Yussef and I had never liked each other; the residue was a lingering wariness and defensiveness. With Luc, it would be different; we would keep a fundamental respect and affection for each other. The thought had sneaked into my mind before I was aware of it. It shocked me to catch myself thinking of my marriage to Luc as if it were a thing of the past. For a moment I couldn't breathe.

The belly dancer had launched into her first number, tossing her hair and clicking her castanets. She was wearing the traditional costume, a sequined silver bikini with a filmy salmon-pink slit skirt. We all sat back and watched. I recognized her face from posters and adver-tisements for shows at the major hotels all over town. It was Fifi `Abdu. She arched her back, her long brown hair whipping her hips as she jiggled her breasts from side to side. The dancer worked the crowd, urging it to clap. The diners, including our table, obliged. The mood was partic-ularly festive after the long month of fasting. Although

251

there was nothing austere about Ramadan, even non-observant Muslims abstained, at least in public, from alcohol and belly-dancing shows.

Tamer had to talk straight into my ear for me to hear him above the din. 'Do you know she headed a delegation of belly dancers who went over to Israel as part of the cultural exchange program?'

'You're kidding!'

'No, seriously. There's this cultural exchange program between us and Israel, part of the so-called "normalization of relations", and belly-dancing was considered one of the distinctive performing arts in Egypt. A whole delegation of dancers just finished touring Israel.'

'And what did the Israelis send in return?'

'Agricultural experts in desert cultivation, I think.'

I laughed. But I thought it was ironic that belly-dancing seemed to be one thing the Islamists hadn't been able to ban, it was just too deeply entrenched.

With a deafening roll of the drums the dancer came to the end of the first number and withdrew to change her costume.

I leaned forward towards Yussef again. 'Have you thought about where Tarek will go to college?'

'Well, American University, I suppose. Then he can go to graduate school in England, as I did.'

'I was thinking he could go to college in the States.'

'He's too young.'

'He'll be seventeen next year. And I would be right there, I would be able to keep an eye on him. He could come home for all the holidays.'

'I don't know. It would be expensive.'

'Not necessarily. And I'd be glad to do my part. Especially if that sale goes through!' I leaned back. 'Anyway we've

252

got some time. Talk it over with Mervat.' I felt sure she would be in favor of the project, if only to get her stepson out of the house. On the other hand, I knew Yussef would not make up his mind without consulting his father, and Kamal Zeitouni was a hard nut to crack.

But I was counting on Mervat's influence even more. I could see that she had learned to handle Yussef. Under her self-effacing, pliant exterior I recognized the kind of relentless manipulativeness which nature and nurture combine in women like her. This subtle skill is learned at their mother's knee and reaches its apotheosis in the capture of the most eligible suitor possible. It is not abandoned in the aftermath. I was willing to wager that Mervat was one of those married women who called her mother every single day to discuss strategy: how to handle a husband's mood, how to confound a social rival, how to deal with the sudden reappearance of the ex-wife of one's spouse.

She need not have worried about me. Feminine wiles were one social skill which my parents had neglected to inculcate in me. Yet without it I had had no chance in a marriage with a man like Yussef. Mervat had succeeded where I had only butted my head against a blank wall. I was sure she had transformed him into a dutiful husband and a doting father, and that she had even managed to get into the good graces of her in-laws.

The dancer reappeared, in an even more provocative outfit: a gauzy black sheath completely slit from shoulder to ankle, held together at strategic points with rhinestone clasps. I looked at my watch. It was past midnight. I leaned over and whispered in Tamer's ear. 'Can we leave after this number?'

He nodded.

* * *

253

I stood on the sidewalk in front of the houseboat, waiting for Tamer to fetch the car. He had parked half a block away. Even at one o'clock in the morning the well-lit Nile embankment was far from deserted.

'Kleenex!'

The pedlar's cry caught my attention and I looked down. At my feet a beggar on a skateboard held up a box of tissues. His legs were bare puckered stumps below the knees. This was not a child, as many beggars were, but a grown man with a moustache and sharp, angry eyes. I fumbled around in my handbag, found a pound, dropped it in his lap without looking and hurried after Tamer.

I caught up with him as he was pulling out of his parking spot. He opened the door for me and gave me a sidelong glance as I slipped in beside him. 'Everything all right?'

I nodded but I was upset, not with the beggar but with myself for reacting to deformity as to blackmail. Many of these beggars were self-mutilated, or mutilated as children, in order to follow this profession. But what if the man were genuinely the victim of an accident? Should I have taken the box of tissues, at least allowing him to save face? The one trait I was most ashamed of was my squeamishness: the impulse to shrink from contact with deformity and desperation, as if they were contagious.

'What's wrong?' Tamer insisted.

'Oh, it's just – there was this beggar. A cripple, with no legs. That's what I'd forgotten about Egypt. The misery.'

'Beggars aren't the worst thing you could have.'

'How do you mean?'

'Think, Gigi. It was a beggar, not a mugger or a rapist. In the States it could have been.'

254

'That's true, but in the States you don't see misery like that!'

'You don't see it because you're buffered from it in a hundred and one ways. Would you have liked the doorman at the restaurant to have kept this beggar out of the way?'

'Of course not! Poor man.'

'Some people would like to crack down on beggars and peddlers. They think it's bad for business when tourists are exposed to disturbing encounters like that. They should get a controlled, packaged experience. Fly straight to Luxor or Hurghada and back out again.'

'I'm not talking about tourists. I'm talking about people like us. How can you enjoy life when you look around and see how most people live?'

'So which is better? To run away and live abroad or stay and try to make a difference?'

'I don't know, Tamer. Sometimes I wonder if there's any future here. Like the man walking on water. Or the dervish spinning. How long can they keep it up?'

255

20

Luxor

The phone ringing woke me the next morning. It was Janet Glasser.

'Hello, Gigi! Guess where I'm calling from? The Gezira Sheraton!'

'Really? That's wonderful! What are you doing in Cairo?'

'Well, I'm here for the symposium on Francophone writers – didn't I tell you about that? I presented my paper yesterday and the symposium ends today. Toussaint just flew in to Cairo today to join me.' Janet paused, clearly relishing the effect of her bombshell. 'I know this is rather sudden, but didn't you have at least an inkling about Toussaint and me?'

'No! Honestly.'

Apparently they had been seeing each other since his divorce, but had kept it very discreet in order to avoid the inevitable gossip in the department. But when he had decided to attend the symposium, they had seized the chance to take a trip together for the first time.

'I almost told you the night of your party, Gigi, when you mentioned you would be in Egypt around then. But we were interrupted. I knew I could trust you not to let it get out.'

'Of course, I won't tell a soul. So that's why you asked Luc for my phone number in Cairo!'

'Right! Although I did nominate you to head the refreshments committee, I didn't make that up.'

'We'll have to talk about that later. This is such a nice surprise! What would you like to see first in Cairo?'

'That's just it, we're flying to Luxor tonight for five days. Can you come down for a day or two?'

'I don't know. Anyway, wouldn't I be *de trop*? Isn't the whole point for the two of you to be alone together?'

'We'll have plenty of time for that, and it would be great fun to be together in Luxor.'

'I'll see what I can do. Where will you be staying?'

'The Luxor Palace. We're getting an incredible rate. I guess it's because there aren't many tourists this year.'

After she hung up I thought about it. I hadn't been to Upper Egypt since I was at school. I knew Tarek had been once, on a school trip, at the age of ten. I was suddenly very tempted to go. If Tarek came along, then I could have him to myself for a while, and I wouldn't feel like the proverbial third wheel around Toussaint and Janet.

I called Tarek.

'Darling, how about spending the weekend with me in Luxor? We could fly down on Friday morning and fly back Saturday evening.'

'Friday? But that's tomorrow, Mummy.'

'Right! Don't pack a lot of stuff, it's for one night only. Check with your father first, of course. I'll pick you up

257

around nine and we'll take the eleven o'clock flight. We'll be there a little after noon.'

Luxor. Already on the road from the airport to the hotel it is a different world. A world of primary colors: clear blue skies and clover-green fields, smiling dark faces and flapping white robes. I feel an instant release of tension and turn to look at Tarek. He smiles back at me.

The taxi pulls up in front of the Luxor Palace. In the lobby of the elegant turn-of the-century hotel, 'Dreaming of a White Christmas' is playing, an incongruous reminder of an American shopping mall. At the reception desk I need to provide identification to show that Tarek and I are related. Unrelated members of opposite gender are not supposed to share a room. I am reluctant to produce my American passport because I made the reservation as an Egyptian in order to take advantage of the lower rate for nationals. I succeed in convincing the receptionist that Tarek and I are indeed mother and son, and that he is only sixteen. There is a message from Janet and Toussaint that they will be back for dinner around eight. Tarek and I go up to our room and change into swimsuits for a quick dip in the pool before sundown.

The pool area is deserted but for a British family. The mother, lobster-pink in her bikini, is spread-eagled on a lounge chair. She has unhooked the strap of her top and when she raises her head to call to the two little boys in the pool she exposes more of her front than she realizes. Yet the waiter who serves her a drink seems oblivious. It occurs to me that this smiling Nubian with his serviceable English probably has a wife he keeps under close wraps at home. The natives of Upper Egypt seem blasé; it is nearly a century, after all, since their region became

258

a mandatory stop on the itinerary of the European on a world tour. The Englishwoman calls to the boys and the family go into the hotel, leaving the pool area deserted but for Tarek and me. The terrorist threat has effectively flushed the tourists out of the country and the few diehard foreigners who do come are bargain-hunters.

We take a last dip in the pool and wrap ourselves in the thick towels. We lie back on the lounge chairs and look out across the Nile at the west bank, the Valley of the Dead. Suddenly the sun dips behind a palm tree just as a felucca glides into view. The delicate sail and the palm fronds are silhouetted against the blood-orange orb for a breath-taking, postcard-perfect instant. Tarek jumps up.

'Quick! Where's the key? I want to get the camera.'

Even as he rushes upstairs to our room, towel around his shoulders, the felucca glides on past and the sun dips lower. I sigh. One day he will learn to enjoy the moment rather than to try to capture it. When he comes back to face a disappointing view I will console him with the promise that tomorrow we will be better prepared to take advantage of the minutes of magical light between the flat glare of full day and the swift dark of an Egyptian night. But since my return to Egypt I am beginning to realize myself that there never really is a tomorrow that repeats the lost moment of today. I draw the towel tighter around my shoulders as the temperature plummets with the abruptness peculiar to nightfall in southern deserts.

Saturday morning. The west bank is mercifully undeveloped; no hotels or restaurants, no cars but the few licensed taxis. Access is limited to the ferries or feluccas that shuttle back and forth from the east bank, that of the

259

living, to the west bank, that of the dead. Even the bridge that was expressly built for the duration of the presentation of Verdi's Aida at the Hatshepsut Temple in November has been dismantled.

The taxi we have hired for the day deposits us at the base of the plateau and the driver joins the other waiting taxi men. We stretch our legs in the cloudless sunshine. Janet is wearing dangling earrings and a caftan of the sort sold in souvenir shops; her new look suits her. Toussaint is wearing a hat, sun block, a video camera and the combative grin of the fearless adventurer. The objective of this preparedness becomes clear when he breaches the phalanx of souvenir stands selling everything from scarabs to sun visors.

Tarek stops at one of the stands to buy camera film and I move on with Toussaint and Janet. A few stands away the portly vendor holds out a display of scarabs. Toussaint is very business-like. He brings out a small wallet and makes a great show of displaying that it contains very little money.

'Look, this is all the money I have with me today. Now I'm only going to spend five pounds on souvenirs because after I pay for the tickets that's all I'll have left over. So if you can find me a scarab for five pounds, fine. If not, I'll try the next stand.'

'Look around, take your time, I'm sure we'll find something for you,' the man smiles under his moustache.

'Toussaint's been pulling the same trick in every souvenir shop we've been,' Janet whispers in my ear.

Tarek catches up with us and asks the vendor, in Arabic, the price of a tiny silver ankh, or key of life. I wonder if the pendant is destined for a girlfriend.

'For you, twenty pounds.' The vendor holds up the

260

case for Tarek and adds in an aside, nodding towards Toussaint: 'Have you seen this guy here? I'm giving him a special break, I swear to Allah, because he has two wives and seems to be hard up. Of course I have two wives myself but I can afford them. Not that I wouldn't give up both of mine for one of these *Frenjis*, especially the one with the shorter hair, she's like honey!'

'That's my mother!' Tarek snaps.

The man is sincerely embarrassed. 'Don't get me wrong, but how was I to know she was your mother? Did she understand me?'

I find all this amusing, and am a little surprised by Tarek's annoyance. Even at sixteen he already has the typical, male protective reflex towards a female relative. He was raised in Egypt, after all. It makes me aware of the distance the years have put between us.

Our first view of the Hatshepsut temple is disappointing, obscured as it is by the scaffolding and bleachers which have not been removed after the opera production in November. The approach to the funeral temple, designed to be an awe-inspiring ascent up broad steps and steep ramps, has been reduced to the backdrop for an opera set.

We wander around the temple, occasionally turning a corner to avoid a group of Japanese tourists who are the only visitors this morning. Janet has a book on the monuments of Luxor and reads out loud from it.

'Although Hatshepsut was known to be a woman, as Egypt's pharaoh she is portrayed in statues wearing a ceremonial fake beard held in place by loops over her ears . . . hmm, the equivalent of the modern power suit, I suppose.'

We have reached the top of the steps. Tarek aims the camera at the opposite shore.

'I can't get a clear view of the Karnak temple because of the scaffolding.' He gives up in disgust.

I reach for his hand and draw him down beside me.

'Bored?'

'No. But I'm just thinking that I've got a test to study for when I get back.'

'That reminds me. I need to get a transcript of your academic record to take with me when I leave. It's high time to start applying to colleges for the fall.'

'But I haven't even sat for my baccalaureate exams yet.'

'I know, but the system in the States is different.' I give him a hug. 'Everything is different. There's so much for you to do there, you'll love it.'

'You've never seen ice sculptures, have you?' Toussaint interposes with a smile. 'The college students in the town where we live have this competition, they build ice sculptures. Whole houses, cars, people! It's amazing. They make panes of 'glass' made of transparent sheets of ice.'

Janet and Toussaint disappear behind the columns. Tarek looks down at his feet and kicks up the dust.

'Mummy, I don't know.'

A minute ago I was warm, now I feel a chill.

'What do you mean?'

'I'm just not sure I want to go to the States. My friends are here, my life is here.'

'But you'll love it over there, you'll see. I miss you so much, darling. Don't you want us to be together at last?'

'Sure, Mummy, I miss you too. But I could come visit in summer. Maybe you could come here more often.'

'There you are.' Janet comes up behind us, still holding

262

her book. 'It says here that the architect who built this temple for Hatshepsut was her lover and the father of her children. Romantic, isn't it?' She realizes by my forced smile that she is interrupting something and wanders off again. I turn back to Tarek.

'But sweetheart, going to college there, it's for your own good, for your future.'

'I know. But I'm just not sure I'm ready yet. Maybe for my graduate degree, okay?'

Graduate degree. I groan. But I bite my lip and keep quiet. Perhaps I have been pushing too much, taking too much for granted. I have been treating him like a child with no mind of his own. I lean back, take a deep breath. I try not to sound as if the hope by which I have lived for ten years hangs on his decision. I will not blackmail him emotionally. I have no right.

'All I'm asking you to do is to keep an open mind about this, darling, all right? You don't have to make up your mind this minute. Okay?'

He nods, but he keeps his eyes on the ground.

Toussaint comes up, looking flushed and triumphant. 'They have these signs posted everywhere: "No video-taping or camera flashes in the tombs". But the guards just stand by and let you do as you like in exchange for bakshish. It's amazing!'

Janet consults her book. 'Do you know that Hatshepsut had this temple specifically built so that it would be in the direct line of the sun god Ra rising behind the Luxor temple? And now the view is obscured by all this scaffolding.'

'That's true,' I nod. 'Hatshepsut must be turning in her grave. If this sacrilege isn't enough to bring down the wrath of Ra, I don't know what is. Shall we head on down? You must be hungry, and I know Tarek is.'

263

As we make our way back through the persistent souvenir sellers and chirping children, Toussaint takes the lead. 'Here, let me go ahead. I know how to make these people scatter. *Yalla, imshi, yalla!*' He flourishes the wallet, open, upside down.

He is clearly relishing the role of great white tourist. I realize that he is the sort of person who revels in exotic travel for all the wrong reasons: it gives him the occasion to rise above his real-world self and to feel his existence justified merely as a member of a taller, fairer, finer, altogether superior race. I cannot decide which I wish to disassociate myself from more urgently: Toussaint's obnoxious sense of superiority, or the grinning vendors' lack of self-restraint which fuels it.

21

The Visit of Condolences

I have been in Cairo almost three weeks now, and my life has settled into something perilously resembling a routine. I still cannot sleep through the night. On the other hand I feel more alive than I have in years. Perhaps it's because I look forward to spending the weekends with Tarek, although the question of his plans for college remains unresolved. Perhaps it has to do with Tamer. I call him on the phone, late at night, and we talk. Sometimes we see each other.

Perhaps I can't sleep because I hear the time ticking away. It seems hard to believe that I will be going back to the States soon. I could just stay. It has happened that way before. Looking back, I realize that the sea changes in my life have been sudden, and that at the time I thought they would be temporary. Five years in England came to an abrupt end in three hours of packing. I received a phone call that Papa had had a serious heart attack and I grabbed Tarek and some clothes and headed for the airport. Papa recovered that time, but I stayed. There

265

seemed no point in going back to London when I had completed my studies and Yussef had nearly completed the work on his thesis.

When I left for France, I expected to be back in a few months. I never went back to Egypt to live. When Luc and I went to the States, it was with the idea of his accepting a temporary assignment as a correspondent. We ended up making New Hampshire our home, finding it easier to settle on territory that was neutral for both of us.

But there is nothing to hold me there. The past ten years seem like an interlude, a sharp zigzag in the flat line of experience, a detour around an insurmountable bump in the road. It's only when I think of Luc that I feel a pang; I am too fond of him to ever want to hurt him. We burned our bridges together. But we have led separate lives for a long time now; he would be all right without me. Perhaps I would even be setting him free to pick up the unraveled threads of his own life and weave them into a new pattern? Or am I only deluding myself to ease my conscience? But is it not my turn, now or never, to seize the fleeting chance of happiness? How can I give up what I have been looking for, waiting for, for so long? How can I leave, now that I feel I have come home?

In my life, endings and beginnings seem to be marked, not with a bang, but with a whimper. I know that it would be just as easy for me to stay in Egypt as to go back. The curse of the chameleon is that, once it has blended into a new environment, it cannot imagine itself anywhere else.

That Sunday I wouldn't be seeing Tarek, as he had a lot of studying to do. I thought of dropping in on Leila for lunch.

266

'Gigi darling! I was just wondering if you were coming. The driver went to fetch the girls from school half an hour ago, but with traffic as bad as it is, there's no telling how long they'll be. Come and tell me what you think of my new dress for this wedding next month. The dressmaker just sent it over, I haven't had a chance to try it on since she made the alterations.'

I followed Leila to her bedroom, and made myself comfortable on the chaise longue. She tried on a seashell grey chiffon dress with tiny seed pearls embroidered on the neckline.

'Leila, it's stunning! Turn around, let me see if the hem drags in the back. No, it's fine.'

The doorbell rang, and in a minute Leila's nine-year-old twins burst into the room, still wearing the navy jumpers and blazers of the Sacré Coeur school uniform. Leila cried out in alarm as she fended them off her delicate chiffon, and they flung themselves down on the chaise longue on either side of me. Leila slipped out of the dress and looked at her watch.

'Two-thirty. Amin is picking up his mother on his way home from the clinic. They should be here any minute. You two –' She eyed her daughters critically. 'Go wash up before lunch. And brush your hair, your barrettes are sliding off. There's Amin now. Come on, Gigi.'

We joined Leila's husband and her mother-in-law in the salon. 'Hello, Gigi, what a nice surprise. Mother, you remember Gihan Seif-el-Islam? Leila's cousin?'

Amin's mother, like her son, was on the stocky side and good-natured. 'Of course, dear, I knew your late mother quite well, Allah rest her soul. But you have more of the Seif-el-Islam about you.'

Amin looked at his watch. 'Is lunch ready, Leila?'

267

'Well, I'll tell the *suffragi* to serve lunch, but I just wanted to check if Tamer's on his way. I told him Gigi might be coming. Gigi, would you call him for me?' She headed for the kitchen.

I went over to the phone and tried Tamer's office number, then his home number. I put down the receiver and shook my head. 'There's no answer.'

Leila reappeared. 'Did you try the office?'

'There was no answer there either.'

'Good thing you know both his numbers by heart.' She looked at me with a curious smile. 'Well, let's go to table then. You know how Tamer is, he might not show up at all.'

At table the twins kept interrupting each other in their eagerness to tell their grandmother and me how they had participated with the other twenty-odd girls in their class at school in sponsoring an *iftar* at a 'Table of the Compassionate' during Ramadan.

'Each girl had to bring two kilos of beef stew and ten loaves of pita bread and –'

'And a dessert! The cook prepared the meat but Mummy ordered the dessert from Koweider –'

'Palace bread with the thick clotted cream. I cut it with a knife when I served it –'

'We helped serve the whole meal ourselves! There were so many people –'

'But at the end it got kind of scary, they wouldn't leave, they sort of mobbed around the table, asking for a cash handout –'

'So the teacher took over and –'

'Times are hard for the poor,' Amin pointed out.

It occurred to me that there was something incongruous about Muslim students in a Catholic girls' school

268

performing acts of Islamic charity under school supervision. But Egypt had always been a country of anomalies; I was the one who had been gone too long.

We were half-way through lunch when the doorbell rang. As soon as the twins heard Tamer's voice greeting the *suffragi* they pushed back their chairs and scrambled for the door. When he appeared in the doorway of the dining room one of them was hanging on his back and the other was hopping up and down at his side.

He went around the table greeting everyone in turn. When he came to me he gave me the usual peck on the cheek, but I wondered if anyone had noticed anything awkward about it. He sat down and helped himself.

'Oh, before I forget, Tamer,' Leila passed him the chicken in walnut sauce, 'I was in Khan Khalili this morning, and Haj Zein said to tell you he has a lantern you might be interested in. He says it's the same style as the one you bought last week.'

'What kind of lantern?' I asked Tamer.

'It's an original brass mosque lantern; I had it wired as a lamp. You've seen it, Gigi. The one in the living room, on the table closest to the bookcase.'

'Oh.'

'I must say, Gigi, you seem to be seeing a lot more of Tamer than I do!' Leila's tone was slightly brittle.

I changed the subject. 'So, tell me about the wedding, Leila! Your dress will really stand out.'

'You really should come, Tamer.' Leila served him a piece of *biftek panné*.

'You know I don't care for these big fussy weddings.'

'Well, at least come and look around. There will be any number of young women you should meet.'

'Leila, you're unbelievable! You're almost as bad as

269

Nana Zohra. Even she's given up match-making for me. Don't you know by now I do things my own way?'

'All I'm saying is come and meet them. Then make up your own mind if somebody interests you. Gigi, don't you agree with me he should at least come to the wedding?'

'Absolutely!'

'I especially want him to meet a friend of mine who recently got divorced. Camelia Bindari. Tamer, don't you remember her? She used to have a thing for you, only at the time you were going with Dina, and she married someone else.'

'I don't remember her at all.'

'Really, Tamer.' Amin pushed his chair back and lit a cigarette. 'All the women your age are married, or else divorced, usually with children. If you want to start a family –'

'That's putting the cart before the horse, isn't it? I've told you enough times, I'm not interested. Now can we drop this?'

'But she's just your type, tall, with long hair,' Leila insisted. 'Don't you think that's just his type, Gigi?'

'Absolutely! You should go to this wedding, really, Tamer.'

'I have no intention of going. And if you'll excuse me, I'll leave you to discuss this fascinating subject without me. I have to get back to work.'

He left the table abruptly. The twins accompanied him to the door, chattering all the way. Leila's mother-in-law got up and went to a bedroom to perform the afternoon prayers. In the few minutes before the girls rejoined us Leila took the opportunity to confide to me: 'He's still as wary as a cat that's been singed after that experience with

270

the Sirry girl. You wouldn't know about that, Gigi. This girl turned out to be really neurotic, and she put him through the worst kind of emotional blackmail. He just shies away from involvement now.'

'That was just before he up and married Lorenza – his Italian wife,' Amin explained. 'I think it was a sort of reaction, really, to get everyone off his back. Even after the marriage she stayed in Milan. She only came to Egypt twice, and both times she caused quite a stir.'

'She's so outspoken and unconventional! I think that's what attracted Tamer most, that she was so outrageous. But it didn't last.' Leila sighed. 'I wish he'd settle down.'

I called him that evening. 'Hi, Tamer.'

'Hey.' He sounded strained.

'That was awkward at lunch today.'

'Really? I hadn't noticed.'

'I'm sorry I sort of chimed in about your meeting women, and all that. I didn't mean to tease you. Don't you see, it would have looked odd if I hadn't? They expected me to.'

'And you always do what's expected of you, don't you? That's your business, as long as you stay out of mine.'

'Oh, I will!' From apologetic I was now on the defensive, and passed to the offensive. 'But I'd appreciate it if you were a little more discreet where I'm concerned, too. Did you have to make it clear that I'd been to your apartment so often?'

'Don't be silly! Besides, what's the harm in that? Who do you think is going to read anything into it? And what do you care if they do?'

'Your sister, for one! And I do care.'

271

Tamer sounded exasperated. 'Does it matter that much what people think any more?'

'It's easy for you, you have nothing to lose. I'm married. You forget that.'

'You don't always seem to remember, yourself.'

I was taken aback for a minute.

'Tamer, I'm just saying perhaps we should avoid awkward situations like that in future.'

'That's fine by me. I can't stand all this hypocrisy anyway.'

'What hypocrisy?'

'I don't know. Acting like nothing's changed.'

'What do you mean?'

'Like nothing's changed between us. Acting like nothing's changed since you went away ten years ago. You think you can come home and weave yourself back into the fabric of everybody's life, then rip it out again when you leave.'

I was quiet. I had done that to him before, years ago, when I had left for France. He would not let me do it again.

Gina died in Lebanon on Wednesday. Her body was flown to Egypt and she was buried in the Makhlouf family mausoleum. Leila sounded numb over the phone: 'She was suffering so much; Allah rest her soul.' I wasn't able to reach Tamer.

Thursday was the first of the three days of official visits of condolences for women – the men paid their respects in separate ceremonies. I dressed in black and went to Tante Zohra's. Her two salons were packed with women in mourning. Her three daughters presided over the proceedings, greeting guests and directing the flow of

272

sugarless Turkish coffee. Dark Nazli, who had always been considered the plainest, was now a striking, elegant woman in her fifties, married to a highly successful man. Mimi, the youngest, had never married; it was said she had been unstable since that day the *fellahin* had torched the Makhlouf's country house and she had been smuggled out hidden in the trunk of the car.

Leila sat in the outer salon, surrounded by the younger women. I hugged her as I murmured the customary formula of condolences. She seemed composed and dry-eyed, much as I must have seemed during Papa's three days of mourning.

I looked for Tante Zohra in the inner salon. She was slumped in a chaise longue, propped up with pillows, her legs covered with shawls. She seemed dazed, as if sedated, and only focused momentarily as each new visitor came up to her and offered condolences. From time to time she released a long, shuddering sigh, and wiped her eyes. I was sure she must have guessed about Gina's condition, and that the news had not been a total shock to her.

'Ah, Gigi,' she murmured as I leaned over to kiss her, 'my poor Gigi.' I couldn't decide whether it was a slip of the tongue or her slurred speech that made 'Gina' sound like 'Gigi'.

I turned away from Tante Zohra, fumbling in my pockets for a tissue, and looked around for a place to sit. I saw a vacant chair in a far corner and headed for it. It was right behind a small loveseat occupied by Lamia El-Salem and Zeina, my ex-mother-in-law. I murmured a brief greeting; the *fikki* had started to chant verses from the Koran. The two women responded with the reserved nods that befitted the circumstances, but in Zeina's eyes

273

there was a chilly curiosity. I took my place behind them. I closed my eyes and listened to the *fikki*'s powerful sing-song rise and fall.

> 'Seek refuge with the Lord of Mankind
> The ruler of Mankind, the God of Mankind
> From the mischief of the evil Whisperer
> Who whispers in the bosom of Mankind
> Among the Djinn and among Men.'

In the pauses I could hear Lamia and Zeina gossiping in the effective but undisruptive whisper perfected over years of practice at visits of condolences.

'Of course Zohra knew. Zohra always knows much more than they tell her.'

'Well, it's a mercy Gina finally died, she was suffering so much. They tried everything, you know – clinics in Switzerland, everything. It was her second husband who paid for it all.'

'Really? Weren't they divorced years ago?'

'Of course, at least ten years before. But he still cared for her, I suppose, so when she fell ill –'

'Didn't I hear that she had remarried a third time?'

'Yes, although very briefly, and the family has always tried to keep it quiet. You wouldn't think Gina would fall for a man like that, a much younger man, absolutely the wrong sort. But then I suppose she must have been depressed and lonely. Anyway she soon realized that she'd made a mistake, but it was too late, she'd married him, and she couldn't get out of it. He wouldn't divorce her.'

'I see. I suppose he had to be bought off?'

'Exactly. It was done very quietly, I'm not sure how. I heard her son was involved somehow.'

'That can't be right, he would have been too young then. Twenty, twenty-one. He wouldn't have come into his father's trust fund yet.'

No, I thought, the only thing Tamer would have had in his own name would have been the new car his grandmother had bought him as a graduation present. He would have sold it and pretended he had wrecked it, in order to have the cash to buy off his mother's cad of a husband. And Tante Zohra must have guessed.

'Speaking of Tamer Tobia, Hala Bindari was asking me about him just now,' Zeina picked up the conversation as the *fikki* paused for breath. 'I'm sure she was thinking he'd be a suitable match for her daughter Camelia. But she'd heard the rumors. You know, about his reputation with women.'

'So what did you tell her?'

'Well, Hala's a friend of mine, so I didn't beat about the bush. Did you hear about the Sirry girl a few years ago? She lost her head over him completely and started to make a fool of herself. I heard that old Wassif Sirry – Allah rest his soul – practically begged Tamer to marry his daughter! So I warned Hala, but I don't know, he's quite a catch –'

'In any case once a man has a reputation like that, deserved or not, just being associated with him is compromising enough. Why –'

'Shhh!' Zeina hissed suddenly.

'Hmm? Oh.' Lamia El-Salem darted a glance over her shoulder at me then turned around quickly. I realized that Zeina had remembered my presence and silenced her friend on the subject of Tamer.

I sat there, digesting what I had heard. I hadn't known that Tamer had a 'reputation with women', but then I

275

had been gone so long, I wouldn't have. When I came back it had seemed the most natural thing in the world to pick up our relationship where it left off. It never occurred to me that being seen with him might set tongues wagging. I had forgotten the relentless, insidious gossip, that hydra-headed monster which the old crones used to keep their society in check. I had forgotten the imperative it imposed of circumscribing one's every move within the confines of 'what would people say'. I felt claustrophobic, suddenly. Nothing had changed since I had been a girl. It was depressing.

All my girlhood I had been protected from 'men like that'. It was against that unspoken danger that I and my peers had been watched over by mothers and chaperones and been raised like little princesses by those formidable authority figures, our moustache-twirling, chain-smoking papas. Unlike less sheltered girls, we were never exposed to the risks of pitting our charms and wits in the matrimonial game against possibly unscrupulous men who did not play by the rules. From the initial encounter to the wedding trousseau, every detail was discreetly arranged and orchestrated so that we were spared the faintest blush or the slightest taint of unseemly strife.

But the tone of the gossiping women reminded me that the old double standard still held. Whatever a man did, after all, was in his nature, rather like a domesticated wolf could be understood, if not excused, for preying on the chicken in the coop. For the chicken, however, or the farmer who left the coop unlocked, there was no sympathy. The same antediluvian dynamics still held sway.

The Tamer I had glimpsed through the eyes of the gossip-mongers was a total stranger to me. But after all I knew nothing of him as a man, as an adult. I had never

276

asked myself what psychic scars he may have carried all these years, a boy abandoned by the mother he adored. But I had sensed his cynicism.

Suddenly I thought of Tarek. I wondered what psychic scars *he* might be carrying around, a boy abandoned by his mother. I wondered what they told him about me, his father, his stepmother, his grandmother Zeina. I still had a chance to redefine my relationship with him, if only he came to stay with me. But my being seen with Tamer could jeopardize that.

During the pause in the *fikki*'s recitation I got up and made the round of subdued goodbyes. I was nearly at the door when I heard a voice I didn't recognize whisper from somewhere behind me in the salon: 'Well, it's a mercy Gina finally died. She suffered for such a long time. Maybe it was Allah's way of giving her a chance to atone for her sins on earth.'

The words hit me like a punch in the stomach.

22

Insomnia

The Pasha has set the date for the family gathering. We would meet at the Cairo House the following Tuesday. As I drove Tarek home after his weekend stay I asked him if he remembered the house.

'Didn't Grandpa Shamel take me when I was little? On a feast day? I remember being given those shiny coins. I don't remember much else about it.'

'Oh, but you should! It was your grandfather's home. It's where I was married. Come with me on Tuesday. If the house is sold soon, you might not get another chance to see it.'

'I don't know, Mummy. Won't it be all grown-ups?'

'Sure. But you look so grown-up yourself. I'd be so proud to show you off! And I do want you to see the house again, and meet the Pasha and the others.' I drew my fingers through the curls at the nape of his neck. He needed a haircut. 'Do it as a favor for me? Otherwise I'll have to go all on my own.'

'Will I have to wear a suit and tie?'

'Not if you don't want to.'

'Okay.'

That evening I wandered around the apartment. For once I had no particular engagement. I switched on the television set; unlike many homes in Cairo, there was no satellite hook-up, only local programming. The first channel was showing a repeat episode of Dynasty. The second had a talk show on which a sheikh from the Azhar University debated whether or not a belly dancer's 'wages of sin' were acceptable funding for a Ramadan 'Table of the Compassionate'; the dancer in question, Fifi `Abdu, was interviewed in rebuttal. The news in English was on the third channel: after the mandatory journal of Mubarak's activities that day the anchor moved on to international news, followed by the world-wide weather report. There were severe snowstorms on the American Eastern seaboard. Kennedy Airport was closed. I wondered what it must be like in New Hampshire.

I felt unbearably restless. I thought of going for a walk and immediately dismissed the idea. It was perfectly safe to do so, but the narrow sidewalks were pockmarked with potholes and obstructed by parked cars, and the air was heavy with the exhaust from passing traffic. If Ibrahim saw me leave without the car he would immediately offer to hail a taxi for me or to accompany me wherever I was going. It would be hard to explain that I wanted to walk, and alone.

Suddenly, for no special reason, I was homesick: for snow, rain, changing skies, pure air; for a long walk on a Fall day; the brilliant russet and gold of leaves that change color; the snow-muffled silence of the woods when I went cross-country skiing; my neighbor's yard in Spring, a triumph of tulips and daffodils; even the stone rabbit

279

coyly nestled among them. I missed the ease and simplicity of shopping malls: their clean, controlled, virtual reality environment, their indoor 'sidewalk' café tables with purely decorative parasols. I missed the Sunday paper, with its crossword puzzle and advertisement inserts; the bounty of libraries and bookstores; rock music on the car radio; cruise control and instant parking. I longed for a world in which you did not constantly lose the battle against dust and bakshish; for release from the pressures of traffic and people; for freedom from watchful eyes, for anonymity, an uncomplicated existence.

I was homesick for cosy evenings back in New Hampshire: alone, but with the edge of solitude blunted by the presence of Luc nursing a drink in the next room; a pile of unread papers, mail, magazines and books on the table competing for my attention with the multitude of channels on television, the new CDs by the stereo, the computer with its screen-saver image of undulating dolphins, a reproachful reminder of work uncompleted. From the media to junk mail: a world of sensory overload.

In Cairo you make your own entertainment. I understood why people here were so gregarious, why they clustered in homes and cafés, why they were on the phone twenty times a day. I thought of Leila and other women I had grown up with. Their lives were one endless round of social obligations and engagements.

Every day there were a dozen courtesy phone calls to make: an aunt was unwell, a niece fell down and chipped a tooth, a friend had a baby. Every week brought its quota of visits of congratulations or condolences and its standing lunch engagements: Friday at your mother's; Saturday at your mother-in-law's; Sunday it was your turn to receive

280

your mother and mother-in-law. Every month brought its complement of weddings, engagement parties and dinner invitations. Every year the winter and summer holidays came around, and there was the beach chalet or country cottage to air and dust, and more entertaining.

I could not imagine keeping up on that frantic tread-mill; you would fall off if you tried to slow down. So much of it appeared unnecessary to me, a cycle of esca-lating social obligations that could not be broken without throwing the slacker out of the social orbit altogether. The delicate web of this network was so sensitive to the most imaginary slight or oversight that it required constant maintenance and repair. I knew I could not live that way.

My peers among my contemporaries were the privi-leged few, and yet they had not really gained ground in the past generation. They tried to fulfill the same social obligations as their mothers, with a quarter of the house-hold help. Their higher education imposed the expecta-tion of 'doing something' professionally, while in no way dispensing them from their family and social duties.

I switched off the television set and looked out the window, trying to catch a glimpse of the Nile. The tall buildings that had sprung up around the villa made me feel claustrophobic. Wherever I looked the lighted windows made it hard to avoid the unwelcome intrusion into other people's privacy. I could barely glimpse the river, but in my mind's eye I saw the city stretched out like a vast, three-dimensional map, with lights glittering here and there, like markers, to pinpoint the homes of relatives and friends. The thought of going out was particu-larly inviting at night here: there was less traffic and, mild as the weather was even in winter, the city was wide awake till dawn.

281

I glanced at the telephone. I could call Tamer. If he were home, it would take me twenty minutes to be there. I hadn't had a chance to talk to him since Gina's death.

I picked up the phone to call him, then put it down. What had seemed so simple a few days ago now seemed fraught with complications. The serpent had entered the garden. For the next hour I vacillated, picking up the receiver half a dozen times only to put it down again.

That night I felt as if I didn't belong here, as if I spoke the language but didn't understand it. In some ways the country seemed to have changed too much, in others not enough. Perhaps the feeling was brought on by Gina's funeral and the gossiping women. Perhaps it was the layers of impressions building up: the Pasha's detachment at the *iftar*; the Sirdanas' all-Filipino staff in the midst of the *fellahin*; the sight of the women in Islamic dress all over town. Sometimes it seemed as if the country now belonged to the *Infitah* millionaires and the Islamists.

Sometimes it's like looking through a kaleidoscope: the individual slivers of colored shapes are the same, but the tiniest shift in the angle of the lens changes the composition to form an entirely new pattern. So it was with my mood that evening; a few days before I could not imagine leaving; now I felt there was no place for me here. I had been gone too long. I should claim what was mine, tie up loose ends, and leave. After the family council took place at the Cairo house, I would leave. I would have my say on the sale of the house, and do my best to convince Tarek to join me the following year. Then I would leave.

I called Luc.

'*Âllo*? Gigi! How's everything?'

282

He sounded distracted. I wondered if he'd started to drink this early.

'You weren't – napping?'

'No, no. I'm watching television. We're snowed in.'

'I know, I saw that on the news. How've you been?'

'Fine. There's some fresh gossip to liven things up in the department. Apparently Toussaint Hopkins and Janet Glasser spent Spring break in Cairo. *Together.*'

'I know. I met them in Luxor. I'll tell you all about it when I see you. Listen, I'm coming home on Thursday. The family meeting is taking place on Tuesday, so I can leave by Thursday. I'm calling the airline tomorrow to confirm my reservation.'

'Thursday? Good. Then you can take care of this. Mrs McMurty left a note on the kitchen counter with a list of things. Pinesol, Windex, I don't know what else. I have it somewhere. What's it supposed to mean?'

'That we're out of those things and we should replace them before she comes to clean again next Friday. Don't worry about it, I'll be back by then. So, don't forget to pick me up at the airport?'

'What time do you arrive?'

'Eight-thirty in the evening your time, assuming there are no weather delays. I'll call you from Kennedy. Would you bring my winter coat with you to the airport? I left it in the car, remember?'

'Then it must still be in the trunk. Okay. Remind me when you call from New York.'

I hung up. Luc had sounded so matter-of-fact. It had not occurred to him that there could be some question about my coming back, only about the timing.

I switched the television on, then off. I looked out of the window again, then I drew the curtains. Finally I got

283

undressed, to put an end to my vacillation. I found some old books and picked a familiar novel by Stendhal to reread. As the hours ticked by and the night grew quiet I heard the intermittent drone of the doorkeepers' voices through the window. Ibrahim was apparently entertaining a few neighboring doorkeepers on the bench in front of the house. They would be smoking cigarettes and drinking endless small glasses of strong, sweet tea as they kept watch through the night. The voices were low but I could tell that they were speaking in Nubian, called *Berberi* in Egypt.

For the first time I wondered if these men were homesick too. The Nubian doorkeepers of Cairo form a caste apart. They migrate north from their far-flung villages in the Nubia and the Sudan, leaving wives and children behind, and take up a monastic life in the basements, stairwells and garages of villas and buildings all over the city. Twice a year they travel home to Upper Egypt, presumably to provide for the next generation of their profession. This entire *confrèrie* seems to be related to one another, forming a formidable basement grapevine running through the streets of the capital. Nothing escapes the watchful eyes of the Nubian doorkeepers, and they are the first resource of the police. But like everything else in Egypt, that institution too is changing and will one day be a thing of the past.

But that night as I tried to fall asleep, there was something comforting in the steady drone of the voices of the watchmen.

I slept very fitfully, and by dawn I was wide awake when the faint rumbling announced the arrival of the *zabaleen*, the garbage collectors. I got up and stood at the window.

284

The clip-clopping donkey cart materialized out of the dawn haze. The shawl-wrapped figure sitting on top of the piles of rags and plastic bags reined in the donkey and jumped off. It was too small to be an adult, but I could not tell the gender in the half-light.

The child pried open the can and started to haul out the bags and newspapers, stopping every now and then to examine an object, then toss it away. It sorted aside some magazines and a bunch of half-withered roses. It snapped off the stem of a rose and stuck it behind an ear. It had to be a girl. Next she emptied what looked like orange peel and fruit rind into a bucket. For what purpose, I wondered in horror, thinking of the rat poison. I remembered that the *zabaleen*, many of whom were Coptic, raised pigs on the peelings from the slop buckets.

My impulse was to run down and warn her. Then I heard Ibrahim's clogs on the courtyard cobbles, and his voice raised in greeting to the child. No, Ibrahim would never have put poison in the garbage cans, no matter what I told him to do.

The child hopped back on top of the pile of garbage on the cart, took up the reins and cracked a whip. The donkey started up, stumbling, and the cart ambled down the street.

Monday morning I read in the paper that there had been a landslide in that part of the Mokkatam plateau where the garbage collectors live in shacks amid piles of rubbish. The mountainside had collapsed under the sewage and waste of the *zabaleen* and their pigs.

285

23

The House

Tuesday morning when I went to pick up Tarek he waved to me from the second-floor balcony and came down a few minutes later. He was wearing dress pants and shoes, a shirt and a blazer. No tie, but he'd had his hair cut. I leaned over to kiss him as he got into the car.

'Thanks for dressing up, darling. You look very handsome and very grown-up.' I thought he looked considerably older than sixteen, like Tamer at his age. 'Do you know, in the States you can start to drive at sixteen. You don't have to wait to be eighteen for a driver's permit the way you do here.' I couldn't resist an opportunity to point out the advantages of coming to America.

'Mummy, I already know how to drive. Papa lets me, quite often, when I'm with him in the car.'

We drove over the bridge and along the Nile Corniche to Garden City.

'So, Mummy, this offer for the house. Is it a good thing?'

'I'm not sure, sweetheart. I need to know a little more

286

about it, and to see how the others feel. As for me, well, I don't even live here. And it would be nice to get this settled. Perhaps invest my share in something profitable, abroad. I ought to try to liquidate what I own and tie up loose ends here in Egypt – not just my share of the house, whatever else I can. With Mama gone, you're my only reason for coming back here. And I'm hoping soon you'll join me. But I'm really glad you'll get a chance to see the house before it's sold. Your grandfather was born there, I was married there, I have so many memories there. You can't imagine what it was like, especially during the heyday of the party, all the people, all the excitement, all the optimism.'

When we arrived at the Pasha's there were several cars already parked inside the grounds. The front door was open, which signaled a formal occasion. Tarek followed me inside the long hall. After the sunshine outside we squinted while our eyes adjusted and shivered slightly as we stood on the chilly marble floor. In the half-gloom Fangali materialized from behind one of the rose marble columns.

'Good morning, Sitt Gigi, the Pasha's in the study. Most of the family has arrived.'

As we followed him down the hall I nudged Tarek and pointed to the second-floor gallery.

'Maybe later I'll take you upstairs and show you the room where I changed into my wedding dress before the wedding party. Such a scene! Mama and Madame Hélène – do you remember her? – helping me dress, and the hairdresser trying to fix my hair and pin on my veil. He couldn't find a convenient outlet for the curling iron near the dressing-table, I remember, and there was a scramble to find an extension cord. And Om Khalil and the maids

287

standing outside the door letting out a *zaghruta* every few minutes.'

We followed Fangali down the hall. The tall wooden double doors to the study were ajar, leaking light and voices. There were a dozen people in the room. The Pasha presided, alone, on a high-backed, silk-upholstered sofa at one end; Lamia El-Salem was conspicuously absent. I made my way over to my uncle and drew Tarek forward.

'Uncle, this is Tarek. I wanted him to come with me so he could meet you. He didn't remember much about his visits when he was little.'

'Well then I'm glad you brought him. How old are you now, Tarek? Sixteen? You could pass for twenty.' The Pasha smiled but he seemed distracted.

I looked around the room. Tante Zohra wasn't there, of course. I shook hands with her daughter Nazli and the third sister. They were both in deep mourning for Gina.

'How is Tante Zohra?' I asked Nazli.

'Mama has been very unwell since Gina's funeral. But she wanted us all to be here. Except for Mimi, she never goes out, you know.'

Leila, austere in black and wearing no makeup, sat next to her aunts. Tamer stood behind her chair. They were there as Gina's heirs, I realized. I hugged Leila and turned to greet Tamer, only having time to whisper in his ear, 'I'm so sorry about your mother! I tried to call you.' He gave me a quick smile and squeezed my hand.

I recognized my third uncle, Zakariah, as he slumped in a large armchair. He had shrunk and his once flaming rusty hair had faded to peach, blending with his freckled skin. When I went up to kiss him he didn't recognize me until I was right in front of him.

'My goodness, Gigi! And this is your son? I can't

288

believe it. Where is it you live again? France? Oh, America? Do you like it there?'

Zakariah, in the way of some younger brothers, was overshadowed by the Pasha's personality. I felt pretty sure that he would go along with whatever his eldest brother decided. Next to him sat my fourth uncle, Nabil. He had not aged much and still had the same dour expression I remembered.

The Pasha, his two brothers and Tante Zohra were the only surviving original owners of the house. The heirs of their deceased siblings were represented at this gathering by the oldest male in each family. Many of the faces were barely recognizable to me. Papa having been the youngest of his brothers and sisters, most of my cousins were considerably older than I, almost another generation. Growing up I had only seen them at weddings, funerals, and feast days. We nodded and shook hands, murmuring conventional greetings. These middle-aged strangers looked gray and tired, as if they wanted this to be over with. They seemed to me a diminished generation, less vital, even physically smaller, than their fathers. Their drab clothes contrasted with their uncles' dapper suits, carefully chosen ties and matching pocket squares. It made me reflect on the hidden costs of the war of attrition the Revolution had waged against my family. It had taken its most insidious toll on the solidarity of this once cohesive, proud clan, reducing them to disputing the crumbs of their erstwhile fortune.

Tarek and I found chairs near Leila and Tamer and sat down. Desultory spurts of small talk did little to disguise the tension. Everyone seemed to be waiting for a signal from the Pasha, who sat, unapproachable, at one end of the room.

Suddenly Tarek tugged at my elbow. 'Look, here comes Grandfather. What's he doing here?'

I looked towards the door. Kamal Zeitouni was being ushered in by Fangali. Still a large man, his hair and moustache were completely white and he leaned on a cane. Tarek stood up and went to the door to greet him. Kamal looked over the boy's shoulder and his sharp eyes picked me out. He took Tarek's arm and plodded across the room to shake hands with the Pasha. My uncle's greeting was cordial but reserved. Kamal's presence, welcome or otherwise, had clearly been expected.

I stood up and waited for my ex-father-in-law to turn to me. Then I sat down again. It occurred to me that he might choose to snub me. But he turned in my direction and I stood up again awkwardly.

'Hello, Gihan. Well, well, it's been a long time.'

'Yes, it has. How are you, Uncle Kamal?' I still addressed him as I did when he had been my father-in-law, out of habit.

'Can't complain, can't complain.'

He made his way stiffly to a chair. Tarek tucked the cane out of the way and came back to his seat next to me.

The Pasha coughed. The instant hush that followed betrayed the fact that everyone had been waiting for a signal.

'Well, you all know why we're here. We need to consider an offer for the house. Kamal Zeitouni is here to represent the buyer and to answer any questions we might have.'

Clearly there were questions, but the younger generation deferred to the older. I wanted to know who the buyer was but didn't dare be the first to speak up. Zakariah was the first to ask a question.

290

'Does he want to buy the house as such, or is he just buying the land to demolish the house and build on the lot? And if so, what will he build? A house for his personal use? A hotel?'

'This area of Garden City is not zoned for high rises, because of the embassies around. The current intention of the buyer is to renovate the house for his own personal use. If, however, remodeling proves to be impractical –' Kamal started.

'The house is perfectly sound structurally,' Nabil interrupted. 'Besides, it's been declared a national heritage, so it can't be torn down. Whoever buys it must expect to renovate it.'

There was a moment of silence. My first reaction was to welcome this news, but then I realized this would inevitably drive down the price of the house by limiting potential buyers to those who would be ready to go to the very considerable expense and trouble of renovating and preserving the house for their personal use.

Finally Zakariah asked the question I was most curious about. 'Who's the buyer?'

'Emir Bandar of Saudi Arabia.'

There was a murmur. The identity of the buyer was apparently news.

I tried to imagine Prince Bandar and Khadija living here. Perhaps this very study, with its gold silk paneling and its heavy green velvet draperies, would serve as their video-viewing room. They would put up a giant wall-to-wall screen, and wall-to-wall sofas. The antiquated, drafty bathrooms would be redone in gilt and mirrors. I somehow couldn't imagine the Bandars in these rooms with their soaring ceilings, elaborate moldings and garlanded Cupids on the cornices.

291

Nabil asked the question that seemed to be on everybody's mind. 'How much is he offering?'

Kamal specified the sum, in dollars. I tried to calculate my share. I divided by eight, because under the Shari`a the two sisters each inherited half a share, the seven brothers a whole. But I would not inherit all of Papa's one-eighth. As a woman, and sole heir, I had to share part of my inheritance with my male relatives: these near-strangers, my cousins.

'The point to consider,' Kamal continued, 'is that the condition of the house is deteriorating rapidly. Buyers for a house like this are few and far between. This good an offer may not be repeated.'

'That's nonsense. Property values are going through the roof in Cairo. It's the best investment imaginable. And this is a unique piece of prime real estate, in the most desirable residential area in the city. Not to mention that all this marble and woodwork couldn't be reproduced today at any price.'

I wondered if Zakariah was speaking for himself or for the Pasha, who sat, sphinx-like, on the sofa.

'True,' Kamal conceded, 'but the demand for a property like this holds up only as long as there is stability. No one can be sure of anything today. Even the rumor of instability can scare off foreign investors. It's happened before.'

'We can afford to wait. A few more years won't make a difference.'

Everyone understood the reference to 'a few more years'. The Pasha was in his eighties. He had already outlived all but two of his brothers and one sister.

'Allah grants long life to those he wills,' Nabil pointed out. 'But I think we have to consider the younger generation. Our children now have to think of their own

292

youngsters. Tying up money indefinitely, when it is needed now, isn't fair to them.' He looked around for support.

There was a general murmur of assent from the cousins. The silence that ensued stretched uncomfortably. No one had brought up the most sensitive issue. If the house were sold during the Pasha's lifetime, where would he live? Presumably he could buy himself a villa or a luxury apartment, but I could not imagine the Pasha living anywhere but in the Cairo House.

Finally the Pasha, as if rousing himself, broke the silence. 'I think it's time everyone took a turn at having their say.' Although he had the most at stake, he sounded detached, above the fray. 'Zakariah?'

'I'm for turning down the offer.'

'Nabil?'

'I think we should accept it.'

'Sharif? I assume you're speaking for your brothers and sisters as Adel's heirs?'

'Yes, Sir. I think we should accept.'

The Pasha called on each of the cousins, and I knew my turn would come. I felt a knot of tension form in my chest, the way it always did when I had to make a decision. Things never came to me in black or white, the way they had seemed to come, so easily, to Papa. I wished he were here, now, to guide me.

The Pasha had run down the list and turned to Nazli.

'Where does Zohra stand on this?'

'Mama said she couldn't reach a decision. It was too difficult for her. She wants us to decide for ourselves, as her heirs. Tamer can speak for all of us.'

'I had a question that I was hoping I wouldn't have to be the one to bring up.' Tamer seemed embarrassed but determined. 'Personally I would be willing to wait a

293

few more years. But what I'm concerned about, and I'm sure I'm not the only one, is what happens, Allah willing after a long life, when you are no longer with us, Sir. You have no children. But you do have a long-time companion living with you in the house.'

'Make your point.'

'Might she not claim to be your common-law wife, and refuse to vacate the house?'

I was in awe of Tamer's boldness; it would not have surprised me if he had been turned into a pillar of salt by a look from the Pasha. There was a murmur of assent. Tamer had clearly voiced a concern that no one else had the nerve to bring up: a potential claim by Lamia El-Salem.

'A common-law wife has no rights under the Shari'a,' Nabil objected.

'But it could tie up the inheritance in legal disputes. That's a point to consider,' Kamal Zeitouni countered. 'It's very discouraging for a buyer to have to deal with so many heirs. Already there must be about twenty! In a few years, it's inevitable, there will be even more. Reaching a consensus, getting everyone to sign at once, will be a daunting task. If, on top of that, there are complications – I mean claims, unfounded or otherwise, to settle – it could discourage many buyers. Far better to settle this now, while at least some of the original owners are here.'

Zakariah turned to his oldest brother. 'I think we need to hear from you now.'

'Not yet. It was Gihan's turn, as Shamel's heir.'

I felt a tightness in my chest, the way I used to do as a schoolgirl when I knew it was my turn next to be called upon by the teacher. I could tell that everyone, including

294

the Pasha, thought they knew where I stood. Living abroad, I was assumed to have severed any sentimental attachments I might have. It did not occur to anyone that, precisely because I had been uprooted, I needed to know that the house would be here for me to come home to. Because my past and present were irreconcilable, I needed to be able to touch base, to reconnect to my old self. The house was my link to the past, to Papa; it was part of Tarek's heritage. I made up my mind. It would all be gone, soon enough. The Pasha would be gone, and after him the house, and one day soon I would only be able to drive past, and it would be flying a foreign flag. It would happen soon enough anyway.

'Gihan?' the Pasha prodded gently. 'Go ahead, Gigi.'

'I don't see why we should hurry.' My voice was even lower than usual, and I cleared my throat and spoke up. 'A few years from now – why not wait?'

A flicker of surprise passed over the Pasha's inscrutable face. Kamal Zeitouni's eyes narrowed, the way they had so many years ago, at my wedding, when I had crossed him for the first time. There was another silence. Finally the Pasha spoke.

'This seems to be the situation: some, even most, of you feel that we should accept this offer from Prince Bandar; some feel that we can afford to wait. For myself, I wish to live out the little that's left of my days in the house in which I was born.' A pause. 'But there is a possible compromise.' Another pause. 'It might be possible to sell the house now, but on the basis of an agreement that I have the use of it for the duration of my lifetime, after which it becomes Emir Bandar's free and clear.'

'You're thinking of some kind of usufruct or lease-back

agreement?' Kamal Zeitouni rubbed his chin. 'I don't know that he'll agree to that.'

'He may be amenable to the idea. From what I understood, he didn't seem to have any immediate plans for using the house. We can get the lawyers together and work out the details. But that should satisfy all parties, I think, as well as lay to rest any concerns about possible claims or disputes.'

He looked around. 'Well, I guess that's all. Thank you all very much for coming. Kamal and I will be in touch, and we'll keep you informed.'

Kamal Zeitouni heaved himself up with the help of his cane. Tarek walked him to the door and out to his car while I joined the line filing past the Pasha to take leave. My uncle remained seated, and had a word with each of us as we bent over to kiss him.

'Give Zohra my love, Nazli, tell her I'll be calling her tonight. Good-bye, Nabil. Is your rheumatism worse, Zakariah? Do you want me to call my specialist? Good-bye, Tamer. Good-bye, Sharif, my best to your mother. Good-bye, Gigi dear. Come for lunch again soon, bring Tarek. Oh, you're leaving on Thursday? Already? Well, have a good trip, and don't be gone as long next time.' He rumpled my hair, a gesture he had not had for me since before I left for France.

I waited out in the hall for Tarek to come back. Looking up at the second floor gallery, I thought I caught a glimpse of a wisp of black veil disappearing behind a door. Lamia El-Salem must be aware, by now, of all that had transpired, through one or the other of the eavesdropping domestics.

'Yes, I saw her too.' It was Tamer who had come up behind me. 'Oh well, someone had to bring that up.'

296

'I hope this idea of the Pasha's works. It's brilliant. I didn't think he would ever agree to sell the house in his lifetime.'

'If you think about it, it's in his interest to sell the house and get his share now. He has no children, no wife. When he goes, his inheritance is divided up among his brothers. This way, he goes on living in the house, but he gets his share in his lifetime, and can do what he wants with it. Spend it, will it to anyone he wants or give it outright as a gift. To anyone.'

'I see. So, Uncle Nabil-?'

'Was playing the devil's advocate. Never underestimate the Pasha. He always has something up his sleeve.'

I smiled. We stood there awkwardly, looking at each other; one of those moments when a hand's breadth of space between two people feels intolerable, and yet – at that moment, in that place – is as impossible to bridge as the length of a room. Tamer was the first to break away and clatter down the stone steps of the front door.

On the way home in the car I suddenly thought of Jeanne Calment.

'What's so funny, Mummy?'

'Oh, it's just that I thought of this Frenchwoman who is the oldest living woman in the world – over a hundred. Jeanne Calment. You never heard of her? Well, anyway, years ago, when she was a mere eighty or so, this lawyer in her town bought her house. He took over the mort-gage payments, on the understanding that she could continue living in it until she died. Well, the irony is, *he* died, and she's still living.'

297

24

The Accident

Loose ends. Some would have to be left dangling. Question marks. The matter of the house was out of my hands. But Tarek? Why did I ever think that I could come back, after all these years, and claim him like lost luggage? I had to resign myself to leaving without him, with no guarantee that he would join me soon. He would make up his own mind. Tarek was not me, at his age. He would not necessarily do what he was expected to do.

Loose ends. Saying goodbye. Last night Leila had a small farewell dinner for me. Afterwards I had more trouble than ever falling asleep, but it didn't matter any more. Tomorrow I would be leaving, and I knew that once I was back in the States, I would rediscover that effortless, opaque loss of consciousness that eluded me here. I had almost forgotten what it was like to sleep through the night, like downing a tall drink in one long draft.

'Tomorrow I am leaving.' I repeated it to myself, but some part of me refused to accept it.

That morning, very early, I went riding with Tarek at the Pyramids. Afterwards, when I dropped him off at his father's, he hugged me painfully hard, the way growing boys do before they know their own strength. It gave me hope. I drove away before he could see me cry.

That afternoon I went to Tante Zohra to say goodbye. I knew I wouldn't see her again.

In the evening I washed my hair; I set out my clothes and the few presents for Luc, the souvenirs for friends. But I didn't pack right away. I took my pocketbook and emptied it out. I switched the Egyptian pounds for dollars, setting aside the Egyptian money in an envelope to give to Ibrahim. I packed my American passport, my credit cards, health insurance card, telephone card, my driver's license – so many cards I have not needed in Egypt, where I carried cash and an I.D. card. In the States there is another stack of cards waiting for me in my desk drawer along with my checkbooks: ATM, library, department store, AAA, car insurance. I switched address books.

My flight would leave at eight in the morning, like most flights to the States from Cairo. This meant I would have to be at the airport at six. Ibrahim had instructions to knock at the door of the apartment at five thirty. He would have a taxi waiting. I set the alarm clock for five, but it would hardly be worth going to bed.

Loose ends. Tamer. I looked at my watch. Eight p.m. I looked at the phone. I walked to the bedroom and tried to start packing. I went back to the phone. I knew I couldn't leave without saying goodbye. I called him.

'Gigi? Hey! What have you been doing with yourself?'

'It's my last night.'

'You're leaving? So soon?'

'Won't you come to say goodbye?'

299

'I can't. I'm expecting a notary to come over this evening to sign some urgent papers and an overseas phone call I can't miss. Why don't you come over?'

'I won't have time. I have to pack, to get ready. I'm taking the early morning flight.'

'It still gives us a couple of hours. Come.'

I hesitated, but his tone, uncharacteristically urgent, made up my mind. 'All right, I'll try.'

Speeding along the Sixth of October Bridge I glanced repeatedly at the time. It was so late, there was almost no point in doing this.

I saw a bus grinding up the Zamalek on-ramp to my right, ponderously swinging its tail behind it. I started to accelerate in order to pass between the bus and the large white van on my left. I had plenty of time. Suddenly out of nowhere a figure sprang into the gap between the bus and the van. A woman in black had jumped off the slow-moving bus and crossed in front of it. I slammed on the brakes even as I saw the van close in on me. The car rocked as the van side-swiped the left rear door. I fought down the lump of fright in my throat and looked in the rear-view mirror at the capacity-filled van. There was no point in stopping in the middle of the fast-moving traffic on the bridge. No one carried insurance in Egypt anyway.

I drove on as the realization sunk in that I had barely missed running down a human being. The sprightly old woman in black had simply hopped onto the narrow shoulder of the bridge and walked away, indifferent to the collision she had caused. The stupidity of her action made me furious. Even if it were not my fault, had she so much as slipped and fallen – I tried not to think about it. The old crone had shot me a malevolent look from kohl-blackened eyes. Something about her triggered a

300

memory. Om Khalil! That's who it was! No, surely Om Khalil couldn't be alive still. Or could she?

I felt a tightness in my chest, a sort of dread, as if the accident had been a warning. It was remarkable, come to think of it, that I had so far avoided having an accident driving in Cairo. But now it seemed as if I had been put on notice that my beginner's luck had run out; my diplomatic immunity had been lifted.

I checked the gas gauge. It was running low. I pulled into a gas station. It would give me a chance to compose myself as well as refueling. The attendant came up with a smile and a windshield wiper.

'Fill it up, please.' I opened my bag to get ready to pay him and realized that my purse contained no Egyptian currency. 'No, wait, stop. I've changed my mind, I'm in a hurry. Sorry.'

I drove off, wondering if I shouldn't just go back home. But I kept going. I was aware of something obsessive about my behavior, coupled with a slight, unreasonable resentment against Tamer.

I parked a block away and walked over to his building. The doorman looked up briefly as I got into the elevator. I got off at the sixth floor and rang the doorbell of the apartment.

Tamer opened the door and greeted me with a smile and a peck on the cheek. 'Glad you made it. Come on in. Are you all right? You look a bit shaky.'

I told him about the accident. 'Tamer, I swear I thought it was Om Khalil!'

'It couldn't have been, Gigi, I heard she died years ago. It must have been someone who looked just like her. Seriously, though – you were lucky. If you had hit the woman –' He shook his head.

301

'I know!' I followed him to the living room.

'Sit down.' He pointed to an armchair beside a table covered with papers and files.

I realized the paperwork must be connected to Gina's estate. 'I'm so sorry about Gina.' I brushed my hand along the scar running from his thumb to his wrist.

'It's all right. Mother left us a long time ago.'

For a moment I was shocked. Then I realized he meant that she had been too ill to be aware of anyone for a long time, not that she had abandoned her children over twenty years ago.

We were both quiet for a minute. Then Tamer shook himself. 'So, all packed and ready?' He was making an effort to sound brisk and detached, I realized, because I had made my decision to leave and only called him at the last minute.

'Not packed, no, I'll do that tonight. But other than that, I'm ready.' I sighed.

'Uh-huh.'

'What do you mean, uh-huh?'

'You don't sound very enthusiastic.'

'It's just that I wish I could take Tarek back with me now.' It was only part of the truth; it wasn't Tarek alone that I would miss – but I had to take my cue from Tamer's tone. 'Anyway, I've waited so long, I can wait a few more months for him to join me.'

'Is it decided then?'

'Not yet. But I won't let myself believe anything other than that he'll come. Guess where I took him this morning? Riding at the Pyramids. I asked at the stables about Haj Hassan. They said he died last year. Did you know that?'

'No, it's been years since I went riding there.'

302

'I'm going to miss everybody so much! Everyone's been so kind. Leila had a little farewell dinner for me last night.'

'Really? She didn't tell me. Who was there?'

'Just two other couples, she kept it very low key because of the circumstances. And do you know what the Pasha did yesterday? He sent his driver over with a big dish of *Om Ali*, because he knows it's my favorite. I was so touched!' I looked out of the French doors at the view over the river. 'It's going to be so hard to leave.'

The doorbell rang. A Sudanese *suffragi* announced the notary.

'Tamer, maybe I'd better go.'

'You just got here. I'll take the guy into the study. You stay put. I'll be done in a few minutes.'

I made myself comfortable on the long sofa in front of the balcony overlooking the Nile. The *suffragi* came back. 'Would you like tea or coffee?'

'Tea please.'

I leaned back against the kilim pillows and closed my eyes. I suddenly felt very tired. I had fallen asleep very late last night, woken up at dawn, couldn't go back to sleep, gone riding at seven. It was now almost ten o'clock at night. The aftermath of the accident, too, was taking its toll. As soon as the man had brought the tea and left I stretched out on the sofa and closed my eyes.

The next thing I was aware of was Tamer's breath on my face. I opened my eyes to see him crouching beside me.

'Shall I get you a blanket?'

'I'll have to leave soon.'

'Doze off if you want, I'll wake you when it's time.'

'Mmm. There's too much light in here.'

303

'I can take care of that.'

He slid his arms under me, scooped me up. The motion made me dizzy and I closed my eyes tighter. He carried me across the living room and through the door.

'Tamer, the *suffragi*!'

'I sent him home.'

I kept my eyes shut, aware of him carrying me down the corridor to the bedroom and drawing the curtains of the window with one hand. Then he set me down on the bed. 'Dark enough?'

I spread my arms on the slippery satin bedspread. 'I'm so tired. I wish I didn't have to leave tomorrow.'

'Then stay.'

Sometimes you hold your life in your hands like a kaleidoscope you look through; the slightest twist in either direction, a decision that could go either way, and the pattern of your life would be changed forever. But you never know, before you twist the lens ever so slightly one way or another, what that pattern will look like.

The phone rang, over and over. He reached over to the console and pushed a button and it stopped.

I drew away from him, kneeling on the bed. 'You won't forget me?'

'I'll try to.'

I knew he meant it. He had been a boy who learned not to count on anyone being around forever.

'Well, I won't. Give me something to remember you by? So I can look at it, twenty-four hours from now, in New Hampshire, and think of you?' I wished I could take some sort of talisman to remind me, in that other world of ice hockey and snow-capped steeples, that this world was just as real.

'Anything you want.'

304

But there was nothing, finally, that I could think of to take with me, but memories.

The phone rang again, but only once this time before the answering machine kicked in. After his recorded greeting, there was a crackling silence, then a hang-up. I slipped away from him, and got up and went to the bathroom.

My reflection in the mirror was flushed and tousled. I ran my hand through my hair. I looked at my watch, it was one o'clock in the morning. I suddenly felt panicky. I ran out to the living room to find my handbag and keys.

'I've got to go.'

'Wait a minute, I'll walk you to your car.' He was pulling on a sweater as he headed down the corridor.

'No, you don't have to. Goodbye.' I was at the front door.

'Wait a minute, can't you wait a bloody second?' He looked back at me, almost angry.

I waited by the door as he went into the study to pick up his keys. My face felt naked, the lipstick smeared off, my hair tousled. Somehow our roles seemed reversed, as if I were suddenly the younger one.

He came to me by the door and leaned his back against the wall, spreading his legs apart and sliding down so our eyes were more on a level. 'We'll go in a minute.' He smoothed my hair. 'Only you're always running away, Gigi. From places, from people. What are you running away from this time? Me? Do you even know what you're running to? You have to stop sometime. Stay and find out.'

There was so much I wanted to say. That I wanted to stay. That he had been an unresolved part of my life, for so long, and that now I would leave, again, and it would never be resolved. That I was afraid to risk the past for

305

the present, to lose the gift of memories. That we could have no future together. That I had come back too late: too late to claim what was mine or could have been. That there was no place for me here now.

That I had no courage to start over. That I could not trust my instincts. I thought of Gina, stumbling from marriage to marriage, each mistake compounding the one that went before. I thought of Tarek. I thought of Luc, waiting for me in New Hampshire, never doubting my return. I wanted to tell Tamer that he had been right, I would go back because I had made my bed, I must lie in it.

In my life, endings are marked with a whimper. I nuzzled his chest. 'I'll write to you.'

The phone rang again, and suddenly I was reminded of the world outside, of the late hour. The world of watchful eyes, of Ibrahim and Om Khalil, of the women gossiping at the visit of condolences.

'I'd better go. Tamer? Will you miss me?'

He hugged me to him impulsively, without lust. 'Yes, I will.'

'Let's go then.' I was glad it was night when it was time to face the street.

He walked me to my car, and we talked in ordinary voices about the accident earlier that afternoon.

'Will you get back all right?' he asked. 'You look tired.'

'I think so. I take a left at the square –'

'No, you take a right at the square, then the next left at the mosque – Never mind. Just follow me. I'll drive ahead of you till I get you on the overpass.'

The last I saw of him was his arm pointing to the on-ramp as he veered away in the opposite direction.

*   *   *

306

On the plane I buckle my seat belt, relieved to be done with the bleary-eyed, tedious routine of checking in and boarding. Lift-off, finally. I look down through a rare morning mist at the dusty, gray city, the gleaming serpent of the great river, and, just beyond, the desert, always the desert, lapping at the outskirts. From the air it is disconcerting to see how narrow the strip of green is, how precarious Egypt's hold on civilization. I wonder how much longer the dervish can keep spinning, spinning and praying. I wonder if one day the *Khamaseen* storm troops will reclaim the city for the sand dunes. I wonder if I will ever be back.

I close my eyes and recline in my seat. I am thrust back through the familiar passage in limbo. I can neither say that I am going home, nor coming from home. This time, though, there is a difference. This time I am aware of turning a chapter.

The world is peopled with the walking dead. You rarely recognize them; they may stride about in perfect health and, perversely, live to be ninety. The difficulty is pinpointing the exact moment at which their life is over, years before they are buried. Rarely is that moment a cataclysmic event that others can recognize: a terrible disabling accident, the death of a loved one. More commonly it is an intensely private moment, the moment in which a person gives up hope.

It is the moment he realizes that nothing will change in his life. There is nothing to look forward to. There is no destination; 'here' and 'there' are the same. The cards have been dealt, the game has been played, and you are out of it, however long you continue to sit at the table.

It was over for Papa long before his heart finally gave out; I had felt him give up. I had felt it in the Pasha too,

307

this last time. His formidable will would hold till he was laid in his mausoleum, but it was over for him years ago when he realized that history had passed him by, and that this time, it was too late to catch up. Sadat had called him a phoenix rising from the ashes. He had outlived Sadat by over a decade now, but the phoenix would rise no more.

People die inside, every day, and keep up their routine with hardly a stumble or a break. Duty and obligations keep them going round and round the treadmill. So it will be for me. I will cling to the hope that Tarek will come one day, but I know the little boy I left behind is lost forever. I will write to Tamer, but time and distance will stretch between us like the desert. All we might ever have is the gift of memories.

Turning a chapter, closing a book. So many metaphors we use for laying the past to rest. I have closed the album of photographs, but the images crowd my head; perhaps one day I will find a way to reconcile my past with my present. Perhaps Egypt, and the Cairo house, will be more real to me, in that town of snow-capped steeples and hockey rinks, than it would have been if I had stayed on in Zamalek. I will find it easier to conjure it from a distance, like Isak Dinesen writing her sun-bleached tales of Africa in the frigid gloom of her drafty Danish castle.

I know it will be easier, now, to lie in the bed I have made. Perhaps I had never given my life abroad a fair chance, or my relationship with Luc for that matter, as long as, subconsciously, I had always held back, dreaming of going back to Egypt one day. It will be different now. If Luc is still waiting for me with his old easy-going smile, if it is all still waiting for me, that world of snow-hushed woods after a storm, I will give it a fair chance.

This much I know. I might go back to Egypt, but I will never go home again. One day I will drive past the Cairo house, and it will be flying a foreign flag.

Glossary

`Abbaya*: full-length cloak with loose sleeves worn by Saudi and Gulf Arab men over their robes.

`Abeddin Palace: the King's residence.

Albanian dynasty: King Faruk and his predecessors descended from Mohamed Ali Pasha, an Albanian officer in the Ottoman empire who came to power in Egypt in the early 1800s.

Allah Akbar: God is great.

Azhar University: at one thousand years old, the oldest surviving Islamic university and one of the foremost authorities in the Muslim world.

Bayram Feast, also known as the Greater Feast or the Feast of the Sacrifice: the most important feast of the Islamic calendar, it occurs on the tenth day of the month of pilgrimage to Mecca. In commemoration of Abraham's sacrifice, a sheep or other beast is sacrificed and the meat partly distributed to the poor.

Belle Hélène: Helen of Troy.

Bey: Sir.

C'est pas la mer à boire: it's no big deal.

Fellahin: peasants.

Fresca: small honey and nut pastries.

Granita: water ices.

Hamdillah `alsalama: expression used to welcome travelers on arrival. Literally: Thank God for your safe return.

Hanem: Lady.

311

Iftar: the meal taken to break the fast at sunset during the month of Ramadan.

Kosha: bower of flowers on a raised dais on which the bride and groom are enthroned during the wedding.

Mabruk: congratulations.

Mahr: dowry the groom gives the bride.

Mihrem: a close male relative, such as a husband, brother or son, acting as a woman's chaperone in order for her to be able to travel to Saudi Arabia.

Minadi: parking attendant.

Muezzin: mosque attendant who calls for prayer five times a day from the top of the minaret.

Om Ali: baked pudding made with pastry, cream, raisins and nuts.

Pasha: Ottoman title for a man of high rank. Bestowed on certain notables in Egypt until 1952, when the revolutionary regime abolished all titles.

Ritza: sea urchins.

Roman à l'eau de rose: fluffy romance novel.

Sainte Nitouche: goody-goody.

Salamlek: the section of a traditional Muslim household where men who were strangers to the family could visit. In contrast, the haramlek was the quarters reserved for the family. In the Cairo House, the term salamlek was loosely used to refer to the bachelor brothers' quarters.

Sitt: Lady, Miss.

Sohour: a meal taken between midnight and dawn during the month of Ramadan, when Muslims fast from sunup to sundown.

Suffragi: butler or waiter.

Tarbouche: a red, felt, fez-like head covering worn by urban Egyptians before 1952, in contrast to the hats worn by Europeans or the turbans worn by rural or traditional folk. The revolution of 1952 banned the wearing of the tarbouche as a cultural and class symbol.

Wahabi, also known as Salafi: fundamentalist, puritanical Islamic movement that spread over Arabia from the eighteenth century.

Zaffa: procession of the bride and groom, followed by a retinue bearing candles, and preceded by musicians and belly dancers.

Zaghruta: a ululating trill of rejoicing.

312

P.S.

Ideas,
interviews
& features . . .

Seeing with Bifocal Vision

What inspired you to become a writer?
You know, the Chinese use the expression
'May you live in interesting times' as a curse,
but for a writer it can be a blessing in
disguise. I grew up in Egypt under a
revolutionary regime at a time of great
political and social upheaval; none were
more affected than politically prominent,
landowning families like my own. But my
memories of early childhood are those of a
happily hybrid culture: Egyptian cuisine and
French governesses; English schools and
Nubian doorkeepers; celebrating the Muslim
Feast of the Sacrifice and licking Italian ices
on the beach in a swimsuit. Then one day, in
the early sixties, this world came to an end.
The Nasser regime's sequestration decrees
designated certain families as 'enemies of the
people'; the men were whisked away to a
camp for political prisoners; everything we
owned was confiscated. The pall of the police
state descended upon us. The thousand eyes
and ears of the Mukhabarat, the intelligence
service, were everywhere; even in the privacy
of our own bedrooms, between parent and
child, we whispered.

At the age of twenty I married and left for
London to study at university. Around that
time, under a new president, Sadat, there was
another great reversal, an abrupt about-face
toward the West. There were brief
expectations of political and economic
reform, but the situation deteriorated rapidly
until it ended with his assassination ten years
later and the rise of Islamic fundamentalism.

I left Egypt for good then and emigrated to the States where I have lived for over twenty years now. But there is a saying: he who has drunk of the waters of the Nile will always return. Every time I went back to Egypt to visit my family I saw such far-reaching changes sweeping the country that it seemed to me the world I once knew would soon be gone. And that was the original impetus to set it all down on paper. Far from being an exercise in 'recollections in tranquillity', as Wordsworth put it, writing turned out to be a very personal and soul-searching effort to reconcile my own present with my past.

Where did the title come from?

While I was writing the book I thought the title was something I could decide on later. But in effect I realized that I would only know what the book was about when I knew what the title was. And the title is *The Cairo House* because the novel, for me, is not just about Gihan, or even just about her clan, but about an entire era of Egyptian twentieth-century history that witnessed the rise of the Pashas, party politics, revolution and counter-revolution. The history and fate of the house reflect this pivotal era that spanned a century and came to an end with the passing away of the last Pasha, my uncle, on the eve of the twenty-first century.

The real Cairo house, my family's residence in Garden City, inspired the title, and the novel. It is still in the family, although unoccupied since my late uncle's death at ▶

LIFE AT A GLANCE

Samia Serageldin was born in Cairo, Egypt, around the time of the 1952 Revolution. At the age of twenty she married and left for England where she studied for her Master's in Politics at London's School of Oriental and African Studies. In 1980 she emigrated to the United States, and has lived in Michigan, Massachusetts and North Carolina. Over the years she has worked as an interpreter for an international organization, a professor of French and of Arabic, a freelance writer and a book columnist. All of these – not coincidentally, she realizes – are occupations connected to words and language in one form or another. *The Cairo House* is her first novel; her short fiction has appeared in several anthologies. She has also published essays on ▶

3

LIFE AT A GLANCE *(continued)*

◀ women's issues and Islam. In the past few years she has been in regular demand as a public speaker on current events in various academic and church forums. She has two grown sons on two different continents and family on a third, perfect excuses for dividing her time between Chapel Hill, London and Cairo. ■

A FEW FAVOURITE READS

Coleman Barks's translation of Rumi's poetry, *Birdsong*

Baudelaire, *Flowers of Evil*

Stendhal, *The Red and the Black*

Gabriel García Márquez, *Chronicle of a Death Foretold*

Marguerite Duras, *The Lover*

Seeing with Bifocal Vision *(continued)*

◀ the age of ninety; as such it is the only one still owned by the original owners in what is known as Embassy Row in Cairo. The Serageldin house acquired particular historical significance on account of its association with the political fortunes not just of the family but of the Wafd party, of which my uncle was the leader, both before and after the revolution. But in other ways it is emblematic of the many grand houses built for Egyptian families in Cairo around the turn of the century, all of which have progressively and inevitably been turned into foreign embassies or museums, as the last generation of occupants passed away and their heirs were dispersed.

What do you think will happen to the house now?
Ideally, it would be turned into a museum or cultural centre. I hate the thought that it will go out of the family, but one consolation is that whoever buys the house will have to preserve its historic character; it has been declared part of Egypt's national heritage.

Since *The Cairo House* draws heavily on your personal history, why did you choose to write a novel, not a memoir?
It is often said that a memoir is fiction in disguise and a novel is fact masquerading as fiction. For me, at least, I could not have written as freely without the fig leaf of fiction; I would have felt far too inhibited by concern for family members and friends, given the personal and political sensitivity of much of the material. Moreover a memoir

4

would have made for a less interesting narrative. Fiction allows one the licence to conflate two aunts into 'Tante Zohra', for instance; to incorporate historical material seamlessly; and best of all, to explore the 'path not taken' at a crucial juncture in the story. But even as a novel *The Cairo House* has been read as a *roman-à-clef* by Egyptian readers, and a far more accessible key than I realized, at that. And that has brought controversy.

What kind of controversy?

Well, the story of the Revolution had never been told from the point of view of the class victimized by its regime, and some diehard Nasserites, in particular, took umbrage against what they considered revisionist history. But I had never intended to write an overtly political work; the book was simply based on my life, and my life was inevitably caught in the slipstream of history. I had anticipated the political fall-out to some extent, but I was blindsided by the controversy on religious issues. Some Muslim readers expressed concern about depictions of the Feast of the Sacrifice and the citation of verses from the Quran. Although entirely inoffensive in my intention and in context, a few readers felt that such passages might be misunderstood by non-Muslims. This, it is worth noting, was when the American edition appeared several months before September 11. Today, the reluctance to contribute to anti-Islamic prejudice is likely to weigh on writers of Middle Eastern heritage in an unprecedented manner. ▶

A WRITING LIFE

When?
Whenever the inspiration hits, even in the middle of the night.

Where?
At my desk, distracted by squirrels and red cardinals hopping about on the tree outside my window.

Why?
To leave a footprint of one's passage through this world.

Pen or computer?
Computer.

Silence or music?
Music.

What started me writing was . . .
Realizing the world I remembered would soon be gone with the wind.

I start . . .
By working out scenes and even entire chapters in my head.

I finish . . .
With an overwhelming desire to go out and be sociable again.

Do you have any writing rituals?
I take long walks in the ▶

5

A WRITING LIFE *(continued)*

◄ woods to do my thinking before I put finger to keyboard.

Or superstitions?
Fear of jinxing my manuscript by showing it before it's done or telling people about a book before it's published.

I admire...
Gabriel García Márquez.

I am inspired by...
Passion, romantic and otherwise.

Guilty pleasure?
Reading during the day when I should be writing or working.

Favourite trashy read?
Political comic books, especially by the irreverent Doonesbury and Kudzu. ■

Seeing with Bifocal Vision *(continued)*

◄ **You write in English. Is that out of choice or necessity?**
I grew up trilingual, but my schooling has mostly been in English, and I have lived in England or the States more or less continuously since the age of twenty, so English is now my dominant language of written expression. But that choice is significant in positioning me on this side rather than the other of the cultural divide between the old country and the new, and in defining my 'ideal reader'. Language is also an entire codification of culture and, for me, I admit that Arabic carries certain cultural inhibitions. I was asked once after a talk I gave in London if I could have written the book in Arabic. And I answered that I could have *written* it in Arabic, but I couldn't have *thought* it in Arabic. It would have been a very different book if I had. That doesn't mean that it can't be translated into Arabic successfully by someone else; indeed, chapters of it have been.

But regardless of the language, the 'hyphenated' writer brings a unique perspective to literature: that of the insider/outsider. It is the ability to see with bifocal vision, to be at home in more than one culture while continuing to observe them all with an outsider's fresh eye.

Some of this material previously appeared in *Scheherazade's Legacy: Arab and Arab American Women on Writing*, Praeger Press. ■

6

The Alternative Universe of the Imagination

By Samia Serageldin

Every writer's relationship with books must surely start as a passive one, absorbing and internalizing, until the day you begin to create. For me, growing up, reading was my refuge. It was around the time when the world around me turned confusing, when the adults in my life took to speaking in anxious whispers, that I became a compulsive reader. I was too young to understand about revolutions and house arrest and 'enemies of the people'. I escaped to my alternative universe of books.

Enid Blyton's Famous Five series; the Comtesse de Ségur's stories; selections from Librairie Hachette's rose imprint, colour-coded for age-appropriateness. I was omnivorous in both French and English. As I grew older I graduated to Walter Scott and Thackeray; Georges Sand from Hachette's green imprint; Stendhal and Balzac from the black. I was the kind of child and, later, adolescent who couldn't go anywhere without a book in hand, the kind who, temporarily bereft of reading material, would resort to reading the ingredients on sauce bottles and the labels on shampoo. Reality intruded feebly into my alternative universe. I remember raising my head from the mist-shrouded moors of *Wuthering Heights* and blinking in disoriented resentment at the blinding glare from the Mediterranean sun glancing off the water at the beach in Alexandria.

I began writing sporadically as a teenager, entirely imaginary, escapist short stories, but also a few surprisingly real, stark poems. ▶

The Alternative Universe of the Imagination *(continued)*

◄ But as I grew into a woman I seemed to lose my voice. Living abroad as I did, from the age of twenty on, there was no room in this brave new world for my memories of jasmine and dust; I locked away my photo albums of Egypt in the attic. My sons grew up playing ice hockey in Michigan and Massachusetts, baseball in North Carolina.

But I returned to Egypt constantly, in my mind, weaving my memories into stories I stored away in that virtual filing cabinet all writers carry around in their heads. I'd be walking in the woods, and make up entire chapters in my head, down to the last comma. Then one day I finally sat down at my computer and put finger to keyboard, so to speak. As soon as I started writing I became so lost in my invented universe that the tangible world outside of my imagination receded in the background. I became a moving hazard at the wheel of a car, so distracted by the stories in my head that I had several accidents in a two-year period. If, before, I had been lonely sometimes, once I started writing I always had company. I woke up every morning impatient to get back to my characters, imagining them waiting for me on the page like friends eager to take up an interrupted conversation.

I discovered what other writers have found, that it is easier, if anything, to evoke a place from a distance than if I had been living there. Isak Dinesen wrote *Out of Africa* after she returned to frigid, gloomy Denmark; she wrote her Gothic tales in the stark sunshine of Kenya. And of course Cairo is a city with such a unique sense of place of its own, even the

❝I returned to Egypt constantly, in my mind, weaving my memories into stories I stored away in that virtual filing cabinet all writers carry around in their heads. ❞

8

night air has a memorable quality. You become more aware of it, rather than less, at a distance. You can live along the banks of a great river and not be actively aware of how its rhythms punctuate your daily life. Growing up in Cairo on the island of Zamalek in the middle of the Nile, I crossed the river several times a day, but it is only after living abroad for years that I realized how much it had marked me. I always felt restless in any land-locked place far from a great river or a sea; I missed a point of orientation. There was no 'there' there.

When *The Cairo House* was finally published, it came as a complete surprise to most people who knew me, since I had kept my writing strictly private. It was also a coming out of sorts for the reserved person I had always been; people who had known me for years looked at me in a new way. I had always tried to blend in like a perfect chameleon. There was no hypocrisy involved; only the need to compartmentalize in order to survive. When glimpses of my former life transpired, I dreaded the slightly sceptical question that inevitably ensued: 'So what are you doing here in Houghton (or Newton, or Chapel Hill)?'

And that is why the central metaphor of the book is that of the chameleon, someone who has more than one skin and is an expert at blending into more than one culture. I was pleasantly surprised to find out that what resonates, even with a reader who has no connection to the Middle East, is the universal sense of exile from an idyllic place or time, ▶

❝Cairo is a city with such a unique sense of place of its own, even the night air has a memorable quality. ❞

The Alternative Universe of the Imagination *(continued)*

◄ even if it is remembered through the rose-coloured lenses of childhood.

For me, unearthing the essential metaphors in a novel helps me to see how each part relates to the others. The palimpsest is another such image: the idea that each of us is a palimpsest of sorts, with hidden layers of the past, of memories and experiences, underlying the superficial image we present to the world; layers hidden even from ourselves, very often, and only visible under strong light and careful scrutiny. The kaleidoscope, too, has always fascinated me as a metaphor for life: how a seemingly slight incident can alter the course of one's destiny, just as an almost imperceptible shift in the angle of the lens changes the composition to form an entirely new pattern.

That is the pleasure of writing for me: shining a light to uncover the palimpsest under the surface; tracing the changing image to the shift in the kaleidoscope; exploring the path taken and the path not taken. The great satisfaction of being read comes from taking others with you on that fascinating journey. ■

> ❝The central metaphor of the book is that of the chameleon, someone who has more than one skin and is an expert at blending into more than one culture. ❞

Samia in the real Cairo house in Garden City, photographed by Ramy in 2000.

If You Loved This,
You Might Like . . .
Be one of the first to read an extract from Samia Serageldin's new novel, El Greco's Illusion

Robert folds the scrap of paper in his hand and looks out of the window. The view outside is very different from the one that this same desk faced only a few months ago, before he sold his business. He looks out at the garden in the back of the house; the dead leaves drifting into the drained pool, the umbrellas folded over the tables on the patio, the shrivelled geranium heads in the stone planters.

He should get a yard service, or a proper gardener, he thinks, instead of Professor Ilya. Russian ornithology professors do not make good gardeners. It is supposed to be a temporary arrangement, but there are not many jobs available for an elderly Soviet refugee who doesn't speak much English.

One ring. The man pushing the French Minitel telecommunications deal. Sounds interesting, but it would take too much energy. Robert does not pick up.

Three rings. Susan, suggesting he join her and some benefit committee for lunch. Sounds concerned. He doesn't pick up.

One ring. His accountant. Sounds worried. Needs to speak to him quite urgently about an audit on back taxes. He doesn't pick up.

Three rings. Dr Berenson. Reminding him this is the second appointment he's missed this week. Sounds concerned. ▶

Read on

11

If You Loved This, You Might Like . . .
(continued)

◄ Missing appointments is a bad sign. Robert doesn't pick up.

He puts the scrap of paper in his pocket. Is this what retirement is like? He doesn't know what he expected. Not having to take any calls. Not having to wear a watch. Time. Switching off the treadmill under his feet for the first time in his life. He stares out the window. A squirrel scrabbles up the tree in front of him.

Robert takes the small scrap of paper out of his pocket and unfolds it slowly. He picks up the phone and dials the number he has copied on the paper. Two rings.

'Hello?'

Robert is taken aback. Her voice is high and light. He expected it to be low-pitched and throaty, perhaps with a slight accent. This voice does nothing for him.

'Hello? Hello?'

He hangs up. He thrusts the scrap of paper into his pocket.

He picks up the phone and punches in Drew's number. Perhaps he can talk him into coming home from college for the weekend. He hasn't been back since fall semester started. There is no answer.

One ring. The stockbroker he was supposed to have lunch with today. Sounds as if he were trying to hide his annoyance at being stood up. Robert doesn't pick up.

He takes the scrap of paper out of his pocket and dials the number again. This time her voice is more wary. 'Hello?'

'Hi. This is Robert Bauer. We met at Caroline Norton's party last week?'

'Oh – yes. Excuse me, I didn't quite catch . . .?'

'Robert Bauer. Caroline told me a little about your research, and that you're new to Boston. I may be able to help you meet some people.'

'Oh, that's very kind of you.' She sounds doubtful, Robert thinks with a grin, because she is trying to remember meeting him.

'Why don't you and your husband come over for coffee tomorrow morning? You can tell me a little about what you're working on. And Susan – my wife – would like to meet you.'

'My husband's out of town right now.'

'I'll expect you around ten o'clock? Let me give you the address.'

'Tomorrow? Perhaps we could put it off till my husband gets back?'

'I'm afraid tomorrow might be the only time I have available for a while.'

'All right, tomorrow then.'

Robert hangs up. It was easier than he thought. She hadn't even asked him how he got her number. ■

Find Out More

READ...

Similar novels such as Isabel Allende's *House of the Spirits,* Ahdaf Soueif's *Map of Love* and Diana Abu Jaber's *Crescent.*

VISIT...

Samia Serageldin's favourite places in Cairo and Alexandria

Any visit to Cairo begins with the **Pyramids of Giza**, where, in *The Cairo House*, Gigi and Luc go for a horseback ride and Tamer has his accident in the desert. Souvenir hunters never miss the **Khan-al-Khalili Souk** or bazaar, the setting for another chapter in the book, the one where Gigi and Tamer watch the whirling dervish at the **Naguib Mahfouz Café**. Order mint tea and an apple-flavoured nargileh, just for fun. Be sure to visit the grand **Hussein Mosque** at the entrance to the souk; tourists can visit outside of prayer times, but remember to take your shoes off at the door. Bring along thick socks or knit booties if you'd rather not walk barefoot on the carpeted marble floors. After your tour of the mosque and the souk, visit the lovely new **Azhar Gardens** just up the hill, overlooking the mosque and the thousand-year-old Azhar University. Take in the view of Old Cairo while you enjoy French pastries at Alain Le Notre café, or go for a stroll along the terraced walks.

At the other end of town, on the island of Zamalek, one of my favourite restaurants is **Le Pacha**, a houseboat on the Nile converted into a restaurant. I used it as the backdrop for one of the scenes in my novel. It is a stationary houseboat, permanently moored near the Marriott Hotel, but cross the bridge to Garden City if you'd like to take a cruise. The grand hotels along the Corniche all have pleasure-boat restaurants that you can take for a two-hour cruise down the Nile and back. Work up an appetite by going for a stroll along the tree-shaded **Nile Corniche** and go off the beaten path to tour the lovely turn-of-the-century villas in **Garden City**. Be sure to keep an eye out for the real Cairo House at No. 10, Ahmed Basha St, and for Fuad Serageldin St, named after my late uncle.

If you have the time, a side-trip to **Alexandria** on the Mediterranean coast is well worth the two-hour trip by train. The ambitious **new library** is a marvel of architecture, with its futuristic hemisphere looming low like a rising sun on the horizon. You can drive along the Corniche from the fifteenth-century **Qait Bey Fort** at one end of the Bay of Alexandria to **Montazah Palace** at the other, and with the palm trees swaying in the breeze, and a willing imagination, it can almost remind you of Nice. Be sure to try the refreshing water ices; lemon and mango were Gihan and Tamer's favourites in the novel. You can go for a walk around the Montazah gardens and grounds, and if you know where to find it the guards will let you see the drowned ruins of Sadat's summer villa, built below sea level with glass walls, like an aquarium. You can stay at the **Salamlek Hotel**, which was once a little ▶

15

Find Out More *(continued)*

◄ folly the Khedive built for his Austrian mistress, and relive the heyday of King Faruk.

THE REAL CAIRO HOUSE

I am often asked if the Cairo House really exists. Unlike Isabel Allende, who writes that a Japanese reporter went all the way to Chile to see the real 'House of the Spirits' only to find out that there never was such a house, I can answer in the affirmative. In my case the Cairo House certainly does exist, in fact it is still in the family. The history of the real house is a little different, and perhaps even more interesting, than that of the house in my novel. It was originally built as a small palace for Kaiser Wilhelm of Germany to use as a residence on his visits to Cairo. The First World War intervened, and the Kaiser never came, but my grandfather Serageldin Pasha bought it and moved there from another mansion nearby. Vestiges of the Kaiser's taste linger in the library with its stained-glass windows, wood panelling and high-backed 'Bishop's chairs'. There are photos of the exterior and interior on my website: www.thecairohouse.com. ■